A
HEART,
SO
COLD
AND
WICKED

A WICKED DARLINGS NOVEL

REBECCA F. KENNEY

First Edition: October 2024

Kenney, Rebecca F.
A Heart So Cold and Wicked / by Rebecca F. Kenney—First edition.
Cover art by Fay Lane

PLAYLIST

"God Needs the Devil"—Jonah Kagen

"Coventry Carol"—City of Prague Philharmonic

"Eyes Closed"—Imagine Dragons

"Feather"—Meg Myers

"Is It Love"—Loreen

"Lady in the Wall"—Danny Knutelsky

"Easy to Love"—Bryce Savage

"Other Boys"—Dove Cameron

"Once Upon a December"—Alala

"Sugar"—Sleep Token

"Miracle"—Story Of The Year

"Stay"—Ghost, Patrick Wilson

"Who's Afraid of Little Old Me?"—Taylor Swift

"I Was Made For Lovin' You"—YUNGBLUD cover

READING GUIDANCE

Child murder (off-page),

child physical abuse and other abuse (mentioned but not depicted on-page),

brief mention of a corpse being violated (not depicted on-page),

horror, violence, gore, murder, kidnapping, vomit, brief mention of rape and sexual assault (mentioned but not depicted on-page),

age gap between Fae and human, a sort-of racism against the Fae by a few humans, light BDSM, punishment play with a switch, light CNC play, spit

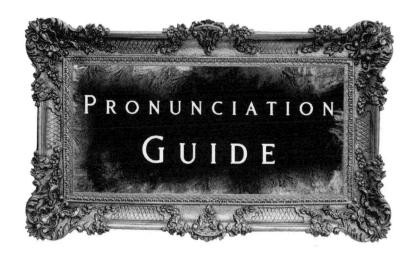

PRONUNCIATION GUIDE

Krampus: CRAM-puss

Perchta: PARE-ktah

Bahkauv: BAH-kowv

Wolpertinger: VOL-peh-TING-ah

Meerwunder: MEER-voon-dehr

Geistfyre: Geist has the "eye" sound (long I), fyre = fire

Nocturis: Nok TOOR iss

Andregh: Ahn-DRAY

Feather has severe mental trauma from the confinement and abuse she endured as a child. In this fantasy setting, she doesn't have access to therapy, so she processes it in a different way. However, in real life, it's always best to seek therapy and counseling for mental and emotional health issues. Please do not treat this fictional book as a guide for processing trauma. If you have such struggles, please be kind to yourself, and seek professional help from a therapist or physician as needed.

This book is a spin-off of the Wicked Darlings and can be read as a standalone. However, certain concepts, like the Wild Hunt and its hierarchy, as well as the nature of the Unseelie, will make more sense if you have read *A Hunt So Wild and Cruel*. For those who haven't: the Wild Hunt is a myth which spans many cultures and usually features ghost riders in the sky. In the Wicked Darlings universe, the Wild Hunt is made up of Fae who were especially wicked during their lifetime and were doomed by the god-stars to ride between worlds eternally as bodiless ghosts, warning cruel people to change their ways and punishing those who refuse to better themselves. Most of the members of the Wild Hunt were once Unseelie, the darker and deadlier kind of Fae, who are more prone to violence and cruelty than their Seelie counterparts.

Ready? Here we go.

Art by Zoe Holland

1

HER

For trigger warnings, a pronunciation guide, and a note about how the Wild Hunt functions in the Wicked Darlings universe, please turn back a few pages.

We aren't the first girls he has taken.

He reminds us of that sometimes, when we do not perform to his satisfaction. He warns us that we are replaceable. He can always drop us into the river at the bottom of the fjord, and take someone new.

There must always be three girls living with him in the cabin. One is Mother, one is Little Sister, and one is Wife.

I pity Wife the most.

There is a new Mother every few years. A Wife might last a week, or several months. It depends on how well she performs.

I'm Little Sister. I've been here the longest, because I am the best at my role. He took me when I was six years old, and I'm twenty now... at least, I think I am. I can't remember my birthday. To him, I pretend I am the same age as when he first took me. I'm short and thin because he demands I eat child-sized portions, and I'm glad of it. My small frame helps me play my role.

The first time I had my bleeding, Mother helped me. She gave me rags, scented herbs, and a poultice for pain. She told me to hide all signs of the bleeding from him. Taught me to put my hair in two fluffy knots on my head, or in two braids, so I would appear younger. She told me to pitch my voice high and wrap my chest flat so I would remain a child in his eyes. So I would not have to be Wife.

Mother told me that any normal man would be able to see that I'd grown and changed, but *this* man was trapped inside his own mind, living contentedly in the fantasy he'd created. Mother said that as long as we didn't disturb the fantasy, we would be alright.

That Mother lasted three years. When he killed her, I cried for eight nights. Never where he could see me. Always in my room.

This evening I'm sitting on the hearth, trying to absorb the warmth of the fire. Nothing is ever thoroughly warm here. We live too far north for that.

The book I'm reading is one of ten in the cabin. Once, when I asked him if we might have new books, he burned one of my favorites, a book about all the creatures of the world. The next month he brought me this one, a book about natural disasters. Hurricanes, floods, tornadoes, landslides—terrible things. "Be glad you live here, in the cabin," he told me. "It isn't safe elsewhere in the world."

In the book, pencil sketches depict each disaster. I like the picture of the hurricane best. The book says that areas prone to hurricanes often have warm, sandy beaches. I like to imagine what the coastline must look like without the high waves, the torn trees, and the wind.

As I stare at the picture, Mother chops the potatoes for dinner. *Thunk, thunk, thunk.* Mother wears a chain around her ankle so she will stay by the stove, because she misbehaved yesterday. She's allowed to use one very dull knife for preparing food.

Wife is curled in *his* chair, the big one draped with animal hides. She's beautiful, with long auburn hair, thick eyelashes, and a saucy red mouth. I have sometimes wondered what it would be like to kiss her. He certainly seems to enjoy it.

This new Wife isn't chained to the bed like the last one, because she's been good. Well-behaved. He allows her some freedom. Besides, it's not as if any of us can get out while he's gone. The logs of the cabin are too thick, packed with chinking that's solid as a rock. The floor is made of sturdy boards as well. There are no windows, and the door is bolted from the outside. Once, a Mother tried to remove the door's hinges, but she was caught and given to the fjord. After that he reinforced the hinges and removed anything we might use to pry at them.

"You're late making dinner tonight," Wife says sullenly from the chair. "He'll be unhappy."

Mother keeps chopping. *Thunk, thunk, thunk.*

"You may think it only affects *you*," continues Wife. "But I'll be the one who has to put him in a better mood." She glares at me. "What about you? You should have to do *something*."

"I'm Little Sister," I reply. "I help with the cleaning and the laundry. I read quietly. I play prettily with my toys. I sing to him. I let him tuck me into bed at night. That's what I do."

3

"But you're a grown fucking woman."

Hearing her say it aloud terrifies me more deeply than she can understand. She's only been here a few weeks. She still has hope. She thinks if she obeys him in everything, she might be able to escape.

"Don't," I say faintly. "I'm Little Sister."

She hears the tremor in my voice and laughs wretchedly. "You're both just as sick in the head as he is."

Thunk, thunk, thunk.

"Admit it," Wife continues, staring at me. "You like living this way, playing his twisted game. Otherwise you'd be long gone. Either you like it, or you're too stupid to scheme a way out."

I shrink against the warm bricks beside the fireplace and clutch the book to my chest. I've seen what happens to those who try to leave, and fail.

"What about you, *Mother?*" Wife says mockingly. "Have you tried to leave?"

Thunk. "It's useless," Mother says, low and hoarse. *Thunk, thunk.*

"If it's so useless, why don't you jam that knife into your neck and be done with it?" asks Wife.

"Because then he would take someone else," replies Mother. "If I endure, I can spare another soul from this fate."

This Mother has been here for several months. Beyond the games we all play when he's around, she barely speaks. I like her plain face, thin mouth, and keen eyes. I like the set of her shoulders. And I love her for those words.

If I endure, I can spare another soul from this fate.

My motives are not so lofty. I simply want to survive. I have no other goal.

A thump outside startles all of us. Wife curls in on herself more tightly, takes a stiff breath through her teeth, then rises with fluid grace as he opens the door.

4

He slams it at once. Stamps frozen mud from his boots. "I don't smell dinner."

"I'm sorry, dear," says Mother. "I was feeling poorly today, so I'm a bit behind."

He lifts a key from a cord around his neck and inserts it in the two locks on the inside of the door, one after the other. Wife's eyes follow the path of the key as he tucks it back in his shirt. When he swallows, the owl tattoo cloaking his throat seems to move. Its enormous eyes are always watching.

He keeps the key around his neck while he's with us. And since he never falls asleep in the cabin, there's no chance to steal it. I've seen women try to knock him out and take it, but he's a big, powerful man with a hard skull.

Every night, after he has eaten Mother's dinner, put me to bed, and fucked Wife, he leaves and locks us in again from the outside. He sleeps somewhere else. Another cabin, I think.

Sometimes he gives us extra food, and then we know that he'll be traveling for days, and that we must ration the supplies. When he isn't traveling, he always visits in the evening. Once in a while, he'll come for breakfast or lunch. During those extra visits, he sends me into the bedroom so Wife can suck his cock.

A Little Sister shouldn't understand such things. He wouldn't be pleased if he knew that a previous Wife told me all about a man's sexual hunger and how he sates it. She said it smells, and it hurts, and it makes you wish you were dead.

Tonight he sets down his leather pack, seats himself in his big armchair, and props his feet on a stool so Wife can remove his boots. Then he looks at me. "Well, Little Sister, aren't you going to welcome me home?"

I lay my book aside and run to him, wrapping both arms around his thick neck and his bushy beard. The hug is quick, our bodies barely touching for more than a second or two. "Welcome home, Big Brother!" I say in the light, childish voice I always use around him.

5

But instead of letting me fly back to my hearth seat and my book, his giant hand wraps around my arm. "Have you been a good girl today?"

"Oh, yes," I say brightly. "Haven't I, Mother?"

Mother finishes dumping potatoes into the boiling water, then turns around. "She's been very well-behaved. Playing so nicely."

"I think she should be rewarded," says Wife.

My spine chills. A reward isn't part of the game. This is new. What is she doing? The safest thing for all of us is to play the game the exact same way, every time.

"Rewarded?" he asks.

"Yes. I think she should get to sit on your knee," says Wife.

He frowns for a second, but then he spreads his legs wider and pulls me onto his knee.

I perch there nervously, not sure what I should do or say. He's staring at me far too closely. "You've gotten heavier."

Wife sets his boots on the mat by the door and returns, perching herself on his other knee and draping her body against his. "Put your head on his shoulder, Little Sister. It's so comfortable."

I know exactly what she's doing, and it's horribly cruel, but I can't step out of my role and protest, so I stick out my tongue childishly at her. When I glance back at him, he looks confused. I can't tell if he's unsettled by the change in our usual patterns, or by something else. But he pulls me closer, and I gingerly lay my head on his shoulder. I didn't wrap my chest quite as tightly today, and the side of my breast presses against him.

"Little Sister," says Mother. "Come and set the table."

She's trying to help me. But when I try to move, the burly arm wrapped around me tightens.

And my breathing stops.

Everything stops.

"I knew this day would come," he says slowly. "You've changed."

I'm breathing again, but it's fast and shallow and too loud.

"Stand before me," he orders. "And let your hair down."

I rise from his knee. "Please, Big Brother…"

"Do as you're told."

I remove the ribbons from my hair and it tumbles down around my shoulders.

"Turn, slowly."

I obey, revolving to face the heat of the fireplace, then Wife's triumphant sneer, then Mother's pale, stricken face.

He inspects me from head to toe. "You can no longer be Little Sister. Usually that would mean a gift to the fjord, but you've been with me for so many years that I've grown… attached. Maybe I can learn to see you as someone else. Perhaps you will make a good wife."

"But… you have *me*," falters Wife.

"You may be Wife to me for one more night," he tells her carelessly. "Tomorrow I will go and fetch a new Little Sister."

Nausea twists through my stomach, but I can't be sick, or that will make everything worse.

Tomorrow he will kidnap a new Little Sister. And then either he will keep this Wife and kill *me*, or he'll murder her and I'll take her place. I'll have to let him put his cock in my mouth and between my legs. My life and my role will change forever.

Wife remains on his knee, despair in her eyes. I'm not sure what she expected. Perhaps she thought I would share in the duties of Wife and take some of that burden off her. But there must always be three people living with him in the cabin. One is Mother, one is Little Sister, and one is Wife. He would never accept anything else.

"Ah, I almost forgot." He leans over the side of his chair and opens the top flap of his pack. "It's Midwinter's Eve. I brought each of you a gift. Here, take this to Mother." He holds

7

out a package to me. It's heavy and awkwardly shaped, wrapped in stained brown paper the color of old blood.

When I hand it to Mother, she unwraps it with trembling fingers and exclaims in false delight over the small cast-iron pan inside. It's just large enough to fry one egg.

"You're so good to me, Son," she tells him, with a bright, shaky smile.

He grins, pleased, then gives Wife her present—soft, lacy panties and a black silk bustier. She manages a trembling "Thank you," which isn't at all convincing and earns her a dark frown from him. He pushes her off his knee so abruptly she nearly falls.

Then he turns to me and offers up a package with a red tag, on which he has written, "To my little sister."

Forcing an excited smile, I rip aside the paper. Inside is a tiny red cart made of wood, with gold curlicues painted on it and a jointed wooden horse at the front.

"This toy was made by a man called Drosselmeyer who lives far away from here. If you flip this lever, it moves on its own. Watch." He kneels on the wooden floor and sets the toy down. With a flick of the tiny lever at the back, the little jointed horse begins to walk, leg after leg, with the cart rolling behind him.

Never have I seen anything like it. On another night, I would be charmed, and my heart would swell with warmth toward him, as it sometimes does. He can be kind when he wants to be.

"It's exquisite," I breathe, and he laughs—a big, hearty laugh. It's a travesty that someone like him can laugh like that.

To please him, I rebraid my hair and play with the toy until dinner is ready. He enjoys watching me; I know it because he says wistfully, "You've done so well, Little Sister."

It's a tribute to my fourteen years in this role, and a farewell to what I've been to him. The finality of it terrifies me.

When dinner is ready, we sit around the table, and Mother brings the food one dish at a time, the chain on her leg clanking as she walks. She fills our cups with water and his cup with the wine that we're never allowed to touch. He raises it high.

"Merry Midwinter's Eve," he says jovially. "I'm thankful to be here with my family."

"Merry Midwinter's Eve," Mother and I echo dutifully.

But Wife laughs.

It's a sneering, unhinged laugh. A wretched laugh, like the sharp ends of broken bones.

He goes utterly still. Mother and I freeze.

"You think I'm going to let you fuck me tonight, just so you can kill me tomorrow?" Wife's voice rises with every word. "You think I'm going to keep playing this sick game, pretending we're a family instead of a monster and his captives? You think I'm going to wish you a merry fucking Midwinter's Eve?"

"Watch your language," he growls.

"My language?" She laughs, her eyes frenzied and glittering with tears. "You *raped* me, and you tell me to watch my—"

He's rising, red-faced, his beefy hands gripping the edges of the table. I've seen him like this before; I know what happens next. I cringe down into my seat, making myself as small as possible.

But before he can rise to his full height, Mother reaches under her chair, then lunges, swinging the tiny cast-iron pan with all her strength.

It rings as it strikes his skull.

He stumbles… wavers… then crashes face-first onto the table.

"Get the key," gasps Mother. "The key, get the key!"

Wife scrambles out of her chair. "Help me push him over."

They struggle with his body, but he's heavy, lying in a mess of smeared food and broken dishes. Fear clamps my limbs to my chair, but my mind is screaming. *Not the key, not the key. Kill him first, make sure he's dead. Kill him, kill him, kill him…*

His left arm moves, lifts, and his great hand closes around the back of Wife's neck. A flex, and a *snap*.

She slumps, slides off the table limply, and hits the floor at my feet, a lifeless doll.

He pushes himself up, covered in potatoes and grease. Mother tries to hit him again, but he grabs her arm and picks up the cast-iron pan.

His first blow dooms her. But he doesn't stop. Maybe he likes the splattering and squelching noises.

When he's done with Mother, he drags Wife's senseless body into the bedroom. I don't know what he does to her in there, but I'm glad she can't feel it anymore.

There is one clock in the cabin, a polished wooden piece with a gleaming pearly face. It sits on the mantel, ticking softly, punctuating the grunting sounds from the bedroom.

It's nearly midnight when he finally emerges, crusted with the remnants of the dinner, soaked with blood. He trudges over to the cabinet, takes out the bottle of wine, then stumbles to his chair and drops into it.

I'm still sitting at the table. That's why he doesn't kill me— because I didn't fight him. I wasn't trying to escape.

"Come play with your new toy, Little Sister." His voice sends a twist of panic along my spine. "Let's salvage what we can of this night. Be a little festive, eh? Just you and me."

I count to three. Then I force myself to stand. I pretend I'm a puppet on strings, and I'm controlling myself. It's the only way I can move at all. The only way I can step across the slick red mush that used to be Mother.

He'll carry away the worst of it tomorrow, and make me clean the rest. Like always. I've gotten very good at cleaning.

When he leaves the cabin for the night, I'll be imprisoned here with two corpses. The smell alone will make it impossible to sleep.

Sitting on the floor between his chair and the fireplace, I run the mechanical horse and cart back and forth, back and forth, while he drinks and the wind howls in the chimney.

Before long, a low, droning sound mingles with the ticking of the clock and the soft rattling of the tiny cart. He's snoring, with the bottle tucked beside him and his head lolling against the back of the chair. The key glints in the thatch of curly brown hair on his chest.

I can't get that key over his head without waking him, and there's nothing with which to cut the cord. The dull kitchen knife might eventually be able to saw through it, but he'd wake up before I managed that. I could get a burning splinter from the fireplace, lift the key carefully, and burn through the cord, but the heat and smoke would rouse him. Plus I might set him on fire, and I have no doubt he'd overcome me before I got the door open, even if he were burning alive.

I rise, my bare feet soundless on the floor. I press one hand to the massive logs of the cabin wall.

I've spoken to these walls often since I came here. Sometimes I whispered, and sometimes I pressed my thoughts outward, toward them, into them. I imagined I was speaking to the trees they'd once been, mighty and towering, until *he* cut them down, killed them, made them into walls, stuffed chinking into their cracks.

The cabin is my prison, but it is also my friend. We are both his victims.

With the smell of Mother's entrails in my nostrils, and his grating snore in my ears, and the rough bark under my palms, I close my eyes, a single, powerful urge filling my soul. *I want to get out.*

11

A vibration shudders through my palms as the cabin trembles. Bits of chinking tumble from between the logs onto my toes.

I snatch my hands back and glance over my shoulder.

He's still asleep.

That has never happened before. The wind must be strong tonight. Or perhaps there was an earthquake, like in my book of disasters. Or… perhaps my will to escape has never been this strong.

Whatever it was, I can't risk him waking up and finding me anywhere but on the floor, playing with my toy like a good Little Sister.

Heart racing, I return to my spot. As I sit cross-legged and stare down at the little red cart, I notice something new—a miniscule latch on the edge. When I lift it, the top of the cart opens. Inside, in a tiny square space lined with red velvet, is a single round sleigh bell on a thin black ribbon.

The bell is a strange contrast to the rest of the toy. It's tarnished, slightly dented.

Taking the loop of black ribbon in my fingertips, I lift the bell out of the cart. It jingles slightly, and for a second my breath stops as I look over my shoulder.

But the sleeping man in the chair behind me doesn't wake.

The sound of the sleigh bell was eerily beautiful, so I ring it again, gently. It chimes prettily at first, and then the note changes, dips into a lower key, and echoes darkly through the cabin. I wrap my fist around the bell, trying to silence it, but the ringing continues, growing louder and louder, reverberating until it fills my head.

With a snort, he wakes up. "What are you doing?" he shouts over the ringing of the bell.

I drop it on the floor and scoot back, tears welling in my eyes. "I'm sorry! I don't know what's happening!"

"Blasted Fae magic," he yells as the ringing sound thunders through the cabin. He seizes the bell and flings it into the fireplace. The instant it hits the logs, scarlet flames explode across the hearth, making him leap back.

The ringing stops.

The fire keeps crackling merrily, as if nothing happened.

"A strange night." He heaves himself up off the floor. "Enough play. You should get to bed, Little Sister."

"Was it really Fae magic?" I venture.

One of the Mothers used to tell me stories of the Fae. She said they were beautiful, wicked creatures with great powers... which sounded like an improvement over my current captor. Whenever I couldn't sleep, I used to fantasize about a handsome Fae prince coming to steal me away from the cabin, away from the bearded man who now pulls me close, against his blood-soaked, food-stained clothing, and says, in a voice heavy with wine, "If it was magic, it's over now. Don't worry, Little Wife. I'll always take care of you."

Little Wife...

I can't suppress a shudder.

He feels it. Holds me at arm's length, frowning, the flush deepening along his cheekbones. A vein thickens in his forehead.

I sense the impending storm, and I brace myself.

He backhands me across the mouth. Grabs me and throws me to the floor so hard I feel as if all my bones and teeth have been knocked loose.

He stalks forward, grabs my hair—

But before he can do anything else, a great heavy Something crashes onto the roof of the cabin.

I scream, and he startles.

Something stomps across the roof, accompanied by a clanking, dragging sound with which I'm all too familiar. The sound of chains.

13

The next instant, a giant chain slams down through the chimney into the center of the fireplace, striking the stone hearth with a sullen boom and scattering the logs. The orange flames shrink down low and turn a deep, bloody red.

"What's happening?" I whisper. But he doesn't answer. On his face is the same look I've seen on Mothers and Wives throughout the past fourteen years—a look of abject dread and fear.

A dozen slender chains descend through the chimney and seal themselves to the bricks of the fireplace, pushing outward. It's as if they're stretching the chimney wider, forming a pathway for something... or someone.

None of this is possible. I must have fallen asleep. I'm dreaming... perhaps I dreamed it all... the murder of Wife and Mother, the terrible ringing of the bell, the chains stretching the chimney...

But I didn't dream being thrown to the floor, nor did I imagine the pain blooming through my body.

He's heading for the door, readying the key—but a pair of spiked black chains come snaking out of the fireplace and coil around his ankles. He falls, yelling, straining to get up and reach the door, but the chains hold him tight.

Two giant cloven feet slam into the center of the low-burning flames. The mantel and the fireplace and the hearth all warp so strangely it makes me dizzy. Black claws curl around the edge of the mantel as the Thing inside the chimney bends and looks out.

It's wearing a mask—a goat's skull. Black goat's horns sprout from the mane of blood-red hair blanketing its head and its massive shoulders. I can't see much of its hulking body because it's wearing a voluminous dark cape or coat, multilayered and ragged, trailing black tattered streamers across the floor as it climbs out of the fireplace. Tarnished sleigh bells jingle here and there among the folds of its garment.

The monster wraps one clawed hand around the chains holding my captor in place and drags him closer. The chains' spikes bite into his flesh, tearing it, leaving streaks of blood on the floor.

"Help me!" he screams. "Little Sister!"

He's reaching out, and by some twisted impulse, I stretch out my hand as if to save him.

For fourteen years he has been the one constant in my life. No matter who came or went, he was there.

I hate him, and I don't know how to exist without him.

His fingertips brush mine, but the monster yanks him back with a snarl. Between its jagged teeth, an impossibly long red tongue lashes through the air. That tongue must be as long as my forearm, and there's a glint partway along its writhing surface— an embedded nub of silver, possibly more than one.

The chains come to life again, wrapping around and around their victim before cinching horrifically tight. I don't try to save him this time. I can still smell the reek of Mother's remains, and there's blood on my frilly nightdress where he hugged me.

I watch him die. I hear him gasp, see his eyes bulge like boiled eggs. His mouth gapes, a raw hole in his beard—and then the chains tighten again, and all the bones inside him *crack*.

The goat-monster lets go of the chains for a moment and unslings a huge sack from his back. Perhaps it used to be red, but it looks as if it's been dipped in a lake of blood, over and over, until it's only dimly red at the top, with rings of deepening brown to the bottom of the bag, which is drenched in deep black.

The mouth of the bag gapes open. The monster picks up the misshapen, chain-wrapped corpse in one clawed hand and flings it into the maw of the sack. He cinches it tight.

Then he turns and looks at me, firelight gleaming on his curved black horns.

I shrink into a crouch and retreat to a corner. The curled ends of my dark braids trail on the floorboards.

The monster takes a step toward me. When his hoof nudges the toy cart, he looks down at it, then back up at me.

"Where is the child?" His voice is thick, deep, grating.

"There is only me," I whisper.

"Fate gives the bells to children who are suffering," he growls. "When a child rings one of the bells, I come to enact justice upon their abuser."

His words assuage my fear a little. It sounds as if he isn't here to murder me, crunch my bones, and stuff me into the sack.

"Who rang the bell?" he persists.

"I did."

Again he looks at the toy, at the open lid of the cart. "This plaything was given to you?"

I nod. "For Midwinter's Eve."

He steps over the toy, and a snuffling noise comes from beneath the goat-skull mask, as if he's scenting the air. "But you smell ripe. Like a woman."

I cringe deeper into the corner, unsettled by the word "ripe."

"One of my powers is discerning age by scent." It's almost as if he's trying to soothe my fears by the explanation.

"Are you Fae?" I ask.

He sniffs again before apparently deciding to ignore me. He glances at the fireplace, then twitches a clawed finger, and the chains hanging down the chimney vanish. Hoisting the bloodstained bag over his shoulder, he heads for the cabin door, his cloven hooves clopping on the wooden floor.

"The key," I venture. "The man you killed had the key…"

But the monster produces a huge chain from thin air and whirls it a few times before sending its metallic weight crashing against the door—that heavy slab, the portal through which food, supplies, and terror have come to me daily. I haven't passed through it since I was six years old.

At the impact of the chain, the door explodes, fragments scattering on the snow outside. Wind slithers eagerly into the cabin, its frigid breath soaking my nightgown with cold.

The monster adjusts the bag over his shoulder and stomps outside. That's when I notice his sinuous tail, with a tuft of red hair at the end.

His dark, hulking silhouette vanishes from the doorway, into the gloomy pallor of the snowy night.

I rise and take a tentative step. My toes curl into a slick pool of blood, but I keep walking, faster, faster, heated by a sudden panic that the door might reassemble itself and close again, trapping me inside forever.

I lunge for the exit—but I stop short at the threshold. Cold air burns in my lungs. Snowflakes dance and perish against the warmth of my cheeks.

The snowy meadow is a gray blur, the forest a smudged expanse of threatening black under the charcoal flatness of the night sky.

I know the fjord is somewhere nearby. My captor described it to me, and he even brought me a sketch of it once, drawn by an artist in a nearby town.

The fjord is where he put them all—the Mothers and Wives who weren't right, and the Little Sisters before me. He dropped them into the river. He says it's bottomless. Nothing given to it ever resurfaces.

The monster has stopped walking. He's holding the chain out, swinging it around so its end draws a big circle in the snow. When the circle is complete, tiny red flames spring up from it, glowing like fluttering crimson veils, turning the snow pink without melting it.

That's a Faerie circle. And he's leaving.

When he leaves, I will be alone. Alone in a giant dark world where I have no one and nothing.

For a moment, that reality seems far more terrifying than the monster himself.

I don't think. I run. Bloodstained bare feet on the snow, carrying me in one leap over the red flames, into the circle with the monster.

My toes have barely touched the ground again when everything changes… transforms into a great gray room of weathered boards, heavy drapes, and towering piles of furniture coated with dust. Huge speckled mirrors with ornate frames hang on the walls, and cobwebs flutter from the candle sconces. Only two of the candles are lit, and they gutter in the draft of our arrival. The ceiling is so high I can't see it.

The monster slams his burden onto the floor and drags it toward a door with a pointed, asymmetrical peak at the top. He yanks the door open, then lugs the sack down a stairway into darkness.

I don't think he noticed that I came with him to—wherever this is.

I kneel and press my palm to the tiled floor, my fingers creating a stark handprint in the deep dust. A faint image fills my mind—lights and dancing figures, music and motion. Life. The room used to be a grand and glorious one, but its beauty has faded. Now the air is stagnant with death, and the rooms are so clogged with mountains of dusty furniture that the house can barely breathe.

Strange thoughts to have, about a house *breathing*…

Frowning, I stand up and shake off the vision.

This one room is larger than the whole cabin. Maybe I can live here. Maybe the beast needs a Little Sister. He might be frightening, but I'm already used to living with a monster.

Cautiously I slink toward another door and open it.

Beyond lies a hallway with more impossibly high ceilings, lit by lamps with frosted glass chimneys shaped like teardrops.

The carpet is worn through in places, threads stretched taut and clinging to each other, scarlet thatch over visible floorboards.

As I proceed down the hall, the floor creaks here and there, as if it needs mending. There are holes along the corridor—gaps in the wallpaper and plaster, where the slatted wooden ribs of the house show through.

As I'm eyeing one of those gaps, something moves.

Something behind the wall.

Something enormous.

I suck in a breath and shrink against the opposite side of the hallway. Farther down the corridor, through two more broken places, I glimpse the creature again, slinking through the space behind the wall. Its legs are bone-thin and tall—taller than I am, with a hunched body at the top. My skin prickles with the awareness that I'm in the presence of something very, very old and very, very hungry.

The wall I'm leaning against groans and gives a bit, as if rotted wood is about to yield under my weight. A sense of pain spirals along my limbs, making my breath catch.

The house is in pain.

But it can't be. It's just a house, a building. Dead trees and plaster.

It can't breathe. It's suffocating, suffering, dying...

Frantic, I break contact with the wall, and the horrible sensation of pain and suffering eases immediately.

Wanting some distance between me and that long-legged entity, I turn and head in the opposite direction, which brings me to a staircase. The light fades partway up the stairs, and from the inky shadows I hear the huge, wet, heavy sound of something breathing—something gigantic, with jaws and a tongue and massive lungs.

Then I see the eyes. Two of them, glowing red in the darkness.

One monster I can handle. Not three.

I flee back to the door I came from, barrel through it, and slam into the cloaked form of the goat-masked monster.

"Fuck," he exclaims. "What are you doing here?"

I pull back, frowning. He sounds different than before. He still towers over me, but he's a little narrower in the shoulders, and instead of cloven hooves, bare toes peek out from beneath the ragged hem of his garments. His nails are still sharp and black, but they're not the long claws he had before.

"You changed," I say.

He grabs my arm and pulls me to the center of the big gray room where we first arrived. "I'm taking you back."

"No!" I wrench free and run from him. I'm too scared to go back to the hallway, but I scurry into the piled-up furniture, ducking under crooked stacks of chairs, dodging behind wardrobes and bureaus, and finally crawling under a table.

"The children whose abusers I punish are cared for by Mother Holle after I leave," Goat-Mask declares in a tone threaded with frustration. "She finds them safe places to live. You should have stayed in the cabin and waited for her."

"But I'm not a child. She might not have come to help me," I point out. "If you take me back where I came from, I'll die. There isn't much food in the cabin. And you broke the door, so I won't be able to keep warm."

"You are not my problem. You're an adult. That bell shouldn't have worked for you."

"It came to me too late," I reply quietly. "If I'd gotten it when I was six, when he first captured me, then maybe..."

Maybe then I would remember my real family. Maybe I would have been returned to them, and we would have lived safely and happily together. Maybe I wouldn't have witnessed so much pain and death for years...

Goat-Mask clears his throat and mutters, "I'll take you to a nearby town."

A town, where people draw and sew and play music and laugh with each other. That sounds much better than a house full of monsters.

"Yes," I breathe. "Thank you."

"Come on out, then. Don't make me crawl in there after you."

I scramble out, braids swinging. My nightgown rips on a sharp nail from one of the bureaus, and the sound of it tearing hurts me, because it is the only thing I own.

Goat-Mask grabs my wrist and yanks me close to him. Chains slide out from the wide sleeve of his garment, and he swings them around, painting a circle of red flames on the floor.

"Are you Fae?" I ask him again.

He doesn't answer.

Our environment changes, gray boards melting away, leaving us on a snowy road at the outskirts of a lamplit town. It's the prettiest place I've ever seen—stone cottages with tiled roofs, golden light gleaming from the windows, wood smoke drifting into the frozen sky, music floating in the air. I can smell fresh, warm bread.

Goat-Mask steps away, and I grab at his cape, intending to thank him, but he's already drawing another circle around himself. When he vanishes, I'm left holding one of the sleigh bells from his garments. A long black thread trails from the little hoop on top of the bell.

After gazing at the bell for a moment, I tie it around my neck with the long black thread. It's almost like a necklace. A few of the Wives and Mothers had such items when they first came to the cabin. They usually lost the privilege of owning them through disobedience. I always wished I could have one, and now I do.

The road into town is ice-cold and stony, painful to my tender feet, which haven't walked on anything but wooden floors and woven rugs. I wander past the first few buildings, then pause at one with a sign over the door: "The Frosty Radler: Best Beer in Town."

That sounds appealing, so I push the door open and step inside.

The warmth greets me first—a wave of it, blessing me down to my bones. The heat carries a savory aroma that makes me feel weak with hunger.

I've never seen so many people at once—or if I have, I don't remember it. I blink, dazzled by the sheer brightness and noise of the place, all the glowing lamps and chunky tables and polished chairs of yellow oak. It's overwhelming—the colors and patterns of the clothes, the clink of dishes, the rattle of cups... and the voices, so many voices.

As the door closes behind me, the merry conversation falters and dies.

Someone murmurs, "Gods, what is *that*?" and someone else exclaims, "Is she covered in blood?"

More voices: "Where did she come from? What is she doing here? What's that around her neck? A Fae talisman? The devil's bell... evil magic... Fae-cursed... witch..."

The last few words travel from mouth to mouth, growing sharper each time they're spoken.

A big man with beefy forearms and a stained apron comes out from behind a long counter. "You there. We don't want any trouble with your kind."

"My kind?" I survey him, mentally comparing him to the only man I've seen for fourteen years. "What is my kind?"

Instead of answering, the man spits on the floor and brushes off both shoulders.

"Fae whore," hisses a woman behind him.

I want to explain, but there are too many eyes. My breath quickens, and my heart begins to pound horribly fast. I feel as if my throat is closing up, like I'm choking on nothing, like my brain is overheating and burning, sizzling inside my skull. This is a new kind of fear.

"Help me," I gasp, reaching for the man.

He jumps back. "Get out, witch, before we throw you out!"

"Make her leave, before she casts a spell on us," someone cries, and a woman yells, "Cut the bell from her neck! Don't let her call for the Krampus!"

More men leap up from the tables. I don't give them a chance to throw me out; I burst through the door and flee down the street. I duck into the darkness between two buildings and huddle behind a barrel until the shouts and the running feet pass by.

I wait longer, until I hear them walk back to The Frosty Radler, apparently satisfied that they've driven me out of their comfortable town.

My feet are growing numb with cold. I can't stay here any longer, yet I'm terrified to emerge. My captor was right—the world is a dangerous place. But surely not everyone in it is cruel. There are kind people. I know this, because some of the Mothers and the Wives were kind. If I can find one kind person in this town, I will have what I need for the night. Food, warmth, and a place to sleep.

So many women passed through the cabin that I made it a game, to read their faces when they first arrived and place a bet with myself about how long they would last. A pitiless game, I suppose. But I didn't have much entertainment.

Perhaps I should make a bet with myself. How long will *I* last, now that I'm in a new place?

Resistance steels my spine at the thought. I did not escape the cabin only to die in the cold, in the dark.

The bell around my neck seemed to frighten the people at The Frosty Radler, so I unfasten my makeshift necklace and slip it into the pocket of my nightdress.

Keeping to the shadows, I continue down the street. The next corner leads into a narrower road where the shops are crammed closer together. One of them catches my eye because it has two red lanterns on either side of the door. The red lanterns remind me of the goat-monster's flames.

Two women lounge on the steps under the red lights. One arches a long leg from beneath the shelter of her cloak, showing off stockings made of black netting and a lace band around her thigh. The other is smoking a pipe.

"Where are your shoes, poppet?" calls the pipe-smoking one with a hoarse laugh. "Where are you off to?"

I pause, eyeing them. "I'm looking for a place."

The one with the netted stockings hooks an eyebrow at me. "What's your gig, then? Forlorn waif?"

"I'm Little Sister," I reply.

"Little Sister, eh?" She glances up at her pipe-smoking companion. "That's a new one. What do you think, Gabi? We need another girl around here. Someone young. Fresh."

Gabi removes the pipe from her painted lips. "We'd have to ask the Mister. How'd you like a bed, some shoes, and a square meal, poppet?"

"Yes." I step closer, barely able to suppress my shivering.

"Go on in, then." Gabi jerks her head toward the door. "Oda will show you around. I'm gonna finish my pipe."

Oda pushes herself to her feet and hustles me into a short hallway with a green-tiled floor and low-burning lamps. There are three curtained archways on either side and a stairway ahead. Faint murmurs and muffled moans come from behind one of the curtains.

Once we're inside, Oda takes a closer look at me. "Gods, what is that on your dress? Is that blood?"

I hesitate. "No. It's berry jam."

"Oh, well, if that's all..." She laughs and mounts the steps unsteadily. "I'm a bit sauced. Could've sworn it was blood. Wait here, I'll fetch the Mister."

Once she has disappeared upstairs, I sit down on the bottom step and massage my feet, which are beginning to sting now that warmth is returning to them.

Between two curtained archways stands a narrow table with wine bottles and silver cups. On a chipped platter sits an assortment of sliced cheese, grapes, and small cakes like the ones *he* would bring to the cabin sometimes, when he had beaten me and wanted to make amends.

My mouth waters, but I don't dare steal anything. At the cabin, we were only allowed to eat at mealtime, or we'd get a beating. They might have the same rule here.

Before the sight of the food can wear down my resolve, a shrill cry attracts my attention. It almost sounds as if someone has been stabbed and has cried out in pain. If this is another place where people murder each other, I'd best not stay too long. At the very least, I should learn the rules so I can avoid being the murdered one.

I sidle over to the archway from which the sound came, part the curtains a crack, and peek through.

A naked woman reclines on a green velvet couch, her thick thighs spread wide. Between them is a slender, nude man who appears to be licking her tender bits. Her fingers curl into his hair, holding him there, encouraging whatever he's doing.

He pauses and murmurs, "Look at this plump little clit, so pink and swollen. It's been well-tended. Do you want my cock now, my lady?"

Cheeks flushed, she exclaims, "Yes, yes!"

He rises on his knees on the couch and takes himself in hand, guiding his length inside her while she moans.

They're having sex. And that terrifies me more than murder. She seems to be enjoying herself—for now—but I've lived in mortal terror of my captor invading my body that way, and I can't bear to watch any longer.

I stumble back, letting the curtains fall into place.

Should I run?

Footsteps on the stairs catch my attention as Oda returns with a large man in a greasy-looking leather coat. A few strands of black hair are scraped across his shiny bald head.

He leers at me. "I hear you're looking for a place, my dear."

"You could do a lot worse than here," Oda puts in. "All you got to do is play Little Sister real cute and let customers slip you the sausage. It ain't so bad. We get plenty of wine and smokes, decent meals and beds, plus a tonic every week so nobody gets with child."

"Slip the sausage?" I falter.

The man's smile fades as he looks me over. Then he lifts a round, brass-rimmed piece of glass and peers through it at me. "Oda, the girl is covered in blood and bruises, and she has no shoes. Where did she come from?"

"Didn't ask," Oda replies. "This was Gabi's idea."

The man approaches me, peering suspiciously through his eye-glass. "Lovely face. Nice enough body. You got tits under there?" He reaches for my chest, and I spring back, quick as thought.

A frown creases his forehead. "Where are you from?" he asks, in a tone that's no longer welcoming.

"From a cabin in the woods," I reply.

"And how did you get here?"

I fumble for a reasonable lie, but I don't know enough about the people who live in towns. I don't know what explanation they would accept. So I speak the truth. "A man in a goat-mask brought me here."

"Oh shit," whispers Oda. "She's been consortin' with the Fae."

"And you let her in," hisses the bald man. "Fae-cursed... sprite... witch... whatever you are... I suggest you leave now, before we call the constable."

Oda spits on the carpeted steps and brushes off both shoulders, then begins twirling two locks of her hair in opposite directions, muttering indistinct words.

So it isn't just the bell that makes these people afraid. It's my association with Goat-Mask.

This time, instead of running, I consider how I might use their fear.

My fingers dip into my pocket and curl around the bell. I withdraw it slowly and hold it up by its black thread.

Oda and the Mister recoil with stricken faces.

"I'll go," I say. "If you give me food, shoes, and a cloak. And something to make a fire."

"I'm not sure—" begins the gentleman, but I move the bell ever so slightly, and he says hastily, "Of course, of course! Oda, give the visitor your cloak and shoes. I have some matches, and take this platter of food. Leave us be, for pity's sake! Tell your master we don't harm children, see? This ain't that kind of place."

Minutes later, I leave the red-lantern house with my heels slipping out of Oda's too-large shoes, her feather-edged cloak around my shoulders, and the chipped plate of food in my hands. When I glance back, Gabi, Oda, and the Mister have all gone inside and shut the door. The red lanterns have been put out, and the street lies in darkness.

I find a narrow gap between houses, out of the worst of the wind, and I nibble at the grapes, cheese, and cakes.

The food fills my belly, but the cloak and shoes don't keep the wind from slicing through my flesh and sawing at my bones. Soon I'm as cold as I was before, with no kindling or firewood in sight. From my pocket, I take the box of matches the gentleman gave me, and I strike one, enjoying the flare of light and the bit of temporary warmth it offers my chilled fingers.

The cold has turned my joints creaky and stiff. It's difficult to move, so I strike another match, hoping it will thaw me enough so I can get up. I need to head for the woods and make a fire. That's the one thing I know how to do. That, and cleaning. At the cabin, I was in charge of sweeping the floors, scouring the pans, shoveling the ashes, rinsing the chamber pots, washing the clothes, scrubbing away the blood, and keeping the fire fed.

I'll burn one more match, and then I'll get up. I'll go to the woods and build a fire, and then I'll be warm.

Strangely, I'm almost warm now... or at least I'm feeling the cold less. I'm stiff, numb, drowsy—

The third match bites my fingers, a savage nip of fire, and I jump. I must have dozed off—I don't remember watching it burn down.

In taking the matches from my pocket I dislodged the bell, and when I startle, it tumbles out from under the edge of my cloak, ringing as it rolls.

With cold-clumsy fingers, I manage to grip the black thread tied to the sleigh bell, pinning it to the icy cobblestones, keeping it from rolling farther. As I pick it up, it jingles.

I'm not sure why I ring it again. Maybe I'm hoping the sound will pierce the heavy numbness creeping through my body.

The ringing of the bell stretches this time, like it did in the cabin. It grows louder, echoing down the black hollow of the alley.

But I can't hold on any longer. I slump back against the bricks, and the bell rolls away from my limp fingers.

2

I've just settled myself and two fine-looking women into a booth at the Cornflower & Crane and ordered three tankards of barrel-aged beer when I hear it—a damned bell reverberating through my brain.

It's insistent, demanding a response. At the same moment, a scroll unfurls about an arm's length in front of my face, invisible to everyone except me. The scroll is a missive from Nocturis, my overseer in the ranks of the Wild Hunt. Usually the message carries a location, a full-color image of my intended victim's face, a list of their sins, and the assigned punishment.

This time, the scroll shows me a map of the town where I left the girl, the surviving victim from the cabin. A red dot glows briefly to mark the location, an alleyway. Then the scroll vanishes from my sight.

"Fuck," I growl.

"What's the matter?" purrs the olive-skinned woman to my right, petting my chest. "Relax, love. You're with Lotte and Bettina."

The rosy, curvy blonde on my left coos in agreement. I was looking forward to watching their pretty mouths travel up and down the sides of my dick as they worked on me in unison until I splattered their faces with my release. Alas, that is not to be.

"Excuse me, ladies." I shoo Lotte out of the booth and shove my way through the milling crowd of revelers in the Cornflower & Crane. I can't ignore the summons. The change will come upon me within a handful of minutes, whether I'm ready or not.

This is wrong. I'm never called twice in such close succession. There's always a respite of a day or two, sometimes longer. I've already meted out justice tonight… though it was perhaps the strangest scenario I've encountered so far. I shouldn't have to answer the call again. But the ringing in my brain is growing louder.

I'm running out of time.

I burst out of the tavern into the cold air and run for the nearest copse of trees. I've barely reached its shelter when my body surges and expands into the hulking, broad-shouldered, goat-legged form of my other self, the Fae demon called Krampus. Black fur cloaks my lower body, and black horns emerge from my skull. My cape and my bone mask settle onto my frame, their weight as familiar as the heft of the huge bag that appears over my shoulder.

Chains rattle when I move, and the bells tucked among my garments clink faintly, unable to ring out unless they're held by a child in pain.

I seethe as I draw the flame-circle around myself and prepare for transport by geistfyre. It's a kind of travel permitted to only a few of the Fae, specifically those like myself who operate under the purview of the Wild Hunt. I don't ride with that majestic band, firstly because, although I'm immortal, I'm not dead—and secondly because the crime that doomed me to this existence was not against my fellow Fae, but against humans. The Fae have a long history of using and mistreating humans, but my sins were of such a shocking and egregious nature that I drew the attention—and the anger—of the god-stars. They doomed me to an existence of being forever summoned by bells in the hands of desperate children.

For many riders, their service to the Wild Hunt has a limit, an end. A final task or challenge, which, if they complete it successfully, results in them receiving corporeal form again, along with a span of years. If they fail the Final Task, they are annihilated. But not all members of the Hunt receive such an opportunity. For me, there is no foreseeable end, no reward I can anticipate. Nothing to hope for.

When I'm summoned, I may only travel to the location I've been given. Between tasks, however, I can transport myself anywhere I like, simply by summoning my chains and using them to conjure geistfyre.

Once the geistfyre circle is complete, the transfer is immediate, and I find myself standing between the brick walls of an alley. My breath issues in white puffs from beneath the bone mask. The musty smell of mold and rat droppings is barely distinguishable through the stark cold.

I'm never summoned without a target—a face, a name. This time, all I have is a location. There's a lump of something near the mouth of the alley, so I trudge toward it, sniffing, filtering out the wood smoke, the rat shit, the frosty scent of impending snow—

Her scent hits me, and I stop short.

As I feared, it's her again. The pale slip of a girl with the long brown braids and the giant dark eyes—the one from the cabin. The one I dropped off at the outskirts of town not three hours ago. And now here she is, nearly frozen to death by the look of her. Stupid human—did she not have the sense to ask for shelter and warmth?

She's wearing a cloak and shoes, and some food lies on a plate nearby. Someone gave her those things... or perhaps she stole them.

One of my bells lies near the curved tips of her blue-tinged fingers. She must have snatched the bell off me and rung it out of desperation.

But why did the bell work for her? By her scent, she's around two decades old—too old to summon me. Yet here I am.

I look up at the strip of clouded night I can see above the alley. "Nocturis, what are you up to?" As my superior within the Wild Hunt, Nocturis has some control over my missions. The ultimate authority, though, resides in the hands of the great god-star Andregh, champion of justice and balance, patron of the Hunt.

No one from the Hunt has contacted me directly in ages, although I still receive assignments. I don't know if this girl's ability to ring the Krampus bells is a mistake or intentional. Perhaps I'm meant to save her life, though I can't imagine why.

I bend, carefully sliding my clawed hands under her body and lifting her. With the extra strength I possess in this form, her weight is nothing. Feather-light.

I drape her over my shoulder so I can summon a chain and draw the geistfyre circle. She quivers suddenly, then begins to flail with panic.

"No," she gasps. "No, not *you*..."

Her half-frozen limbs flutter against my powerful bulk. I ignore her, finish the circle, and transfer us back to my house. She'll have to reside here until I can figure out an alternative.

Hopefully my housemates won't eat her. Though if they do, I suppose it would solve the problem.

I always appear in the ballroom when I transport home. The moment I set the girl down, she scuttles away from me, shivering so hard she can't speak. I can't have her hiding in the pile of old furniture again, like a little worm in a potato—she might die in there, and then rot, and I'd have to live with the smell because it would be far too great a bother to drag out each piece of furniture until I finally uncovered her corpse.

So I grab her ankle and drag her back toward me before she can crawl farther away.

She screams faintly, kicking at my hand with her icy bare foot, since both her shoes apparently fell off while I was carrying her. She kicks at the wrong angle, slicing the bottom of her foot on one of my claws. Blood flecks the floor.

I can't have her escaping and getting lost or eaten, nor can I let her keep hurting herself, so I unsling my bag with my free hand and shake it open. The mouth of the bag widens, prepared to swallow and preserve whatever I stuff inside it.

Clumsily, trying not to scratch her with my claws, I attempt to stuff the girl into the sack. She writhes, screams, and kicks, but I have more than my share of Fae strength in this form, so I manage to get her inside. I cinch the top of the bag and step back, while her small feet, knees, and fists hammer against the inside of the sack, distorting its shape slightly. She's a feathered bird in a snare, who doesn't yet realize her struggle is useless.

"Hush, girl," I order, and the bag stops moving for only a moment before she continues to fight.

With a shrug I lift her onto my back, then carry her down the hall and up the stairs to my room. It's the only safe place in this house. Besides which, there's always a fire burning in my chamber, and she needs heat.

On the way to my room, my usual form returns. I retain the mask, cloak, and bag for now. They appear whenever I'm summoned, and I can keep them as long as I need to and dispel them whenever I'm ready to do so.

Once we're inside my room, I close the door. It's not bolted, but my chambers are marked with sigils invisible to the human eye, designed to foil my housemates if they decide we're no longer allies and I'd be the perfect snack. In my Krampus form, they usually give me a wide berth, but they've made it known how delicious I smell in my regular Fae form. The beasts and I have maintained an uneasy truce for centuries. They don't devour me, as long as I keep them fed.

I open the bag and dump the partly-frozen human onto the hearth rug. She's shaking uncontrollably, her teeth are chattering, and there's blood at the corner of her mouth. She probably bit her tongue.

That scarlet gleam sends a greedy buzz through my brain. Her blood smells hot, rich, and salty-sweet.

Still draped in the cloak, wearing my mask, I sink to my knees beside her.

Blood is part of my work, a commonplace substance, and I don't typically desire it like most Unseelie Fae do. But *this* blood… it's like a well-marbled beefsteak when you're used to bland fillets of fish. It's irresistible.

The girl's pupils are huge, her lips tinted faintly blue. She's breathing rapidly, shallowly, unable to do more than tremble as I unfurl my long tongue and flick it through the blood at the corner of her mouth.

That tiny taste zings through my nervous system like lightning. I groan, dazzled by the flavor—and yet there's an aftertaste I don't like. A faint yet unmistakable marker in the blood, proof that her body is going into a shocked state which could end in death.

I need to get her warm, and fast.

Throughout my centuries, I've picked up plenty of information about humans, including the fact that when one is deathly cold, skin-to-skin contact is the best way to restore heat.

I slice off the girl's cloak and nightdress with my claws, leaving her panties intact. Her chest is constricted by a band of cloth, wound in tight layers, and I cut through it so she can breathe better. She whimpers and covers her chest with her arms while her breath grows even faster and shallower.

"Not going to hurt you," I mutter. I take off my cape, lie down on the hearth-rug, and drag her shivering form against my bare body. Then I envelop us both with the great ragged cloak. It's layered, and heavy. It will trap the heat well.

She sobs at first, horrible hitching gasps of terror, but when I don't move for several minutes she begins to settle, to breathe slower. The compulsive shaking eases as warmth flows from my body into hers.

I'd planned for this night to end very differently, in a distant town, in a different room, with two naked beauties curled up on either side of me. This waif might be nearly naked, and she might have delicious blood, but beyond that, she doesn't appeal to me at all. She's a lost scrap of humanity. An anomaly in the endless nightmare of my life.

A feather on the winds of Fate.

3

HER

Warm. I'm warm again.

My toes and fingers are soft and pliant. I don't have to fear them freezing solid and snapping clean off.

I'm swathed in layers of dark fabric, with my nose barely poking above the bulk of a cloaked arm. I don't open my eyes at first, because I'm so warm and relaxed, and I know when I look at the creature holding me, I'll panic.

So for a moment I simply *feel*.

My arm, my bare breasts, and my hip are all pressed against hard, smooth, hot skin. My legs lie parallel to his, thighs and knees touching.

He smells like darkness. Like the middle of the night, when the fires are out and the air itself seems frozen in place. Like ice with the faintest hint of peppermint. It's a violent kind of freshness, a bladed hit to the nostrils. And there's a thread of coppery blood under the scent, too. I can almost taste it.

I know the scent and taste of blood all too well. I've been intimately familiar with it since the age of six.

When Goat-Mask stuffed me in that dark red sack, I nearly vomited. The fabric reeked of death, as if he'd soaked the bag in decades' worth of mortal blood. I thought he'd crush me inside it, break my bones to splinters. Pulverize me.

But he saved me instead. He's lying with me now, his large chest surging and sinking with slow, deep breaths.

I open my eyes.

He's still wearing the goat-skull mask. Beneath the toothy lower edge of the mask, I can see a pale, sharp jaw with a crisp corner. Locks of red hair drape across his throat, like scarlet slashes on his snowy skin. A ruff of black fur and ebony feathers form the collar of his cape.

Behind me, a fire crackles, its glow dancing on the grayish-ivory bone of the goat skull. The sockets of the mask are too deeply shadowed for me to perceive his eyes. Is he asleep?

I need to move away from him. I've never been naked with a man, much less a monster. The quiver that runs through me isn't cold, but anxiety. The need to escape. And yet my skin and my flesh crave the warmth of him, the heat of this hollow beneath his cape.

Conflicted, I remain tense and still for several moments before easing myself backward, out from beneath his arm, away from his shelter. I cover my breasts with my hands and stare at the ruined fragments of my nightgown. The bloodstained scraps aren't the only garments on the floor—it's littered with discarded shirts, tunics, trousers, socks, lounge pants, vests, and jackets. A giant wardrobe, which takes up half an entire wall, stands open, disgorging an avalanche of clothes.

At the cabin, I usually wore nightdresses or frilly frocks that were much too small for me. I had perhaps a dozen pieces of clothing, not counting underthings. The careless abundance in this room shocks me. But I'm nothing if not opportunistic, so I select a loose, cream-colored tunic, oversized for a frame as small as mine. Even buttoned, the neckline scoops low, grazing the tops of my breasts, and the hem falls just below the middle of my thighs.

The cut on my foot has stopped bleeding, but I rip a piece from my ruined nightgown and bandage it anyway, in case it decides to reopen. Thus attired, I begin to explore.

This room is as messy as the big gray one, except instead of a forest of furniture, this chamber holds precarious stacks of unwashed plates and mugs, tumbled piles of ornate clocks, and tilted paintings propped crookedly against the walls, with pocket watches on chains looped over their corners. The crystal watch-faces twinkle in the firelight.

Unlit candelabra, some as tall as me, stand in corners, draped with necklaces of multicolored beads. Trinkets and mechanical toys form careless heaps. Feathered purple scarves and gauzy green veils flutter from bookshelves crammed with papers, tiny carved statues, and painted glass vases. He has tacked embroidered tapestries and exquisite sketches to the walls, and between them I catch glimpses of elaborate maps and gorgeously illuminated pages from ancient books.

From the ceiling beams overhead, long strings of crystals twirl and twist, their facets catching the light and tossing it against the walls in triangles or diamonds of emerald, lavender, ruby, and yellow.

It's a nest. A dragon's hoard. A collection in which his massive, dark bulk looks out of place. And it's terribly dusty, as well as disorganized. My fingers twitch with the urge to set the room to rights. It would take days, though… maybe weeks, if I intended to wash and sort everything properly. Most of these items are only familiar to me because of the books I read in the cabin, or because of stories told by a Mother or Wife who was feeling talkative.

A painting of a beautiful nude woman petting a lion catches my eye. As I step toward it, my foot sinks to mid-calf in a pile of clothes… and my toes encounter something *slimy*. With a gasp I leap back and gingerly inspect the clothes. Some of them are seamed with dirt, others crusted with unidentifiable grime, perhaps food spillage. Two of the shirts reek of wine, and one pair of pants has a large stain across the front which smells strongly of piss. The slimy thing I stepped on is a pair of undershorts. There's a glossy, whitish substance on them—a lot of it. A recent addition to the pile, I think.

Apparently monsters don't like doing laundry.

"Nasty creature," I mutter under my breath.

Even as I speak the words, a plan forms in my mind. A way to make myself useful and to claim a place here, at least for a while. The monster saved my life. Didn't eat me or hurt me. If I repay the debt and prove my worth, maybe he'll keep me around.

After surveying the room again, I pick my way over to a big basket full of colorful yarn balls, rolled-up papers, and two rotting apples. After dumping out the basket's contents, I begin filling it with the foulest of the discarded clothing.

There must be a kitchen or a bathing room somewhere in this house. The monster is obviously magical, yet he has physical form and physical needs. If I can find the bath or the kitchen, I might also find soap, and a sink or a washtub where I can give these clothes the thorough scrubbing they need.

With the basket propped on my hip, I open the bedroom door and slip out into the hallway. I close the door quietly behind me, hoping the monster will stay asleep until I can finish at least one batch of laundry. I'd like to surprise him.

The basket is heaped so high it's almost too heavy for me to carry. My legs still waver a bit from the terror and exposure of last night. Is it still night, or is it morning? The clocks in the bedroom all told different times, and I've yet to see a window in this place, except for the curtained ones in the great gray room. What joy it would be to live in a place with real windows—to feel the sun shining through the glass, onto my skin! My captor used to tell me the sun was dangerous, that it would burn me and blind me; but the other women said that if you were careful, the sun could be a wonderful thing. I'm not sure what to believe, but I would like to experience the sun and decide for myself, even if it's dangerous.

Everything is dangerous, after all. The cabin, the town, and this house. I haven't forgotten the monster in the walls, or the heavy-breathing creature on the staircase. As I walk the halls by the light of the occasional guttering candle, I scan the gaps in the walls and cast glances upward, into the shadows that cloak the high ceilings. But nothing interferes with my progress, and after a while I descend four broad stone steps and open the large door beyond them to find the largest, messiest kitchen I've ever seen.

I step inside, onto a flagstone floor. There's a huge fireplace arch with a spit across its middle and stone ovens flanking its sides. The fire is nothing but faintly-glowing coals, so I stir it up with a poker and feed it a few sticks of kindling from a nearby bucket.

Both the kindling and the logs in the firewood rack are dry and dusty. It seems no one has fed the fire in days, yet the coals were alive. And the candles in the hallway were long and fresh, without a drip of wax, even though they must have been burning for hours. Strange.

"Magic." I speak the word aloud with a shrug. It's the only way to explain the inexplicable.

The kitchen cabinets, counters, and tables are piled high with grimy pots and crusty dishes. When I attempt to move a stack, several pots and spoons clatter to the floor, and a flood of brown insects scurry away, disappearing into the cracks between the wall tiles.

I freeze for a moment, stunned by the sheer number of them. But I've had plenty of practice swallowing my distaste for unpleasant surroundings, so I recover quickly.

Lucky for me, there's a jar of soft soap near the sink, its lid filmed with dust. I'm doubly pleased to find that the huge sink has a spigot with two handles, one of which produces hot water without the trouble of heating it on a stove. It's a modern convenience the most recent Wife bemoaned when she first came to the cabin and discovered that our water only ran cold. I've never experienced hot water flowing from a pipe before, and I'm beyond delighted with it.

My first task is to empty the sink, piling the grimy dishes aside for now. Then, with my two new allies, hot water and soap, I fill the sink and attack the laundry, immersing myself in the familiar comfort of making foul things fresh again.

When the first batch of laundry is done, I hang the well-wrung items on some half-moldered string I found in the pantry, so they can dry near the fire. Next I clear and scrub down one of the tables so the clean dishes can have a place to sit and air-dry. And then I attack the piles of filthy plates, mugs, and bowls.

I'm elbow-deep in suds when I glance toward the fireplace and nearly scream.

Something is hanging upside down inside the chimney, peering out at me with eyes the size of saucers. Short gray fur covers every bit of its body that I can see, including its long pointy ears, which both look as if something has chewed mercilessly on their edges. It has stubby horns and a wide, wide mouth—*terrifyingly* wide and thankfully closed. One tiny pointed tooth protrudes over its lower lip. Clawed fingers grip the bricks as it watches me.

It drops a bit lower, allowing me a glimpse at its scaly, serpentine tail, probably thrice the length of its body.

Heart pounding, I turn back to the soapsuds and keep scrubbing, debating if I should run. The creature resembles the sketch of a lemur in the book of animals I received a few years ago. But lemurs don't have horns, and their tails aren't scaly.

I steal another glance, only to see the creature catching live sparks on a tongue as long as its tail. Parallel rows of small triangular teeth line the inside of its mouth.

Definitely not a lemur.

The pot I'm scrubbing is clean, so I rinse it and set it down on the table, eyeing the creature sidelong to see how it reacts to the sound. Its attention swerves back to me briefly before it hops down to perch on the spit. It wraps its snakelike tail around the metal bar and leans over to lick at the flames. After it slurps a whole flame into its mouth, its eyes glow briefly purple and orange, like a sunset, and it smacks its lips.

"Fire-eating lemur with horns," I murmur. "Nothing like that in the mortal world, I think. You must be Fae."

The creature tilts its head and makes a clicking sound.

"Perhaps I should give you a name," I say evenly. "Or do you already have a name? Are you a pet of the Goat-Mask? The—" I search my memory for the word the townspeople used— "The Krampus?"

The creature's ears twitch, and it looks toward the kitchen door. I follow its glance, but the door is still shut. I'm still alone in the gigantic mess of a kitchen, in the small space I've cleared for myself.

"Once I wash all these dishes, I'll need a broom and a mop," I tell the creature. "I don't suppose you know where those might be?"

Filmy eyelids close sideways over the creature's enormous eyes, and it leaps down into the fire with startling suddenness. Unaffected by the flames, it bounds over the hearth, then springs lightly across the stacks of pots and moldy rags on the flagstone floor. Its speed sends my heart into my mouth.

The creature bounces up onto the counter by the sink, its claws scratching against the thin slab of stone laid across the wooden cabinets.

"Hello there." I wipe my hand on my borrowed shirt before reaching out to the creature. It sniffs my fingertips delicately with slitted nostrils that are barely visible through its gray fur.

"Wait here." I move away slowly, smoothly, careful not to startle it. I step over to the fire, retrieve one of the last sticks of kindling, and light it. Holding the unlit end, I return to the little creature and offer it the flame. Quick as a blink, it grabs the stick from me and shoves the burning end into its mouth, sucking it clean of the fire. Its eyes turn violet and orange again, and I laugh.

"You're kind of beautiful, aren't you?" I say softly. "Fiery and tiny and beautiful. I don't know why that makes me want to cry." I shake my head and return to scouring the next pot.

I've never been one to talk much while working. I was always afraid of saying the wrong thing—something Wife or Mother might repeat to *him*, to my detriment and their own benefit. In all those years, I only trusted one of them with my true thoughts and feelings—the Mother who saw me through my first bleeding.

I don't talk much to my fire-eating friend, either. A few words, here and there. Once, when I mention that the water is getting cold, the creature leans over the sink, submerges its mouth in the water, and breathes superheated bubbles into the liquid. It seems pleased by my exclamation of delight.

"Full of surprises, aren't you?" I croon, reaching out. I'm not sure what I plan to do—let it sniff my fingers again, maybe pet its fur—but before I can attempt either, a voice barks, "Stop! Don't move."

THE WOLPERTINGER

4

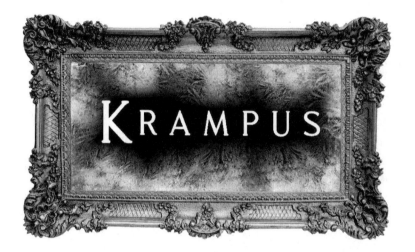

KRAMPUS

When I finally wake up, I'm instantly furious.

That was the best sleep I've had in months and I can't stand the thought that maybe it was because of the girl, because I needed something to hold, like a fucking toddler with a stuffed toy.

I'm also angry because the girl ran off and she's probably already been eaten, which means I'll have to dispose of the wet skin and melted flesh the Bahkauv will have left behind, after extracting and gulping down her bones. Wolpertinger is neater with his meals, but if he got her first, there will still be leftovers to get rid of. Worst of all, the Imp may have found her before the others. If so, the girl will be diced into bloody bits within seconds. The Imp will pick up one cube of flesh at a time, set it afire, and swallow each flaming tidbit with clicks of pleasure. I've seen him do it before. His meals take hours and always result in a lake of blood. Not to mention I'll be stepping on bits of diced bone for days—they always seem to get scattered through the entire house.

God-stars, I hate cleaning.

I used to have the same abilities many other Fae possess—the skill to swiftly clean entire rooms or to conjure food with magic. But I was separated from those powers when I was exiled to the mortal world and turned into a demon. I've often imagined the god-star Andregh snickering with satisfaction as he condemned me to centuries of mopping, dusting, and washing my own clothes. Joke's on him, because I simply purchase new dishes or clothes when the old ones are too filthy. Some of my targets are obscenely wealthy, and in those cases I always take some of their money and possessions for myself. Nocturis has never rebuked me for collecting such treasures, so I continue to do so, liberally, whenever I get the chance.

After pulling on a pair of undershorts and shrouding myself in the cape again, I hunt for the girl, traversing this huge carcass of a mansion, marching up staircases and down hallways, checking each unlocked door. I slam one quickly when I see the Wolpertinger lunge up from his resting place and gallop toward me, his red rabbit's eyes glazed with greedy hunger and his huge front teeth snapping. Each of Wolpertinger's four legs is far taller than I am, so I doubt he could fit through the door and get to me, but I'd rather not test the theory since he seems out of sorts today. His body is that of a huge brown hare, skinny and stretched to impossibly tall proportions. He always looks half-starved, even though I bring him most of my victims. Hawk wings protrude from his back, narrow antlers stick straight up from his skull, and the tail that lashes behind him is reddish and bushy, like a fox's but longer.

I didn't expect him to be in one of the rooms. He's usually slinking through the gaps between the walls, making a *shushing* sound as his lanky body drags along the slats and plaster.

He doesn't have the girl, so I keep looking. The Bahkauv doesn't show himself at all.

As I approach the kitchen, I hear the clank of a pan, and I curse myself silently for not checking there first. Of course the human would be looking for food.

I push open the door, surprised by the warmth and humidity of the room, and by the pungent smell of soap.

The girl stands by the sink, smiling, her tender little fingers held out to the Imp.

My whole body tenses in horrified shock. This foolish mortal has no idea how deadly the Imp can be. Another second, and her soft human flesh will be chopped into pieces no bigger than the end of my smallest finger.

"Stop!" I command her tersely. "Don't move."

The girl looks my way, startled. The Imp hisses at me, then ducks and rubs its head along the girl's palm. She smiles and scratches the Imp's ragged ears. Then, with another angry hiss at me, the Imp bounds across the floor, jumps up to the fireplace spit, and disappears into the chimney.

"You scared it," says the girl reproachfully.

"*I* scared it?" I stare at her, incredulous. "Do you know what it is? What it would have done to you?"

"We've spent a couple of very pleasant hours together."

"You... you what?" I brush aside a few mouse droppings and sit down heavily on a stool. "You're lucky you're not in its belly right now."

"That little thing?" Her eyebrows rise.

"Oh yes. The Imp can devour a full-grown human. Dices them up first with those sharp teeth. As it consumes each morsel, it transforms the flesh and bone into magical energy. It's a powerful, intelligent creature."

"Oh." She rubs her forehead with the back of her soapy wrist, leaving a smear of tiny glistening bubbles on her brow. "I didn't realize. I thought it might be dangerous, but… I think it likes me."

"Imps don't *like* anyone." With a sigh I take off the skull-mask, lifting it free of my horns. I wore the mask while I searched for her, since it seems to elicit respect from my monstrous housemates—but I'm weary of its weight on my face.

The girl stares as I toss aside the mask and it vanishes in midair. With a groan, I shake out my long red hair and massage the roots of my black horns. I could banish the horns, as I do when I go out drinking and carousing among humans; but they're impressive, and I like the way the girl looks at them with such awe. She needs to know I'm someone to be feared and respected, even in this form.

After a few seconds of staring at my unmasked face, she turns back to the sink, runs the hot water, and rinses off a frying pan. After she has cleared the suds from its surface, she adds it to a stack of freshly washed dishes on the table between us.

"Why are you doing that?" I challenge her.

"Making myself useful. I'm a good worker." She opens her brown eyes very wide. "And this place is filthy."

I know it is, of course. But her judgment irritates me. "It's fine," I snarl.

She shrinks a little at the force of my tone. "I could help. I could make this a comfortable, clean place for you. Isn't that something you'd like?" Her voice is softer now—light, delicate, and soothing, with a coy playfulness that's almost childish. It grates on me, because it's false. An affectation.

"What's your name?" Again my tone is harsh, and she looks as if she might sink down and melt right into the floor.

Her dark eyes turn mournful and liquid. "I'm Little Sister."

"What is your name?"

She shakes her head.

"You don't have a name?"

"Sometimes a Wife or a Mother would try to give me one. But I never allowed it. I was afraid I might accidentally answer to the name in front of *him*. And he wanted me to be Little Sister. The role was the thing, not the person playing it. Whenever he killed someone and they went to the fjord, we called the new person 'Wife' or 'Mother,' and the game continued as if it never stopped."

As an instrument of death upon the wicked, I've seen my share of twisted souls. But it sounds as if the man I killed last night was a whole new kind of demented.

The girl wipes her wet fingers on the shirt she's wearing—*my* shirt—and comes around the table toward me. She clasps her hands in front of her, tilts her head to one side, and looks up at me, blinking her long, dark lashes prettily.

"I'll be your Little Sister," she says in the same childish voice.

"Stop talking like that," I growl. "We haven't yet discussed the fact that you summoned me *again*. No one summons me a second time. How did you do it? You stole one of my bells, didn't you?"

"I didn't mean to." She's in earnest now, no longer playing a role. "It was an accident. I thought I could wear it as a necklace, but when I entered the tavern, everyone was terrified of me. They said I was Fae-cursed, and that I would summon the Krampus. They were ready to throw me out."

"Shit." I rub a hand across my face. "The bell is a telltale sign. You should have discarded it."

"I didn't realize that at first." She looks down at her feet, one bare and one bandaged. I can smell faint traces of blood from the injured foot. I'm shocked that one of the monsters didn't gobble her up the second she ventured into the hall, with that fresh blood scenting her steps.

She continues speaking, with a shamefaced expression. "I went to a place with red lamps, where they said they could use a Little Sister… but I don't think it was the same kind of play I'm used to. They asked where I was from, and when I told them, they were frightened and told me to leave. But I made them give me food and some other things first."

"How did you make them give you things?"

"I held up the bell and told them if they didn't do what I said, I'd call the Krampus."

The corners of my mouth tense, and I have to frown ferociously to keep from smiling. "That was incredibly foolish."

"It was the only thing I could think of. I was alone. You left me." There's a faint accusation in the last three words.

"And you want me to, what? Let you stay here?"

She nods, blinking prettily at me again.

"Stop that," I snarl.

Her eyes widen. "Stop what?"

I rise from the stool, towering over her. Fuck, the top of her head only comes to mid-breast on me. Though there's fear in her eyes she stays perfectly still, her expression smooth, controlled, and submissive.

"Let's get one thing clear," I tell her. "I'm not like the piece of shit who kept you prisoner. Simping and fluttering won't work on me. This isn't a safe house, nor is it a jail. It's a fucking carnival of ravenous monsters who will devour you in a moment and make it hurt so much that moment seems to last forever. You don't belong here. You'll die here."

"I'll die out *there*." Her voice is frail, but her chin is set. "I made friends with the Imp, didn't I? I saw the other beasts, but they didn't eat me, and they could have."

My heartbeat kicks up at the thought of her encountering either Wolpertinger or the Bahkauv and surviving. "That's very fucking strange."

"I'd like to stay and clean. I'll do your laundry, clean the house, organize everything—and change your sheets. When was the last time you had clean sheets?"

Couple decades ago, maybe... "You want to be my maid?"

She hesitates as if the word is only distantly familiar. "Yes."

"It's a big job. There are many rooms, and this house has a personality and a mind of its own."

She raises her eyebrows at that, but determination conquers the caution in her gaze. "I can do it."

"Fine. I'll allow it, on a trial basis. But if you get eaten, it's your own fault."

"I'll remind myself of that while I'm being chewed."

Again I feel the ridiculous urge to smile, and again I scowl. "Very good. You'll need clothing that's appropriate for the task, and more cleaning supplies. I'll take you into the city with me today and we can purchase the necessary items."

At that, she retreats to the other side of the table. The pile of clean dishes is so high she's nearly concealed behind them. "No."

"No?"

"I don't want to go into any more villages, towns, or cities. Not yet."

"You'd rather stay here alone, with the monsters?" She looks as if she might scurry away and hide in a cabinet if I deny her, so I shrug and say, "Fine. Suit yourself. I'll go alone, then. You stay here and keep doing... all of this." I wave my hand at the wreck of the kitchen. Mountains of dishes, years' worth of moldering food. In my line of work, I'm used to foul odors, but that doesn't mean I like them. I burn magical incense both here and in my room every so often to keep the smell under control, but the odor still annoys me. I'm not sure how she can stand it.

The girl turns her back to me as she picks up a stack of plates. Her soft brown braids swing against the cream-colored shirt she's wearing, their curled ends brushing the swell of her ass. I remember how she felt in my arms—feather-light.

"Feather," I say suddenly.

She looks at me, suspicious and alert.

"That's your name now. Feather."

Her lips pucker as she considers my statement. She has a pretty mouth. I didn't notice it before.

"Feather," she says. "Yes. And you? What's your name?"

"You haven't earned that knowledge yet. You can call me *sir*, or *my lord*, or *master*."

I'm half-joking, though my tone doesn't change to indicate the sarcasm. But she accepts my statement with an earnest nod. "Yes, sir."

Her compliance makes me irrationally furious, and rather than yell at her, I leave the room.

I don't bathe often. Fae don't generally smell, so there's little need for it unless I'm coated in blood, and even then I usually just sponge off the gore. Today I wash myself a little more thoroughly than usual. Once I've dispelled my horns and put on a suit of human clothes, my geistfyre takes me to the city of Rothenfel.

When the Wild Hunt gave me this role and restricted my magic, they allowed me the ability to glamour or dispel a few telltale aspects of my person, like my horns and my pointed ears. In my regular form I have no tail, but my tongue is noticeably longer than that of most Fae. When I am judging the wicked, my tail appears, my size increases, and my tongue grows longer and turns venomous. With one lick, I can paralyze a human for several minutes.

Sometimes I use my tongue on the innocent, to keep them quiet and out of the way while I do my work. Other times I use it to immobilize my target if I'm feeling particularly lazy and I'd rather not deal with them struggling or screaming. But I like it best when I'm in my Fae form, when there's no venom involved, and I can use my tongue for more pleasurable purposes. During my jaunts into various cities and towns, I usually leave it un-glamoured. I find that showing its pierced length to women has a tempting effect. I've lured many pleasant lovers into bed that way. But I rarely reveal its full extent, lest someone suspect my Fae origins.

Few kingdoms in this world are friendly to the Fae, and Nocturis has made it clear that the Wild Hunt will not help me if I get myself captured by humans or attacked by Fae-hunters. I'm expendable. There are plenty of wicked Fae, and they could replace me easily. So when I'm out among humans, I must remain glamoured, and I must keep my guard up, despite the influence of beer or bawdy women.

I make a stop at a general store in Rothenfel, hand a bag of silver coins to the owner, and ask him to pack up everything that a new maid in a large household might need, including clothing, linens, and cleaning supplies.

"My new maid is about her size, but slightly smaller," I add, pointing to the owner's petite assistant. "I want her to look the part."

"Of course, sir," replies the shopkeeper.

I've been to this shop before, and as far as the owner knows, I'm a wealthy young lord from a nearby estate. He'll fill the order to my satisfaction, I have no doubt. Meanwhile I'll be drinking at The Holy Boar down the way.

As I stroll along the street, looking into the occasional shop window, I notice several pieces of paper tacked to a wooden lamppost, their tattered edges fluttering in the cold breeze. Sketches of missing men, women, and children from this province, which is called Visseland. Most of the posters are badly frayed, but two are recent. One is a girl with a pert face and braids wrapped around her head. But it's the second, an image drawn with bold black lines, which catches my eye. I spread the paper out so I can see it better.

It's a "Wanted" poster—or perhaps more of a *warning* poster—of me. The people of this region and the other provinces I've visited call me Krampus—an old trollish word from the northern cave systems of Faerie, where I was raised. No doubt the term was carried to the mortal world by some realm-traveler. The paths between worlds are fewer now, but they still exist, though all of them are closed to me. I am forbidden from returning to Faerie ever again.

My nails scrape shavings of wood from the lamppost as I crumple the poster and cast it aside. The artist's depiction isn't a goat mask, but an ugly, demented visage with a rictus grin. The long tongue, the black horns, the goat hooves, and the heavy cape—those are accurate. But the manic glee on my face, the stooped posture, and the arrow-shaped tail are all wrong. I'm not some hideous fiend.

Worse still, the scrawled lines at the bottom of the poster blame *all* the disappearances on me. And while that may be true in some cases, I'm certainly not responsible for all the kidnappings, runaways, murders, infanticide, and cruelty that go on in Visseland.

Still seething from the sight of that poster, I shove open the doors of The Holy Boar, my favorite pub in Rothenfel. I saunter to the bar and take a stool, flinging down a few coins.

"Lord Brandt!" The bartender uses my false name. "A pleasure, I'm sure. What'll you have?"

"Beer, with a wedge of lime and a dash of heat, and salt the rim."

He nods and hurries to prepare the drink.

I hesitate to broach the topic of the Krampus with the bartender, but I'm concerned about who might have pinned that notice to the lamppost. If suspicions are riding too high around here, I may need to move my house elsewhere.

Geistfyre magic requires a stationary anchor point, creating a radius in which I can move from place to place—and the house serves as that anchor. When my reputation in a certain part of the world becomes too dramatic and the stories becomes too vivid, I use geistfyre to move the whole house to another country or province. It's a difficult process which weakens the house's energy, so I try not to do it often.

When I came to Visseland, I anchored my geistfyre magic—and my house—in an abandoned quarry not far from Rothenfel, where the natural aura of the quartz in the ground provides a strong energy source. It has been a good enough place, and I've grown attached to certain pubs, brothels, and gambling houses in the region at large and Rothenfel in particular. It would be a shame if I had to move away.

Besides, I have plenty of work here, without having to travel far. The people in the northern reaches of this continent are a depraved lot—and it's not the commonplace sort of acceptable depravity, either. No, this goes far beyond drunkenness, thievery, or licentious behavior. Maybe it's the length and severity of the winters, or the parts of the year when they go days without seeing the sun. Maybe it's the bone-deep ache of the freezing air, a cold so ferocious I feel it myself, though the Fae are typically resistant to temperature variation.

Whatever the reason, the people scattered throughout these ravines, mines, and mountains are a cruel kind, with hearts as cold as the landscape and wicked as the Unseelie. Vices run rampant among them, more so than in the other places I've visited. Here in Visseland, I've judged many a family where a parent, friend, or relative was beating the children... or committing worse acts upon them.

I don't deal out death in every case. Depending on the severity of the offense, sometimes it's just a warning—a mutilation, a dismemberment, or a brutal thrashing, with a caution to do better, lest I return for a more final judgment. It's those survivors who report my existence, who give rise to rumors and legends and posters like the one I just ripped down.

The bartender slides my drink toward me, and I catch the tankard in my hands. "I saw a strange picture on a poster during my walk here," I say. "Fucking ugly creature with horns."

"The Krampus." The bartender speaks low, with an anxious glance around. "He killed my wife's brother a while back. Not that we missed my brother-in-law much—he was a rotten bastard. But the way he went... the blood all over the floor..." He shakes his head. "His daughter was four at the time. She came to live with us afterward. Hasn't spoken a word since."

It's not my place to worry about the ones I save. I judge, I punish—I do not rescue. When I do take payment, I'm careful to leave plenty of money for the care of those left behind. Mother Holle follows in my wake and ensures that any orphaned children are found and cared for, or she takes them to a safe place herself. I merely remove the wicked; I don't waste time rehabilitating their victims.

But the tale of the silent child troubles me, even though I know her speech difficulty is likely due to her father's wickedness, not my judgment.

"How awful," I murmur.

The bartender nods. "The Mayor is interested in finding the beast and destroying it, so it can't terrorize good, law-abiding folk no more."

I almost spit out the swallow of beer I just took, but I manage to control myself. "No, we wouldn't want good people to be terrified."

"Don't you worry," the bartender assures me, swiping at the polished counter with his cloth. "The Mayor called in some help. Couple of Fae-hunters from a southern province. Experts in all things dark and magical. They should be here in a month or so. They'll catch the monster."

"Perfect." I fake a smile as he moves off to polish a silver tankard.

Fae-hunters. Shit.

Other members of the Wild Hunt, being ghosts and all, don't fear Fae-hunters; but since I'm corporeal, I have to be more careful. The house, in its role as a geistfyre anchor, is a noticeable piece of magic, and it will blaze out like a fucking beacon to anyone who knows what they're looking for. That could be a problem if these Fae-hunters venture too far from Rothenfel.

I'll need to find out who they are and gauge the severity of the threat. Which means attending one of the Mayor's parties, where wine flows freely and loose tongues spill secrets. As "Lord Brandt," I have a standing invitation to all such gatherings. There's one coming up five weeks from now, in fact.

No use worrying about the hunters until then. Right now, I require distraction and delight.

I survey the room, displeased that there aren't many women here at this time of day. I need to see admiration and desire in someone's eyes when they look at me. I need them to want me, to crave me so badly they're willing to make fools of themselves to gain my attention. Being wanted like that—it makes my life bearable, somehow.

A young man down the bar nods to me, appreciation shining in his eyes. I devour that look, basking in the scent of his lust, and I give him an answering smile, which encourages him to abandon his seat for one next to me. Men aren't my preference in bed, so this won't go farther than a little flirting and a few drinks. But for now, that's all I need.

5

Feather.

I like the name.

Feathers are light and pliant, yet resilient. My book of creatures had birds in it, with sketches of their bones and wings, and I've examined feathers that worked their way out of the down pillow on Wife's bed. Feathers can survive all sorts of circumstances. They might come through a storm looking wet and ragged, but a little preening and they're good as new again.

"Feather," I say aloud to the Imp, who returned to me shortly after Krampus left. "How do you like my new name?"

The Imp lashes his scaly tail and gnaws on a pair of iron tongs that I heated red-hot for him in the fireplace.

Somewhere in the house, a door bangs.

It's not the first strange sound I've heard during the hours I've been working. The old mansion creaks almost constantly. Various rustling, scraping, and shuffling noises echo through its walls and corridors.

But there's a sharp definition to that slamming door, an intentionality that catches my interest. Is Krampus back? He's been gone for at least a couple of hours. I wipe my hands and go to the kitchen door, eager for the supplies he promised to bring me.

When I open the door, my breath catches. The kitchen is huge, rambling, and piled with dishes and debris that cast frightening shadows, but it seems downright cozy compared to the hallway that stretches away into the dark.

The Imp slinks past my feet and scampers a little way down the hall, his immense round eyes glowing like yellow lamps.

"I rather wish I hadn't offered to clean and care for this house," I confess to him.

He makes a clicking sound and bounces away into the dark. Without him, I feel horribly alone.

I'm used to having *someone*. At the cabin, there were always three of us. Wife, Mother, Little Sister. Even if one died, a replacement would arrive within a week at most.

A scratching sound rasps down the hallway, distant but coming closer. Like nails dragging along the wall… dragging slowly, jerkily, constantly. No footsteps, only the interminable scraping.

The sound grows louder, until I can see grooves forming in the wallpaper. I can't see what's making the scratches, but it's headed straight for me.

A cold breath stirs the stagnant air, and the sudden aroma of cinnamon makes my nostrils twitch. I want to rub my hand under my nose, but I resist the urge. I stay perfectly still, because I know predators. I know what it is to live alongside someone whose control could snap at any moment. Sometimes hiding is best, and sometimes, when it's too late to hide, you must watch, and wait, and be absolutely motionless.

A whisper seems to come from within the wall itself. "Nerves of stone, with skin so soft. Pretty thing. Mortal, yes?"

"Yes," I answer.

"Only monsters live here," croons the voice.

"Monsters, and me."

The voice laughs—lilting feminine merriment. It sounds bodiless, untethered, without the warmth, solidity, and dimension of a voice that comes from a chest, lungs, and a throat. This laugh is a thought or a memory. It has no physical source.

Pale mist slithers from the scratches on the wall and condenses before my eyes, taking on opacity and color until a woman stands there. She's tall and wistful-looking, with pale, translucent skin, white antlers, and golden eyes. Blond hair cascades down her body, all the way to the floor. Streamers of white mist surround her, fluttering and billowing like the ragged remnants of a white gown, its design fluid and ever-changing.

"Krampus didn't tell me he had a guest," she says.

My mouth is dry with shock. When Krampus took off his mask, I was stunned by his beauty, and she's just as lovely, in a ghostly way. Eddies of icy mist whisper across her skin when she moves, and I suspect if I tried to touch her, my hand would pass right through.

"I'm the new maid," I manage to say.

"The maid?" She titters softly. "He could use a servant to keep this place in order, but a *human*? Seems dangerous, with the beasties loping about, don't you think? What's your name, pretty thing?"

"Feather. May I ask... what are you?"

She sweeps her golden hair behind one pointed ear. "I was Fae once. Now I am nothing, a mere ghost of myself, except when I have a task to complete. Then I receive physical form for a short while. My name is Perchta of the Wild Hunt. Perhaps you've heard of me."

I shake my head.

A quiver of displeasure distorts her lovely face for a second before she smiles gently. "No matter. I am not so dramatic and dreadful as Krampus." She drags one long nail through the wallpaper. "Like him, I can appear in two different guises. But I doubt you'd want to see my other form. People tend to piss themselves with fright."

"I can handle terrible things," I reply.

She sweeps forward suddenly, while her hair lifts and floats around her like a writhing cloud of frothy gold. Her gaze pries me open, as if she's peeking into the parts of my soul that I don't want anyone to see.

"Oh," she breathes. "You're a wicked one, aren't you? Does Krampus know what you've done?"

My heart turns into cold stone.

She *can't* know. Anyone who knew is dead now. Which means she must be reading my mind.

"Stay out of my head," I hiss.

She retreats, mist draining off her translucent shape in curling tendrils. "As you wish, Feather. Is Krampus here?"

"He went to purchase supplies."

"That's a new term for 'fucking, drinking, and gambling,'" she muses. "Ah well. I'll roam the house a bit and wait for him. Maybe I'll come back later and we can have a real conversation. This house is much too full of males—we girls have to stick together. I know you and I are going to be excellent friends."

She drifts away down the hall. Once she's out of sight, I go back into the kitchen and close the door. No doubt she could pass right through it, but still… I feel better with a barrier of solid wood between me and ghostly Perchta of the Wild Hunt.

Krampus returns like a blizzard, like the wild winds that used to batter the cabin and howl through the chimney. He bursts into the kitchen and flings two large bags onto the floor, along with a bundle of sticks.

"There." He gestures to the supplies with a lazy flourish. "Everything you need." His words are slurred, his balance uncertain. I know the signs of drunkenness. Caution flares through me, tightening my nerves as I gauge whether to hide, to run, or to stand my ground.

He doesn't have horns at the moment, and he's dressed in a fine sky-blue shirt with white pants, a dark overcoat, and black leather boots. As I watch, his rounded nails turn sharp, while his human ears grow pointed. But the horns don't reappear.

Last time I saw him, I understood his beauty as a fact, as an essential piece in the puzzle of his character. A potential weakness. Beautiful people are far more likely to believe themselves beloved or invincible.

I'm wearier now, exhausted from my hours in the kitchen. More vulnerable to his striking features. His jaw has such sharp corners, such straight, crisp lines. His nose is perfect, decorated with a small ring between the nostrils. Bold, angled cheekbones slash along each side of his face, accentuating the subtle hollows of his cheeks. His ears and brows glitter with jewelry, and he wears rings on every finger. I could have sworn his eyes were red last time, but they're green now, and glowing faintly.

When he takes off his overcoat, I can't drag my gaze away from him. His body is obtrusively gorgeous, commanding the room. It's almost offensive how broad his shoulders are, how smoothly they taper to his waist, how fluidly his hips move, how long and strong his legs look in the close-fitting white pants and the tall boots. I never imagined a man could have such a form, that he could project masculine power and sinuous grace at the same time.

"A friend came by to see you," I tell him.

"Friend? I don't have friends." He scoffs and flings himself into a kitchen chair. One of the chair legs has rotted, and it snaps before I can warn him, dumping him onto the floor. He glances around in offended consternation, like he's unsure what happened or how to get up.

I step forward and extend my hand. He blinks at it and frowns ferociously. "What the devil are you doing?"

"Helping?"

"Well, stop it."

Withdrawing, I watch him climb to his feet with many a muttered curse. He stares around at the kitchen, which is far cleaner than when he left, though I still have hours of work before I'm satisfied.

"You have too many dishes and pots," I tell him. "They won't all fit in the cabinets."

"I buy new ones when the old ones are too dirty to use," he says. "I hate washing things."

I can't imagine such wastefulness and laziness, but I only say, "What shall I do with the extras?"

"Fuck if I know."

"Your friend... she may still be here if you want to speak with her."

"I told you, I have no friends. Who is it?"

"Perchta of the Wild Hunt."

He frowns. "She's floating around here again? God-stars. How did she behave?"

"She was pleasant enough." Then I venture a question. "What is the Wild Hunt?"

"A collection of assholes," he replies. "Wretched bastards who did terrible crimes in life, who are now condemned to ride between worlds as ghost-Fae and bring justice upon those who do similarly terrible crimes."

"You're not a ghost."

"How well you state the obvious," he sneers. "Do you want a treat for your cleverness?"

"You punish those who are cruel to children. Does that mean you once did something terrible to a child?"

Instead of answering, he strides through the kitchen to an area I've not yet tackled. He kicks aside some rubbish and opens a cabinet, brushing away the bugs that instantly swarm up the inner walls. "There should be a fruit pie in here," he mutters. "Ah, there you are."

He knocks more bugs off the crust and digs his fingers in, scooping up a dollop of cherry-red filling. His long tongue snakes out, and this time I definitely spot more than one piercing along its length. His fangs glint as he licks the pie filling from his fingers.

"Don't eat that, I beg of you." I cringe as a small insect scurries along his knuckles and down his wrist. "Surely there's some food in those bags you brought. I can fix you something."

He evaluates me out of the corner of his green, glowing eye. "I need something sweet. If my eating habits offend you, go away."

His sharp tone reminds me how precarious my position is. I duck my head and give him a small curtsy. "Yes, sir. Tell me how to get back to your room, please. I'd like to collect more of the laundry and bring it down for washing."

He holds my gaze while his long tongue snakes around his fingers, polishing them clean. There's something wicked in the way he does it—something in the wet slither of his tongue that makes my knees weaken and my pulse flutter. Something flutters between my legs, too—a soft, insistent, ticklish sensation. Something I've only felt a few times.

The glow of Krampus's eyes intensifies. "Do you like what you see?"

"Please tell me how to get to your room," I repeat.

In a disgruntled mumble, he gives me a few words of guidance, then advises, "Check the bags I brought. There may be a set or two of clean linens in there. I asked the shopkeeper to give me everything a maid would need for taking care of a large house." He goes back to eating the terrible pie.

Sure enough, one of the bags contains brand-new sheets, towels, and kitchen cloths, as well as a few sets of clothes and underwear. I select clean sheets and a set of clothes before heading for his room. I don't ask for his company or protection, even though I'm fearful of meeting monsters on the way.

Lucky for me, no monsters materialize. Once I'm in Krampus's bedroom, I quickly change into the maid's outfit he purchased for me. It's far different from my nightgown or the childish frocks I'm used to wearing. The black, lace-trimmed dress is very short, barely reaching the middle of my thighs, and the neckline dips low in the front. White thigh-high stockings and buckled shoes complete the outfit, but I leave the shoes off, for now.

There are a few mirrors in the room, half-buried in clutter, and from what I can glimpse of myself, I like my new look. Far from hiding my breasts, hips, and legs, these clothes seem designed to celebrate them. Which is new for me, and a little terrifying—yet it feeds some part of me that has been hungry for a long time. Revealing myself like this, as a fully grown woman, is a satisfying kind of defiance.

Once I'm dressed, I strip the bed, fighting back queasiness as I notice how stained and filthy the sheets and pillowcases are. The feather pillows will need a good airing. Back at the cabin, when bedding needed to be aired out, we simply moved it to the front room for a while, where a little fresh air leaked through the chimney. Here in the house, cool currents of air circulate through the hallways periodically. The air doesn't have an outdoor freshness, exactly, but it's better than stagnant mustiness.

Under the bedsheets there's a thin pad, also soiled, so I strip that away as well. The mattress beneath looks and smells decent enough, so I proceed with making the bed. It's a much wider bed than I'm used to, but I manage to get the sheets in place. I crouch to tuck them under the end of the mattress, then lean across to smooth out a few wrinkles in the center.

I'm in that position, bent over the bed with my arm outstretched, when my skin prickles with the sensation of being watched.

6

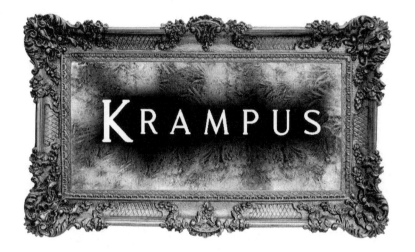

I drank too much, and the pie isn't soaking up the liquor. I need to sleep.

I stagger down the hallway, drawling loudly, "Listen well, beasties! If you want to gobble me up, now's your chance. Come on, bitches. Come out and get me. Wake up, Wolpertinger, you mange-riddled old bastard. Let's end this now."

It's stupid to call them out like this. But I'm in a doleful, dreadful, reckless state of mind, and I can't help taunting my housemates as I stumble through the halls, crashing into corners and tripping on steps.

Why haven't they come to devour me? Perhaps they're munching on the girl at this very moment, too full of her tender flesh and sweet blood to bother with me.

The thought sobers me for a second—just enough that I'm quiet as I approach my room. The door squeaks faintly as I push it open, but my maid is too involved in her task to notice. She's crouching at the end of the bed, tucking in the sheets. Her brown braids swing as she stands up—and then she bends over, reaching to flatten a crease in the center of the bed. Her ridiculously short skirt rides up, exposing her ass to me.

The panties don't conceal her entire bottom, and the lower curves of her ass cheeks peek out. Between her thighs I glimpse a little mound of white—her pussy, covered only by thin, soft fabric. The lace-trimmed black skirt frames the picture for me as I stand dumbfounded by the door.

She tenses suddenly. Straightens and whirls around.

Her thin fingers smooth the black skirt of the dress, and her breasts swell against the neckline as her breath quickens.

"What the fuck are you wearing?" I rasp.

"The… the clothes you bought me." Her eyes widen, dread pooling in their brown depths. "Is something wrong?"

Something is wrong because I want to bend you over that bed and fuck you so deeply you scream my true name…

The drunken part of my brain sees nothing amiss with doing exactly that, but a sober remnant of my mind protests. She may be a woman, but she's been treated like a child for years. She has no experience with sex, and little understanding of it, I would guess. She is exactly the sort of person that a debauched bastard like me should never touch.

"Those clothes are all wrong for you," I snarl. "You look ridiculous. Take them off at once and put something else on. I'll return these to the shop tomorrow."

She makes a little face, like a child's pout of displeasure. I know immediately it's a face she used to make for her captor, to soften his anger and appeal to whatever flecks of affection resided in his merciless heart.

I hate that she's making that face for me.

"Stop pouting," I tell her.

"It's just that… I rather like the dress."

The quiver in her voice tells me she's not used to choosing things for herself, or expressing her own preferences.

I know what it is to have your path marked for you by another being, to have that path barricaded on both sides so that you must trudge onward without hope of escape. I know what it is to live with survival as the only goal. And for a moment, I cannot speak.

"Do you really think I look ridiculous?" Her fingers toy with the little black-velvet bow at her waist.

"What I think shouldn't matter to you."

"You're my master. You've given me a place to live and a new role. Of course it matters." She keeps her head low. Her lashes droop, and her lower lip still protrudes with a slight pout.

I blink away another hazy flush of pure lust and try to ignore the increasing tightness of my pants. I don't want her to see the shape of my erection, so I gather up a great armful of filthy clothes and hold them in front of myself.

"Keep the fucking dress, then," I snap. "I'll take these to the kitchen."

"That's *my* job, sir. You need sleep." She approaches, holding out her arms. "Give that to me, and I'll leave you to rest."

Reluctantly I place the laundry in her arms. I can smell the staunched blood on her wounded foot; I can feel the flushed warmth of her body. A subtle fragrance of earthy florals and spiced citrus emanates from her. Humans can smell each other, of course, but the Fae are uniquely sensitive to the scent and taste of humans. And the longer I'm around this one, the more strongly she seems to affect me.

Or I'm drunker than I thought.

"Go," I tell her, and she hurries away with the laundry.

Dimly I wonder if I should have told her to rest, too, or given her a room. Other than her brief time sleeping on the hearthrug with me, she's been on her feet, working. She's probably exhausted.

The image of her pretty round ass and lovely stocking-clad legs surfaces in my mind as I move toward the bed. I keep picturing the glimpse of her pussy—that little mound peeking between her thighs.

As if the god-stars are conspiring to tempt me, I spot the panties she discarded when she put the new frilly ones on.

For a moment I refuse to touch them. I fight the impulse to—fuck, I'm bending down, snatching them up. They're still warm.

I drop onto the bed, lie back, and hold the delicate garment over my nose and mouth, inhaling through it.

Her scent. Fuck. It spirals through my nostrils up into my brain, sending a violent thrill through my belly, down to my cock. Again I breathe, and the fragrance curls sweetly in my lungs, in my chest, around my heart... turns me dizzy and sick with want.

How can anything smell this good?

With one hand I hold her panties over my face, while my other hand works open the buttons of my pants, tugs out my cock, and begins to stroke.

This is a temporary drunken indulgence. After a nap, I'll be in my right mind again.

Long legs... perfect ass... I picture myself nudging aside the cloth of her new panties to reveal her pussy... and there they are, two rosy lips, pink and shining, and between them a tempting little slit just right for my cock to squeeze inside, slippery and tight... I'd push deep into her body and then I'd come inside her...

I wrap her panties over my cock and groan while hot jets of cum spurt into the fabric. I'm gasping, almost sobbing at the intensity of the pleasure coursing through my veins.

After a few moments of recovery I force myself to get up and toss the cum-slicked panties into the fire. Much as I'd like to keep them and soak them with my cum again, I can't risk her finding out what I've done. My depravity is my own. I refuse to corrupt her with it.

As I'm leaning a forearm on the mantel, watching the flames blacken the fabric, I hear a wispy female voice. "Naughty, naughty Krampus. Stroking yourself to the fragrance of that sweet, innocent girl."

Shit.

Perchta emerges from the wall, taking on misty form. She blinks innocently at me.

"You shouldn't spy on someone when he's... occupied," I mutter.

"Not much of a greeting for one of your oldest acquaintances."

"I thought you'd been reassigned to another world."

"Mmm," she hums softly. "I was, yes. But I came back here, because I like this one."

"Perchta, you must be careful. You've broken the rules too many times. One more act of rebellion, and they'll annihilate you."

"I've *bent* the rules, not broken them," she says. "And I had to come back to see if you've considered my idea and perhaps changed your mind."

"Your plan won't work, Perchta. No one defies the Wild Hunt, and none of us can alter the existence we've been given."

Perchta's situation, like my own, sets her apart from most of the Wild Hunt's members. Because of her continued defiance, she lost her chance at a Final Task. There is no longer any opportunity for her to complete one last challenge and regain corporeal form. Her service to the Hunt is now eternal, but she lacks the one advantage I possess—a physical body. Ever since it happened, she has been hounding me to help her find a way around the dictates of the Hunt.

"There's no harm in trying my idea," she says. "If you could harness the magic at the heart of the house—"

"I said *no*."

Her ghostly form flares brighter for an instant. "You refuse to think of anyone but yourself. You have a *body*, even when you're not performing a task. You can *feel*. You can eat. You can fuck."

"My existence isn't the blessing you seem to think it is," I counter.

"And yet I envy you." Her laugh is quiet and hollow. "I envy you until I think I might go mad with jealousy. Maybe I *have* gone mad. It's been so long, I barely know what I'm doing, or why. Nocturis never checks in anymore to see if I'm performing my duties correctly. No one cares, and no one would notice if we took the power of the house and used it for ourselves."

"They *would* notice, and our punishment would be worse than anything you suffer now." I push myself away from the fireplace and head for the bed.

"The house is weak, Krampus," she says. "But it's growing a little stronger with *her* here. It's waking up, recovering its old spirit. If your maid can stay awhile and keep herself alive, she and the house will grow stronger together, and its power will be replenished. More power is a good thing, for all of us. So I'll wait until the time is right. But I will be back again, with the same question."

"And you'll get the same answer." I bunch the pillow under my head and lie back on the bed. "I am not the architect of your existence, Perchta. I didn't put you in this state, and I can't

76

change it for you. You have your work, as we all do. You must find satisfaction in that."

She drifts nearer, a low moan echoing through the chamber. *"Satisfaction,* you say. My work was never as satisfying as yours, Krampus. You are an avenging demon of death. I turn into a monstrous, ugly old crone and rebuke disobedient children. I frighten the cruel little brats who terrorize their parents and torment their peers." Her tone shifts to one of mockery and disgust. "They are wretched, whining, disgusting creatures, and yet I'm only allowed to scare and admonish them. Just once, I'd like to deliver the punishment they truly deserve. Set me free, Krampus, before I do something dreadful."

"You're asking me to risk my own existence, as well as that of the house and those who live here."

"The girl could go back to her own kind," Perchta says. "And the other creatures have existed long enough. It's their time to dissipate, to become one with the Void. Besides, you don't know that my plan would destroy the house. And if it did, you could always live elsewhere."

"And be vulnerable to humans and their hunting parties? Or risk drawing the anger of the god-star Andregh himself? We could be annihilated for even talking about this, Perchta." I sigh, throwing an arm over my face. "You need to leave. And stay away from Feather, do you hear me? She doesn't need your despair added to her own sadness."

A faint chill passes over my body, as if icy mist rolled through the air of the bedroom. When I lift my arm and look around, Perchta is gone.

I don't know where she'll go. Out into the Void, perhaps, where she'll float until there's a task for her to fulfill, at which point she'll appear wherever she's needed. She has no home, no dwelling place.

Since I have physical form, I was given this house. I don't know its whole history, but I do know that it's sentient, temperamental, and filled with enough power to draw the attention of Fae-hunters if they have tools that can detect magical energy. All the more reason for me to attend the Mayor's next party and learn more about the hunters he hired.

The Mayor has complained that he's growing bored of the same crowd, and he has made it a requirement that for the upcoming gala, every invited guest must bring someone new. If I know the wealthy citizens of Rothenfel, they will make this into a contest of sorts, as they do with everything. They'll vie with each other over who can bring the most beautiful, the wealthiest, the most interesting, or the most lascivious guest to the event.

I have a few potential companions in mind, but I also have concerns. I can't very well conduct a thorough investigation with a lady hanging on my arm all night. And what if I'm summoned as Krampus while I'm at the party? I'll have to leave my companion, and that's sure to draw attention and raise questions.

What I need is a companion who already knows who I am and what I must do, and who understands that I might be called away suddenly.

My brain is too beer-addled to think on it further, so I roll over in bed, pushing the troublesome thoughts aside and yielding to the pleasant oblivion of sleep.

Finding a companion for the party is a problem for my future self.

I have no schedule, no predictable routine of nights and days. I sleep when I can, eat when I'm too hungry to ignore the need, and fuck whenever the opportunity presents itself.

When I wake up, my stomach is growling. I push myself upright, noticing once again how much smoother and fresher the bed feels with the new sheets. I should have purchased a set sooner. I could have been lying in comfort all these months. But it hasn't occurred to me to do so, not for at least a year. I've been busy dealing out the wrath of the god-stars and gorging myself on beer and pussy.

Speaking of pussy—I haven't had sex in almost a week, which is a long time for me. Most Fae need frequent sexual encounters to fuel their magic, and while my powers remain sufficient whether I fuck or not, I find my existence easier to endure when I'm balls-deep in a beautiful woman. When I don't fuck often enough, I grow profoundly uneasy, and my body hums with a frantic, restless energy I can't subdue.

I head for the kitchen, intent on finding something more substantial than moldy pie to sustain me. If there's nothing appetizing there, I'll go to Rothenfel, or into one of the towns or villages within the range of my geistfyre. I have a collection of favorite eateries that I visit often.

When I push open the kitchen door, I stop short on the threshold and gaze around in shock.

It's clean. Every single dish has been scrubbed till it shines, and those that won't fit in the cabinets repose in neat stacks in one corner of the room. Gleaming copper pans hang from the racks overhead. The counters are bare, the hearth has been swept, and the wall tiles are glossy and vibrant, rather than grimy and dull. Not a cobweb remains, and no insects are visible. The flagstone floor is so spotless I would eat my dinner off it without a second thought.

Laundry hangs on lines tacked across the ceiling, from beam to beam, most of it near the chimney where the heat from the fire can dry the clothes. More damp clothes and sheets are draped on the half-rotted kitchen chairs.

A pot bubbles heartily over the fire, with an occasional hiss as a drop or two spills from beneath its lid into the flames. Its contents smell savory and delicious, but there's a faint tinge of something beginning to burn, and I suspect if it stays there much longer, the meal will be ruined.

Using a folded towel to protect my hand, I unhook the pot and set it on the hearth to cool. As I straighten again, I see her. Slumped in the entrance to the pantry, with her head tilted against the doorframe as if she sat down to rest for a moment and nodded right off.

Her braids have loosened, and tendrils of brown hair lie across her face, fluttering with each slow breath from her parted lips.

Slowly I ease myself onto the floor, lean back against a cabinet, and look at her.

Her neck is slender, elegant. Graceful. I like the delicate lines of her collarbones and the dip between them, at the base of her throat. Her breasts form two points against the tight bodice of the black dress; she isn't wearing a corset or bustier. Her ribs jut out a bit above her flat stomach, a sign that she's been underfed for years.

Her hands are red and swollen from cleaning for hours, and two of the fingers have been hastily bandaged. I glance at the bandage on her foot again and shake my head. There must have been shoes among the supplies I brought, and yet she didn't put them on. Maybe they hurt her feet. Or maybe she didn't want to stain them with blood.

The cut on her foot needs care, and so do her hands.

When I receive wounds, they heal rapidly. I haven't tended a human's injuries since I was very young, but I do know that a wound requires cleansing first, then some sort of herbal poultice to prevent infection and promote healing. I'll have to visit an apothecary's shop for the necessary items. Until then, water and soap will have to do.

I'm tempted to remain here and stare at the girl for a while. But the angle of her neck looks uncomfortable, and she did more work for me in a day and a night than I could have imagined possible. She deserves a bed. Since there are no safe bedrooms in the house except mine, she'll have to rest there.

First I collect a few items from the bags—a small bar of herbal bath soap wrapped in paper, a couple of clean cloths—and I tuck them into my pockets.

Bending down, I gather the girl's body in my arms and head out of the kitchen, back toward my room. But as we round the first corner, I stop short, a gasp in my throat.

Wolpertinger stands in the corridor. His legs are the legs of a hare, long and crooked, the bones barely covered by a thin layer of light brown fur. Those legs end in cloven hooves. His hunched rabbit body is shrouded in the shadows of the ceiling, but I can distinguish the outline of his wings and the plume of his tail.

His antlered head snakes down, the neck stretching unnaturally, and his red eyes fix on the girl in my arms. His rabbit nose twitches, and he champs his huge yellow teeth. Two tiny arms, like those of a raccoon, protrude from his chest. The little raccoon fingers open and close, grasping, begging.

I let my horns emerge, and I snarl at him, monster to monster. When I'm angry, or when I'm in my avenging form, my eyes change from their usual green to scarlet pupils in a sea of black. I allow it to happen now, hoping the effect will make Wolpertinger back off.

He lifts one towering leg and stamps his foot. It's a demand. He thinks the girl is a sacrifice of food, and he's tired of waiting for me to offer her up.

I lay her down on the floor and step in front of her, my fangs lengthening as my tongue lashes between them. "She's not for you."

He howls, loud and sudden, a hideous scream that sends terror twisting through my gut. This creature is an eldritch thing, much older than I am—old as the bones of the world, and he's been trapped in the house for centuries, if not longer. His sole purpose, his one delight, is devouring human flesh—but he'll take Fae when he can't get anything else.

"She isn't yours," I shout at him. "I'll bring you something later, but this one is not to be touched, do you hear me? She's mine."

She's awake now. I can hear her rapid breathing behind me, but I don't dare take my eyes off Wolpertinger or speak a word to reassure her. Not that reassurance would do much good. We're both about to die.

7

FEATHER

I wake up on the floor in a hallway of Krampus's house.
He's standing in front of me, legs braced and claws out, snarling
at the monster I saw behind the walls—the one with the
stretched-out legs. When I sit up and lean to the side for a peek
at the creature, I wish I was still asleep. It's so much more
horrifying than the glimpses I caught before.

I crouch, both hands pressed to the floor, ready to spring
away and run.

But Krampus thunders, "She isn't yours. I'll bring you
something later, but this one is not to be touched, do you hear
me? She's mine."

Despite the bold words, there's a tension in his voice that I know far too well. I'm intimately familiar with the way a person's voice sounds when they're trying to act normal or cheerful, while they're actually terrified beyond reason.

Palms to the floor, I close my eyes, debating what to do.

And suddenly the house is there in my mind, a monumental presence, yet shockingly intimate. I could always sense the cabin somewhat, but this is a far stronger connection to a much more powerful consciousness.

The house is pleased with me. It approves of my work in the kitchen, and it wants me to stay here, to free more rooms of grime and clutter, to bring it back to health. It doesn't speak—no definite words, only an impulse, a voiceless bargain that I will relieve its pain, and in return it will help me.

An image flickers through my mind—walls detaching and shifting, boards slamming into place between us and the monster.

"Yes," I whisper. "Yes, do it. Please."

The long-legged monster yowls, shrill and mindless and ravenous. My eyes flash open in time to see it charging Krampus.

But a piece of the wall detaches with a grinding crunch, swivels, and slams across the hallway, like a door. Krampus and I are now facing a dead-end. At the same time, boards shift and creak as another corridor opens up on my right.

"Come on," I call to Krampus. I scramble up and race down the new corridor. More boards swivel and shift as whole sections of the walls fold back or slam shut. Floors move and slant, stairways adjust themselves to new angles to accommodate us. We're being guided through the house, by the house itself.

"What the fuck?" exclaims Krampus. He sounds shaken. But my whole body feels wonderfully alive, thrilling with a strange excitement, a sense of power and connection I've never experienced before. When the house deposits us at the door to Krampus's bedroom, I burst in without waiting for him.

It's been years since I entered a room first when in the company of a man. *He*—my captor—always told me I should follow him, not precede him, even when we were entering my tiny closet of a room so he could put me to bed.

The thought of *him* drains my energy and quells the power racing through my veins. I feel the house withdraw slightly from me, returning to its usual state, its walls and passages assuming the same positions as before.

Krampus darts inside and slams the bedroom door. Through its thick oak, we both hear the monster howling in the distance.

"That's Wolpertinger," Krampus says breathlessly. "He can't come in here. My chambers are off limits."

When Krampus turns to me, I shrink, certain he'll rebuke me for entering the room first. If not, there will be something else to punish me for. There always is.

Sometimes big brothers have to punish their little sisters...

I crumple to the floor, holding my head in both hands, driving my nails into my skull as if I could claw my captor's voice from my mind.

"Feather." Krampus crouches at my side. In his Fae form, his voice is younger and smoother, like liquid gold. It's the complete opposite of the grim, raspy voice in my head, so I cling to it, to *him*. I reach out and clutch his wrist.

"He can't get us in here," repeats Krampus, and I know he means Wolpertinger but I'm still thinking of the man from the cabin. The one whose true name I never knew.

What if I imagined the sound of those bones cracking inside Krampus's bag? What if my captor isn't dead? What if he comes back? What if...

"What did you do with him?" I whisper, my lips trembling as I look up and meet Krampus's eyes. "The man from the cabin—what did you do?"

"I killed him," he answers quietly. "And I fed him to the Meerwunder."

"That's another monster?"

He nods. "The Meerwunder lives below."

"And there's no chance—" I swallow, trying to keep my voice from shaking. "No chance that he'll come back?"

"None."

"Good." I release his wrist and press my hand to my chest. My heartbeat is slowly returning to normal. "That's good."

Krampus gazes at me with a blend of suspicion and wonder. "Can you tell me how you did it?"

"Did what?"

"You spoke to the house. It shielded you. Helped us."

"Hasn't it done that before?"

He scoffs lightly. "No. This house hates me. But apparently it likes you."

I chew my lip thoughtfully for a moment. "I think it's grateful that someone is cleaning it, after so long. It just wants to be able to breathe. To have a caretaker."

A sneer twists Krampus's beautiful mouth. Right now he has two little fangs that overlap his lower lip, and two small tusks that jut upward, denting his top lip.

"The way you look… it changes," I say. "Why?"

"I used to be skilled with glamours and with shifting my appearance," he replies. "I've lost much of that ability. But my eye color still alters with my mood unless I consciously control it. For example, my eyes glow green when I'm happy, excited, or lustful. They're red when I'm angry or vengeful. And I can conceal or reveal other aspects of myself, like my fangs, claws, tail, horns—"

"And your pointed ears."

"Yes."

"Do you have wings? I've heard that some Fae have wings."

For some reason, the question seems to irk him. "No." He pushes himself up, off the floor. "Fae with wings are annoying bastards who think they're better than everyone else. Enough of this. You should sleep. I was bringing you here so you could rest after your labors."

"Rest where?"

"Where do you think?" he says sharply. "The only safe bed in the house. Get in it, and go to sleep."

I stand up, eyeing the mussed sheets and the slight indentation where he was obviously lying not long ago. The thought of my body nestling in the same spot makes me feel odd and jittery.

Almost every night since I was six years old, I've been put to bed in exactly the same way, by the same man. Sometimes he would let Mother do it, if he was eager to begin his time with Wife. I came to understand that the hard roll in his pants, like a stick of wood, meant he was ready to be with Wife.

My favorite Mother used to sit with me while he went to Wife's bedroom. Mother would cover my ears if Wife sobbed or screamed. Each new Wife quickly learned not to make such sounds. It only angered him, and made everything worse.

"Why are you staring?" asks Krampus. "It's a bed. Surely you know what it's for."

"It's *your* bed," I murmur. "And I'm not used to simply… going to sleep. Someone always put me to bed."

He tosses a clawed hand through his long red hair. "Right, the sick game of 'Little Sister.' That asshole put you to bed at night?"

I nod.

"Did he…" Krampus grimaces. "Did he hurt you in such a way—I mean, did he put himself in—shit… how do I say this?"

"He didn't have sex with me. He made Wife do that."

Krampus looks somewhat relieved. "Do you know how many he killed?"

I count on my fingers. I don't have enough fingers for all of the deaths I remember. "Many."

"Fuck." He strides away, his shoulders and back tight with anger. He's not angry with me, though, which is a relief. "Why didn't they send me after him sooner?" He slams the side of his fist against the mantel.

"Who?"

"The god-stars. Fate. The fucking leaders of the Wild Hunt. I swear, sometimes they make no sense."

Suddenly, I understand him. The realization is like a brilliant flash of light in my mind. "This house is your cabin, and the leaders of the Wild Hunt are your captors. You are playing a role for them. Acting out the part they set for you."

He wheels around and looks at me, his eyes wide and stricken. My stomach flutters with triumph at that look, at the tension thrumming in the air between us. It's as if our souls have suddenly been bared to each other.

"We are not the same," he says through gritted teeth.

"No. You are Fae. You have magic, and you are beautiful."

A quiver of emotion crosses his face. "That's not what I meant. We are different because you did nothing to deserve your fate. You were innocent. I was not."

"What did you do?"

His long red tongue skates out and he growls through his fangs.

"You don't have to answer," I say.

He turns away and stares down at the flickering fire. He's quiet for so long that I'm convinced he isn't going to tell me.

At last he says slowly, "You're living here. You deserve to know what you're living with."

Wildly curious, but feigning composure, I seat myself on the edge of the bed and wait.

"I was three years old when my mother sold me to the trolls," he says, low. "The troll female who bought me decided I was too pretty to be cut up and used in her spells, so she raised me as a pet instead. It was a brutal life. No sunlight, no trees, only rocks and slimy subterranean creatures. The other trolls despised me, so to escape their fists and teeth, I used to wander deep into the cave system. One day, when I was around ten, I found a long-forgotten notch between worlds, just big enough for a Fae child to slip through. I emerged in the hills of the mortal world, near a home for orphaned children—an isolated place full of miserable little creatures who had been abandoned by human society."

His claws are driving deeper into the wood of the mantel with every sentence he speaks. I'm not sure he realizes it.

"I was lonely," he continues. "I became friends with one of the children. He told me all the terrible things that went on in the orphanage, and I told him all the terrible things the trolls did to me. We were both nearly starved, but I learned how to hunt rabbits and find quail eggs in the nearby forest, so we both grew healthier."

"Did you try to escape?" I ask.

"I couldn't bring him back to Faerie. We could never have made it out of the trolls' tunnels alive. And in his realm, the orphanage was far from any city or town—too far to walk. There were wolves in those woods at night. I couldn't have protected him from them, any more than I could protect him from the wolves inside the orphanage."

I stare at his broad back, transfixed and on the brink of tears. His voice is so hard, so steady, and yet I can sense pain, waves of it, oceans of it, surging through his body.

"What happened?" I whisper.

"They killed him," Krampus says simply. "By accident, I think, while they were punishing him. Someone took it too far. Lost their head. I'm still not sure who it was. I was thirteen by then. He hadn't come to meet me in weeks, so I ventured closer to the building where he and the other children lived, and I found his remains in the rubbish heap, where they had tossed him. Like a piece of garbage."

"Oh gods." I press my fingers over my mouth.

"I lost my mind. All I could think of was destroying the humans responsible. I went into the orphanage that night, and I slit the throats of every adult in the place. Some of them were doing wretched things to the children in the dark. I cut them open where they stood."

He takes a deep breath. "But I didn't stop there. I saw how miserable the children were. Most of them were starving, many were deathly ill, and they had all been abused. Several were sick in their minds—they had learned cruelty from the adults who cared for them, and they would grow up to be just as wicked."

Slowly he turns around and faces me for the final words, as if he's pronouncing his own judgment. "I thought, if I couldn't set them free in this world, I could release them to the next. So I killed them all. It felt like mercy at first, then desperation. Once I had begun, I couldn't stop until it was finished. I hunted them all down, every last child. Even the ones who hid from me. I told myself I was ending their pain, doing them a kindness. Stop crying, Feather. You didn't know any of the children. Why should you weep for them?"

"I'm not crying for them," I gasp out. "I'm crying for *you*. You were just a child yourself. You were hurting—"

"No excuse." His eyes turn wicked, and his tongue lashes out again, firelight glinting on the piercings. "There's no excuse for my actions. I killed thirteen adults and one hundred and twenty children that night. Then I went back to the trolls, covered in human blood and gore. My troll guardian never asked what happened; she just beat me senseless. That only made me hate her more."

"Of course it did." Memories surface in my mind… scrubbing copious amounts of blood from the cabin floors, soaping up the boards, wringing out the gore, watching the water in the bucket turn from clear to pink to red...

"Once I had a taste for killing the wicked, I couldn't stop," Krampus continues. "I began to murder the trolls, one by one. I started with those at the fringes of the clan—the old, the young, and the weak. When I went out killing in the tunnels, I'd wear a mask of bone and a cloak of furs. Sometimes I was spotted, and they would chase me, but I was smaller than them, and I could hide in narrow cracks which they overlooked completely. They begin to say the cave system was haunted by a 'Krampus,' an eldritch demon cobbled together from earth and bone."

"They didn't suspect you?" I ask.

"No. They thought of me as a Fae weakling. They suspected nothing, not even when I killed five of them in one night, including my guardian. I unmasked myself just for her, so she could look into my eyes as she died. After that, the troll clan decided to leave the caves altogether."

"You didn't go with them?"

"Fuck no. With my guardian dead, I would have been dinner. No, I hid until they left. Then I followed their reek out of the cave system and saw the sunlight of Faerie for the first time in years. I thought I was free, that I'd escaped retribution for the human lives I'd taken. I lived in the northern forests for a while, and then I killed a Seelie peddler and took his gold. With that, I went south and became a civilized member of the Seelie kingdom. But on my thirty-third birthday, twenty years after the massacre at the orphanage, the Wild Hunt came for me. They gave me a choice—utter annihilation, or an endless existence of wreaking vengeance upon the abusers of human children."

"It seems overly cruel." I rub tears from my cheeks.

"They were merciful. They gave me this house, and they let me retain my life and my physical form. Between tasks, I have the freedom to pursue pleasure, which is a mercy. As I said—I'm not innocent. I deserve this."

I'm not sure he does, but I'm not prideful enough to argue aloud that the god-stars were wrong. After all, he did slaughter over a hundred human children. The most frightening part is, I understand why he did it, what led him to that breaking point. I've been in that place, too. A place where I made cruel choices and did unspeakable things.

"Your wounds need cleaning," says Krampus abruptly, fumbling in his pockets. "I brought soap and cloths."

"No water?"

He points to a shadowed corner. "There's a bathroom. The sink works."

I squint. Past a mountain range of chests, boxes, jumbled furniture, dirty clothes, and unidentifiable trinkets, I can make out the door he's pointing to. Without his help, I would never have known it was there.

"You climb over all that whenever you have to relieve yourself?" I ask.

He glares, and I suppose I should be frightened. He's a fearsome figure, with the black horns and the fangs, not to mention the tongue and the claws. Besides which, he's twice my size.

But I'm picturing him clambering across the clutter to reach the bathroom, and the image is too much to resist, especially with my emotional control so thin. I choke on a tiny laugh.

He hooks an eyebrow and tilts his horned head, the ring between his nostrils gleaming briefly in the light. He eyes me cautiously, as if he thinks I've gone mad.

"I need to use the bathroom," I say. "If you'll give me the cloths and soap, I can also wash and bandage my foot."

"No. You did a poor job of it the first time. I'll do it."

At his commanding tone, I recoil slightly, with a deferential nod and a soft "Yes, sir."

My tone seems to displease him, though I can't figure out why. He heads for the bathroom, navigating the clutter with a practiced grace that astounds me.

The bathroom door can't open all the way, and he has to hold it ajar while I enter. I thought the kitchen was dirty, but the bathroom is ten times worse. Unspeakably filthy. Grime coats the enormous bathtub, and mold creeps between the tiles.

"Did you kill someone in here?" I gape at the dark streaks up and down the walls.

He gives a noncommittal grunt in reply.

"What are these whitish splatters?" I point to one, and he says hastily, "Don't touch that. Do your business, and I'll clean your foot afterward."

"Could you perhaps clean it in the bedroom?" I ask tentatively.

He scowls again, but when I'm done in the bathroom, he directs me to sit on the bed while he fetches a bowl of water and soap. I unwrap the makeshift bandages on my fingers, and when he brings me the washbowl, I clean my hands thoroughly. The cuts and broken blisters start to bleed again, and I notice his nostrils twitching. But he says nothing, only kneels before me, sets the bowl down, and picks up my foot.

His claws have vanished, leaving rounded fingernails. He's gentle as he unwraps the bandage, which is stiff with dried blood.

No man has ever knelt in front of me or tended to my needs. Back in the cabin, my captor was always the one being tended. We knelt before *him*, not the other way around.

I like the way Krampus's warm, strong fingers wrap around my ankle, holding it still as he squeezes out a cloth with his other hand and daubs away the blood.

"So you *can* clean things," I say softly.

He glances up, humor creasing the corners of his eyes. But he catches himself and glares at me again. "Silence."

I pin my lips shut and watch him bow his horned head over my foot, intent on cleaning it thoroughly. Even once the blood is gone, his fingertips trace the arch of my foot, the shape of my toes. Every brush of his skin against mine makes me tremble inside—not the frightened kind of tremor, but something altogether new, a sensation both warm and dizzying.

He dries my foot and slides out a single claw so he can cut a fresh strip of cloth for a bandage. Once my foot is taken care of, he rises up on his knees and takes my hand, inspecting each cut and wiping it carefully. He slices smaller ribbons of cloth to bandage my fingers.

During the process, he pauses once, his hand upturned under mine. We're palm to palm, skimming the heat of each other's skin. The size difference between our hands is striking.

The tip of his tongue glides out and traces his lips. He finishes tying the last bandage.

And then, still on his knees, he looks up at me.

His green eyes are so beautiful I can't breathe. I can barely think—except for some reason, my mind leaps back to the memory of the woman in the red-lantern house, with the man's face between her legs. I can't forget her expression, the sounds she made...

I scuttle backward on the bed as fast as I can, my heart racing, heat pulsing between my thighs.

Krampus looks startled, but he covers it quickly with one of his stern frowns. "Sleep," he orders. Then he storms out of the room, knocking over the washbowl on the way and not pausing to mop up the spilled water.

I try to sleep, because he's my new master, and he told me to. But I can't stop thinking about the spilled water and the soiled bathroom.

Finally, with a resigned sigh, I get up. And I go to work.

8

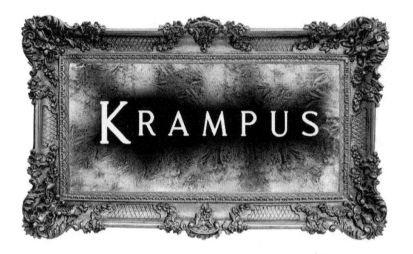

K RAMPUS

I'm called away more often than usual during the next two weeks. Fortunately that means I have plenty of evildoers to feed my housemates, a fact I partly credit for Feather's survival during the first fortnight.

The schedules we keep are so different I barely see her, and yet we develop a routine of our own. When I drag myself and my prey home, she somehow knows I've returned, and when I go to my room, there's food and a hot bath waiting for me.

Now that my bathroom is clean, I've come to enjoy baths, and when I stop by the shops for our groceries, I often swing by the apothecary as well to purchase bath salts, all different colors and scents. She uses them too, when I'm gone. I know because I take note of what's left in each glass bottle after my own bath, and when I return the next time, there's always less. It makes me smile, though I'm not sure why.

She bathes and sleeps when I'm out avenging, carousing, or shopping, and when I'm sleeping, she cleans. We share the bed, but never at the same time. Her scent on the sheets is a delicious torment.

Feather's cooking is simple, so at times I bring food back from my favorite taverns and pubs, and I always leave a generous portion for her on the kitchen table. When we do meet, she curtsies, wide-eyed, and says, "Master," in the soft, thrilling voice I hate so much. After those encounters, I find a desolate corner of the house and stroke my cock frantically, coming to the memory of that quiet voice, those small breasts, and the long, graceful legs beneath the short maid's skirt.

I haven't gotten her any new clothes because she likes her maid outfits. And because I'm a wretched, vile soul and I like how fuckable she looks in those dresses and stockings.

I will never touch her. I've vowed it over and over in my mind, though I stopped short of vowing aloud before the god-stars.

Instead I visit the villages of the region, a different one each time, and I sate myself with lovely women. I try not to picture Feather when I'm fucking them.

I don't always succeed.

9

FEATHER

Years ago, when I had my first bleeding, I stared at the stain on my sheets for several minutes. I investigated the source and determined that the bleeding was ongoing. Then I took the soiled sheets to Mother and quietly told her that I was going to die.

I had considered and accepted my death within the span of several minutes. When Mother explained what was really happening, I felt a faint sort of relief, threaded with a secret disappointment, because death would have meant an end to the strain of playing my part for my captor.

I still miss that Mother sometimes. The way she listened. The way she didn't just survive, but made things better for the rest of us, even *him*. I remember he used to put his head in her lap. I remember the tragedy in her eyes as she stroked his hair.

I remember the night he killed her. I remember how hard it was to pretend she didn't matter to me.

Every time he killed a Wife or a Mother and brought a new one into the cabin, I accepted the change calmly. No outward sign of grief or loss. No visible divergence in my routine, except to give the new resident a little extra help until she adapted. Until she learned what was expected of us.

Perhaps that's why I accept my bond with the house so quickly. The connection simply *exists*. There's no reason to flail and fret about it. I have questions, of course—about the house, about myself—but there's no one I can ask. Krampus has made himself scarce ever since he confessed his great sin to me. Perhaps that conversation made him feel vulnerable. I suspect he doesn't like feeling fragile any more than I do.

If I asked him, he might tell me more about the house. But he knows nothing about me, so it's no use worrying and wondering where I came from, or why I can form connections with the buildings in which I reside.

Whether I understand it or not, I'm linked to this house, a stronger bond than my link with the cabin. When I'm working quietly in the rooms, I feel a current racing through my veins, energizing my limbs. I sense the interest and enthusiasm of the house, its pleasure and pride when I finish cleaning another area.

The Imp follows me around some days, helping out by eating copious amounts of clutter and debris. He'll devour almost anything as long as I set it on fire first. Fortunately, if he sets anything alight that isn't supposed to burn, he can swallow the flames and snuff it out before it spreads.

I enjoy having his company, almost as much as I enjoy transforming the house from an abandoned wreck into a livable place. Whatever clutter and spare furniture the Imp won't eat, I've been moving into the big gray room, until I can figure out what to do with it. But I make sure to leave space for Krampus to return in his fiery circle, and I leave him a wide path to the stairway that leads below. I avoid that stairway. It's where he takes his victims, and I'd rather not see that part of the house.

The other monsters lurk near me sometimes, in dark corners, behind walls, on ceilings, or beneath the floorboards. Mostly I ignore them, or quietly move to a different room. If they become aggressive, the house interferes, rerouting either them or me.

Even after two weeks, I've only touched a fraction of the rooms in this place. An awareness has developed in my mind, a sense of the house's vastness, its age, and its will. It likes me, but it doesn't trust me yet. It's keeping some things hidden. There are certain rooms it's not ready to let me access.

The secrecy doesn't bother me. Earning trust, being patient, and sensing the moods of others is what I'm good at. I can wait. Eventually, the house will open itself fully to me.

Krampus is another matter. He seems to prefer a separate life from mine, so I accommodate him. When he returns, I sense it through my connection to the house, and I do my best to meet his needs unobtrusively.

He knows I'm still here, still alive. Sometimes he brings me gifts of food, the most delicious meals I've ever eaten, in larger portions than I'm used to. He fluffs the pillows and smooths the sheets when he leaves the bed, so they'll be fresh and ready for me. I'm growing accustomed to the winter-midnight scent of him, like a path I can follow to peace and rest, a familiar fragrance that helps me relax and sink into sleep.

On the fourteenth day since I left the cabin, Krampus returns with a crash and a roar that shakes the house. I drop my broom, and the Imp frantically scurries up the chimney in the spare room we're cleaning.

Without thinking, I run out of the room and race toward the source of the sound. Krampus is always loud, but never like this.

The flames of his fire-circle are flickering and dying around his huge cloaked body, which lies on its side in the gray room. His sack is abandoned near him. It's bigger than he is, stuffed full of bodies, and it's still moving. Muffled roars and male screams penetrate the heavy, blood-saturated fabric.

As I approach, Krampus flings up his horned head and snarls at me, fangs flashing and tongue writhing beneath the goat-skull mask. His tongue is horribly wounded, sliced halfway through, hanging on by threads of flesh. The dark fur around his cloven hooves is soaked and matted with blood. Someone has cut off the tufted end of his tail.

I reach for his mask, and he gives a guttural, anguished roar. Blood paints one of the eyeholes, and as I lift the mask free, I notice that his left eye is a ruined mess, while the other one is dead black with a scarlet pupil. Most of his face is coated with blood.

He's panting, his wounded tongue spilling from his jaws onto the floor.

"Gods, what happened to you?" I murmur, tentatively reaching toward it.

"Careful," he slurs. "My tongue—paralytic toxin."

"Will you heal?" I ask.

"Slowly… if at all." Each word is a torment for him. "They had… iron weapons."

I might not be very familiar with the Fae, but I know that iron is harmful to them. "So the men you were after—they knew Krampus would come for them, and they suspected he might be Fae. It was a trap."

He doesn't answer. His chest heaves, and I don't like the wet sound of his labored breaths.

With all my might I push him over onto his back. The bells sewn into his cape jingle faintly.

I fumble with the layers of heavy fabric and fur until my fingers touch hard muscle slicked with blood. He's badly wounded somewhere underneath.

I've seen wounds. And I've assisted with the care and binding of injuries after a Mother or a Wife was beaten. Hell, I've tended my own wounds more times than I can count.

I can do this.

I keep pulling at the cape, but I can't find an opening, only the short slit where an iron blade cut through. The material is too heavily layered and too thick for me to rip with my bare hands.

"I have to get this cape off you so I can tend your wounds," I tell him. "I'm going to fetch a knife."

"I can... dispel the cape," he gasps. But his face contorts horribly, and he cries out in pain.

"Whatever you're trying to do isn't working, and it's hurting you," I exclaim. "Stop it." Glancing over my shoulder, I catch sight of the Imp lurking in the doorway. "Go to the kitchen and fetch me a big knife," I tell him.

With a blink of his enormous eyes, the Imp races off.

Krampus groans. In this form, his voice is so deep and monstrous that I shiver.

"Easy." My tone is calmer than I feel. "You won't die from this. You just have to wait until things get better."

It's something I told myself over and over in the cabin. *You won't die from this. You just have to wait until things get better.*

A thump seizes my attention, and when I glance at the sack, its cinched mouth is widening. A fist thrusts out, followed by another groping hand.

The humans Krampus captured are emerging. Which is bad news for me, since he judges the most brutal and heartless kind of people—those who are cruel to children.

I have no weapons, and even if I did, I don't know how to fight. Krampus is in no shape to defend himself or me.

The first man emerges from the sack with a malevolent howl of rage. He's bloodied, bruised, furious. Another man follows, dragging the third man, who seems to be immobilized, probably from Krampus's tongue. A fourth man crawls out, feeling absently around a large wound in his skull. He won't live long. I've seen a head injury like that before.

The first two men stand up, seething. They spot me at once.

"Come here, little girl," hisses one of them. He lunges toward me, but I'm too quick. I bound away from Krampus's side and dive into the piles of furniture. This room is a wilderness of tables, chests, and chair legs, and I'm the ferret slender enough to slip through the crevices.

"Get her," snarls the man. "I'll finish off this one." He starts toward Krampus.

"Watch the tongue," warns his companion.

I'm already far inside the tangle of furniture, crouched under a table. I slam both hands to the floor, the centers of my palms heating with sudden energy as I feel the power thrumming through the house.

This room is too clogged with objects for the house to help us. There's no space for its energy to flow, not enough air for it to work with.

"Bring the monsters to me," I murmur to the house. "The one that hides in the shadows, and the one in the walls. Guide them here quickly, or Krampus dies. If he dies, *I'll* die, and there will be no one left to care for you."

The floor quakes and the walls shudder as the house responds. The trembling of the structure is violent enough that both ruffians look up.

"A fucking earthquake?" exclaims one.

The other starts a long string of curses as he heaves aside piece after piece of furniture, making his way toward me.

"Come here, girl, and I'll take it easy on you," he offers.

I stare at him from under my table, then slither deeper into the debris.

"That's how you're going to play it?" he spits. "Fine. I'll tear your little cunt apart, I swear."

"I can't choke this bastard without getting hit by his tongue," calls the other ruffian. "His neck's too thick anyway. What should I do?"

"Grab something and bludgeon him," replies the ruffian pursuing me. "Do it quick. I'm about to catch us a pretty little maid."

I climb onto a dresser and stand there, surveying the room. Waiting, while the man struggles toward me.

A cracking, splintering sound draws my attention upward to the shadowed ceiling. Claws scrape and scrabble, and there's a whooshing sound, like a tail whipping through the dark. That's the lurking beast, the one I haven't yet seen clearly. A word presses into my mind—both shape and sound, lent to me by the house's consciousness. *Bahkauv.*

At the same moment, clomping steps sound in the hall, and four long legs appear in the doorway. An antlered rabbit's head with giant yellow teeth and red eyes lowers itself below the lintel and peers into the room. Its small raccoon hands grope the air.

This one I know. *Wolpertinger.*

The man with the head injury screams.

At his shriek, the creature on the ceiling drops with a crash onto a pile of furniture, fully visible for the first time. And I almost scream, too.

Its form looks similar to a large, hairless, deformed calf. The head and nose are bovine, but the skin is like a seal's, taut and gray. A tapered tail, like a lizard's but without scales, wraps around a chair leg. The creature's front legs are muscular, similar to a panther's, but with elbow spikes and three massive toes that end in fat, ridged claws. It opens its mouth and bawls, its voice calf-like but wretched, hollow, mad with hunger.

Wolpertinger howls in answer and hunches down, fitting itself through the doorway and entering the room. Krampus's unmoving form lies between the monster and the men, and Wolpertinger lowers its rabbit head toward him, sniffing the blood seeping from beneath his cape. Its teeth chatter eagerly, and then its maw opens to bite.

"No!" I cry out.

Wolpertinger's head whips up. Its neck is uncannily long and flexible, and I have to stifle the frightened wail that wants to escape my throat. But I know how to steel my legs so they don't wobble. I know how to pretend I'm not afraid for my life.

"No," I repeat loudly, staring into Wolpertinger's red eyes. Then I turn and give the Bahkauv a firm stare as well. "Do not touch Krampus. Eat *them*. Those men." I point to the ruffians who came out of the sack.

The two monsters pounce with horrifying swiftness. One of the men makes a break for the stairs, and I don't warn him about the Meerwunder below. He'll find out soon enough.

The Imp appears at the door, holding a butcher knife. I climb through the furniture toward him, trying not to listen to the crunching, slurping, and shrieking as the monsters feast on their victims.

The screams don't last long.

Untangling myself from the last of the clutter, I grab the knife from the Imp, who bounds off to join the carnage. I lift Krampus's cape and saw through the layers of fabric until I can part them and see his chest.

He's bigger in this form, with thick veins snaking over his bulging muscles. His sinewy neck, huge pectorals, and packed abdominals promise brute strength, and yet he's weak, nearly unconscious, his one good eye quivering half-open. Two large gashes cleave his chest and stomach. The edges of the wounds look burned, as if the iron blade seared going in and out. And yet he bleeds.

"Tell me how to help you," I murmur.

His lips twitch back over his fangs. "Your blood."

"My..." I gulp down a surge of panic. "My blood?"

"Human blood... can help."

Human blood... does it have to be mine? I glance at the leftovers of the ruffians and immediately wish I hadn't. I choke down a retch as bile surges in my throat.

Krampus notices when I glance at the dead men. "*Your* blood," he whispers. As if it makes a difference.

I chew my lip, frowning.

"Or let me die," he breathes, and his good eye closes.

I know that yielding, that acceptance when the end looks like relief. Like peace. I've been there, too.

But I'm glad I did not perish in the cabin. It was the only life I could imagine for myself... and yet here I am, doing something new, growing stronger.

I lean close to his pointed ear and say softly, "You might think this is all you will ever be, all you will ever do. But you can't know what's going to happen, or what joys might lie ahead, if you just wait... if you take one more step, survive one more day. Besides... we need you here." *Bath salts, plumped pillows, gifts of food left for me on the kitchen table...* "I need you."

A long breath rattles from him.

Holding my arm above his mouth, I slit my palm with the knife, curl my fingers, and squeeze blood between his lips.

10

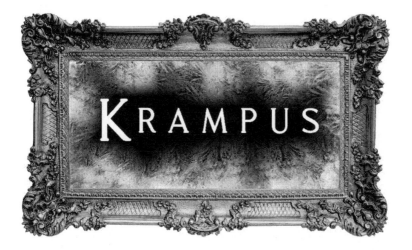

KRAMPUS

Stoic, silent tears stream from her eyes as I swallow her blood. She stares unflinching at some point in the distance.

I heard her command the house. I witnessed, through my one bleary eye, her stalwart courage before the monsters, the bold way she ordered them to leave me alone and devour my attackers.

I had no idea that in a single fortnight she had developed such a bond with the house, or such bravery with my housemates. It would astonish me more if I weren't so torn and twisted with pain.

After the first few trickles of blood, I'm able to revert to my usual Fae form, no longer the hulking, veined Krampus. Thanks to her, I won't die. But my recovery will be slow.

With my tongue no longer a toxic danger to her, I seize Feather's forearm and sink my teeth into her flesh. It's an impulsive act, needy and reckless. She doesn't protest, but her lips press together more tightly.

Rich and hot, savory and sweet, her blood flows down my throat. My sight glazes and I moan, lost in the dizzy euphoria.

"Krampus," she says urgently. "Stop."

Dazed, hardly comprehending, I growl in protest.

"Stop," she orders, louder. "They're coming closer. Stop, stop!"

With a violent surge of willpower, I unlock my jaws from her arm. She clamps her hand over the wound and gets to her feet.

I turn my head so I can see, with my remaining eye, the threat she's facing. My stomach drops into harrowing darkness as the Bahkauv and Wolpertinger, finished with their meal of men, prowl closer to Feather and me. They can smell her blood, more delicious and tempting than that of the wretches they ate. And they have even less restraint than I do.

My gaze switches to Feather, standing there with her slim legs braced apart, gripping her wounded arm. She's tiny compared to the colossal monsters, but her chin lifts in regal defiance.

"Run," I rasp.

"No." She speaks quietly to me, then louder for the beasts, her tone cool and firm. "You've had enough to eat. You did well. Good boys."

She stalks around me, her pace slow and measured. She's wearing shoes today, and her heels clip sharply against the floorboards. She goes right up to the Bahkauv.

My panicked breath hisses through clenched teeth, and I struggle to sit up, but I can barely manage it. I'm in no shape to defend her.

A frenzied, grievous terror shakes through my bones. She can't die here, she *can't*, not after saving me. "No, Feather." The words rattle from me in a broken groan.

Feather holds her injured arm against her stomach and reaches out with her other hand. Reaches for the Bahkauv.

"Fool," I whisper, and two hot tears spill from my eyes as I lurch upward, onto my knees. I nearly keel over and I have to prop myself with one hand, blood dripping from my chest onto the floor.

The Bahkauv bawls, loud and startling, but Feather doesn't recoil. She presses her bloody fingers to the creature's calf-like nose, stroking the broad, soft space between the immense nostrils.

"Good boy," she says quietly. "You played your role well. Now go."

My body quakes with pain and panic as I wait helplessly for her to be eaten.

But my panic turns to wonder as the beast shuffles backward, snorts, and then bounds away, clambering up the wall with shocking speed and disappearing into the shadows of the ceiling. There must be a hole up there, because I hear him scrambling through and scuttling off to some distant part of the house.

Wolpertinger lowers its head and starts to bite, just as Feather whirls around, snaps her fingers, and says sharply, "No!"

His teeth click shut a handspan from her face. She doesn't flinch. Just stares him down. Not even a glare, really—just a look of pure, icy dominance. Sheer fucking force of will.

Wolpertinger screams again, like a hare being flayed, then skitters around her on long legs and wedges his lanky form back through the door. His shriek of discontent fades as he gallops away down the hall.

The Imp sits on his haunches in the blood, licking his tiny fingers. Apparently the idea of eating Feather doesn't even enter his mind. When she clicks her tongue, he leaps onto her leg and scrambles up her body to perch on her shoulder.

Then she turns to me.

Between the bloody footprints the Imp left on her dress, and the blood from her own wounds, she's a mess. She's less emaciated now, but her skin is still bone-white from lack of sun, and shadows paint the hollows around her huge dark eyes. Her wavy brown hair forms a cloud of darkness around that delicate white face.

I've never seen a mortal look so wholly inhuman.

"Can you walk to your room?" she asks. "Because I don't think I'm strong enough to support you."

"I'll manage," I tell her. "I'll crawl if I have to."

I can barely crawl, as it turns out. But when she and I reach the door to the hallway, somehow my bedroom door is directly across from us. The house shortened the distance we have to traverse.

"In all the centuries I've lived here, the house has never done such favors for me," I mutter, grasping the wall for support as I drag myself into the bedroom. "I might be a little jealous."

"You didn't listen to the house, or respect it," she replies. "You filled it with foul odors and choked it with trash. I'm not sure it will ever forgive you."

"Perhaps not." I watch the blood dripping between her fingers. "You need medicine and bandages for that wound. I purchased those a while back—you should find everything in the bathroom cabinet. There's a staunching ointment to help lessen the blood flow and promote quicker healing. I thought it might come in handy."

"Stop worrying about me and get into bed," she says.

"You're the one who nearly died."

"So did you." I start to heave myself onto the bed when she exclaims, "Wait! Don't get blood all over the sheets!"

I sink back onto the floor. "What the fuck else am I supposed to do?"

She chews her lip, then says, "Let me bandage my arm, and then I'll wash some of that gore off you."

While she's in the bathroom, I stare at the ceiling, trying not to think about her washing me. Sex is another way that the Fae can speed up the healing process, but I'm not about to suggest it and frighten her.

When she returns, her arm and hand are so neatly bandaged that I'm sure the Imp helped her. He pauses near me, sniffing and blinking before darting through the flames of the fireplace and disappearing up the chimney.

I could try dispelling my cape again, but instead I let Feather take it off me. Her eyes widen when she realizes I'm fully naked underneath, now that my furred lower half has reverted to Fae form. Swiftly she tosses a bit of the cape over my crotch, and I fight a painful smile.

The sponge squishes against my stomach, warm water dribbling along my skin. I close my eyes and inhale her scent while she mops away the blood. Occasionally her fingertips brush my flesh, and a tingle runs through my body.

"So who were those men?" she asks.

"The worst kind of wretches. They had a girl of twelve. They were using her."

The sponge pauses. "Where is she now?"

"As I told you, Mother Holle takes care of the children. Sometimes she's able to soften the memory of what happened, though she can't remove it entirely."

Feather's voice falters over her next question. "Why couldn't you have been summoned *before* those brutes hurt the girl?"

"I cannot judge humans until a crime has occurred," I reply. "After the sin is committed, or once the ongoing abuse has reached its peak, the child is sent a Krampus bell by the god-stars. Unless they ring it, I can't find them."

"Seems like an ineffective way to punish the wicked," she mutters.

"I didn't make the rules."

"What about when a child is murdered? They can't ring a bell if they're dead."

"No. In those cases, the Krampus bell is sent to their killer. It possesses a compulsive magic that makes them want to ring it, and when they give in to that desire, I find them and judge them."

The sponge sweeps low on my abdomen. "Those men knew you're Fae, that iron would hurt you."

"I haven't spent as long in Visseland as I have in some other regions, but I'm already a legend here. Not all the people believe I'm real, and most of them don't realize what secret crimes their neighbors are guilty of, so they think I'm a villainous beast who preys on the innocent. Apparently these men suspected my true purpose. They knew I might come for them, and yet that fear wasn't enough to deter them from wicked deeds."

"So they prepared themselves in case you showed up," Feather says.

I sigh, and the movement causes my chest wound to flare with pain. "Either that, or it was a trap, a test conducted on the advisement of Fae-hunters."

"Hunters?"

"Yes. A bartender told me the Mayor of Rothenfel has hired Fae-hunters to come to the region and track me down. I thought I had plenty of time before they arrived, but perhaps they got here early… or perhaps they sent instructions, something for the locals to try before their arrival."

Feather wipes the sponge along my thigh with quick, angry strokes. "If those Fae-hunters orchestrated a trap with a young girl as bait, they're as bad as any of your other victims."

"Agreed."

"And they'll try again."

"Perhaps."

"How will you defend yourself?" she asks.

"I need to figure out who the hunters are, what they look like, how much they know, and what supplies they have. They'll be staying with the Mayor, so I'm planning to attend one of his parties and do a little investigation while I'm there."

"Isn't that terribly dangerous?" Feather squeezes the blood-soaked sponge into the bowl of water beside me. "What if they spot you as Fae immediately?"

"They won't. I can glamour away all telltale signs."

"And what if they can detect a glamour?"

"There are relics in this house which can conceal the energy residue of small glamours. I'm more concerned about the hunters finding this house by tracking its geistfyre energy. The quarry where the house resides is a bit too close to Rothenfel for my comfort. I could move it, but it's a strain on both me and the house. And unless the Fae-hunters have certain detection charms or devices in their arsenal, they won't be able to find it. So I'd rather not move it if I don't have to."

Feather dips the sponge again and moves forward to bathe my face. She starts with my horns—I suppose they must be spattered with blood from my fight with the men. Then she mops my brow gently.

"When is the party?" she asks.

"In a few weeks." I let my good eye close as the sponge glides along my temples and cheekbones. "I need to find a companion for that night. It must be someone the Mayor has never met, who has never attended one of his gatherings. I have a few women in mind to invite, but I'm afraid they might not be too pleased if I leave them stranded while I wander off to explore the Fae-hunters' quarters."

I'm musing aloud, talking more to myself than to her, and I barely realize what I'm saying until the sponge stops moving at the corner of my jaw. It leaks warm water down my neck.

"What if I went with you?" Her voice is so small and faint I barely hear it.

My eye opens. Feather looks petrified by what she just said—more frightened of a party than of a sentient house full of monsters.

"No," I say curtly.

She frowns, offended by my abrupt refusal. But I hate the vulnerable, scared look I saw on her face just now, and I refuse to be the one who puts it there again.

"This is an elegant gathering," I continue. "You wouldn't know how to act. You haven't had an education, or learned social graces. You don't belong there."

Her eyes narrow. "That may be true. But if a big dirty brute like you can pass as one of them, I'm sure I could learn as well. You can teach me these 'social graces.'"

I imagine this delicate, shy girl dressed in a luxurious gown, floating into a room teeming with the Mayor's careless, greedy, self-absorbed guests. The vision makes my stomach clench with anxiety. Brave as she was against the monsters of this house, the monsters of that mansion are worse.

"You can't learn everything you'd need to know in just three weeks," I growl. "It's impossible."

"So you think I'm stupid."

"That's not what I said—" My protest chokes off as she slaps the wet, bloody sponge over my mouth. Bitter salt tinges my tongue.

Despite my weakness, I summon enough strength to grab the sponge and fling it back at her. It smacks wetly against her chest, then plops into her lap.

She blinks loftily at me. "Just as well. I need to clean up, too."

She puts the sponge in the bowl, rises, and takes hold of the hem of her short black dress. She lifts it, exposing her lace panties, her smooth stomach—then she drags the dress over her head and tosses it aside. Her breasts are sharply peaked into rosy tips.

"What the fuck..." I breathe.

"You've seen me like this," she says. "Remember? When you kept me from freezing?"

"Yes, but..."

She kneels beside me again, her eyes as soft and innocent as her nude form. My cock twitches and hardens—I can't stop the reaction.

"Gods-*fuck*," I choke out.

"What's that?" She pretends to lean in and listen closely. "You agree to teach me the social graces I need so I can accompany you to the party? How kind of you, Krampus."

"You think exposing yourself to me will get you what you want?"

Her cheeks flush a delicate pink. "I saw one of the Wives do it. I thought I would try."

"Well, you're out of luck. You're not the type of woman who tempts me. The opposite, in fact."

Her flush deepens and she cups her breasts, concealing them. "Am I too small? Too pale?"

"You look like a fucking child," I snarl. "And you act like one. Go to bed."

"But *you* need the bed."

"Well then... find another room."

She gets up, grabs a blanket from the end of the bed, and wraps it around herself. "What about the monsters? What if they eat me? You said this was the only safe bedroom—"

"I know what I said!" Gripping the bed frame, I haul myself up and heave my wounded body onto the sheets. "Fine. For now, I suppose we'll have to share. You've lost blood and you should rest."

"You've lost blood too. I'll fetch you some food to bolster your strength. And what about bandages? The bleeding seems to have stopped, but do you need—"

"Lie the fuck down!" I bellow.

I regret the outburst immediately. She shrinks from me, her gaze wary. When she slinks to the other side of the bed and lies down, I can practically taste her tension, her caution.

I want to tell her she doesn't need to fear me. That I would never hurt her. But fuck me, I don't know how to do this. I can feign merriment and gallantry out in the world, but here in the house, with her, I can't be suave and charming. I don't know why. My whole body grates and growls in her presence, turns stiff and gruff and thorny.

Am I protecting her from me, or protecting myself from her?

Much as I hate scaring her, I can't make myself apologize. The Fae don't say they're sorry.

Instead I turn my back to her, my muscles aching from my iron-poisoned blood.

After a moment, her thin voice drifts into the silence. "We're not done talking about this."

Resistance flames in my chest. "You're not going to the party."

"I am. Because you have no one else. You'll realize it when your brain isn't addled with iron and pain."

My tongue flicks out, running along my lips—a habit when I'm aggravated or excited. It's half-healed, but still sore. "You're alone, too."

"I have the house. And the Imp. And possibly the other monsters as well." She speaks in the softest, lightest, most childish tone, as if she's talking about toys she has collected, but there's an undercurrent of acid in her voice. She's reveling in the fact that she took the monsters' allegiance from me.

"I could banish you from this house whenever I please," I tell her.

"Do it, then," she snaps.

I vent a hoarse, mocking laugh. "I would, but I need someone to wash my underwear and scrub my floors. 'Maid' is a role you play well. Stick to it."

The silence between us is thunderous.

Finally she says, in a tight, pinched voice, "I hate you."

"And yet you saved my life."

"Foolish of me." The bed creaks as she gets up and heads for the door.

I want to roar after her, to demand her return. But I stay silent.

When the door closes behind her, I roll onto my back, the tips of my horns scratching the headboard.

She's right. I have no one else. And as much as I hate the thought of taking her with me into the Mayor's world, I'm not sure I have a choice.

Surely I could teach Feather enough to get by in society for just one night. She is the traumatized victim of a psychotic kidnapper, but she is also a tireless worker and a bold commander of eldritch beings. Among those identities, perhaps there is another—a poised, well-spoken young woman who could appear on my arm at a party.

I hope I can shape her into such a woman, because otherwise we may both end up dead.

11

FEATHER

"I hate him," I seethe aloud as I scrub gore from the floor of the gray room. After leaving Krampus's room, I changed into a nearly-dry nightdress that was hanging in the kitchen, and I've been trudging back and forth with buckets of water, ignoring the pain in my injured arm. When blood starts to soak through my bandages, I simply add more strips of cloth. I can't stomach the idea of resting in that bed with him. Exhausted though I am, I'd rather be working.

"Oh my," says a faint, glittery voice, and Perchta appears, seated in midair with one knee hooked over the other. "Is there trouble between you and Krampus?"

"A disagreement," I reply.

"He can be terribly disagreeable." She tosses her floating golden hair. "You know, darling, I've been wandering the hallways a bit and I have to say, I love what you've done with the place."

"Thank you."

"The house must adore you." Her smile widens.

"We have a bond."

"And has it shown you every little nook and cranny?"

"Well…" I wring out the sponge with more vigor than necessary. "Not everything."

"Oh." She lifts a misty brow slightly.

For some reason, her expression makes me even angrier. "Trust takes time to build," I mutter, scrubbing the floor savagely.

"Of course, of course. And so very few people are worthy of knowing all the secrets of a place like this." Her laugh tinkles. "Perhaps, once you've cleared more of the rooms, it will reveal to you the truly important areas—like the library."

"The what?" My head snaps up, a chill of excitement ghosting over my skin.

Ten books. That's all we had in the cabin. A book is a new horizon, a doorway into the world, a window into the hearts of people. But a *library*—that is a fantasy, a dream, a universe of possibilities. A whole *room* full of books. I've only heard of such places—I've never seen one.

"Yes, the library." Perchta inspects her frosty white claws. "So many beautiful books. And there are a few interesting artifacts in that room as well. Some of them have been here as long as the house. You might say they're part of the structure, in fact. Integral to its power."

I'm barely listening, still trying to grasp the concept that this house, the one I'm connected to, has an entire roomful of books that it has kept secret from me. Before, I didn't mind waiting for the house to slowly reveal itself, but now that I know books are involved, I can barely contain my eagerness.

I drop the sponge and splay both hands on the floor, tapping into my mental awareness of the house, hunting for the library. I can't sense its location, but there's an entire area that's dark, as if someone spilled ink on a map. I can't see those rooms.

I let my displeasure flood through my connection with the house, and it returns a vague pulse of aloofness tinged with guilt. I can tell it's close to relenting. Close to letting me in.

A little more work, and those darkened areas will be unveiled to me.

"Fine," I hiss, and I keep working.

Perchta drifts around me aimlessly until I ask, "How long have you known Krampus?"

"Oh, ages. I mentored him a bit, at the beginning. Helped him get used to his new existence, until the overseer decided I wasn't obedient enough to be a guide for him. But we've stayed in touch. I used to pop in on him at odd times and surprise him, just for the fun of it. In fact, not long ago I went to his room and caught him stroking his cock while smelling your underwear." She titters.

I'm not quite sure why Krampus would do such a thing, but I picture it without meaning to, and my cheeks flame as I rinse the sponge again. I remember what I was told about a man's pleasure, how it results in the expulsion of liquid seed.

Perchta swoops closer. "Why, darling, have I embarrassed you? Have you never pleasured a man before?"

"No," I murmur.

"You've touched yourself, though, of course." When I don't reply, she gasps. "Is it possible you haven't? Oh, what fun! Shall I teach you? It's really quite simple. Of course I can't actually make myself come, not without corporeal form, but I could explain the process. The easiest way to begin is to place your

121

fingertips over your clit—that's the little bud between your legs, and move them around—"

"Please… no." I clap both wet hands over my ears. "I don't want to hear it."

She nods, and when I remove my hands from my ears, she says, in a tone softer than I've ever heard her use, "I won't tell you anything you don't want to hear. But you should know there's nothing wrong or frightening about pleasing yourself or someone you like. No matter what you've heard or seen… that sort of pleasure can be healthy and beautiful."

I swallow hard, but I don't reply. After a moment, she says, "It's been a delight, Feather. I look forward to our next meeting."

She vanishes, and I continue with my task, trying not to think about what she said—which proves impossible, because my brain keeps repeating her words over and over.

There's nothing wrong or frightening about pleasing yourself or someone you like. No matter what you've heard or seen… that sort of pleasure can be healthy and beautiful.

I work until I'm beyond the point of exhaustion and the floor of the gray room is clean. Then I drag myself back to Krampus's room.

Darkness shrouds the chamber, the shadows barely disturbed by the low-burning fire. Heavy breathing tells me that Krampus is sound asleep, hopefully recovering from his wounds.

Carefully I crawl into the opposite side of the bed. It seems safer to do so, now that he's asleep.

My body craves sleep as well, but my mind is desperately curious. If I can't explore the library tonight, maybe I can explore myself.

Beneath the sheets, I draw my nightgown up and slip my fingers into my underwear. I have the little sensitive spot Perchta mentioned—the *clit*, and the moment I touch it, I feel a soft flutter through the entire area between my legs. My captor called it the "pussy." Sometimes he would grab Wife's pussy in front of

Mother and me. That always happened right before he took her to their bedroom.

No. I won't think of him while I do this. I'll think of the woman in the red-lantern house, and the man between her legs. I'll picture how he grabbed her thighs, how he moved his mouth on her enthusiastically, as if she tasted like the finest cake or the most delicious wine.

My fingertips toy with the small bud, and then I run them farther along the delicate folds of my sex, parting the seam, discovering a light dampness. It isn't blood, but something else.

I hesitate, glancing over at Krampus, but his back is turned, and he's still breathing slowly, heavily. Deeply asleep.

I wonder if his tongue has healed yet. I wonder how his tongue would feel right here, slithering over my pussy, the piercings rubbing against this sensitive bit at the top. My fingers move in slow circles, then faster as I imagine his beautiful face and horned head between my legs, his mouth devouring me with eagerness and devotion, a deep hum rolling from his chest...

I feel awake and warm and deliciously alive. With every pass of my fingertips, a surge of fragile pleasure trickles through my pussy. But I want more—I *need* more. And I'm not sure how to get what I need.

I give a faint moan of frustration, then clamp my free hand over my mouth.

When did I bend my knees and spread them wide? When did the sheet slip down dangerously low across my waist? And I think I was panting aloud. I became so lost in chasing the pleasure that I forgot where I was.

Krampus still has his back to me. But as I hold my breath, I realize the pattern of his breathing has changed. It's still heavy, but it's faster than the slow cadence of sleep.

I press my hand to my pussy, staying perfectly still.

"Are you trying to kill me?" he says, low and venomous.

"What... what do you mean?"

"Filling the air of this room with your fragrance. With the scent of arousal. Do you know what that does to a Fae like me? Especially a wounded one?"

"I don't understand."

He rolls onto his back with a weary sigh. "Blood isn't the only thing that helps us heal. Sex does, too, if it's with another Fae... or a human. And *you*, lying next to me with your little fingers nestled in that sweet-scented pussy—it's like you're dangling a healing charm in front of my face while forbidding me from taking it. Is this your vengeance because I refused to go along with your plan?"

"No," I mutter shamefacedly into the darkened room. "I didn't know what I was doing. I haven't done it before. Perchta said it was fun, but it seems more frustrating than enjoyable. I can't... I need *more*..."

"Perchta?" His tone is a blade, keen and combative. "She spoke to you? I warned her—"

I yank down my nightdress and pull the sheet up to my chin. "I don't want to talk any more. I'm going to sleep."

"Well, now that you've gotten yourself excited, you won't be able to sleep until you come," Krampus replies, then adds in an undertone, "Nor will I."

"What do you mean, 'come'?"

He groans, and it sounds like pain, but there's an undercurrent of wild hunger, too. A gentle thrill traces along my pussy, and my fingers twitch with the longing to touch it again.

"This is too cruel," he mutters. "But I suppose I must teach you, since you have no one else. If you keep playing with yourself as you did, but with a faster rhythm in just the right places, you will achieve a burst of exquisite pleasure. It's called an orgasm, a shock of euphoria when your body comes. It's a relief and a delight when the act is performed alone—even more so when achieved by two partners."

"Is it the same thing as sex?" I whisper. "When a man puts himself inside a woman? I always thought it pleasured him and pained her."

"Only if she isn't willing," replies Krampus, in a gentler tone. "Sex between willing partners shouldn't hurt. A little the first time, perhaps, but after that, there should be no pain. There are many ways for bodies to join, whether male, female, or other, and all such connections should be delightful, not harmful. Unless one of the participants enjoys the occasional playful bite or the sting of a whip to intensify their pleasure."

I frown. "How would pain intensify pleasure?"

He's quiet for a while. All I can hear are his quick breaths.

When he speaks again, his words are thick and strained. "I can't tell you about this anymore."

"Why not?"

"Because I'm so fucking hard it hurts," he growls. "I need you to be quiet, and cover up that luscious-smelling cunt of yours before I drag you over here and use you as a cock-sleeve." He vents a frustrated snarl, then mutters, "Not that I would ever touch you. You need not fear that from me. But in my current state, I am sorely tempted."

I bite my lip. Though my limbs are trembling with apprehension, my pussy is slick and warm and tingling. "One more question, please. Is it normal for me to be… very wet in that place?"

"Yes," he rasps. "That liquid eases the way when a hard cock penetrates you. It means you're ready to be fucked. Now shut up."

We lie there silent, unmoving. Eventually I risk a glance at him. He's barely visible in the glow of the fireplace embers, but I can make out his elegant profile and the parallel ridges along the curve of each black horn. He has thrown off most of the covers, but the sheet still drapes him from the waist down. Beneath the sheet, below his waist, something large and thick is poking up.

His cock. *So hard it hurts,* he said. And sex helps the Fae heal.

I don't understand the wild, dark need inside me, the sudden yearning to lift the sheet and see all of him again... maybe touch him this time. Two weeks we've lived together, and we've never shared the bed. Perhaps this is why. Perhaps he feared this sort of connection, or temptation.

He doesn't really like me, any more than I like him. He's simply aroused by my scent, by our conversation, and by his desire to heal. It's more than a desire—it's a need. Perhaps it's a need that his maid should fulfill.

I shift nearer to him under the sheets, until I can feel the heat of his bare skin all along the side of my body. Cautiously I move one hand toward him until my fingers touch his thigh.

"Get out," he rasps.

I freeze.

He practically snarls at me. "I would leave if I could, and give you the bed, but I'm not strong enough yet. Take pillows, blankets, whatever you need, and go. Sleep in the bathroom or the kitchen. Go."

"I want you," I whisper.

"I said, *get out.*"

Hot, angry tears stain my cheeks as I tear a pillow and a blanket from the bed and stalk out of the room. I make my way to the kitchen, conscious of the Bahkauv trailing along in my wake. He doesn't come too close, nor does he try to enter the kitchen when I do. Frustrated and weary, I lie down on the hearth, roll myself in the blanket, tuck the pillow under my head, and fall into a tormented sleep.

THE BAHKAUV

12

KRAMPUS

We don't speak of that night for three days. She brings me food, tidies the room, then flees my presence. When I need to relieve myself, I crawl to the bathroom alone.

Halfway through my recovery, I remember a set of charmed silver armbands that might help speed the healing process. I have no idea where they might be, but when I mention them to Feather, she locates them immediately, having noticed them before when she was organizing my room. I suppose there's some benefit to keeping things neat.

She stays long enough to place the silver bands on my forearms and wrists, but then she hurries away again, like a skittish animal who has been wounded and is now leery of me.

I'm angry with myself for the conversation we had. Not for the information I imparted, but for letting myself come so close to fucking her. Over and over I have vowed that I won't touch her that way, and yet each time I see her, my resolve evaporates.

On the third day, when she opens the bedroom door and carries in the tray, I spot the Bahkauv right behind her.

"Shut the door, quickly!" I cry, sitting bolt upright.

"What? Why?" She glances over her shoulder at the beast with its dull red eyes and its calf's muzzle full of fangs. "Oh, it's just him. He's been following me around." She jerks her head at the Bahkauv. "Go. Run along."

With a strange, bawling cry, he slinks away. Feather kicks the bedroom door shut and brings the tray to my bed. "Close your mouth, Krampus. Your tongue is sliding out."

I retract my tongue and close my gaping jaws. "He… follows you around?"

"He's not as scary as I thought." She shrugs, pouring out a cup of tea.

"Yes he fucking is."

"To *you*, maybe."

I take the teacup, my lip curling with faint resentment. "I think you've become comfortable here far too quickly."

Triumph sparkles in her gaze and *fuck*, where did she get such huge, gorgeous eyes? No wonder that piece of shit kidnapped her. She must have been adorable as a child. And her family—how they must have missed their small, beautiful daughter, and mourned her when all hope was gone.

"Do you remember anything about your life before you were taken?" I ask.

"No." Her expression becomes shadowed, furtive, and she retreats toward the door like a deer about to bound away through the forest.

"Wait!" I call, with all the strength I can summon.

The dress she's wearing today is the same one she wore when she saved me. She has washed it, but it still bears discolored splotches where the bloodstains wouldn't quite come out. She isn't wearing stockings or shoes; she stands bare-legged and barefoot, and somehow that's worse. She has such tiny, crooked, kissable toes.

I drag my gaze back up her body, trying not to linger too long on the twin points of her breasts beneath the tight black fabric. Locks of wavy brown hair lie against her chest, shifting lightly with her breath.

"What is it, master?" Her voice is crisply polite and cold.

"I'm feeling better. We should begin your lessons."

"Lessons?"

"I need to prepare you for the party at the Mayor's house."

Color drains from her face. "You're going to bring me with you?"

"It was your idea."

"Of course, yes. But you said—"

"I changed my mind."

"Perhaps I've changed mine as well." She winces. "I want to help you. But I've been thinking about it, and I realized… there will be *people*."

"Yes, there generally are people at a party," I reply. "That's rather the idea of it all."

Her thin fingers twist together. "I'm not used to people. When I walked into that tavern, in the town where you left me, it was terrifying. All the faces, the voices, the noise and the eyes…"

"We'll go out at least once before then," I assure her. "In fact, you can come with me tonight, to one of my favorite pubs. With practice, you'll acclimate to being around other humans."

"Are you sure you feel well enough to go out?"

"I'm healed. A little stiff, but it's nothing a stein of good beer can't mend. In fact, a drink would do you good as well, I'd wager."

"And should I wear this?" she asks, indicating her maid's dress.

"God-stars, no. If I had all my Fae powers, I'd conjure you a dress…. Though I was never much good at making clothes. We'll have to find something of mine for you to wear. Go on, take a look. You've laundered and organized it all anyway—you should know if there's anything that might suit you."

"I'm not sure what suits me," she answers quietly. "I've always worn what I've been given. I dressed only for *him*."

For her captor. Fuck him. Fury spikes through my veins, a rush of violent heat. "I should have killed that bastard more slowly. Taken my time. Made it hurt."

"No." She comes a step closer, her face white and earnest. "I preferred a quick death for him. Quick is better. It's the end. No fear of him returning."

"You wouldn't have wanted to torture him yourself? Paid him back for all the years he kept you prisoner?"

She looks down at her hands. "I don't think I could have."

"Why not? He was a rotten motherfucker, a murdering asshole."

"Yes. And he was the only constant in my life since I was six years old," she says softly. "He put me to bed every night. Held me. Kissed my cheeks. Brought me presents and clothes. He beat me sometimes, but he always cried afterward. I would comfort him, and then everything was alright between us. He always brought me something especially nice after a punishment. A few times he brought cake."

I stare at her, immobilized by the storm of emotions in my chest. It's too much for me to cope with—I'm half afraid I might explode.

I've been alone for so long, moving through my usual routine: doing my work, then transporting myself to some tavern to drink away the memory of the carnage—fucking a stranger to make myself feel something again.

But with Feather, I am *always* feeling things. Rage, lust, longing, disbelief, sorrow, surprise. And another feeling—the sense that I, a rejected Fae infant sold to a trollish clan, the murderer of over a hundred mistreated children, the master of bloody vengeance and emissary of the Wild Hunt, am laughably ill-equipped to help this woman heal from all the wounds to her heart and mind.

I don't know how to respond to her revelation. So I clear my throat awkwardly and say, "Look in the wardrobe and bureaus. Find something to wear. Something *you* like."

While she selects a few items of clothing, I devour the food she brought. We're nearing the end of our supplies, but she managed to create a delicious meal of sausages, potatoes, and carrots, with a thick gravy.

"Your cooking has improved," I tell her.

"I found some old cookbooks in one of the kitchen cupboards." She holds up a sky-blue silk shirt, some brown pants, and a fur-trimmed leather vest. "May I wear these?"

Her slight frame will be lost in them, but I nod. "Try them on. I want to see how they look."

She starts to remove her dress, and I exclaim, "In the bathroom! Try them on in the bathroom."

Her lips tighten, but she goes into the bathroom without protest. When she comes back, dressed in my clothes, she looks so stunning I nearly drop the cup of tea I'm finishing. The sky-blue silk contrasts beautifully with her porcelain skin, and her brown hair perfectly matches the fur trim on the vest. But she's holding the pants up with one hand, and the shirt is much too long and baggy.

"You need a belt." I rise from the bed, and her eyes widen with horrified anticipation until she sees I'm not naked; I'm wearing a pair of undershorts.

My body is still stiff in places, particularly across the chest, even though the gashes have nearly healed. A normal Fae would have taken even longer to heal from such wounds, if they healed at all. But I have the charmed jewelry and an extra dose of strength, thanks to my status as a member of the Wild Hunt.

Powerful as I am, those men should have been quick work for me. But I was caught completely off guard. I didn't expect so many, didn't know they were anticipating my arrival. I didn't move fast enough when the first man swung his iron ax.

I crack my stiff neck and walk over to a dresser. "Where did you put the belts?"

"Second drawer down, on the right."

In the drawer I find belts that I haven't seen for years, including two of my favorites. I choose a wide one of soft leather, imprinted with swirling leaves and flowers. Then I walk over to Feather. "Take off the vest."

She sheds the vest, and I can't help noticing the way the silken shirt moves against her breasts.

"Lift the shirt out of the way," I tell her.

She gathers the folds of blue silk and holds them up, baring her slim waist. Her belly is flat and smooth, except for a gentle swell right below the navel, and I find myself compulsively yearning to run my fingers over her stomach, to settle my hands on her waist.

Instead I run the belt through the loops on the pants, my chest tightening each time my knuckles graze her skin.

"Before I fasten the buckle, we'll tuck in the shirt," I say hoarsely. "Let go of it."

She obeys, and I lower the pants just below her hips, correcting the fall of the fabric, smoothing the shirt as I tuck it in. Then I cinch the belt tight and buckle it slowly, conscious of how close my fingers are to that tender spot between her legs. I have to bend nearer as I'm fastening the belt, and her light, soft breath stirs my hair.

I loosen the shirt, ensuring that it's not tucked in too tight. "It looks better if there's a bit spilling over the belt, like this."

"Oh," she says faintly. "Thank you."

Her shoulders curve inward, hitched up slightly, as if she wants to withdraw her head inside herself like a tortoise. It's a position of cowed submission. And her spine arches like someone who spends days on her knees, scrubbing floors.

"Stand up straight." I place one hand on her back, between her shoulders, and I lay the other hand on her stomach, exerting firm, gentle pressure in both places. "Shoulders back, chin up. Like a woman who owns the world and expects every man to worship her."

She lets me adjust her body. Her pliant obedience heats my blood, and I struggle with the urge to place her in the most wanton of positions, with her hands on the floor, her ass in the air, her legs braced in a wide triangle, and her damp little slit open for the taking.

God-stars... I haven't fucked anything in far too long. I need to find someone tonight, at the pub, or I might lose my mind.

"Master?" she says tentatively. "Am I not doing it right?"

She's asking because I haven't removed my hands from her body. In fact, the one on her belly has slid lower. My traitorous fingers want to dip between her legs and show her the pleasure she's capable of enjoying.

With an effort, I let her go. "Chin up."

She lifts her face to mine. "Like this?"

"You should look even more arrogant. Lower your eyelashes, relax your mouth. Good. Now give me the slightest of haughty smiles."

Feather tilts her head and gives me an imperious little smirk.

She is truly a wondrous actress. Her talents were wasted in that cabin—or perhaps they were honed by the demands of her captor. Either way, I can't take my eyes off that pert, conceited mouth.

I'm standing too close to her. If she keeps smiling at me in that naughty way, with those dark lashes draping her lovely brown eyes, I'm going to seize her and crush her against myself and kiss her until—

"Walk," I bark, stepping back. "Walk the room. Elegance and grace. Go."

Her walk is good, if only she can remember to keep her shoulders back, her chin up, and her chest out. When she looks to me for approval, I nod. "No more cleaning today. I'll bathe and dress, and then we'll go into town. Don't worry, it's not the town where I left you last time."

She chews her lip thoughtfully for a moment. "I know you can transport to various places with your chains—"

"Geistfyre," I put in.

"Geistfyre. And you said we're near Rothen-something..."

"The house is at the bottom of an abandoned quarry near Rothenfel, the largest city in the region."

She nods hesitantly. "I do think it's odd that this house has no doors leading outside, not even from the kitchen. And behind the drapes, there are no windows, just walls."

"Ah… well, that's because the only way to get in and out of this house is transportation by geistfyre."

"Then why are you afraid of the Fae-hunters finding it? Even if they find it, they can't get in."

"They could neutralize its magic, disrupt my geistfyre so we can't leave, and then burn it down with us inside. This place is powerful, but not invincible. Once they discover it, there are many ways they can cause us harm."

"Seems like an escape route might be wise," she mutters. "Or at least a window where someone might look outside."

After a moment's hesitation, I confess, "There is one very special door, but I'm not sure you're ready to know where it leads. You might go mad."

Feather arches one eyebrow. "I'm sure I can handle it."

I'm tempted to deny her, but I'm also curious to see her reaction, to gauge the extent of her courage. So I relent. "Come along then."

The iron poisoning has made me more sensitive to temperature, so I snatch a fur-lined cape from the wardrobe and pin it around my bare shoulders. Since the vest alone might not keep her warm enough, I toss her a blue cloak that nearly matches her shirt.

We make our way to the cluttered ballroom where I collapsed from my wounds just a few days ago. The floor is spotless—not a bloodstain in sight.

"You cleaned this well," I comment.

"I've had plenty of experience with blood," she says. As if it's the most natural thing in the world for a young woman to be familiar with mopping up gore.

When I head for the stairway leading below, she hangs back. "You said the Meerwunder is down there."

"So is the door I want to show you."

Still she hesitates, her dark eyes huge in her pale face. "What if he doesn't like me?"

"Do you think I would let anything hurt you, if I could prevent it? I'd die first." The last three words jerk out of me, an impulsive snarl that sounds more threatening than reassuring.

But instead of recoiling in fright, Feather seems to relax a little. "Very well."

As we descend the stairs, I mutter, "I think everything down here is dead. It should be. Except for the Meerwunder, of course. Stay close."

"What do you mean, you *think* everything is dead?" She crowds against my back, clutching my elbow as we descend into darkness.

"Sometimes I bring my captives back here for torture. It depends on the crime, the dictates of the god-stars, and my mood. Sometimes I need something to ruin."

"If you found out that I was very, very bad, that I had committed some great sin, would you ruin *me*?" Her soft voice flutters in my belly. The sound of it, blended with the suggestive nature of the question, takes me utterly by surprise, and my cock stiffens. Which makes me helplessly furious at both her and myself.

"You've done nothing worthy of death," I reply roughly.

"You don't know that."

I whirl around, conscious that my eyes are glowing green with arousal in the dark. I can see their reflection in her gaze. "Where is this nonsense coming from? What happened to you wasn't your fault. You were a victim, not a perpetrator."

"You don't know me." Her voice cracks with pained anger. "I spent years *watching* him kill women. I did nothing to stop him. Didn't try to escape, not once, because I was too frightened that I would fail and end up dead myself. I was *loyal* to him, don't you see? Loyal, because I wanted to survive. That mattered more to me than helping any of them. And one time I even—"

She goes abruptly silent, unable to voice whatever she was about to confess.

"I don't care." In my fervor to make her understand, I clasp her upper arms. "None of it was your fault. It was *him*. You

138

could never be deserving of the kind of punishment I deal out. If I ever ruin you, it will be in a very different way."

"What do you mean?" She's trembling in my grip. When I inhale, I can smell her shame, her raw grief... and her arousal.

Little deviant. She may not know exactly what I mean by *ruining* her, but she suspects it, and her body is responding to the idea.

Maybe it's the fact that I'm nearly whole again—maybe it's the depth of her emotion in this moment, maybe it's the delirious scent of her, but suddenly I can't resist. I shove her against the wall of the stairway and crush my body against hers. Her position, one step above me, brings us into better alignment than usual—chest to chest, cunt to cock. My lips ghost over her mouth, and I let my long tongue emerge to trace her jawline.

"When I ruin a woman," I whisper, "I take every hole she has. Mouth, pussy, ass. All mine. I go balls-deep and fill each hole with my cum until she's dripping my seed everywhere. I make her scream, make her thighs shake with ecstasy, and when she thinks she can't come for me anymore, I coax the most exquisite, most violent orgasms out of her body. Afterward, each time she has sex with another partner, she'll picture me. She'll come for them while thinking of me, and she'll wish she could feel the shape of my cock inside her again. That is what I mean by *ruin*."

I breathe the last words hotly into her ear while she remains motionless, crushed against the wall, the thick roll of my cock pressing between her legs.

She's panting, the scent of her arousal stronger than ever. But this sweet, tragic girl doesn't know what she really wants. I'm determined that when she finally has sex, it won't be with me. She will never experience the brutal passion of my depraved mind. Someone like her needs a calm, steady, human partner to keep her safe, treat her gently, and help her heal. I would only break her. I have the lurking sense that if I did fuck this girl, it wouldn't be just once. I couldn't stop there. I'd need more. I would want to use her up.

My thoughts end abruptly as her soft mouth touches mine. I go rigid, motionless with shock.

It was tentative, barely a graze of lips... but she kissed me. A keen thrill traces through my whole body at the realization.

No. This cannot happen.

A guttural rebuke leaves my throat. "Don't ever do that again if you know what's good for you."

"I'm sorry," she gasps. "I don't know why I did it. I'm sorry. Don't throw me out, please."

"Be silent, and walk behind me."

As we continue down the steps, the smell worsens. It's the odor of rancid flesh, rotting and melting from bones. Feather makes a choking sound.

"Hold the edge of your cloak over your mouth and nose," I advise, and a rustle of fabric tells me that she's following my guidance.

When I reach the bottom of the steps, the house automatically lights two lamps for me. The moment they flare up, something heavy slithers and thumps rapidly across the floor, retreating from the blaze. Meerwunder hates light. He stays in the distant shadows, the bulk of his body barely distinguishable from the darkness. I've never seen all of him, only flabby tentacles and the occasional slimy claw.

Along the edges of the huge room are the cages where I sometimes keep prisoners. The reek comes from a newish, rather gooey corpse I'd forgotten about. I open the cage door so Meerwunder can take care of the remains after we leave. Once that body is gone, the smell will improve.

In the center of the room are long narrow tables with manacles and shackles attached. Various torture implements, whips, and straps are strewn across the floor, lying where I left them. There's a pile of switches, too, which I carefully selected for their pliant strength. They're perfect for beating my victims.

Still holding a fold of the cloak over her mouth and nose, Feather crouches and picks up a long leather bullwhip. It's one of my favorites, since I can use it to cause pain from a distance. I've even used it to keep the monsters in line occasionally.

Feather inspects the whip, then lays it on the table. The next second she spots the pile of switches and exclaims, "Oh, firewood! How perfect! We're almost out."

"No, that's not—" I protest, but she's already gathering an armful of the switches. "Fine," I sigh. "We'll use them as firewood. Give them to me, I'll carry them."

While she inspects more of the torture implements, I tie the switches together and swing the bundle onto my back.

"What's this?" Feather gestures to a huge ring bolted to the floor.

"The trap door. The house's one exit. I'm going to open it now, but don't try to understand what you see, or you'll go mad. You must simply accept it."

She nods, wide-eyed.

I reach down and hoist up the trap door.

13

FEATHER

Krampus climbs down through the trap door, then pulls me up with him.

Up, because though we went *down* through the bottom of the house, when we emerge we are standing upright, as though we climbed out of a skylight and we're standing on a flat roof.

"Are we upside down?" I gasp.

"Don't try to understand it. Just know that there is gravity to hold us here, air to breathe, and just enough warmth to keep us from freezing solid. Look."

I lift my eyes, and my mental horizons explode into infinity.

Space is all around us, a black and endless void reaching above, and below, and far away on every side. Stars and suns sprinkle the depths, sometimes alone, sometimes in great colorful swirls and clusters. There are clouds of green gas threaded with luminous pink, bursts of dazzling blue flecked with a white so pure it's painful to behold. In the middle distance, I spot a pathway of pale clouds streaking across the universe.

"One of the paths of the Wild Hunt," says Krampus. "Sometimes you can see them riding between worlds and realms. Walk this way. Don't be afraid—you won't fall."

But I'm locked in place. My feet refuse to move until he gathers my hand in his. When he walks me to the edge of the house and we peer beyond it, there is nothing. The house appears to be floating in emptiness.

"We're at the bottom of a quarry in Visseland," I say breathlessly. "And we're here, in the middle of nothing."

"In the Void," he replies. "Yes."

"We are occupying space in both places. At the same time."

"Yes."

I nod, taking a moment to adjust my definition of reality. I may not comprehend how both states of existence are concurrently possible, but the truth isn't contingent on my understanding. It simply *is*.

Besides, the Void is beautiful. Astonishing. Mind-shattering in the most brilliant way. I let go of Krampus's hand and look up, trying to take in the glory of it all. "I've been longing for a nice view."

Krampus looks surprised. Then he throws back his head and laughs, showing his fangs, while his long tongue lashes the air. His eyes glow green, brighter than ever. "I thought you'd be cringing and wailing at the vastness of this place. Yet here you are, taking it all in stride. You amaze me."

Heat floods my cheeks. He clears his throat and glances away, as if he didn't intend to say those last three words.

Desperate to break the awkwardness, I blurt out a foolish question. "Why is your tongue pierced?"

He lifts his long black claws to his mouth, and his tongue twines around them as if it has a mind of its own. He touches each silver stud, then retracts the tongue. "These piercings have a purpose. They offer greater sexual stimulation when I'm pleasuring someone."

I suspected as much, but my stomach does a wild little flip when he says it aloud. "And the ring in your nose?"

"That's simply an accessory, like these." He touches the little bar through his eyebrow and the jewelry along his ears. "Sometimes I remove the one in my nose. Depends on my mood. Of course then it heals over and I have to pierce it again..." He frowns, shaking his head. "Why are we discussing my personal modifications?"

I shrug. "Maybe I want one or two. At least in my ears. I wasn't allowed to have earrings in the cabin. Little Sisters don't wear jewelry."

"Fuck that." His eyes flash. "You shall have earrings, and soon."

I follow him back to the trap door. "Where does our water come from?"

"It's elemental magic. A convenient feature of this house."

"And where does the house's magic come from?"

"A centralized locus of power called the Nexus."

"And where did that come from?"

"Fuck if I know. I only live here." He climbs through the trap door and crouches on the floor on the other side, extending his hand to help me through.

It strikes me suddenly, how strange we would look to a faraway observer. Two creatures, entirely dissimilar, crouching on opposite sides of a wall—one above, one below. Me, the frail human in borrowed clothes, my brown hair and blue cloak billowing around me, caught in the eddies of some mysterious wind of the Void. Him, the gorgeous Fae with black horns, scarlet hair, and a furred cape, reaching out with elegant, claw-tipped fingers to draw me back inside his magical house.

His expression shifts, turning anxious as I linger outside. In a tone of velvet and blood, he urges, low and insistent, "Come, Feather."

I place my fingers in his palm. His hand closes around mine, and he pulls me through, out of the vast maw of the yawning universe, into the security of the house.

We rise together, and for a moment our bodies tilt against each other, my silk-covered breasts touching his bare chest. The contact sets me on fire, like it did when he grabbed me on the stairs. It's tantalizing in a way I've never experienced.

But he moves away, lowers the trap door into place, and stamps on it to make sure it's tightly closed. "Upstairs. Now. And don't come down here trying to make friends with the Meerwunder. It won't work."

I had no intention of doing so until he said I couldn't. Rebellion flares in my chest, an unfamiliar yet appealing fire. With him, I like pushing boundaries. It's subversive, yet safe.

"You thought I couldn't make friends with the Imp or the Bahkauv," I retort. "But I did."

"And I still don't understand it." He begins climbing the steps. "Even if they seem friendly, I beg you to keep their bloodthirsty natures in mind and realize that no matter how much you like them, they could decide to devour you at any moment."

I laugh a little. "I'm used to volatile beings."

He turns, glancing over his shoulder at me. "Of course you are." His tone is thoughtful, almost sorrowful.

"It's alright, you know," I tell him impulsively, sensing his anxiety, wanting to soothe it. "I'll be alright."

His throat moves as he swallows. "This is no place for you to heal."

The comment terrifies and unsettles me. I want to scream at him that he's wrong—that this house is exactly the right place for me. I want to dig my nails into the floorboards, claim this mansion as my own, and make him promise he will never send me away.

"I'd rather be here than anywhere else," I tell him.

"That's because you don't know any better." He turns away, continuing up the steps. "I'm going to bathe. I'll come fetch you when I'm ready to leave for the pub."

Once he's ready, we travel by geistfyre and spend a couple of hours in a small town, at a seamstress's shop where I'm measured and fitted for lovely, comfortable clothes with more coverage than my maid's outfits. I'm allowed to select the styles and the fabric—soft colors and subtle floral patterns—but Krampus chooses the material for the gown I'll be wearing to the Mayor's party. It's a flowy, plum-colored fabric which the seamstress promises to decorate with lavish appliques along the shoulders and waist. Krampus also commissions a pair of plum-colored lace gloves.

"All the women wear gloves, at least for the first part of the evening," he explains. "While they're still pretending to be chaste, elegant ladies."

For our foray into town, he has glamoured away every sign of his true nature—horns, fangs, ears, and claws. His eyes are green, but they don't glow like they often do at the house. His red hair trails over the huge, rolled collar of his coat like tendrils of scarlet silk. He looks human, except for the stunning beauty that sets him apart. The seamstress keeps bobbing curtsies to him and tucking stray curls behind her ears while beaming broadly. For my part, I have to fight the impulse to kneel at his feet and beg him to touch me.

"Look through the ready-made clothing rack," he tells me. "Choose anything you like."

The seamstress eyes us both, faint envy in her gaze. "You two are courting?"

"No," Krampus barks out, so sternly that the woman looks startled.

I interpose with the innocent, charming smile I cultivated in the cabin. "I'm his little sister," I explain. "An accident occurred while I was traveling to visit him. Both my trunks were lost in the river. That's why I need new clothes."

"Sister." The woman glances between us, somewhat unconvinced. "Well, I'm happy to provide you with what you need. We have some very fine underthings and nightwear as well, and a beauty enhancement kit with cosmetics of the highest quality. And a dressing gown so plush you'll think you've been wrapped in a cloud."

"We'll take all of it," says Krampus. "And a scarf. And those fur gloves with the matching hat."

He hands over an assortment of coins, and the seamstress is so delighted she doesn't question us any further. When we leave her shop, Krampus's arms are piled with bundles. I skip beside him, wearing my new hat, scarf, and gloves, barely able to contain my joy.

"I always thought choosing pretty clothes must be delightful," I exclaim. "But I never knew how much fun it really is."

"It was more fun than I've had in a while," he admits. "And I've worked up an appetite."

"I didn't realize how late it was getting." I glance up at the deepening blue of the evening sky.

"The rest of the shopping will have to wait," he says. "We're off to The Spinning Sow for dinner."

He takes me into a shadowed alley and puts the packages in my arms while he conjures his chains and swings them in a circle around us. The alley vanishes, and we're transported to a broad, snowy field.

The cloud cover is thicker here. Not far away stands a line of bare gray trees, interspersed with bushy evergreens. I'm knee-deep in soft snow, while large flakes drift lazily down from the heavy clouds above us. The flames of his geistfyre circle dissipate quickly, leaving us in semi-darkness.

"Well, fuck," mutters Krampus. "I didn't realize how much snow there would be in this spot."

"There's snow in my shoes," I gasp, giggling. "At least *you* have tall boots."

He swears again, then bends and lifts me off my feet, packages and all. I scream a little, but it's partly a laugh.

"I've never seen snow falling so heavily before," I tell him. "It's lovely. And it's so quiet."

The snow has a pale luminescence all its own, as if it's absorbing any trace of starlight from the gaps between the clouds. It muffles sound, too, creating a thick, beautiful silence.

Krampus is looking at me, and I hold my breath, because he's even prettier when our faces are this close. Snowflakes are caught in his dark lashes.

"You've never played in the snow before?" he asks in a low voice.

I shake my head.

"Well then." He strides over to a large rock, one of a few boulders in the field. He sets me down long enough to brush the snow off the rock and place our packages on it. Then he scoops me up again, spins us both in a fast circle, and flings me into a drift of fluffy snow.

I squeal and flounder, my smile so big that my cheeks hurt.

Krampus gathers a double handful of the snow, cups it firmly, and shapes it into a ball. The moment I scramble to my feet, he flings the ball at me, and it bursts into white powder against my chest.

He laughs, his long tongue slithering out for a moment. But his merriment is short-lived, because I'm a quick learner, and within seconds I've formed a similar snowball and sent it hurling toward him. It strikes his stomach.

"Little devil." He snatches up more snow and presses it hastily into a ball.

I run from him—or I try to, but running in deep snow is more difficult than I expected and I keel over face-first into the pillowy white. His snowball hits my rear, and then he's on top of me, rolling me over. I grab a handful of snow and toss it into his face before wriggling out of his grasp and backing away.

He jumps up to chase me, but one of his feet sinks into a hollow beneath the snow, and he teeters, off balance. I barrel into him, shoving him flat before jumping astride him and dropping a lump of fresh snow into his laughing mouth.

"Delicious," he croons. "Try some." And he presses a generous clump of snow into my mouth, too. It melts instantly, leaving a fresh, sweet taste on my tongue.

"It's wonderful," I say, panting. "Thank you. Not just for this, but for… everything."

His eyes soften. "You deserve better than I've given you."

Guilt seeps into my soul, a familiar acidic burn in my stomach. If he knew everything I've done…

But why am I even thinking about *that*? It's not as if tormenting myself will change the past. I have to move on and pretend it never happened.

Krampus lies beneath me, his arms splayed wide, his pale face and throat tilted up to the sky, and his red hair spilled like blood on the snow. He looks so human like this, so vulnerable.

Not like a hulking beast of vengeance. When he looks at me, I see tenderness in his eyes.

Still, I can't shake the memory of how he rejected me the other night. My foolish admission: *I want you.* And his voice when he replied, *Get out.*

"I'm wet and cold and hungry." I climb off him and stand up. "We should find the pub."

His expression changes, the tenderness veiled by cool composure. "It's just down the road. Stay here, and I'll get the bundles."

Once he has fetched them, he hands everything to me again and picks me up, heedless of my muttered protest. His long strides carry us swiftly to a road that's half snow, half frozen mud, which we follow until a large stone house becomes visible ahead.

"The Spinning Sow is a wayside inn and pub, situated between two towns and popular with the citizens of both, as well as with travelers," Krampus says. "They know me as Lord Brandt here. The host is a kind man, welcoming to all and open-minded to trysts, but with a low tolerance for thievery and brawls. It's a safe place, with good food."

I nod, trying not to notice how good his arms feel around my body. "How long will we stay?"

He clears his throat, which tells me I won't like what's coming. "You should walk the rest of the way."

After putting me down and taking a few of the bundles, he keeps walking, and I hurry alongside him.

"I told you that sex helps the Fae heal," he says, staring ahead. "But that's not the only benefit for my kind. Sex also bolsters our energy, enhances our magic, and feeds our very life-force. We need it to function properly. And I haven't bedded a woman for too long. So tonight, I will be leaving you in the common room for a short time while I take care of that need."

"You're going to leave me alone? With strangers?"

"I told you it's safe," he replies. "Would you rather stand in a corner and watch me fuck the woman I choose?"

"Maybe," I retort. "Perhaps then I could see how it's done, and how it works between two people who both desire it."

He glances sharply at me. "You're serious?"

Truth be told, I'm not sure I could bear to watch. But the thought of him leaving me alone for even a short time is terrifying. What if someone steals me away and locks me up again?

"I'd be happy to observe... unless it would bother *you*." I let a hint of challenge seep into my tone.

"Why would it bother me?" He's walking faster, striding ahead with such restless ire that I can barely keep up. "Watch if you want. It won't disturb me in the slightest. The women who come to The Spinning Sow to have their needs met are generally amenable to all sorts of things. I'm sure I can find one who doesn't mind an observer."

"Then it's settled," I snap.

"So it is," he replies caustically. "I'm very pleased about it."

"So am I."

Thanks to our furious pace, we're approaching the inn already. The pale snow of the yard has been shaped into hollows and crusts by dozens of hooves and boots. Warm yellow light spills from the windows.

Once inside, we leave our outerwear and packages with a servant boy in the coat-room before proceeding into the pub. I stay close behind Krampus as we enter the common area.

This time, I'm better prepared for the noise, the lights, and the people. I hold my head up, like Krampus taught me, and I pretend that I belong here, that I've been coming to places like this all my life.

With a few quick glances, I observe the women in the room. One is balancing trays, sidling between chairs, laughing as she returns the friendly jibes of the patrons. Another woman, long and slim, has draped herself in a booth between two men who both seem fascinated with her.

A square-shouldered woman with short, sandy hair and freckles is playing a game of cards and dice with three men. Judging by their expressions, she's winning. Three young women about my age are chatting and chuckling, sharing a large platter of chopped vegetables and sauces.

A few other women are scattered through the pub, conversing or drinking. I wonder which of them Krampus will pick. At least I'll get to see what sort of woman appeals to him.

Someone yells "Lord Brandt!" and Krampus returns the greeting with a genial, raucous shout of "How are you, you motherfucking bastard?"

At the exchange, the languid woman looks up, her hooded gaze latching onto my escort. She has olive skin with gold undertones, and her black hair shimmers like a waterfall of ink. Her purple lips are small, plump, and pouted.

She shoos the two men away from her and gestures imperiously for Krampus to approach.

"Do you know her?" I whisper.

"Rather well," he replies in an undertone. "It so happens she's the sort of person who might let you watch."

"Oh," I respond glumly. "How wonderful."

He leads the way toward her, and we both slide onto the bench opposite her in the booth.

"Midrael," he says.

"I haven't seen you in ages, Brandt." Her voice is mellow, liquid. "And who is your... friend?"

"This is Feather," Krampus replies. "She and I are looking for some good food—and some pleasant company."

"Is that so?" Midrael surveys me. "Well, you know I can be very pleasant. And very open to new friends, especially pretty ones."

She reaches across the table and strokes my hand lightly with her long, delicate fingers. She has perfectly tapered nails, smooth and pink. A jeweled ring sparkles on her central finger, and there's a lacy tattoo across her wrist.

Krampus clears his throat. "Let's have some food and wine."

"Something light," suggests Midrael. "I prefer not to consume too much before a dalliance."

"I remember. The soup, then?"

"Perfect."

"I'll speak to our host about the wine." He rises from the table. "You two can get acquainted."

When he leaves, Midrael cocks her head, surveying me. "Interesting choice of clothes for someone who's seeking pleasure."

"My trunks met with an accident while I was traveling." The lie rolls easily from my tongue.

"Indeed. And where were you traveling from? How do you know Lord Brandt?"

"Um…" My mind races, trying to conjure answers to questions I wasn't prepared for. *Play the role, Feather.* "I was traveling from a village on the southern border. Lord Brandt visited my family there a while back, and we became acquainted—"

"I actually don't care." She gives me a wide, vicious smile. "I may be open to sharing my bed, but I do have standards. My choice of bedmates reflects on me, and frankly, you look as if you've been rolling about in the snow. You're dreadfully flushed and disheveled, and those hands… ugh. What are you, a farm girl?"

"Do you have something against farm girls?" I reply coolly.

"Not at all, provided they stay in their place," she answers. "Here's what we're going to do. You'll stay down here and stuff that pasty face of yours with the inn's best dumplings while

Brandt and I take our wine upstairs. A man of his beauty belongs with someone like me, not with a farm wench from the south."

Heat flushes my cheeks. "You know nothing about me."

"I know he deserves better than some uncouth trollop, and you're certainly not the kind of woman I'd share a bed with. I like my ladies shaved bare and well-perfumed. Judging by the state of you, I suspect you're smelly and hairy as a sheepdog down there. Leave Brandt to me, and stay put. There's a little reward in it for you if you do."

She produces a silver coin and holds it up between two fingers.

The only other woman who angered me this much was the Wife who came to the cabin when I was eleven. She said her real name once: Colletta. And from the moment she was brought to the cabin, she treated me like a crusted piece of shit on the bottom of her shoe.

I hated her, because she almost took everything from me.

And I made sure she didn't last long.

Midrael hasn't won, but I need her to think she has. When people believe they have triumphed, they reveal their true intentions.

I pluck the coin from Midrael's fingers. "Agreed."

"At least you're smart enough to know when you're bested." She smirks, fiddling with her empty wine glass. "I have the right of first claim, anyway. I've slept with him twice. He has more stamina than any man I've bedded, and he's rich, too. We're perfect together. All I need is a little more time with him, and he's mine—his fortune, his cock, and his pretty face. Ah, here he comes."

As Krampus approaches with a bottle and two more glasses, she coos, "Brandt, my precious one, your friend has graciously allowed me to have you all to myself tonight. She can order anything she likes, on my tab, and have a grand time here while you and I take our wine upstairs."

Krampus looks down at me, his brow furrowed.

"It's true," I assure him. "We had a lovely chat. Go on, I'll be fine."

His frown only deepens, but he lets Midrael tow him away from the booth toward the stairway at the back of the pub. They both pause briefly at a small desk where a woman hands them a key. As Krampus accepts the key, Midrael reaches up, laces her hands around the back of his neck, and pulls him down for a long kiss. Her eyes flick open during the kiss, looking at me over his shoulder.

A dark, bloody haze creeps inward from the edges of my vision. My chest tightens until I can hardly breathe.

She touched him. She kissed him.

She is going to *take* him. Take him with her body, take him away from me, take his heart and his thoughts, and I can't fucking bear it.

My ears roar with my pounding blood. I can't form coherent thoughts through the hideous red storm in my brain. The coin slips from my fingers, rolls off the table, hits the floor with a ringing sound like a Krampus bell.

I wait until they're almost out of sight, and then I blow out the large candle on the table, yank it out of its iron holder, and leave the booth with the holder gripped in my hand. The woman at the desk doesn't stop me from going upstairs; perhaps she saw me sitting with Midrael and she assumes I'm going to join the tryst. I keep the iron candlestick low at my right side so she doesn't notice it.

I reach the narrow second-floor hallway just as Midrael and Krampus are unlocking their room. As they move inside, I run lightly and silently along the carpeted hall and catch the door just before it closes.

Krampus heads for the bed while Midrael follows him; but he hesitates and begins to turn around, saying, "Perhaps this was a mistake—"

At the same moment, I strike Midrael's skull with the candlestick.

She crumples instantly, unconscious. Not dead. I knew exactly how hard the blow needed to be.

A smile teases the corners of my mouth. I like her better this way. Quiet and still. Less boastful.

"Feather!" Krampus exclaims. "What the fuck have you done?"

14

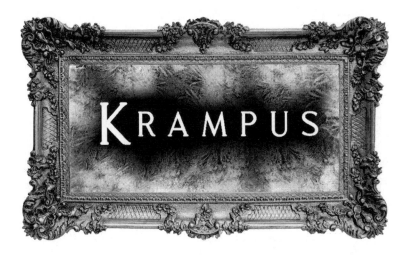

KRAMPUS

Feather stands over Midrael's insensate body. Her right hand shakes so much she can barely grip the candlestick, but her smile is bright and cruel. I've never seen her wear such an expression. It shocks and excites me at the same time.

"Too bad," she says softly. "You can't fuck her while she's unconscious. Well... I suppose you could, but I don't think that would be right."

She's out of her mind. Violently jealous. Most humans would keep her at arm's length after seeing this new side of her character.

But I am a child of the Unseelie, raised by trolls, steeped in the poison of vengeance. I understand her more deeply in this moment than ever before.

She did this because she desires me with a ferocious longing much darker and deeper than I gave her credit for. I can still hear her soft plea from the other night: *I want you.* She'll never know how much it cost me to repel her after she said those words.

All I have craved, in my long, long life, is to be wanted. And she wants me so violently that she injured another living thing out of willful passion. I'm wildly thrilled by it, and yet I can't let her know that I'm pleased. I can't let her believe that this is acceptable behavior among normal humans.

First I set down the wine and glasses on a side table. Then I check Midrael's pulse and sniff deeply of her scent to reassure myself that the wound is not mortal and caused no deeper damage.

With that done, I shut the door and grasp the back of Feather's neck. She cringes a little, her eyes widening, as I drag her past Midrael's body, toward the bed.

"I need sex, because of what I am," I grit out. "It fuels my vitality and keeps me sane. Yet you took away my chance to enjoy it. Worse still, you harmed this beautiful woman. Why?"

She won't answer. She's trembling.

"Look at what you've done." I point to Midrael. "Why did you hurt her?"

"You didn't hear what she said to me," Feather whispers. "She despises me. She thinks I'm worthless."

I release her neck and seize her shoulders instead, forcing her to face me. "You can't knock someone unconscious because they despise or insult you."

She stares at me with tormented eyes.

My heart clenches at the hurt, anger, and confusion in her gaze. When I found her, she had bruises on her body from the man who called himself her brother. He beat and killed dozens of women. He punished Feather in the name of false love, out of cruelty and selfishness, and he fractured her psyche, perhaps beyond repair. The darkness in her came from him. I must tread carefully here, so as not to damage her any further.

"This isn't how humans behave," I say, more gently. "You know that, don't you?"

Her lips tighten. No answer.

"God-stars, Feather." I vent a rueful laugh. "We were just playing in the snow. I thought you were this soft, harmless creature—"

"Well, I'm not," she snaps. "Not when you crack me open and look deep inside. I'm a thing of blades and iron. That's how I found the strength to pretend I was weak, for so long. That's why the monsters in your house like me, you see." Her smile is agonized, beautiful. "They can sense it. They know that I'm a monster, too."

"But you weren't born one," I tell her. "You were made into one, by *him*. And he's gone. He has no more power in your life. Which gives you the freedom to transform yourself into something wholly new."

She wrenches her shoulders out of my grasp. "And you think you can teach me how to do that?"

I touch my chest, thinking of all the things I have been... a bargaining chip, a slave to trolls, a friend to one solitary human boy, a mass murderer, a careless member of the High Fae in the Seelie capital, and a servant of the Wild Hunt.

If anyone knows how to exchange one existence for another, it's me.

Perhaps the god-stars *are* at work in this. Perhaps I am not so unfit to help her as I first thought. She has awakened me, roused me from a doleful, endless existence. Can I sacrifice myself, subdue my own lust, and instead be the teacher she needs, her guardian and guide until she is ready to live with her own kind?

"Yes," I say aloud. "I can teach you. I may be the only one who can."

At my reply, something fractures in her gaze. "I'm sorry. I got so angry... I couldn't stop myself."

"I'm not the one who deserves your apology." I stride over to Midrael, pick her up carefully, and lay her on the bed. There's a lump on the side of her head, but no blood, and she's already beginning to stir.

"She will be alright," I tell Feather. "But we should leave. Quickly."

We hurry out of the room and head downstairs to gather our things from the coatroom. Once we're outside, in the shadow of the barn, I draw the geistfyre circle around us, and the cold night disappears. In the blink of an eye, we're safely embraced by the gray walls of the house, far from any stories Midrael might tell or any vengeance she might seek.

"I can never go back there." I dispel the chains and sit down heavily. "That was one of my favorite pubs."

"I'm sorry." Feather places the packages on the floor near me, then walks with measured steps toward the stairway that leads Below.

"What are you doing?" I exclaim.

"That's where you punish people, right? I deserve to be punished for what I did. I ruined the night. We didn't get to eat or drink, and you didn't get your... your sex. Because of me, you can't sleep with Midrael again, or return to the pub." She descends a few steps, then looks back. "I need you to punish me. It's the only way I'll learn."

The spirit of the Krampus inside me agrees with her, rises up eagerly at the idea of punishing her tender flesh. But I resist the urge.

"I'm not the man from the cabin," I say. "I won't hurt you."

"Then the beast will." She descends lower.

I leap up, springing over to the stairway. "Don't be self-destructive. Get back up here."

"You don't understand." Her voice is wrecked, pleading. "I need you to hurt me. I've done things... terrible things. I should pay for them."

I hesitate, drawing a long breath.

Tonight she showed me that she isn't the pure, innocent young woman I thought she was. Her soul has a cruel streak, a darkness that screams to my own tenebrous heart. She's no less worthy because of it. In fact, I respect her more—her strength, her pain, her beauty.

Right now, she's weighed down by the realization of what she did tonight and by the shadow of some past sin that haunts her soul. Guilt is a beast with venomous teeth, and she's been taught that violence is the only way to purge the poison. If I'm too gentle, if I flat-out refuse her the punishment she's accustomed to receiving, she'll rebel and fling herself into the tentacles of the Meerwunder, either right now or sometime when I'm not watching. I have to walk this line carefully.

"One day, when you're ready to tell me everything you've done, I will punish you in the way you deserve," I tell her. "But for tonight, will you come to bed?"

I hold out my hand.

She hesitates, poised to spring away from me into the yawning black throat of the stairway. If I'm not present, the Meerwunder will devour her the moment her feet touch the floor of the torture room.

Desperate, I speak a word that I haven't voiced in years. "Please."

The volatile anguish in her gaze softens. She bites her lip, then places her fingers in mine and lets me draw her out of the dark.

Silently, we retrieve our packages. Back in my room, she puts away her new clothes while I head to the kitchen to fetch a few scraps of food—bread, butter, cheese, the end of a ham, and two apples, only slightly shriveled. We eat quietly and companionably before the fire, and then we take our own sides of the bed. She doesn't approach me, and though I lie awake a long time, I resist the temptation to touch her.

I'm called away shortly before dawn. A pair of toddlers this time, subjected to the cruelty of selfish parents. There's no sign of a trap, and when I arrive, one of the boys is still holding the sleigh bell he found in the yard. Both children are grubby, bruised, and malnourished. I enter the cabin, wrestle the parents into my sack, and drag them away, out of the cottage and across a field. In a thicket of trees nearby, I wait a few minutes until I see the familiar glow of Mother Holle approaching on her white reindeer.

I've grown to believe that all humans have the capacity for great wickedness. Some do wicked things because of a cruel upbringing, or because grief, rage, or desperation drive them beyond reason. Others have a sickness of the mind that limits or confuses their capacity for empathy and kindness. But there is another group with a deeper malady—a rot of the soul that makes them truly evil. They are born with malice inside them, a diseased root so deep that neither a physician of the mind nor a healer of the body can offer aid.

I have judged all three kinds, meting out torture, death, or both, depending on the will of the god-stars. The parents screaming and thrashing in the sack I carry are the worst kind— they take a sick, selfish pleasure in abusing their own children. I transport them back to the house and set them loose for the monsters to hunt. As I head back to my room, a shrill, gibbering howl tells me that Wolpertinger has already caught their scent.

"I wish you joy of the meal," I mutter, shoving open my bedroom door.

My Krampus form has not yet faded, so my hooves clop loudly on the floor when I enter. Feather startles out of a deep sleep, hastily yanking all the pillows against her chest in a protective wall, then blinking groggily at me.

"I did not mean to wake you." I dispel the goat-skull mask and the cape. "There. Better?"

"Not really." She's staring at my lower half, including the long, thick strands of fur that mostly conceal my cock in this form.

"I'll revert to my usual shape in a moment," I assure her.

"Did I hear something howl? Or was that in my dream?"

"Wolpertinger," I explain. "I've just given him a snack. I'm going to the market today to purchase food and firewood. Would you like to come? When we return, we'll begin practicing what you'll need to know for the Mayor's party."

She seems relieved when I don't mention Midrael. "I think you should go out alone," she says. "I'll need to clean up whatever Wolpertinger leaves behind."

"Very well." Even as I'm speaking, my bulging muscles shrink and the veins disappear as I revert to my usual lean, toned form. I'm utterly naked, but Feather doesn't look away, and I don't attempt to hide anything. I saunter over to the bureau, select some clothing, and pull on my pants slowly, taking my time as I fasten them.

"Promise you won't do anything rash while I'm out?" I ask.

"I won't." She winces. "I'm sorry about… everything. I feel much better now. I think I was just tired."

Of course. You knocked out the woman I was going to fuck because you were tired. How perfectly normal and reasonable.

Maybe Feather suspects what I'm thinking, because she says, "I'm also sorry for asking you to punish me. That was strange and wrong. I won't ever say such things again."

"Very well. But remember, I made you a promise, and I'm willing to keep it if you should ever crave… punishment." On the last word, I cast her a significant glance, and she flushes rose-red.

165

"I'll remember," she says faintly.

"Be ready for lessons when I return."

"Alright. And you be careful," she adds as I'm buttoning my vest and heading for the door. "Watch out for iron."

"Of course." I hesitate, turning back. "There is something you could do for me while I'm gone, after you're done cleaning. In this house there's an artifact that could help me withstand touching iron for a short time if I need to, without visible effects. It's designed to conceal the energy signature of glamours as well. I haven't used it in ages. I think I left it in the library. It's a necklace with an amulet bearing the sign of a half-closed eye within a crescent moon. If you happen to find it, I would be grateful."

"I would be happy to look for it, but the house hasn't let me into the library yet," she admits.

"Ah. Interesting, but not surprising. The library is home to the Nexus, the soul of the house—the source of all its magic and some of mine. The Nexus sustains the monsters who live here, and it also binds them so they can't run amok through worlds."

Feather hugs the pillows tighter to her chest. "What does the Nexus look like?"

"I couldn't tell you. It often takes on new shapes, especially when revealing itself to someone new. If you do gain access to the library, be cautious. The Nexus can be unpredictable."

"So can I," she says quietly.

She's avoiding my gaze again, looking small and withdrawn behind her mound of pillows. I hesitate in the doorway, wondering what a normal human or Fae might do in this situation. A comforting hug, I think. But I never hug anyone unless I'm out in the world playing the role of the genial Lord Brandt, and even then I only embrace potential lovers in a seductive context. Comfort isn't something I know how to offer. God-stars know I never received any myself, except from the first human I ever befriended.

And he ended up in the refuse pile.

Turning my back on the girl in my bed, I leave the room and close the door behind me.

15

FEATHER

He probably thinks I'm insane. At least, that's what I fear
for the first week after the incident with Midrael. But he doesn't
bring it up again. We simply proceed as we did before—him
going about his tasks, and me accomplishing mine—except that
we share the bed more often, and we spend hours in a room I
recently cleaned, which he calls the "smoking room."

There are a few books on the shelves in the smoking room,
but I'm disappointed to discover they're all in languages I can't
read. Krampus says it's mostly obscure dialects from various
regions of Faerie, along with a few ancient human languages.

He teaches me how to walk smoothly and elegantly, how to
respond to certain types of greetings, and what to say in response

to any questions about myself and my origins. In the story we've concocted, I'm a family friend of Lord Brandt's who just moved to Visseland. I'm a lady of good birth and fortune, looking for a cooler climate because my fragile health can't handle the arid heat of my birth nation.

"There are all types of people at these parties," Krampus says. "Merchants, lawyers, singers, modistes, nobility, bankers, generals, entertainers. But all are expected to conform to a certain standard of behavior, at least for the early part of the evening. Once everyone has enough liquor in them, the gathering becomes rather more raucous and degenerate."

I must look nervous, because he hastens to add, "The most salacious activities take place upstairs, in various rooms of the house. You won't be subjected to the sight of people fucking in public, never fear."

An uncomfortable silence tightens the air between us for a moment before he says, "Let's move back some of these chairs and try a bit of dancing."

"Dancing?" I frown, curling deep into my armchair and tucking my legs up close to my chest. "You never said I would have to dance."

"It's a *party*." He cocks an eyebrow. "Of course there will be dancing."

"Perhaps I could claim that I have an injured ankle."

"You're brave enough to command eldritch beasts, yet not brave enough to dance in a crowd?"

"Fuck you," I mutter.

He tries to keep a straight face, but the grin sneaks through. "That's the first time you've said that to me."

"Is it? I'm sure I've thought it more than once."

"Give me your hand, Feather."

Sighing, I climb out of the armchair and stand before him.

"I'll teach you the most popular dance first. Your partner's hand goes just here." He cups my waist with his palm. "And you hold his hand like this. I'll step, and you follow. One, two, three... one, two, three..."

I do my best, but it's difficult to concentrate with our hands entwined and his firm grasp on my waist. I can feel the heat rising to my face, and I hate that telltale flush. I hate that so many of the experiences I've had with him involve physical closeness and confusing emotions. Back in the cabin, we had a routine, and we rarely deviated from it. When we did, there was blood to clean up, wounds to dress, or a body to ignore... and even that was another part of the routine.

Here, so many things are new. And dancing with a tall, handsome Fae male in my bare feet on the floor of a magical, sentient house is so dreadfully new that I begin feeling lightheaded after he has hummed through the song a few times.

"Can we stop?" I ask breathlessly. "I don't think I can do any more."

"You're tired?"

"Yes." I seize on the excuse. "I've been working hard cleaning the house, and I'm still not as strong as I should be. I didn't have much exercise when I lived in the cabin."

He picks me up instantly and carries me over to a sofa. Then he flings himself into a nearby chair and lights a long-stemmed pipe whose musky fragrance is oddly enticing.

"We'll try again tomorrow," he says.

But I'd rather not try again. Being that close to him, knowing he doesn't want me... it's torture. I can't bear the anguish of it. So I'm glad when he has to go out unexpectedly the next day to end the life of some dreadful wretch. It gives me time to push a bit farther into the house and clear out more of the rooms.

I'm batting copious clouds of dust off an old rug when Perchta floats out of the wall and drifts lazily to rest on top of a china cabinet. The cabinet's doors are so thickly coated with grime that I can't see inside it.

"You haven't visited in a while." I reach into my bucket and sprinkle water in the air to settle the dust.

"Busy, busy," she says. "Frightening the pants off wayward children. It would be so much more fun if I were allowed to really *hurt* them, you know? My approved methods of correction are so ineffective."

"Punishing children with pain only makes them angrier inside."

"Speaking from experience?"

"Speaking for myself, yes."

"Hm. Why are you cleaning this dull room?" she asks, and I arch a brow at the abrupt change of topic. "Why not explore somewhere more interesting, like the library?"

"Gods, why is everyone talking about the library lately?" I exclaim, rather disgruntled.

"Who else has been talking about it? Krampus?"

"Yes. He wants me to find something for him—an amulet, so he can touch iron for a few minutes at a time."

She sits up. "Why would he need to touch iron?"

I tell her briefly about the Fae-hunters, the Mayor's upcoming party, and Krampus's plan to search the hunters' things and determine whether we need to move the house or not. "He wants to be able to touch iron in case they use that method to test the guests at the party."

"Interesting. And this amulet is in the library? Why don't you simply fetch it?"

"The house won't allow me in there yet."

"I could take you there."

I nearly drop my duster. "You can? How?"

"I'm a ghost of the Wild Hunt. I can pass through walls, and I can take someone with me if I need to. If I attempt such things outside the course of my duties, it makes me rather thin and faint, and I can't transport anyone very far, but as it happens, the library is right on the other side of this wall." She strokes the plaster with wispy fingers. "All we have to do is pop through, and there you are."

It sounds simple enough. But it makes me vaguely uncomfortable to think of entering the library without the house's permission. And if Perchta had this convenient ability all along, why didn't she mention it to me the last time we discussed the library?

"I wanted to wait until the house lets me in," I say hesitantly.

"It's your choice." Perchta rolls onto her stomach and props her chin on both hands. "I only thought, if Krampus really needs that amulet for protection, you'd want to help him. Have you seen what iron poisoning does to Fae-kind?"

"I have." I chew my lip, picturing the anguish he endured after the attack by those four ruffians.

"If I were a close friend to Krampus, as you seem to be… if he relied on me, trusted me, like he seems to trust you… then I would risk it, for him. But I can understand if you prefer not to spend your time hunting for a dusty old artifact. After all, it could be anywhere. The library is enormous. So many books. Volumes of fairy tales with lovely illustrations, books about the world and its creatures with detailed sketches, leatherbound collections of maps and charts, tomes full of historical and scientific wonders, and thick novels packed with romance and adventure. Not to mention chapbooks of the loveliest poems you ever read. Most of them in the common tongue, too."

My mind hungers for those books like a starving woman for a hearty meal. Still, I'm unsure.

"I confess, I'm dreadfully bored," Perchta says, her face and shoulders drooping. "Not to mention depressed and despairing. I'd love to explore with you… it would lift my spirits. If you can spare a little time, I promise we'll have fun. And I'll help you do your hair for the Mayor's party. Krampus may know a thing or

173

two about clothes, but he can't hold a candle to me when it comes to fancy hairstyles."

I hadn't even considered what to do with my hair. Thanks to one of the Wives in the cabin, I know a bit about arranging hair, but I've never prepared for a gathering of fine gentlemen and ladies. I'll need all the help I can get.

"I have a little time," I concede. "I suppose we could visit the library, just for a bit. But if the house becomes angry, we must leave."

"Of course. Of *course* we will," Perchta assures me, her eyes bright as she floats down from the top of the china cabinet. "Come here, then. Take my hand."

She grimaces as if making a huge effort, and her smoky fingers solidify more than usual. I can feel her hand, but I hold it lightly, sensing that if I squeeze too hard, my fingers will go right through her cold, translucent ones.

Perchta whisks through the wall, pulling me with her. It's like going underwater. Objects that were once solid now shimmer and shift, and I can't breathe or speak as we move from one space to the next. The wall is thicker than I realized, with a hollow space behind it—one of Wolpertinger's passageways.

We pop out of the slats and plaster into somewhere new, and I drag in a hoarse, screaming breath as my shriveled lungs reinflate. My body aches, as if all my organs have been rearranged. With a strange, jerky, swollen thump, my heart starts beating again, and I realize it stopped altogether when we passed through the wall.

"That seems—very unsafe," I gasp.

"Unsafe?" Perchta's voice is fainter than ever, and she's barely visible—little more than a breath of mist in female shape. "Is anything in this house safe? Or is anyone safe in this house?" She titters as if she has said the cleverest thing. "Never mind that now. Look where we are."

The library is a glimmering Faerieland lit by glass-bellied lamps branching from ornate sconces. No one tends the lamps, so perhaps they are self-sustaining, as seems to be the case with many of the light sources in this house. Their glow touches the dark, glossy wood of endless bookshelves, each one soaring up to astonishing heights. The bookcases are arranged in a maze-like series of aisles, with an open space at the far end, where I glimpse leather chairs and plush couches. Some of the bookcases curve inward, while others belly outward, and so the aisles form wavy lines instead of straight ones, like an undulating sea of knowledge and fantasy.

The shelves hold more books than I've ever imagined. Some of the spines are beautiful—crimson leather stamped with gold foil, or black leather with silver foil, but other spines are cracked, brittle and brown. I find every single one of them enticing.

Between the books are countless timepieces. Pocket watches hang on the necks of bronze busts or drip from the limbs of silver statuary. At a glance, I spot at least two dozen ornate shelf clocks, some with their own tiny pendulums. Some are circular, some square, others carved of wood with tiny figures that go round and round, performing repetitive movements. There's a row of magnetic rocks that swing back and forth, clicking together in an eternal, unceasing rhythm. And I can't fathom how many hourglasses there are—every third shelf seems to have one, each containing a different color of sand—gold, blue, emerald, scarlet, lavender.

Beyond the books, there's another shocking thing about this room… the plants. Nowhere in the house have I found a single growing thing, and yet here, tiny potted plants stand between the books, and lush waterfalls of ivy spill from shallow gutters along the edges of the upper shelves.

"How do they grow without sunlight?" I ask.

"Magic," replies Perchta, her wispy voice so close to my ear that I startle.

"This room is enormous. I don't know where to begin."

"Let your heart lead you," she says, a subtle excitement in her tone. "If you feel that you're being drawn somewhere, or that something is calling to you—follow the urge, and listen to the voice."

"Alright." I drift along the wavy rows of shelves, scarcely daring to reach out and touch the books with my fingertips. But after a few bracing breaths, I risk it. I touch them.

Amid the gentle ticking of the many clocks, a faint hum reaches my ears. As if the library itself hummed in response to my touch.

I sink to my knees for a moment, not caring if Perchta thinks my behavior odd. There's a patterned carpet slithering down the aisle, following the curves of the shelves, but I touch the bare strip of wooden floor on either side of it, palms to the ground so I can feel the house.

"So you're not angry?" I whisper.

My eyes close as I listen for the answer. The house always replies with impulses, with images, or with surges of intent or feeling. What I sense from it now is a grudging acceptance, a reluctant fondness. It would have preferred that I wait to enter this place… but it isn't angry. And I sense something else, too—that during past years, it has rerouted Krampus away from here many times, to keep him from cluttering the place up. He's only allowed inside on rare occasions when his actual intent is reading.

I smile. "Wise choice," I murmur to the house.

Another pulse of emotion, this time threaded with suspicion and displeasure, tied to the image of Perchta in my mind. The house doesn't trust her, because it can't read her. In fact, it can barely perceive her, which is unsettling for it.

"Perchta is alright," I tell it. "She's a friend."

The caution recedes, and a gentle thrill passes through my stomach as I realize how much the house trusts me. Perhaps all it needed was a little push to let me in here. Perhaps I wasn't crossing a line after all.

Perhaps this was meant to be.

"Look around," Perchta urges. "Explore. Remember, you have to find the amulet for Krampus."

Rising, I follow the aisle I'm in, letting my palm graze the rows of books. Finally I pause and take one gently out of its row. I'm delighted to find I can read the title—*A Compendium of Fables*. A perfect starting point, and just the sort of thing I like. Which the house knew, of course. I have no doubt it guided my selection.

As I move on, my gaze catches on several items that aren't books or timepieces. There's a tiny globe, a sextant, a compass, several music boxes, and an enameled puzzle box. I also spot a marble hand with rings on each finger. The middle finger is bare, and there's a faint area of discoloration as if a ring once rested there.

A little further on, a stone bust braces up a row of books. A tiny placard in front of the bust reads, "The Amulet of Lugus," with a sketch that closely resembles Krampus's description of the necklace he wants. And of course, there's no necklace or amulet anywhere in sight.

"It's just like him not to put things back where they belong," I mutter.

"You'll never find it in all this mess," says Perchta. "You could ask the house."

"I could, but I've imposed on the house's good graces enough today," I tell her. "I'd rather search for it myself."

We exit the aisle into a large reading area. One of the biggest leather armchairs has a pronounced ass-shaped dent in the seat, and beside it are several messy stacks of books, folios, and papers, surrounded by a few empty goblets, a music box or two, a scarf, a plate with moldering crumbs on it, and a tangle of jewelry. Warmth rushes into my heart at the sight, and my stomach thrills again—a lower, more poignant sensation this time.

Perchta peers at my face. "You're smiling."

"Am I?" I try to rearrange the expression.

Truth be told, I've never seen a more accurate portrait of Krampus... no, not Krampus, but whoever he is beneath his monstrous identity. This is a reflection of his true self, the one linked to his real name. For some reason, I want to hug the chair and the whole mess around it.

If I hugged *him*, I think he would push me away.

The thought wipes the smile from my face. "Someone really needs to teach him how to clean up after himself," I mutter as I kneel to pick through the knotted jewelry.

Sure enough, one of the necklaces is the amulet with the half-closed eye and the crescent moon, the one he's looking for. It takes me several minutes to disentangle it from everything else. I'm not sure how he got all this jewelry into such a mess in the first place, but undoing the knot taxes my patience.

While I work, Perchta flits back and forth in midair, inspecting first one bookshelf, then another. She floats up near the ceiling for a while, perhaps to investigate the topmost shelves. It's almost as if she's also looking for something.

"Can you read books?" I ask.

"I can turn a few pages," she replies. "It's difficult to interact with any physical object for very long."

"I could read aloud to you," I offer.

She spins toward me, her gauzy garments whisking around her. "How sweet. But shouldn't you spend a little time familiarizing yourself with the other artifacts in this room? As the new caretaker of the house, you should be aware of any objects that possess notable powers."

"I suppose so." I say it casually. But I was the little sister of evil, the daughter of darkness, and I know when I'm being manipulated. Perhaps it took me a little too long to realize it, because I like Perchta, and I wanted to believe I had a guileless friend, incapable of using me for her own ends. But it's clear to me now—Perchta wants something from this library. From me. I pull Krampus's amulet free and tuck it into my pocket along with its chain. "What are you looking for, Perchta?"

"Me?" She giggles softly. "I'm not looking for anything."

"You are. You want something. What is it?"

"Nonsense. Wherever did you get that idea? I'm a *ghost*."

"Enough games." My tone is sharper than I intended, and she flares brighter for a second, her brow furrowing with momentary anger.

When she answers, her tone is colder. "I'm interested in anything that might help me become corporeal. You don't understand what it's like, being a ghost always. I only receive a body when I'm chastising wayward children, and it's a hideous, gnarled form, meant to terrify them into obedience. Once my task is done, I don't get a single spare minute to do anything—I revert to ghost form instantly."

"That must be frustrating."

"Frustrating?" She practically shrieks the word, and an unsettled vibration runs through the bookcases. "I haven't enjoyed a meal in centuries. Not a drop of wine, not a morsel of food. I crave one night's sleep in a comfortable bed, or the glow of warm sun on my skin, or the clasp of someone's hand around mine, or the hot, scented water of a bath. I'm so tired of watching humans waste their lives. Their ungratefulness starts in the early years, and it only gets worse. They don't understand the riches they possess just by *existing*. Sometimes I hate them so much that I—"

Her words choke off into a garbled wail of furious agony.

"So you want magic that will help you obtain physical form," I say quietly.

"Yes. And Krampus refuses to lend it to me. He won't even let me try."

"As a member of the Wild Hunt, you're in this position because of something you did... isn't that true?"

She bares her teeth, looking momentarily more demonic than ghostly. "Yes, but my sin was no worse than what Krampus did. And yet he receives *life*, while I languish like this. Why should he be able to eat, and drink, and fuck, and waste every imaginable privilege, while I suffer this cold, bodiless existence? Why, Feather?"

"I don't know," I admit. "Don't the god-stars have something to do with it? They make the decisions."

"And why should they decide my eternal fate? Why shouldn't I strive for a chance at something better?"

"I'm sorry for you," I tell her. "Truly, I am. I know what it's like to be trapped, and to yearn for things you believe you can never have."

"Do you?" She laughs, brittle and bitter. "Do you know what it's like to be a ghost for centuries? To take physical form only as a monstrous, horned, gap-toothed crone who scares children into obeying their parents and being kinder to their friends? Do you understand my life, little human girl? Do you?"

"No," I reply simply.

"No. You *don't* understand. No one ever can, and no one cares. My overseer never speaks to me anymore. No one in the Wild Hunt cares that I exist, and no human ever believes the witness of the children to whom I appear. I might as well not exist at all. I must do something to make the humans believe. To *force* the Hunt to remember me."

"You want to be seen." In my limited human way, I do know what she means. I spent my earlier life playing my role, controlling my actions carefully so I would be lovable but not too noticeable, because disturbing the fantasy could mean death. Despite the danger, part of me thrived on my captor's attention. Whenever he was gone on one of his trips, I felt purposeless. Empty. And I understood that if he killed me, no one in the outside world would know or care that I existed at all. Even Mother and Wife would quickly forget me.

At least here, in this house, I know I would be missed. If I die, Krampus won't replace me with another maid, and even if he did, the house won't have the same connection with any other girl. The Bahkauv and the Imp will notice my absence. They see me.

Sometimes that's enough, and sometimes I want more. When I go to the party with Krampus, I will hate the exposure to strangers, but I will love it too, because it will mean I am visible. My existence will be noted by the outside world.

Perchta is sobbing quietly near the ceiling, and I want desperately to comfort her.

"I will help you if I can," I say. "If there's an object of power that might grant you physical form for a while, and it's something the house can spare, you may have it. I'm sure there's some sort of charm, necklace, orb…"

"Do you mean it?" She flies down toward me so swiftly that I gasp.

"I do. But only if the house allows it. And I would have to ask Krampus first, of course…" Even as I speak, I sense his return, the tremor of his power and his own connection to the house—different from mine, but no less real. There's a distinctly masculine rawness to his aura when I feel it through the house. It awakens an ache low in my belly, a flutter between my thighs.

"He's back," I say.

"I should go." Perchta begins to fade, and I call after her, "Wait! You have to take me back through the wall."

"I think you'll be able to go in and out whenever you like now," she says. "Look."

I turn around, and in a deep recess with bookshelves built in a tunnel over it, I spot a door with a brass handle.

"Imagine that," I murmur.

I turn to say goodbye to Perchta, but she's already gone.

Clasping my book of fables and the amulet, I stand for a moment, listening to the ticking of the clocks, breathing in the freshness of the lush green plants. Krampus is back, which means I should prepare his bath and a snack... after which he'll probably want to practice dancing with me again.

Somehow, in light of Perchta's predicament, the idea of dancing with him seems far less terrifying. Torturous as it is knowing that he doesn't want me, I should enjoy his touch while I can, and be grateful for the privilege of his nearness.

He witnessed the most dark and wicked impulses of my heart, and his behavior toward me did not change.

He saw the monster in me, and he did not run.

16

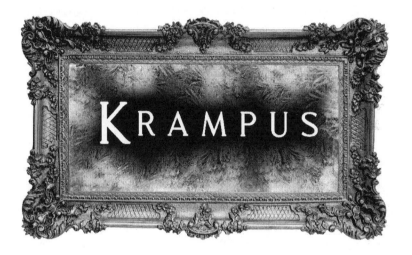

KRAMPUS

Weeks after the incident with Midrael, on the day of the
Mayor's party, I transport myself to town to fetch Feather's
gown and a suit I commissioned for myself. When I return, as
I'm approaching my room, I could swear I hear voices. But when
I push the door open, Feather is alone.

Two days ago, she moved an antique dressing table into our
room. It's a slender, elegantly carved piece of furniture, with an
oval mirror and several tiny drawers with mother-of-pearl knobs.
She chose a stool with a puffy pink cushion to accompany it, and
while neither piece is precisely my style, I didn't protest, mostly
because I liked the pleased little smile on her face when she
showed it to me.

She's perched on the stool, clad in lacy white undershorts and a white corset whose cups barely cover her nipples. Her hair is swirled around and pinned up in a most bewitching way, leaving her slim, delicate neck bare. She leans toward the mirror, arranging one of the curls that frame her face.

"Do you think this will do?" Her eyes meet mine in the mirror.

I open my mouth and am surprised to find that I cannot speak. Not a single sound will emerge from my throat. The only thing in my head is her exquisite face, her lovely form. No words, just an all-consuming wonder.

Feather turns around on the stool, frowning slightly. "Are you alright? Oh gods… was the gown not ready? Are we not going after all?"

She has stenciled her brows lightly, shaping and filling them until they are perfectly arched, perfectly matched. Her lips shine plump and red, and her cheeks glow pink. God-stars bless the seamstress for suggesting that beauty enhancement kit. Feather has always been beautiful, but the cosmetics celebrate her loveliness in a whole new way.

"Krampus." Her voice sharpens with concern, and she rises from the stool.

Fuck, now I can't help staring at her breasts, the way the corset pushes them up and makes them look so deliciously plump… I wish it was my real name, not my title, falling from her lips.

"Krael," I say hoarsely.

"What?"

"My name. Krael."

"Oh." Her mouth forms the most kissable shape, and her eyes widen.

I stand there stupidly, with my arms full of boxes.

"Does one of those boxes contain my gown?" she ventures.

"Yes." I swallow and walk to the bed, where I set down the packages. "Yours is the large flat one."

She struggles with the string for a second, so I bend down and slice it with my teeth.

"Thank you." She removes the lid and gasps at the sight of the plum-colored gown. "It's beautiful. Absolutely gorgeous."

"Yes, it is," I manage to say, staring at her.

She doesn't look at me. Her whole face is aglow with delight. I want to buy her a new gown every day just so I can see that look.

What the fuck is wrong with me?

Feather draws the gown out of the box. "It looks rather complicated." She eyes the row of buttons at the back.

"I'll help you," I offer. "I've stripped hundreds of women naked, after all. I know how such dresses work."

Feather gives me a look of such soul-splitting malevolence that I feel heat rising to my cheeks. What possessed me to mention that I've bedded hundreds of women? I must be losing my mind.

"Let's put your expertise to good use, then," she says crisply.

I help her with the crinoline, then assist as she dons the dress and settles it over the corset so it conforms perfectly to her lithe body. It's torture buttoning her into that gown when I would much rather strip it off, but I manage to accomplish the task.

If I thought she was lovely outside the dress, she's fucking glorious once she has it on. I can hardly look at her, for fear she'll see the mad obsession on my face.

Anywhere else, if I saw a woman like her, I would turn on the charm and be balls-deep inside her within the hour. But this is *Feather*. The girl I took into my home, where no one is allowed except the monsters and me. This is a wounded girl, a girl with depths and darkness she won't reveal to anyone, a girl unfamiliar with sex except in the context of force. I cannot rush headlong into a dalliance with her, or do anything that might frighten her.

My gaze travels to a stack of books on the dressing table—a frequent occurrence over the past couple of weeks. The house apparently let her into the library, and she's been enamored with books ever since.

"You got a fresh supply of books," I comment.

God-stars, what a stupid thing to say. So obvious and commonplace. I want her to think well of me, to view me as something more than horns, chains, blood, and debauchery, and yet all I can do is make an absurdly obvious statement. *Fuck* me.

"I'm still cleaning and organizing the house," she says defensively. "I haven't slacked off in my duties."

"That's not what I… I wasn't suggesting you had slacked off. I only meant, I'm glad the library has provided you with some solace in this dreary house."

She nods, mollified. "Each book is a gateway to somewhere new."

"Quite so. And I'm grateful that you found the amulet. It should protect me tonight."

"You won't be detectable to the Fae hunters at all? Not even your glamours?"

"The amulet suppresses all signs of my Fae nature and magic," I reply. "Including glamours and the aversion to iron. However, if I'm put in direct contact with iron, I won't be able to endure it for more than a handful of minutes without damage. So let's hope any such experience will be brief."

I open the remaining boxes and Feather exclaims over the fine jacket, trousers, vest, and shirt within. I coordinated my outfit with hers, focusing on shades of plum, lavender, and gray. Once I'm dressed, with my hair in a loose braid, the effect is rather striking. Feather keeps stealing glances, which pleases me immensely.

"Do I look alright beside you?" she asks. "The gown is grand, but I think perhaps I'm rather dull."

"Nonsense," I reply. "Though you are missing something."

She follows me to a bureau, where I open a shallow drawer and stir my finger through dozens of earrings scattered across the faded velvet lining. "Ah, here we are! Perfect."

"But my ears aren't pierced." She looks at me mournfully.

"Will you trust me?"

I see the shift in her gaze, the caution and savagery in her eyes. The animal that will bite the hand that feeds it, if that hand should prove false.

"I *want* to trust you," she says.

"Trust me in this, then. A moment of pain, and then you will have what you desire."

She nods and tips her head aside.

I take her soft little earlobe between my fingers, caressing the supple flesh for a moment. I had planned to use the post of the earring to create the tiny hole, but my mouth is watering for a taste of her—my teeth practically ache for her flesh.

"Hold very still," I whisper, leaning in.

Her delicate scent, the faint heat of the pulsing blood in her warm throat, the light cadence of her breathing—all of it overwhelms my senses. I live for the quiver of her mouth and the curly wisps of hair around her perfect, rounded ear.

Angling my head, I set the point of one fang in the center of her earlobe. And I bite. Just enough to punch all the way through.

She breathes out, as if the pain was a release instead of a torment.

"Good girl," I murmur.

My tongue slides out, bathing the spot I wounded, collecting the precious drops of her blood. Then I slide the earring into place.

"It barely hurts at all," she says wonderingly.

"The essences of the Fae—blood, tears, saliva, and other things—they have physical benefits for humans," I tell her. "So it should heal perfectly."

"Do it again." She turns her head, offering her other ear. There's a rosy brightness in her cheeks, beyond the cosmetics she applied, and her eyes glimmer with arousal. Her body betrays her in another way, too—the intensified fragrance whispering in the air around her, unfurling from a place I have long desired to taste.

"The other ear," she murmurs. "Please."

At that little word, I melt inside. I fucking collapse, mentally sink into a worshipful puddle. Dragging the sloppy remains of my self-control together, I frown mightily at her, glaring as I lean in again, but she only smiles, as if she fucking *knows* that my displeasure is an act.

This time, when my fang pierces her earlobe, she gives a tiny, unmistakable moan.

Perhaps I don't have to teach her about the marriage between pleasure and pain, after all. Perhaps she already understands.

I lick the dot of blood from her ear, then let my tongue trail a little lower, along her neck.

Her head lolls aside, baring her throat to my wet caresses... and for a moment I consider skipping the party altogether. But we've planned and practiced for this. I need the information I will gather tonight, and I can't let my cock decide my fate or Feather's.

Besides, I swore to myself I wouldn't fuck her. Strange how that resolution seems to grow less and less important in my eyes.

I insert the second earring and step back. "Now your ensemble is complete, except for a necklace."

"I found one," Feather says shyly. "In the library. I was going to ask you if I might borrow it."

188

She holds up a long silver chain. Its hourglass pendant is encrusted with tiny emeralds.

"I don't recognize it, but if the house let you take it, it's yours," I tell her. "I'll put it on you, if you like."

She hands it over, and I loop it around her neck, purposely letting my fingers graze her smooth, warm skin as I fasten the clasp.

"Do you think it has magic?" she asks.

"Perhaps. There are many artifacts in that library which possess power."

"Are there any that can give a ghost corporeal form?"

My fingers go still against her skin. "You've been talking to Perchta."

"Yes. She's my... friend."

"I want you to stay away from her. She shouldn't even be in this house. If she shows up again, tell me at once, or command the house to expel her, do you understand?"

Feather pulls away from me. "Why?"

"Because Perchta is a vicious, greedy ghost, that's why. She wants things she can't have. Things that are mine."

"Like what?"

I debate not telling her. But if I really want her to obey me, she must have all the information.

"Perchta wants the Nexus, the soul of the house," I explain. "The item of great power I told you about. No other artifact in that library can grant her the power to become corporeal. I'm not even sure the Nexus can, and if it could, holding her in that form would slowly drain its power. It could mean the destruction of both the house and those who live here. You and I might survive, but we'd be left homeless, without a single possession or a roof over our heads."

I half-expect Feather to repeat that Perchta is her friend and that she would never do such a thing. But instead, Feather's face

189

turns hard, and her eyes empty of all emotion. It's like watching a lake freeze over in a single second.

"Perchta was using me," she says flatly. "I knew it, I suppose… but I didn't realize how much she was willing to risk to get what she wants."

"She's miserable and selfish," I reply. "I am also miserable and selfish, but at least I'm open about it."

"Why can't she find the Nexus herself?"

"As a ghost, she can't locate it on her own. But if a living creature were to reveal its form and location, she might be able to access its power, at least in theory."

"Then we have no reason to worry," says Feather. "Because neither of us will ever show it to her."

She says *we* as if she and I are allied. It's a pleasant word, *we*. I haven't been allies with someone since I was a child.

"Enough about Perchta," Feather adds. "Shouldn't we go? It's getting late."

"Yes, of course." I put on the amulet and conceal it beneath my shirt. With the addition of a loose cravat for me, then cloaks and dancing shoes for each of us, we're ready to leave.

We travel by geistfyre to an inn outside Rothenfel, where we take a carriage I've hired for the occasion. The driver is from another town and has been well-paid to swear that he works for me at Brandywick Hall, the false name of my supposed estate.

After a brief journey, our carriage joins the stream of other carriages traversing the circular drive of the Mayor's mansion. A footman ushers us out of the vehicle, and I instruct Feather under my breath, "Remember to keep your chin up, smile a little, and *glide*."

"I'm gliding," she retorts. But when I glance over, her smile is angelic, not a trace of rebellion. A servant takes our cloaks at the door, and we proceed into the glittering hall to speak with our host.

The Mayor is a thickly built man about a head shorter than I am, with big cheeks that tighten into shining balls when he grins. The sheer jollity of the man has always appealed to me, even if he's better at throwing grand parties than he is at governing. He means well, which is more than I can say of most humans.

His ebony face creases into a broad smile when he sees me. Though he usually wears a wig, tonight his head is gleamingly bald, and he's dressed in a flamboyant scarlet suit, nearly the same color as my hair.

"Brandt, my boy!" he calls. "Come and meet our guests of honor! I've called them in to clean up this Krampus nonsense. Fae-hunters from the south! Abil Amindi and Nikkai Richter."

Abil Amindi is a tall, solemn-looking fellow with brown skin and close-trimmed black hair. Beside him stands Nikkai Richter—brown hair, pale skin, medium build. Both are handsome, in their early thirties, with tattoos covering their ungloved fingers. Even at this distance, I sense the hum of power from those tattoos, and it sends a wave of revulsion through my gut. The tattoos were probably inscribed with charmed or iron-infused ink. They're designed to detect the Fae with a single touch.

Nikkai reaches out his hand in friendly greeting, and I clasp it, arranging a pleasant smile on my face. "Welcome," I say genially. "Best of luck with your hunt."

To my relief, there's no blaze of pain as my skin contacts his. The amulet is working.

Thank the god-stars, the hand-clasp is brief, and the Mayor's attention has already swerved to Feather. "And who is this vision of beauty?" he exclaims. "Brandt, you've been holding out on me! Why have I never seen her before?"

"She's a recent arrival in Visseland," I say. "May I present the Lady Laurelai Montaine."

Feather curtsies like I taught her, with a demure little smile. "A pleasure, gentlemen."

The solemn Abil cracks a smile, and Nikkai looks positively dumbstruck.

"Lady Laurelai." He bows halfway, taking her lace-gloved hand and placing a light kiss on her knuckles. "You are the loveliest creature I have seen tonight. May I trouble you for a dance later?"

"Stealing my companion already?" I soften the question with a chuckle, though I'm seething inside.

But Feather says, "Of course, sir. I would be honored."

"I'll find you, then. It will be easy—I'll simply look for the most beautiful woman in the room." Nikkai bows to her, and she gives him a shy, delighted look which he returns with a besotted grin.

What the fuck just happened? Does she like the bastard? Has she forgotten that he's here to kill me?

Keeping a pleasant expression plastered to my face, I escort Feather into the ballroom, where guests are sipping wine and sampling delicacies from silver trays passed by the footmen. There is no dinner tonight, only light grazing, conversation, and dancing, not to mention kissing, petting, and fucking, once everyone is drunk enough. I have no doubt the Fae-hunter Nikkai had such things on his mind when he was fawning over Feather.

"Why would you agree to dance with him?" I ask her tersely under my breath.

"To get information," she murmurs. "And to distract him so you can do what you need to do."

"Don't lie to me. I saw the way you looked at him, and the way he looked at you." I snort. "You two were practically salivating over each other."

She shoots me a bladed glance. "Yes, he is handsome, and he seemed enchanted by me. It felt nice. And maybe I want more of that feeling. Is that wrong?"

"Well, I—"

"It's *not* wrong. I enjoy being admired. And I like men who aren't afraid to say what they're feeling."

"Is that fucking so?" I mutter. "When did you become so enlightened regarding the type of men you prefer?"

"Just now." She lifts her pretty little chin. "I learn quickly."

"Don't get attached," I growl. "If I decide they pose too great a danger, I may have to dispose of them both tonight."

"Are you allowed to do that?"

"To protect myself? Yes."

Feather steps in front of me, her eyes glittering with the same vicious intent I saw in them the night she struck down Midrael. "I think you should admit what's really bothering you."

"The threat to my very existence?"

"No," she hisses. "The other thing." She shifts closer to me, and my gaze drops to her delicious cleavage for a second. When I look up, her lashes have lowered, and she's smirking. "Yes," she says softly. "That."

"You're not making sense," I say hoarsely.

"I've been thinking you don't want me. But you're acting jealous, so perhaps you *do* want me, and you're rejecting me for some other reason." She moves nearer, filling my space, her scent suffusing the air. I try to hold my breath, but then her fingertips drift over my chest, toying with the lapel of my jacket. She presses her palm flat, and I swallow hard, aware of how fast my heart is pounding.

"This," she whispers. "You should admit to *this*."

Her face crystallizes before my eyes, while everything else fades to dull, distant shadows. Every bone and nerve in my body is screaming for me to cup her face and kiss her, to slide my tongue down her throat, to scrunch up her gown and slip my fingers inside her pussy… to drown myself in her.

"You don't know what you're asking for," I whisper. "You have no experience. I would destroy you."

Her lips part to reply, but at that moment two women approach from the left. I recognize both of them from previous trysts. Simultaneously, a trio of eager gentlemen converge on Feather from the right. I make grudging introductions, but beyond that I'm forced to let her fend for herself, a graceful doe cornered by predatory hounds. My former flings are both determined to monopolize my attention, each hoping to enjoy the pleasure of my tongue and my cock later tonight, though they would never express their wishes so indelicately.

By the time I manage to disentangle myself from the women, Feather has already drifted away with the men, giggling and begging them to excuse her "terrible dancing," while they promise to lead her through the steps and to hold her close so she doesn't fall.

I think I may vomit.

But there's no time to wallow in my murky feelings about Feather. I need to explore the chambers of the Fae-hunters, find out what supplies they brought, and discern what strategies they typically use. I refuse to be caught by surprise again.

My hope is that these hunters are charlatans, cocky and poorly supplied. Anyone can wield iron against the Fae, but it takes a skilled hunter to actually track down Fae targets. These young humans could be braggarts with very little experience or skill—or they could be an actual threat.

In the presence of a serious threat, I should move the house, despite the difficulty of the process. But I'm increasingly reluctant to do so, for one simple reason I haven't divulged to Feather.

She's human. She wouldn't survive the immense wave of energy involved in the transference. Which means, if my life is at risk and I must flee this region, I can't take her with me.

I will have to leave her behind.

17

FEATHER

I've never had so much fun.

I dance with several attractive men and two lovely women. I sample the delicious foods on the silver trays. I drink lemonade and a kind of water full of tiny bouncing bubbles that burst on my tongue with every sip. My skin is warm, and my body feels lithe, lovely, and more awake than it has ever been. My shoes pinch a little, but I don't notice it much.

Sometimes I begin to feel anxious, untethered in a crowd of strangers—but then I focus on the face of my partner, whoever it may be, and I remind myself that I'm no longer a waif in a bloodstained nightgown, wearing a cursed bell. I am Lady Laurelai, and in that role there is both safety and power. Besides which, Krael is here… the Fae who named me. Though he glares and growls, I'm convinced he would defend me if I were in danger. And that knowledge sets me free to enjoy myself, far more than I expected to.

Perhaps part of my enjoyment comes from the spirit of the Mayor's house. When I touched a doorpost on the way into the ballroom, I felt its gaiety even through the lace of my gloves. This is a glittering, glamorous house—a bawdy, boisterous, carefree house. It thrives on lechery and luxury, feeds off the frenzy of greed and lust swirling through its rooms and corridors. And I give myself to it, a willing sacrifice.

When Nikkai Richter finds me, the gentleman I'm dancing with bows out respectfully, and I slip into Nikkai's arms, melting with him into the music. He's an excellent dancer, which is a relief for me. I've improved under Krael's tutelage, and I've held my own over the last hour or so, but I'm far from an expert. Each time the song changes, it's an adjustment.

"How are you enjoying the party?" Nikkai asks.

"Very much." I smile up at him. "You?"

"We're celebrated wherever we go, so I'm used to parties. But this one has particular charm." He winks at me.

Warmth floods my cheeks. "I find you charming as well."

"Is that so?" he murmurs. "Well then… perhaps we should find a quiet place to get to know each other a little better."

Krael said I lack sexual experience. That's why he won't touch me. Perhaps if I gain a little of that experience, he'll give in to his obvious desire for me. Besides, if Nikkai and I are alone, if we become more intimate, perhaps I can get some useful information about his strategies for hunting and capturing Fae.

So I give him a sly smile, and I nod.

Delighted lust leaps into his eyes. We continue to dance, but he slowly steers us toward an arch, then into a quiet hallway with low lighting and several cushioned benches at discreet intervals.

We settle onto one of the benches, and he wastes no time slipping his hand around the back of my neck and drawing me in for a kiss.

His mouth is warm, salty, and delicious. He's not demanding or forceful. The kiss doesn't alarm me—instead, I find myself softening all over, leaning into the sensual luxury of it.

Still, I was hoping for something… more. Something dramatic, powerful, passionate. This kiss is merely comfortable and pleasant, like a trickle of spring rain when you crave a sweeping thunderstorm. Not that I've seen either of those weather phenomena with my own eyes—but I've always liked storms better. I could hear them clearly from inside the cabin, and I could imagine how wild, ferocious, and free they were, compared to the tame pitter-patter of a gentle rain.

I give myself more deeply to the kiss, trying to awaken the passionate tempest I feel when I'm near Krael. But even with my tongue in the Fae-hunter's mouth, all I can picture is Krael, handsome and magnificent in his new suit, frowning down at me with his arms crossed.

I demanded the truth from him, so I should be honest with myself.

The only person I want to be kissing is Krael. No one else will do.

I lean back, gently ending the kiss.

Nikkai smiles and strokes my cheek. "So enchanting. You have a unique kind of beauty. And when I call you beautiful, you must know that I mean it with all my heart, because I've seen the beauty of the Fae, and your loveliness could rival theirs."

A warning twinges through my mind, and my suspicious nature awakens. He's taking the flattery a bit too far. How many Fae can he really have encountered, if he didn't recognize it when one of them shook his hand? Krael is by far the most beautiful being I have ever seen, and I don't understand how these humans can look at him and not guess his nature instantly. Perhaps it's part of the glamour he uses when he's among them. Maybe it does more than alter the shape of his ears.

"Oh yes! The Mayor said you're a Fae-hunter," I exclaim, as if I'm just now remembering it. "How did you get into this line of work? Isn't it dangerous?"

"Of course it's dangerous." He sits up straighter, his chest swelling slightly. He's pleased by my tone of admiration. "But I have a personal stake in seeing that any Fae who visit our world are dealt with quickly. You see, my sister was stolen by the Fae."

"How dreadful," I murmur.

"Yes, it was. The day before her disappearance, we were warned about the presence of Fae in the woods. A peddler stopped by our house for refuge. He claimed he saw the monsters with his own eyes—naked Fae with horns, roasting a human child on the fire while they danced. My parents weren't sure whether to believe him. They thought he'd smoked bad antler-weed. They gave him a bed and some tea, and they tried to calm him down. He left the next morning, and sometime that afternoon my sister was kidnapped by the Fae. She was only six years old."

Six years old.

A blazing chill seizes my body, and my mind snaps back to the earliest memory I have—the memory of a burly man with a brightly-painted peddler's cart, smiling at me and coaxing me closer with a stick of caramel candy. I recognized him, trusted him, accompanied him without question when he promised we would go into town, buy some delicious cakes, then return to my house in the evening. Of course, we never did return. Two days later I entered his cabin and became "Little Sister."

All my prior memories are a vague blur—impressions rather than recollections. As if my mind mercifully blotted out the remembrance of the life I could never get back.

"Are you quite alright?" Nikkai rubs my shoulder. "It's a terrible tale, I know. Perhaps too shocking for a young lady such as yourself."

"Are you sure it was the Fae who took her?" I manage to ask.

He frowns slightly. "Of course it was. The next day my father found outlandish symbols carved into some of the trees at the edge of our property, and there were signs of a bonfire."

"And the, um... the peddler... Do you remember what he looked like?"

"Oh yes. He came by our house every year after that to bring us fine trinkets. He still visits my parents. And he sold me my first iron dagger. He's a big fellow, dark hair, with an owl tattoo on his neck, just here." He taps the front of his throat.

My ribcage feels like it's tightening around my lungs. Another moment, and I won't be able to breathe. "He... he visits your family every year?"

"Yes. He was distraught to learn about my sister's disappearance, and he gave my mother a lovely set of wind chimes which have been a comfort to her ever since."

"And where did you grow up?" My voice is a weak, cracked thing. I barely recognize it.

"Northern Visseland, outside Beirfeld, a couple days' journey from the Gutland Fjord. Are you sure you're alright? You're looking rather pale. Something you ate, perhaps?"

I have a right to be pale, given that I just kissed my *brother*.

I can see the similarities between us now. Our hair is exactly the same shade of brown, and our eyes are wide and dark, with the same thick black lashes, the same slight droop to the outer corners of the eyelids, giving us an innocent, mournful look.

My stomach revolts suddenly, bile surging up the back of my throat.

"I'm going to be sick," I gasp.

199

"Oh gods," he exclaims. "Probably the crab puffs. I always say, never eat shellfish if you live too far inland. There's no way to be sure it was stored and handled safely on its journey from the sea. The privy is right down that hall, on the left."

I leap up and race away from him, locating the privy and bolting the door.

My knees hit the tile and I vomit into the porcelain toilet. It's the finest toilet I've ever seen—so glossy and white that I hate to soil it—but its purpose is to accept waste, after all.

Even when I'm done spilling all the fine food I ate, I stay on my knees, gripping the rim of the toilet, shaking uncontrollably. A cold sweat moistens my forehead and back.

I'm the girl Nikkai spoke of, the sister who was stolen. I was taken, not by the Fae, but by the deceitful peddler with the owl tattoo. All the pieces fit.

He's my brother.

This is too strange and cruel to be mere chance. This is a trick of Fate, of the god-stars, of whoever the fuck likes to play with mortals' lives.

As I kneel there, gripping the toilet, I feel a surge of sinister fascination from the Mayor's house—a dark and merciless greed focused on me. And that's when I realize another startling truth—this house doesn't only thrive on pleasure. It devours pain. Beneath the glitz and glamour, there's a creeping corruption, a sadistic hunger infused into the very walls, floors, and beams. I'm not sure if the mansion has absorbed that personality from the people who frequent it, or if its malevolent nature influences those who enter to perform the most reckless, ruinous deeds of their lives; but one thing is sure—this mansion is a devourer of misery and chaos. It likes having me here, on my knees, crushed by what I've discovered. I can almost picture its eagerness, its slavering jaws widening to swallow my misery.

I rise hastily from the floor. The change of position doesn't eliminate my sense of the mansion's aura, but the effect is less strong when I'm upright, not in such close contact with it. With the mansion's influence lessened, I can think more clearly.

Should I tell Nikkai I'm his sister? No... I can't, because then he would have questions about how I escaped my captor, where the bastard is now, and why I lied about my origins. Answering those questions could endanger Krael.

Besides, if Nikkai knows I'm his sister, he might want me to come home with him. Which I can't possibly do, because I have a life with Krael and the monsters. I have a connection to the house. I have a job as a maid for Krampus.

On the other hand, it might be nice to live a normal life as a human. Back at the house I don't even have my own room. I spend most of my time cleaning out decades' worth of clutter and grime, doing laundry—

At the thought of laundry, I frantically check the bodice of my gown. Thank the gods I leaned over far enough when I threw up—the lovely dress doesn't seem to be soiled.

My lacy gloves are another story. They're flecked with drops of vomit, so I strip them off and drop them in the waste basket next to the toilet.

Once I leave this bathroom, I must find a way to occupy Nikkai while keeping him at arms' length for the rest of the night. When I think of the kiss we shared, I feel queasy again. I'm glad it didn't escalate further between us. Not that I could have pursued anything more, with the image of Krael's handsome, disapproving face in my head.

Someone raps on the door, and I call out, "One moment!" Quickly I rinse out my mouth, take a mint from the dish by the sink, and crush it to powder between my teeth.

Clutching the rim of the sink, I fight another surge of tears. My breath comes in such violent gasps that I begin to see stars winking here and there across my field of vision.

Pull yourself together, I scream inwardly. *Play the role. Wear your mask, Feather. Stop this, right now.*

201

I give myself to the count of five, during which time I manage to regulate my breathing and scrape together some semblance of composure. Then I emerge from the privy with a curtsy and a smile to the woman waiting outside. She lifts her eyebrows at the sight of my gloveless hands, but she doesn't comment.

I've only taken a few steps down the hallway when someone grabs my elbow and an annoyed male voice growls, "My lady."

My stomach thrills at Krael's voice, then thrills again as his tall, broad-shouldered form moves in beside me.

I want to tell him everything. I want to fling myself against his broad chest and sob into his beautiful shirt while he holds me safe. I want to confess that the Fae-hunter hired to kill him is my long-lost brother, my own flesh and blood, part of my past and my family. But I can't make myself say any of it—not here. If I try to speak of it, I will shatter entirely.

"What are you doing out here?" Krampus says under his breath. "I thought you were dancing with Lord Asslicker in the ballroom."

"I was," I reply. "I felt sick, so I went to the privy."

"And how are you feeling now?" He glares ferociously, as if that will conceal the concern in his tone. It doesn't, and I love him for not being able to hide that note of tenderness.

I… love him…

Gods, I'm fucked.

I release a long, slow breath. "I'm fine."

"Good. I've checked Nikkai's room, but I almost got caught. I need you to come with me to the room of the other hunter, Abil."

"Why?"

"Because if I do get caught in one of the bedrooms, I need a good excuse for being there."

I blink at him. My mind has just undergone a cataclysmic shift, and I don't understand what he means. I simply don't have the extra space in my brain to figure it out.

Krael sighs, exasperated, and escorts me farther along the hallway, explaining under his breath. "At these parties, it's normal for couples to slip away to find some privacy so they can kiss, grope, and fuck at their leisure. I'll take you upstairs, and if anyone asks why we're in Abil's room, we'll pretend we were involved in salacious activities. Do you understand?"

"I think so."

"Salacious means sexual."

"I've got it, thanks."

"Good. This way." He steers me toward a staircase. A group of four guests round the corner, laughing over some joke. Krael props me against the wall, presses his lips to my temple, and strokes my bare shoulders while they pass.

At his warm touch, I nearly fracture into helpless pieces. I'm a half-second from exploding into a sobbing mess in his arms. But I manage to stay rigidly still, desperately holding myself together.

Once the other guests have gone, Krael frowns. "Are you still angry with me?"

"Yes," I say, hoping that will serve as sufficient explanation for any strangeness in my behavior tonight.

He doesn't apologize, but he looks slightly repentant. "Fair enough. But try to act as if you like me a little. We're supposedly sneaking away to fuck, after all."

"I'll try," I grit out between clenched teeth. "It's difficult."

"You met the fine Nikkai Richter and you hate me now, is that it?" His tone is dry, but there's an undercurrent of hurt in it. And that angers me, because *I'm* suffering, yet he expects me to pacify his vanity. To be fair, he doesn't *know* I'm suffering—but my sore heart latches onto him as a handy target for my roiling emotions.

203

"Yes," I hear myself saying bitterly. "I hate you."

"Perfect," he snaps. "That will make everything easier."

We climb the stairs together, and when we pass another group of guests I give Krael a feigned look of adoration. He escorts me through the upstairs hallways to a varnished oaken door, at which he listens for a moment before opening it and hustling me into the room.

There's a lamp burning low, and he turns it up while I hesitate by the door.

"You have to stand beside me while I search," he whispers sharply. "If someone comes in and finds you standing all the way across the room while I have my hands in a drawer, we won't have a convincing excuse to offer. Come *here*."

Annoyed by his tone, I approach sulkily. I still feel sick to my stomach. Now that we're alone, I have a chance to tell him about Nikkai. But I can't make up my mind to do it. I don't know how he'll react. He might say, "Wonderful! No need to live with me any longer. Off you go to your real family."

The thought of living with a family I've never met terrifies me. I don't know what sort of people they are. If they abhor magic and the Fae as much as my brother does, we might not get along at all.

How would they react if they knew that I can connect with actual buildings? Would they fear and despise me?

Is family really that vital to happiness, anyway? Isn't it simply a collection of people playing the roles Fate dealt them— rather like my companions in the cabin?

"Feather." Krampus peers into my face. "What's wrong?"

"Thinking," I reply.

"Think later. Be ready to make a convincing show in case anyone pops in." He clears his throat. "We should mess up each other's hair a little and pull our clothes to the side a bit... and you should sit on top of the dresser while I search it."

"Alright, but I'm not sure I can climb up there with this gown—oh!" I gasp as his hands close around my waist and he lifts me onto the dresser.

"Now…" He licks his lips, careful not to let too much of his tongue slither out. "May I touch you? I mean… may I adjust your clothing for the purposes of this ruse?"

But all I hear is, *May I touch you?*

The question is like a healing tonic offered to a diseased soul. Right now I feel dirty—befouled by the kiss with my brother, violated by the house's desire for my pain. I *need* a cleansing touch. I want the grime cleared from my soul. I want to be held, calmed, tethered to something powerful and steady. I need Krael's strong hands, his muscled arms, his solid body, or else I might drift away and be lost forever in a void of pain and uncertainty.

"Yes, you may touch me," I whisper.

"Very well." He moves closer, and I automatically part my legs so he fits between them, his hips nested in the voluminous skirts of my gown.

Krael speaks casually, as if we're discussing food choices at the market. "If I had just kissed you, I probably would have held your head like this, and loosened the pins a little." His fingers slide into my hair just behind my ear, gliding around to cup the back of my head. His nails graze my scalp lightly as he pulls me toward him.

Our mouths hover a breath apart, and it's agonizing. I hope the nearness of our lips is as great a torture for him as it is for me. And if we're playing this game, I refuse to let him make all the moves. So I sink my fingers into his braided hair, pulling some tendrils loose. "And I might have done *this*."

"Of course. And if we were kissing, your lip stain would be smeared." He cups my chin and drags his thumb slowly across my mouth. My lips part, letting the tip of his thumb slip between them.

I don't miss the way his pupils dilate, or the slight quickening of his breath.

"Some of the stain should be on you as well." I swipe my fingertip over my mouth and rub the rosy tint onto his soft, smooth lips.

His tone is still an attempt at nonchalance, but it's quieter, gentler... deeper. "If I were truly groping you, I would place my hand just here."

He cups my breast, warm palm and strong fingers... and I lose every thought that ever existed in my head. I can't remember any trauma or terror; all I know is the heat of his hand as he feels the shape of my breast.

A thrill passes through my body. "Yes," I manage. "That makes sense."

"And having touched you there," he continues, a faint tremor in his voice, "I would not be able to resist tugging down this tempting neckline, just a little."

"That's only logical," I breathe.

His fingertips nudge beneath the neckline of the bodice, grasping one cup of the corset as well. He tugs my clothing lower, slowly, until one of my nipples pops out.

"This would be more sharply peaked and a bit reddened," he says hoarsely. "For the purposes of the scene we're portraying."

"It has to look real," I agree, my heart racing. Is he going to—fuck, I think I might unravel completely into a million anguished threads—

He bends. Takes my nipple in his mouth and sucks gently for a moment, while heat swells between my legs.

It's all I can do not to cry out. *Touch me, hold me, I need more of you, please...*

With a final lick to the rosy circle around my nipple, he straightens. "Perfect. And now to explore the contents of this dresser."

I sit motionless, abandoned, with my breast bared and arousal pooling between my thighs, while he opens one drawer after another. If he moves any items, he replaces them exactly as they were.

My entire soul is begging for him to hold me, screaming so loudly I feel as though he *must* be able to hear it. My need for contact, for comfort, has never been so excruciating as now, but I can't make myself ask him to help me, to *care*. So I remain motionless and silent.

But Krael becomes more flushed with every drawer he inspects, until at last he growls, "Can't you control yourself at all?"

"I'm sitting perfectly still."

"Your *scent*," he snarls. "The luscious fucking scent of that wetness between your legs."

My face grows hotter. "I can't help it."

He glances up, his green eyes luminous and daring. "You want me that badly?"

After the emotional torment of this night, I may not have much pride left, but the little I have won't let me admit how violently I crave him.

"Anyone would be aroused if a handsome Fae sucked their nipple," I counter. "And you should control *yourself*—your eyes are beginning to glow."

"Fuck." He closes them briefly, then opens them again and continues his search.

When he finishes with the dresser, he snatches another glance at my exposed breast before meeting my eyes. "I need to check under the bed. Stand by the bedpost."

I'm about to obey, but as he moves to the opposite side of the bed and bends to look under the mattress, muffled footsteps thump in the hallway just outside the door.

I seize Krael and pull him down to the floor behind the bed, where we're both concealed from anyone who might enter. He lies face-up beneath me while I'm draped along his body.

In this position, with my crotch positioned directly over his, I can feel the immense, rock-hard length in his pants. We're nose to nose, and I meet his gaze with a triumphant glare. How dare he comment on *my* arousal when *his* is just as obvious?

He won't hold my gaze. He averts his eyes, swallowing hard.

The door opens, and leather-heeled shoes clack on the hardwood briefly. There's a thump, possibly from the books on the desk, and then the footsteps retreat and the door closes.

I start to move, expecting Krael to order me off him immediately. But his hands close on my upper arms with a convulsive grip, holding me in place.

Startled, I look down at his striking face, into his green eyes. He's gazing at me with a visceral, compelling hunger that makes my heart race.

He looks as if he might kiss me. It's what I want, and it's also the thing that frightens me the most.

So I say something terribly stupid. "I kissed Nikkai. Or… he kissed me, and then I kissed him back."

His features harden into exquisite stone, but his eyes fracture. "Do you want him?"

"You said I need experience…"

"So you thought you'd jump on the dick of the first man who wanted to bed you?"

His scornful tone angers me. I roll my hips, grinding against his cock, and he sucks in a sharp breath and exhales a soft, agonized, "Fuck."

"He's not the only one who wants to bed me," I hiss.

"Anyone would be aroused if a beautiful woman sat astride their hips." He's lashing out, mimicking my earlier words and tone. "It means nothing. *You* mean nothing."

His face changes the second he speaks those last words, as if he realizes he has made a grave mistake. As if he betrayed himself.

I climb off him immediately and walk to the window. The curtains are drawn, so I can't see outside, but I stand there staring at them anyway. Pretending there's a view, like I used to do back at the cabin.

I hear him rise from the floor. "Feather... that's not what I meant to say."

It mollifies me a little that he regrets the words so suddenly and completely, but they still stung, and I'm not ready to forgive him just yet. I spent years forgiving easily, being so dependent on someone that I'd overlook their most terrible flaws as long as I could be safe. I refuse to do that anymore.

"Maybe I'll go where I'm wanted," I say.

"What does that mean?" He sounds exasperated. "You have nowhere else to go."

"Actually I do. My family home."

"You remembered something about them?"

"No, but Nikkai told me a strange story tonight." I repeat the conversation, along with his description of the peddler, which elicits a low "shit" from Krael.

"You can't kill him now," I say, turning around. "He could be my only family."

Krael's expression is serious, but he arches an eyebrow. "And you kissed him."

"*Before* I knew we might be related," I retort. "And I had to throw up afterward. But I could confess the truth to him now... or part of the truth. I could say that my captor finally died and that I escaped. I could leave you out of it."

Krael shakes his head. "You can't live with Nikkai. He's a wretched snake who hates my kind. Most Fae-hunters are charlatans anyway. When business is slow, they invent 'signs' of

Fae activity and then profit off the backs of peasants by making the local lords pay exorbitant sums for protection."

"Nikkai takes legitimate jobs. Like this one," I retort. "And why aren't you congratulating me? I thought you'd be happy that I found my true family."

"Not if your family includes Fae-hunters!" he exclaims in a half-whisper. "They're dangerous, especially for a human with magical affinities, like your connection to the house."

He's repeating the same reservations I had, but somehow his protest only makes me angrier, especially when he draws himself up to his full height and declares, "I forbid you to live with Nikkai. You're *my* maid."

Part of me wants to submit meekly, as I used to. But I've gained confidence over the past several weeks.

"You can't tell me what to do," I snap.

"I can when you're being a little fool."

"If you try to control my life, you're just like *him*."

We both know who I mean. The man in the cabin. My captor.

Krael bares his teeth. They look human at the moment—no Faerie fangs. Yet somehow he radiates a ferocious savagery that almost makes me step back. I have to fight my instinct to flee.

"I am *nothing* like that bastard." He advances, tall and violently beautiful, a commanding presence that snatches the breath right out of my lungs. "My goal isn't self-serving. I only intend to protect you."

"He said that too," I reply. "He used to say that the outside world was terrible, and that the cabin was the only safe place for me."

Krael looms over me, his fists clenched as if he's trying to restrain himself, trying not to frighten me. His voice is quiet, yet so intense it shakes me to my very bones. "The world is wretched, yes. But it's also wonderful. Meeting *you* reminded me of that. I was beginning to feel like a machine, a thing of gears and clockwork moving dully from one task to the next. Even when I sought pleasure between kills, I found little satisfaction. It all felt like a hollow ritual, endless and inescapable. But now..." His eyes shine intensely bright, vividly green. "Now I suffer from one all-consuming need."

His nearness, his heat, the primal dominance of his body— it's more than I can bear. My survival instinct kicks me in the gut and sends me darting away from him, into the corner of the room by the wardrobe.

He springs after me so fast that I utter a faint shriek right before his hand clamps over my mouth.

"Don't run from me," he whispers. "I *will* chase you if you do. I can't help it. It's part of my nature."

His lean, powerful frame overwhelms my slender one. His nose drifts against my hair and he inhales slowly, while I stay perfectly still. My nerves are thrumming with panic, but it's not the stone-cold fear I felt in the cabin. This is a heady, dazzling, wild feeling that wavers between wanting to run and wanting to be captured, mauled, devoured. I'm a mad doe willingly standing in the snare of the hunter, trembling for the deadly touch of his hand.

My very skin screams to be soothed and swept by his palms, molded by his fingers. I want him with a madness I barely comprehend. If he doesn't touch me I think I might crack open my own ribcage, climb out of my body, and fly away shrieking into the night, a soul who perished from sheer unrequited yearning.

So I do the only thing that I know will make him touch me. I attack him, my small fists flailing against his chest.

He chuckles lightly as his warm hands close around my wrists. "You think you can hurt me with these little fingers?"

I buck against the hold, my body arching against his, and he instinctively moves closer, pushing me to the wall.

I can't restrain a tiny smile of satisfaction at the success of my plan. He sees my expression and presses in tighter.

The firmness of him all along my body soothes me so deeply that I release a sob of frenzied relief. But I crave more—his bare hands on my naked skin. His lips on mine. The force of his lust tearing me out of myself, embracing my soul, swallowing it up in the storm of his strength.

I rise on my toes, seeking his mouth, but he rears back, just out of reach. Embarrassed, frustrated, on the verge of tears, I turn my face aside. I don't understand why he keeps rejecting me. It hurts.

A tear slips from my lashes. Rolls down my cheek.

"Feather." He murmurs the name he gave me. "The Fae never say they're sorry. *Never*, do you understand?"

I nod, more tears flowing down my cheeks.

He continues speaking, low and urgent, a repressed passion suffusing each word. "I'm telling you this so you will understand what it costs me to say it—I am beyond sorry. I lied when I said you mean nothing to me. It's the opposite, in fact. I can't seem to think about anything else, or want anyone else. I'm cruel and selfish to tell you this, to even open this door between us, because there is no happiness in it for you, no future that a human girl like you could want or need. But I cannot bear for you to believe that I meant those words, when you have taken a heart as cold and wicked as mine, and brought it back to life."

He leans in and licks my tears, his tongue sweeping from my jawline up to my lower lashes. Then he licks again, tenderly, right at the corner of my mouth.

My lips part as I turn back toward him, and his tongue slithers into my mouth.

He kisses me with a fervent hum of glorious relief, and I greet him with a sharp, aching whimper. He releases my wrists, wraps both arms around my body, and lifts me against the wall. I

212

cinch my legs and arms around him instantly, tightly, determined not to let him change his mind.

My bones are crying for him, my lungs are yearning for his breath, my skin is scorched with the need for his touch. *Touch me everywhere, everywhere…*

As if he understands, he drags his hands over my breasts, down my sides. He cups my rear, then runs a hand along one of my legs where it's arched, locked around his waist. He shoves the skirts of my gown up, hunting beneath them until he finds the edge of my stockings and panties.

"I can't do this with you here," he breathes heavily against my mouth, his forehead rocking against mine.

"No." I shake my head. "But *yes.*"

He chuckles hoarsely. "You want me to fuck you? When someone could enter this room at any moment?"

I hesitate, thinking of the other women he has bedded. The ones who meant nothing to him but a good time.

I clasp his face between my hands. "If we have sex, will you be done with me afterwards?"

A wicked tenderness threads through his laugh. "Fuck no. I won't be done with you for ages."

Goosebumps flood my skin at that pronouncement. I can't be sure that he means it, but he seems to believe it.

"Fuck me, then," I tell him. "But first, would you… lick me… there?"

His smile turns wicked. "Where?"

A hectic flush scorches my cheeks, and I glance away. He takes my chin in his hand, pulls me back to face him. "Where, Feather?"

"Between my legs," I whisper.

"Never be afraid to tell me what you need." And with that, he sets me down and drops to his knees. He lifts up the skirts of my gown and disappears beneath them.

213

I feel him peeling down my stockings, then dragging my panties down my legs. He shifts me into a wider stance, and then...

His long, long tongue ripples against my pussy, starting at the front and slithering all the way between my legs, until the very tip of it flicks near my asshole. He withdraws the tongue in a fluid glide that rubs every piercing he possesses along the lips of my pussy and over my clit. I cry out, my thighs trembling uncontrollably at the sensation.

I hear him chuckle beneath the muffling layers of skirts, and then his tongue squirms over my pussy again... only this time, its rippling length nudges between the lips of my sex and penetrates my slit, probing deep inside me.

I'm so wet that the beautiful thickness of that pierced tongue glides in easily, and I feel every inch as it coils and quivers within me. There's a brief moment of tension, a flicker of pain as he presses through a momentary resistance deep in my body, but I'm distracted from that tiny discomfort by the hot, soft press of his lips. His mouth is wide open against my pussy while his tongue flexes inside me.

I've never experienced anything like it. I'm galvanized to the wall, my skirts draped over the head and torso of the Fae male whose tongue is surging and swirling inside my belly. Every pulse of that tongue elicits a new wave of hot, quivering pleasure.

Why do I feel like I need something to hold, something to pull, something to anchor me? I'm straining, striving for a goal I don't know how to reach, and yet he's dragging me toward it in spite of myself. His tongue withdraws halfway, part of it still flexing inside while the thickest part undulates against my clit.

"I don't know what to do," I gasp. "I can't, I can't... I need—"

As if he understands, his hand appears from beneath my skirts, and I grip it with all my strength.

He withdraws his tongue entirely for a moment and I moan at the unfulfilled emptiness between my legs. But he only pauses to look up, his face alight and his lips wet, and he says, "Don't fight it, Feather. Let yourself come. Give in to me."

"I can't." I shake my head. "I don't know how."

"You *can*," he insists. "Grip my hand, trust me, and let me take you over the edge."

I nod, whimpering, and he disappears from my view once more. I grasp his fingers and brace my other hand against the wardrobe beside me. When his tongue rushes into my center again, I almost scream, but I swallow the sound, because the last thing I want is for someone to burst into the room and interrupt *this*.

His tongue thrusts into me, rolls against my sex, drives the stimulation to shrieking heights, to an unbearable crest. White-hot flashes of need sear through my body—and then, with a violent squeeze of his hand and a slam of my palm against the wardrobe, the coiling blaze *bursts*, culminates in a stunning, shattering, blinding explosion of the keenest ecstasy I have ever felt.

I can't make a sound. I can only strain, and spasm, and sink my nails into his hand, while jagged blades of pure pleasure raze my whole body.

His tongue strokes me down, settles me until I can breathe again. When he emerges from beneath my gown, I nearly collapse, but he catches me, props me against the wall, and holds me there with his heat, his presence. He kisses my cheek and murmurs words I don't understand, either because my brain is too addled with bliss, or because they're in some language of Faerie.

Yes, it must be a Fae language, because after a few seconds, my brain registers a glow seeping from between the doors of the wardrobe.

"Krael," I gasp, nodding toward the light. "Krael, look."

He twists around. "By the god-stars, there we have it. They possess some device that reacts to trollish words, of all things." He kisses me hard on the mouth—a ferocious, glorious, soul-sucking kind of kiss—then pulls my panties and stockings back up before arranging my skirts in their proper place. "Forgive me for not fucking you properly just yet," he whispers hoarsely, making me shiver with delicious anticipation. "I promise I will fuck you brainless once we're home. But you must allow me a little time."

Weakly, I nod.

Krael opens the wardrobe, moves aside a stack of clothes, and takes out a box. Vivid blue light streams through its keyhole. After fiddling in the lock with two of my hairpins and muttering something that sounds like a spell, he finally gets it open.

Inside the box are trays and compartments full of strange-looking objects, as well as a rack of tiny, jewel-colored glass bottles. The blue glow comes from an oddly shaped crystal.

"Shit," he whispers. "These are no charlatans or pretenders. See that compass? Those markings? It's designed either to track Fae or to indicate the presence of powerful spells. It could find the house."

"Can you break it?"

He touches its surface tentatively, but his hand springs back as if the object burned him. "This isn't just made of iron—it's been charmed against my kind. I can't touch it. And I doubt it will be easy to destroy."

I reach past him and pick up the small compass. It doesn't react to me at all. "At least we can take it away from them." I tuck it into the bodice of my dress. "Anything else that looks particularly dangerous?"

He points out a couple more artifacts, including the crystal, whose blue glow has almost faded. While I find places to hide the objects in my clothing, he empties the bottles into the fire, one by one, then closes the box and puts it back where it was, under the stack of clothes.

"We can't be caught here now," says Krael under his breath. "Come on. We'll go out to the garden. There's something we need to discuss before we leave."

He leads me from the room, then out of the house by a back stairway. The cold hits me like a bracing slap to the face, waking me out of the sensual stupor I've been in since he kissed me. And with the waking comes the crushing weight of remembrance—my brother, my family, my captor.

It makes me sick that my kidnapper visited my family over and over. I can imagine them welcoming him like any other traveling peddler, accepting his gifts, buying his wares, sharing meals with him while I scrubbed the blood of murdered women from the floors of his cabin.

For a moment, I think I'm going to be sick again, but I manage to quell the nausea with a few lungfuls of fresh, cold air.

Krael leads me deeper into the garden, between evergreen hedges dotted with bright red berries, beneath stone arches laden with snow. In a small courtyard, by the side of a frozen fountain, he halts and looks up at the black, star-sprinkled arch of the night sky.

"I wish they would tell me what to do," he says, and I know he means the god-stars.

"Why are we out here, Krael?" I ask him, rubbing my chilled arms. "We can't stay here long. I don't have my cloak."

"I know." He turns to me. "There is something we must discuss without the risk of being overheard. And I want to give you a choice, since you've had precious few of those in your lifetime. The Fae-hunters are a threat, Feather. Maybe not an immediate one, since we've destroyed some of their potions and stolen their supplies… but at most that will be a setback, not a deterrent."

"So let's move the house."

217

"It's more complicated than that. You're not an eldritch creature, and you're not Fae—you're human. You can't be in the house while it's being moved—you wouldn't survive the process. Which means to move the house, I would have to leave you behind."

Dread curls icy fingers around my spine. "You could always come back and fetch me after you've moved to a new spot."

But he shakes his head. "I'll have to move it to another part of this world. And my geistfyre has a limited range. You'd be too far away."

My heart plummets into depths as vast as the Void. "What else can we do?"

"I could kill both of the Fae-hunters. Tonight."

"But one is my brother."

"But one is your brother." He nods gravely. "And no doubt they are well-armed, even beneath those fine clothes. They might end up getting the best of me."

"Don't risk it, then." I can't bear to think of them killing him. He came too close to death once already.

His eyes soften, shining a luminous green in his pale, handsome face. Those eyes, and his height, and his beauty are the only signs that he isn't human.

"There may be other spells for illusion or concealment that I can try, to keep them from locating the house," he says. "None of them are guaranteed to work. If they find it, they can disable my geistfyre, poison the house's energy, burn it with fire—any number of destructive things. And they won't stop until they're sure I'm dead."

"So… we're fucked," I whisper.

"Seems so." He pulls off his tailcoat and wraps it around me. I welcome the heat, but my shivers are more than physical cold. They stem from a bone-deep fear that I'm going to lose the strange new family I just found.

"You can't leave me behind," I tell him. "You *can't.*"

"You think I want to?" His fists curl tight and his voice is strained, with an underlying vehemence that startles and pleases me. "You have become my fucking reason for existence. You think I could bear to be parted from you? I'd sooner cut out my own heart."

I love the passionate violence of those words. I knew he was holding back his emotions, but I didn't realize how much.

"We have time," I say. "A little time to think about it. Don't we?"

"Time." He draws in a long, shuddering breath. "Yes, we can take some time."

"As you said, we've set them back by destroying and stealing their supplies. You could always kill them later, if you have to."

"Yes," he murmurs. "After all, you and I have unfinished business. There are still secrets you must confess to me, and I did promise to punish you, if you desire it."

The way he says *punish* doesn't terrify me, because it's accompanied by a lascivious lash of his tongue and a brighter glow in his eyes. My clit flutters with anticipation, even though I'm not sure what kind of punishment he's planning… or whether he'll still want me after I've told him my darkest secret.

"Let's go, then," I urge him. "The sooner we leave, the sooner we get these objects away from the hunters."

"We'll have to leave the way we came. Using geistfyre this close to a pair of Fae-hunters would be infinitely foolish. Give me a moment to collect myself, and then we'll bid farewell to our host and call for our carriage."

He walks a few steps away from me and bends over, hands on his thighs, breathing deeply. When he straightens again, his eyes are no longer glowing.

On the way back through the house, we almost encounter Nikkai, but Krael spots him in time and we steer clear. The Mayor is in the smoking room of the house, sprawled on a huge sofa, entangled with two plump, silk-clad women and a slim, shirtless young man. Krael compliments the Mayor on the party and makes some excuse about me feeling sick.

"She does look wretched," comments the Mayor, at which I bristle slightly. "Take good care of her, eh, Brandt?" He winks.

"Always, sir." Krael bows deeply.

We hurry to claim our cloaks, then stand on the mansion's steps waiting for our carriage. I start sweating despite the cold, because one of the charmed objects I tucked into my underwear feels like it's going to slip out and fall to the ground at any second. But perhaps the god-stars are smiling on us, because I manage to climb into the carriage without any mishap.

Once the door is closed, Krael pounds on the front wall of the vehicle and it rattles away from the Mayor's house.

"Shut the curtains," I say. "I need to readjust some things."

He obliges, but once the curtains are drawn, the interior of the carriage is pitch black. I drop the blue stone, but since it's no longer glowing, I can't find it on the floor.

"Shit," I exclaim. "Where did it go?"

A moment later, yellow light bathes the carriage interior. Krael is holding his hand palm up, and above it floats a small, glowing orb.

"What is that?" I gasp.

"The Fae can conjure these for light," he says. "I don't usually need to, since the house takes care of its own lighting. But occasionally the ability is useful."

I can't stop staring at the tiny golden orb of light. "Magic," I breathe reverently.

He chuckles. "You've seen me do magic. Geistfyre, glamours…"

"But not like *this*. This is… beautiful."

"This is commonplace," he says, low. "*You* are beautiful."

"I'm not," I whisper. "I'm too pale, too small, too strange…"

"Stop." He lets the orb float to the carriage ceiling while he leans forward, glaring at me intensely. "You have fucking bewitched me, woman. Every flaw of yours turns to glory in my eyes and makes you dearer to me than any other being in the universe."

We're sitting opposite each other on the carriage benches, our knees nearly touching, yet suddenly the space between my body and his seems ridiculous and extreme. I want to lunge toward him, but I hesitate, still half-afraid of rejection.

He must notice my hesitation, because his expression shifts, haunted with pain. "You've come to your senses, perhaps, and realized why you shouldn't want me. Very wise of you. I tried to be wise, too... I promised myself I wouldn't touch you, and yet I was foolishly weak tonight. I took advantage of your sadness and confusion to indulge my own lust. I confessed my feelings without pausing to see if you returned them. It was unforgivable of me, and it won't happen again. You can have my room tonight. I'll sleep elsewhere."

I squeeze my hands into fists. It takes every bit of willpower I possess to keep from flinging myself at him and kissing away his doubts; but if I touch him, I'll lose the ability to form rational thoughts. And before that happens, there's something I need to say. Something that will reassure him.

"You were never wanted." I spill the naked truth into the air between us. "Your mother didn't want you, and neither did the trolls. I suspect you never quite fit in with the Seelie, and then you became *this*. Even the humans who want you only crave your beauty. They don't understand everything you are, and if they did, their craving would turn to revulsion."

His lips tighten, and his eyes spark red for a moment.

"I was always wanted," I continue. "Or at least, that's how it looks on the surface, I suppose. But my birth family gave up on me too easily. They were so blind to the truth that they befriended the man who stole me. *He* wanted me, but only as long as I behaved precisely as he wished. Had I made even one mistake, I would be dead. That isn't the right kind of *wanting*. That isn't the way I want you."

He's tense all over, his eyes fixed on my face and burning—burning green.

"I want you in spite of all the mistakes you have made, or will make," I say quietly. "I want you in this form, or the other. I like *you*. Gruff, glaring, adorable *you*. Charming, graceful, tormented *you*. You in any mood, in any shape, covered in blood or scars or tears. I will have you, just as you are, and as you will be."

He's breaking, right in front of me. Stunned, tears glistening in his eyes, the hard edges of his body softening.

I shift forward and put my hand on his knee, keeping my tone sober. "But you *must* learn to clean up after yourself."

He laughs, and it's partly a sob, wrenched from his chest. He drags me into his lap, and when our mouths meet, I taste his tears.

18

KRAMPUS

I'm so lost in the magic of her mouth that I barely have time to douse the little orb of light, remind Feather to retrieve the stone she dropped, and subdue the glow in my eyes before the carriage driver opens the door for us.

We're at the inn and tavern where I rented our transportation. It will look odd if we go walking off into the night in our party clothes, so for the purposes of our cover, we go inside and I pay for a room.

Originally, I had intended to draw my geistfyre circle in the room and take us home at once. But the moment we enter the chamber and I close the door, my plans change.

Feather wastes no time removing all the objects we stole from her garments and laying them on top of the bureau. "That feels so much better," she sighs. "They were poking me. And this is poking me too." She lifts her arms to adjust one of the pins in her hair.

I reach for the pin, and instead of helping her reseat it, I pull it free and fling it aside.

Startled, she looks up at me.

My heart is swollen full with everything she said to me, words I never expected to hear from another living creature. I didn't realize how deep my own feelings were until I spoke them aloud and discovered the raw truth of them in my soul. And now, I intend to offer her another kind of proof of my affection.

I trace my fingertips along the curve of her face. "If we had just been fucking in here," I murmur, "your hair would be unbound." I pluck out another pin, and another, discarding them one by one until her brown hair tumbles around her shoulders.

She blinks up at me, her eyes wide with panicked excitement.

I cup her chin to confirm her attention. "This is not a game, or a role you must play," I tell her. "My feelings for you will not change if you deny me, or if you speak your own will. Do not go along with this unless every part of you desires it. And if you feel uncertain about anything, tell me. I will yield to your wishes immediately. You have only to speak, and I promise to listen."

The panic recedes in her eyes, replaced with bright confidence, and I smile, adding, "There is nothing so beautiful as a woman with power."

She collects the hand that I curled around her chin, and she kisses my fingers. "I love you."

That phrase is a blade of light through my heart, flooding my chest with a blaze of wondering joy.

"Not lightly do the Fae say those words," I whisper.

"I've only said them to two people, and with one of them I didn't mean it," she replies. "But I mean it now."

"And I mean it when I say that I love you recklessly, foolishly, beyond logic or hope."

Feather unclasps her cloak and lets it fall. "Show me, then."

I want to leap on her, throw her down, tear her clothes off her back. My entire body is shaking with my need to consume her, to be inside her. But I force myself to move slowly, so as not to frighten her. She's been naked in front of me before, but this is a different kind of unveiling.

I'm halfway through with the buttons on her dress when she says tersely, "Is there a reason you're taking so long?"

"I want to be sure you're comfortable, that you feel safe…"

She jerks free and spins around, her brown eyes afire with a ravenous hunger. "If I want you to slow down, I'll tell you. But right now, stop asking. Stop hesitating. Be the predator you were in that room, when you said you would chase me if I ran."

I stare at her, and she blushes deeply, biting her lip. "Maybe it seems strange to you that I would want that, after the way I lived for so long. I don't understand it myself. But I know what I need, and it's not this slow, painful process—"

Her words break off in a squeal as I lift her bodily and fling her face down on the bed. My claws rip through every button on the dress—they can be repaired. I drag her lithe little body out of the gown, throw the dress aside, and toss her on the bed again, this time on her back. I crouch over her, letting my glamour fall away, revealing my horns, fangs, pointed ears, and all. Nestling my face between her breasts, I bite through the corset with my teeth and tear it away in ragged strips. Her breasts quiver with her frantic gasps, but she doesn't stop me.

My tongue snakes out to curl around one of those charming breasts, and as it slithers across her nipple she tilts her head back and releases a faint moan. My cock was already stiff, but at that sound it hardens so violently that I cry out with the pain of it. I have not fucked a woman in far too long.

Reeling, dizzy with need for her, I step back and strip off my own clothes while she shimmies off the crinoline, stockings, and panties. I lunge for her, my bare body settling on top of her slim one. She seizes my hair, pulls my face down to hers, devours my lips with urgent kisses. The kisses melt into each other, sugared and decadent, a languid blaze, a temporary indulgence amid the torment of need.

I'm leaking arousal onto her smooth stomach as I kiss her. When she reaches down, tentatively, and runs her fingers along my aching length, I almost come.

"Stop!" I cry out, agonized. "Have some fucking mercy."

She meets my eyes, startled, but there's a wicked gleam in her gaze. She likes that I'm so helpless to a mere graze of her fingers.

I grip her face with my hand. "I'm coming *inside* you, not on you, do you understand?"

"Yes," she breathes eagerly. "Yes." And with the natural instinct of a sensual being, she lifts her hips and opens her thighs to me.

I grasp the base of my cock firmly and nudge the head into her soaked slit. Her small pussy, unused to cock, can barely accept my girth, and she gasps at the stretch as I enter her slowly. I feel her muscles tighten, her breath taking on a shrill note of pain.

"Relax." I grasp her thigh and squeeze gently. "Don't tighten up. Breathe, and feel your muscles loosening. Take me in when you're ready."

I'm gritting out the words between clamped teeth, fighting every second not to spill inside her immediately.

Feather inhales. Exhales. Relaxes her thighs and her pussy, and shifts forward to take more of me inside her.

I groan loudly at the torturous delight of it, my sensitive length squeezing deeper into the delicate wet center of her. She shifts her hips, accepting me, and I move in until I'm fully seated, sunk to the hilt in the pussy of the girl I've been obsessed with for weeks.

"Is that it?" she whispers.

I laugh raggedly. "No, precious. Now be still, if you love me, or I'll come too soon."

"I like you inside me," Feather says softly, with those lush rosy lips of hers. "You're so big and warm. You fill me right up."

"Fuck..." My cock throbs heavily, and it's agony to hold back. "Stop talking, I beg you. Give me a moment."

Holding as still as I can, I reach down and rub my thumb right above where we're joined. At the first caress of her clit, Feather gives a breathless little shriek and trembles all over. Her tits are peaked and rosy, and I fill my greedy soul with the sight of them while I stroke her clit with the pad of my thumb. I toy with her, circling and flicking, watching her reaction, smiling as the caution and cleverness fades from her gaze, replaced by the blank hunger of pure carnal need. Only when she has fistfuls of the sheets in her hands and she's squirming beneath me do I pull slowly back, partway out of her, and then thrust firmly back in.

"Oh!" she exclaims. "Oh fuck... do that again..."

She's glassy-eyed, flushed, utterly fucking beautiful. She deserves every bit of pleasure I can give her. I've pleased other women as a matter of course, as a polite courtesy in return for the use of their body. But with Feather, I find myself more obsessed with her climax than my own.

"Come for me," I tell her. "Come on my cock, precious. I feel how slick you are. You're ready to come so prettily for your master."

Her pussy flutters around me, and I'm so startled by the rush of pleasure along my nerves that I thrust deeper and harder than I meant to.

"Oh gods, yes!" Feather exclaims, and I thrust again, a forceful rush through her pussy. I ramp up the pace, losing myself to the rhythm, to the expression of tortured intensity on her face, to the increased frequency of her tiny, breathless shrieks.

Her eyes fly open and she gasps. Her pussy squeezes compulsively around my cock and I let out a harsh, savage groan as I come inside her. I flood her with my cum, great spurts of it, pent up for days. My arms are shaking as they hold my body above hers. She lets go of the sheets and grabs hold of me, shrill breaths still bursting from her lungs as she keeps spasming, keeps coming around my hard length. The thrills rocketing through my whole body are like nothing I've ever felt before.

"Oh gods," she whimpers, her fingernails digging into my biceps. "It's happening again… ahh—" And she comes a second time, with a rushing intensity that I can feel through every nerve in my body. I come with her, helplessly, violently, my balls tightening as they spill more cum into her belly.

"What the fuck," I gasp out, trembling from the force of the pleasure.

Feather's arms slip away from me and she falls back, barely conscious, blissed out on the bed. She's panting, eyes half-closed.

When I start to pull out of her, her eyes fly open, stricken with ecstasy. "Fuck," she whimpers. "Stay right there for a minute. Oh…"

A thrill traces through my cock as it hardens again, synchronized with the impulses of her body. I roll us both over so I'm beneath her and she's on top, still impaled on my cock. I tuck two fat pillows under my head to prop myself up, so I can better enjoy the sight of her.

Feather plants both hands on my chest and lifts herself experimentally. She fucks herself on me slowly and clumsily at first, then faster, more smoothly.

It's beginning to register in my mind that this isn't possible. This isn't normal. Even among the Fae, it takes a little time for a male to be hard again. I've never come twice so strongly in such close succession, and if she keeps riding me, I'm going to come a third time.

Vaguely a concept nags at the back of my mind... something I heard about during my time with the Seelie Fae. The idea of a mate bond. But that sort of bond was only possible among royalty, or so I was told. Neither of my parents were of royal blood. Besides which, I'm an outcast wretch bound to the Wild Hunt. The privilege and pleasure of a mate bond would never be permitted for someone like me.

"Krael." Feather leans forward, one hand planted on my breastbone, the other cupping my face. Her long brown hair swings softly against my chest. "Am I doing it right?"

I've never seen such a glow on her face... on anyone's face. No one has ever looked at me with so much trust, delight, and love. It's enough to break my heart.

"You couldn't do it wrong," I assure her. "But you should stop being so fucking beautiful."

She smiles, bright as the stars in the Void. "I love this. Don't you?"

"Fucking come here." I reach up and pull her down to me, her soft form pressed to my chest, her hair cascading over my ribs and my arm. I'm still deeply lodged inside her, tendrils of my pleasure still twined with hers, still sending shivers of delight into my belly. She kisses my mouth, slipping her tongue over mine. Her hands find my horns and she uses them for leverage as she begins to move her hips again, slicking my cock with her arousal.

"Krael," she whispers, blinking pleasure-dazed eyes at me. "Krael…"

"Ride me, sweetheart," I urge hoarsely. "Ride me until you come."

19

FEATHER

Nothing exists but the two of us.

No house, no Fae-hunters, no family, no decisions or dangers.

Only Krael and me, and this bed, and the ecstasy that rolls through our bodies in overwhelming waves.

I come three times on his cock and once on his tongue. While I'm recovering from the fourth orgasm, he stares at my swollen, damp pussy for a few minutes before lifting my legs and pushing inside me again. He comes almost instantly, and he pulls out halfway through, spurting white liquid across my sensitive clit. There's something intensely erotic about seeing his cum on my pussy, especially when he drags a finger through it and traces several lines and swirls across my stomach.

Impulsively I dip a finger inside myself and dab a little of his cum and my arousal on the end of his nose. Then I paint both his cheekbones with it.

"You're making a mess," he growls, crawling over me, burying me in the sheets and blankets while I giggle.

"It's not my mess to clean up," I reply.

"I do pity the inn staff." He gives me a sheepish grin. "There was a lot of cum. Far more than my usual amount, which is already more than the average human male."

"Most of it is inside me," I point out.

"I know." He pries my legs apart and peers between them. "Some of it is trying to escape. Let's keep it where it belongs." He runs a finger up my sex, scooping up the cum and pressing it back into my entrance. "Not that it will have any effect, since I'm not in heat."

"What does that mean?"

"Fae are only fertile when they're in heat," he explains. "So no matter how much I come inside you, you won't get pregnant."

I nod, remembering the bits of information my favorite Mother gave me about pregnancy. In the cabin, my captor made each Wife take a tonic when she first arrived—one that would render her permanently infertile.

He never made me swallow the tonic, but I'm far from ready to contemplate having children. In fact, I'm not sure I ever want to.

"That's good," I murmur. "One less thing to worry about."

Krael's face sobers. He rolls onto his back beside me and stares at the ceiling. "Yes. We have enough worries."

I sit up, oddly pleased at how quivery my limbs feel. I'm sore inside where he fucked me, but it's a warm, pleasant, sated kind of soreness.

For a moment I simply gaze at him, as he lies beside me with one arm tucked behind his head. The bicep of that arm is a smooth bulge, terribly tempting for my fingers. His hair has mostly come loose from his braid. The lamps in the room glitter on the jewelry in his nose, his eyebrow, and his pointed ears. When he smiles at me, my heart flips over at the sight of his sharp upper fangs and the jutted lower ones.

I love the strong male slant of his throat, the smooth expanse of his chest, the neat double row of his abdominal muscles, and the way his hips and stomach taper down to lean, strong thighs. My gaze lingers on the smooth, thick cock lying between those thighs.

"Don't look at me that way," he murmurs, grinning wider. "I'm spent, Feather."

"So am I," I confess.

"Then we should go home."

I wince and look away from him. "I'm afraid we'll go back and sleep, and then tomorrow you'll change your mind. I'm afraid you'll be harsh with me and reject me again."

"I wouldn't reject *you*." He sits up too. "If anything, I'd be rejecting myself. I know I'm being selfish, starting this with you. I'm immortal. You aren't. You need a peaceful life with a normal man, and I'm a condemned Faerie with sadistic tendencies. Soon I may have to flee for my life, and you can't accompany me."

He's right about all of it. That's what he meant when he said he loves me beyond logic and beyond hope.

He can't abandon the house or his duties, and I can't go with him when he moves. Our only chance of staying together is if the hunters fail to find him. And even that is a limited future, because, as he said, he's immortal. Sooner or later, he'll *have* to leave, and then I'll be adrift in the dark, lonely sea of the world.

Not even the idea of my true family is any comfort. I'm more wary of them than I am of being alone.

Krael lets out a gusty sigh. "Fuck reality. I liked it better when I was inside you and I couldn't think of anything except how perfect your cunt feels hugging my cock."

I blush violently and pull a bit of the sheet up to my chest, but I can't stop smiling.

"You're shy now, after what you just did to me?" He smirks. "Too late. I know the taste of that sweet little pussy now, and I believe it's my new favorite flavor."

"Hush," I whisper, smiling wider.

He grins as if he's about to keep teasing me, but his face changes from playful malevolence to resigned ferocity in half a second. At the same time something echoes faintly in my mind—the distant, barely perceptible ringing of a bell.

"What's that sound?" I ask.

His eyes flare wide with shock. "You can hear it?"

"Yes. Are you being summoned?"

"That's not possible," he says, stunned. "Have you heard a bell before, when I've been called?"

"No."

"It's not possible," he repeats. "None of this is possible... Shit, I have to go, and I might not be able to come back for hours."

I'd rather not linger in this inn by myself. The thought of sleeping anywhere unfamiliar without him chills my blood. What if someone broke into the room and hurt me, or stole me away? It's simply not safe. "I'll come with you."

"You can't." Even as he rises from the bed, he's changing. His muscles swell larger, veins snaking over them. His neck thickens while the goat-skull mask appears out of thin air and settles over his face. His legs shift in shape until they're thicker, more goatlike, covered in fur, and his feet transform into cloven hoofs. The ragged cape appears, cloaking his form, turning him into the hulking, horned creature I remember from the night I rang my own Krampus bell.

He stretches out one clawed hand and a chain appears in his palm. "You can't come with me, Feather."

"I refuse to stay here." I'm pulling on my dress, heedless that it's unbuttoned in the back. "You can't leave me alone in a strange place—what if something happens? Please, Krael."

"I don't have time to argue with you about this," he growls.

"So let me come with you. I'll stand aside. I won't be any trouble." I stuff my feet into my shoes, then snatch my cloak and swirl it around my shoulders.

"Fuck," he snarls. "Fine. This one should be simple enough. Once we arrive, you'll wait outside while I enter the house, understand?"

"I understand."

Hastily we sweep the items we stole into a pillowcase, which I hold close to my chest. Then Krael drags me against his huge form. As Krampus, his usual smell of fresh winter midnight is laced with the bitter tinge of blood, the sourness of horror, the dull reek of death.

My heart hammers wildly as he draws the geistfyre circle.

Instantly we're somewhere new, at the edge of a town, behind a snow-covered shed. I spot a crooked wheelbarrow, a stack of old clay pots, a half-rotten wooden lattice. The fence around the frozen garden is bowed or broken in several places. Three cows stand in a miserable clump beneath a sagging shelter.

"Wait here," Krampus tells me. He stomps past the garden, chains dragging through the snow behind him. Then, with a startling leap, he springs onto the roof of the cottage.

I'm not sure why he chooses the chimney as an entry point when he could simply smash through a door or a window. Perhaps it's a means of striking fear into the heart of his target.

Curiosity wages a swift war in my mind. On the one hand, I've never seen live cows. I pity them, and I'm fascinated by them. On the other hand, I want to see who Krampus is after, and how he carries out their judgment.

There will be other chances to experience animals up close, but Krampus may never bring me along on one of his violent forays again. So despite his warning, I set down my pillowcase bag, pull my hood over my head, and hurry toward the cottage. Krampus is up on the roof with his back to me, looking down the chimney, so I make it under the eaves of the house without attracting his notice.

I peer through a narrow window beside the back door. Its glass is grimy and coated with frost, so I can barely make out a table with a lamp on it. But I can hear a woman's voice inside, ranting and shrieking, interspersed with a child's cries. Something slams, and the child's voice cuts off mid-wail.

Terror sends a sickening thrill through my chest. Without really thinking, I locate the handle of the back door and push. To my surprise, it gives way. The hinges creak, but the sound is cloaked by the thunder of heavy chains falling down the brick chimney. Those chains will magically expand the space so Krampus can land among the logs, stalk out into the room, and seize whoever he's meant to punish.

My mind keeps replaying the child's wail and how it ended so abruptly. I have to know if they're hurt, so I slip inside the cottage, finding myself in a kitchen alcove.

Quickly I take everything in. A table in the center of the main room, with a lamp, a bottle, and a cup on its well-worn surface. A woman stands beside the table, staring at the fireplace. A few paces away I spot the outline of a trap door, possibly leading to a cellar. Was that door the source of the slamming sound? Perhaps she banished the child down there.

The house stinks of rot, of water damage, of mildew— something my kidnapper said was the enemy of all wooden houses. He was forever making repairs to the cabin, daubing corners and cracks with a tarry mixture to prevent moisture from taking hold. Apparently this cottage enjoys no such care. The odor of feces hangs in the air, too. I'm not sure if it's from humans or pests.

I can sense the cottage's personality dimly—or rather, I sense the shadow of its former consciousness, before it succumbed to its own rot. The very walls seem to be groaning silently, endlessly, the boards and beams drenched in despair. The poverty and deprivation of this place contrasts starkly with the luxury and abundance of the Mayor's mansion. It's far more difficult to be a decent person in a place like this, with so little hope.

The fireplace widens suddenly, its brick walls flexing, expanding outward. Exactly what happened in the cabin on that fateful night, when Krampus arrived.

The woman whimpers and moves back, putting the table between her and the fireplace. The flames sink low, turning a vivid red as Krampus's cloven hooves crash into the center of the fire.

The woman is gibbering now, backing away, half-swearing and half-sobbing as Krampus bends low and, with jerky, frightening movements, lurches out of the fireplace and rises up. He can't straighten to his full height, so he remains slightly hunched, his horns dragging along the low ceiling as he flings a chain toward the woman's legs.

She screams and bolts for the kitchen alcove, perhaps intending to grab a knife or a weapon. But his chains are too quick. As they snake around her ankles and tighten, their tiny spikes tear through her shabby stockings and into her flesh.

She falls with a scream that shears right through my heart. The abject terror on her face is as familiar to me as my own reflection.

"Stop!" I hear myself cry out.

Krampus looks up. His bone mask renders his face unreadable, but his tone is unmistakably furious as he growls, "I fucking told you to wait outside."

"It's not her fault," I begin, but the woman is shrieking and clamoring so loudly I can barely hear myself speak.

Krampus drags her close, seizes her by the throat, and leans down. His tongue lashes across the woman's face.

The effect is immediate. She goes utterly still and silent, paralyzed by his venom.

"Now that we have a little quiet," he snarls. "What apology were you about to give?"

"No apology," I say. "Only this—that I understand why she's angry. She lives *here*, in this wretched place. The despair, the deprivation, and the loneliness are making her cruel."

"There are many such cottages, in which mothers or fathers struggle alone against misfortune and poverty," he replies. "And yet they manage to be reasonably kind to their children. Perhaps not always, but most of the time. *She* screams at her child. She locks her child in the cellar. She sometimes eats her child's portion of the food herself. When a little money comes to her, she drinks it away instead of using it to repair the cottage. She is not the only one in a situation of dire need. And yet she has chosen to respond this way to her circumstances."

I see his point, but I'm not convinced. "What will you do to her?"

His tone is darker and deeper than ever. "What I must."

"Wouldn't it be better to help her? To teach her how to do better?"

"That is the duty of other riders in the Wild Hunt, yet they have not been assigned to her. I have. This is my role, Feather. It is not for you or me to debate the will of the Hunt and of the god-stars. I've been given my orders, and I will follow them."

My knees are trembling and my lips quiver, but I step forward, willing myself to see Krael through the guise of this

238

monstrous masked figure, this terrifying beast in the cape, this deep-voiced, demonic wielder of chains and death.

"You're just as trapped as I was," I tell him. "Bound to the role they have set for you, whether it's right or wrong. Is there no escape?"

"None. If I do not follow orders, I will be annihilated. Now wait for me outside." The last sentence is a command so ferocious his voice shakes the house.

I retreat a few steps. "What about the child? Are they alright?"

"The boy is alive. Mother Holle will see to him after we leave."

"And how do you know she will—"

"Enough!" he roars, and flames leap high in the fireplace at the explosive thunder of his voice. "Get the *fuck* outside!"

With hot, angry tears spilling down my cheeks, I march back out into the cold and through the snow to the shed. I stand there seething and chewing my lip, clutching the pillowcase bundle, until Krampus blasts up out of the chimney again, leaps down from the roof, and stalks toward me. The large blood-red bag on his back is full now, stuffed with the woman's body. When he reaches me, he drops the bag into the snow with a thump and stands there, huge and dark and furious.

"The back door was open," I point out.

"I chose to leave by the chimney," he snarls. "Are you going to criticize every part of my job?"

"Is the woman alive or dead?"

"None of your gods-damned business, Feather. By interfering with my mission, you put both of us at risk. I took a chance bringing you along, and if you'd stayed out here, there would have been nothing to worry about... but you came into the house. You may have attracted the god-stars' attention, or my overseer's attention at the very least. Do you know what that means?"

I shake my head.

"They could take you away from me." His voice carries all the wretched fury of fear. "They could wipe all memory of me from your mind. And I could be severely punished for letting you become such an important part of my existence. I've been punished by them before, centuries ago. Do you know why it's been that long? Because I learned my lesson so fucking well, thanks to the soul-grinding, mind-eviscerating torture they inflicted on me the first time."

"But the god-stars gave me the Krampus bell," I say. "They let all this happen, didn't they? Maybe even wanted it to happen."

He shakes his great horned head. "I've wondered. I've hoped that might be the case. But the more likely scenario is that someone made a mistake, and once they begin paying closer attention, they'll rectify it."

A low moan from the bag draws my attention and I wince. "Believe what you want. But I don't believe you should kill all of them. What if some of them could change? What if some of them have reasons for doing terrible things? Or if not reasons... circumstances they couldn't handle any other way."

My voice falls at the end, because even though I can't see his face, I sense the keen look he's giving me from beneath the mask. It makes me shrink a little.

"This isn't about *her* at all, is it?" He nudges the bag with his hoof.

I catch my lip between my teeth and look away from him.

"Feather," he says, low. "What did you do?"

If he'd asked me when we were in bed together, I might have told him everything. But out here, in the cold, with a moaning woman in the sack by his side, and his burly Krampus form standing over me like a dreadful judge, I can't. I don't know where to begin, or how to say it.

"Tell me this, then," he says. "Have you done something worthy of punishment?"

Slowly, I nod.

"After what you did to Midrael, I promised I'd give you the punishment you deserve. I could do it tonight. Punish you and elicit the confession. I think it would do you good to say it aloud, to purge the sin instead of letting it fester. Besides, I would prefer that there be no secrets between us. I gave you my darkest secret, after all. Yours cannot be worse."

I lift my eyes to the dark holes of his mask, my soul full of pleading dread.

Maybe I didn't murder dozens of children out of a twisted sense of mercy. But to me, what I did feels worse. It gnaws at my heart with poisoned teeth, veins of rot stretching outward from that spot through every part of my being.

Much as I hate it, I think he's right. I think I need to confess to someone aloud, and experience a dramatic purging of the evil.

Krampus steps closer, planting one cloven hoof in the snow right in front of me. His bulk makes me shiver, as does the deep, growly timbre of his voice when he says, "I need your spoken permission, Feather. Do you wish me to punish you? To coax out your secrets with the most intimate kind of torture?"

"Yes," I say.

"Then choose a safe word. It will be your key to stop the punishment, end the torture, and escape the process." He grasps my chin with his thick fingers, careful not to hurt me with his ragged black nails. "Unless you speak that word, I will consider myself free to do anything I want to you."

"Will you be in *this* form?" I ask.

"Since I am punishing you for a sin, and since my judgment of this other woman is not yet complete—yes, I can retain this form. Is that acceptable to you?"

As I nod, a quiver of pleasure trickles through my clit, along my pussy.

I'm horrified at myself. Why should I be aroused by the idea of Krampus punishing me and eliciting my secrets with torture? It makes no sense. And yet a second soft thrill teases my body as I picture it.

Krampus lowers his bone-masked face near mine, and I hear him sniff. His claws twine through my hair for a moment, toying with the wavy locks. Then he hums low in his chest and moves to pick up his bag again.

My attention swerves to a distant glow across a field, near a line of trees. I squint, trying to make out the pale shape. It looks rather like a tall white reindeer, with a cloaked figure on its back.

"Mother Holle," Krampus says. "She's coming to care for the child."

"She's part of the Wild Hunt?"

"In a manner of speaking, yes."

"How do you know she's helping the children? Have you ever watched what she does?"

"Yes, and I've met her. She is an ancient force, generous and gracious, but not to be taken lightly. We must go. Stay close, little one. No sleep for either of us tonight."

20

KRAMPUS

Once we're back in the house, Feather goes to put the
objects we stole in the library, while I drag my victim
downstairs, paralyze her with a fresh swipe of my tongue, and
fling her body into a back room of the lower level. As I hoped,
Meerwunder waddles into the room after her, eager for a meal. I
close the door behind him. He can get out of the chamber if he
wants to, but I'm betting on his lazy nature and the fact that he'll
want to sleep after his meal and digest his food for a while. If
I'm right, he'll stay put, giving me and Feather several hours of
privacy.

My victim is lucky that I don't have time to visit upon her
body all the pain and deprivation her child suffered. I'd rather be

done with her, so I can focus on the sweet torment I've planned for Feather.

The amulet still hangs around my neck, beneath my cape. I take it off and lay it aside, but I don't divest myself of my clothing or mask just yet. That will come later.

I inspect the tools of my trade, but most of them are too bloody, corroded, or grimy to use on Feather's delicate body. Fortunately I spot one of my switches—a long, smooth, pliable stick of white wood, cut from a sapling. It's as thick as my finger and nearly as smooth as her lovely skin—the perfect tool to make her confess everything to me.

The dungeon smells better than usual, since it's been free of bodies for a while, but I light a censer of magical incense anyway, to purify the air. I want to torture Feather sensually, not sicken her with foul odors.

When she descends the steps into the torture room, I'm still in Krampus form, standing by one of the tables with my arms folded.

"Take off your clothes," I tell her.

She has already shed her cloak, and she slips easily out of the unbuttoned gown. She stands naked in the gloomy chamber, glancing nervously around at my implements of torture.

I take a moment to appreciate the pert plumpness of her breasts, the lithe curves of her waist and hips, and the anxious pout of her plump mouth. She's still wearing the emerald hourglass she found, and the earrings I gave her, but those items are her only adornment.

"Get on the table and lie down," I command her.

She climbs onto it and stretches herself out, her breasts peaked in the chilly air of the dungeon. The sweet musk of her arousal mingles with the fragrance of the incense, but I detect a hint of fear from her, too. Good. It will make her confession and her eventual release all the sweeter.

One by one, I clamp padded restraints around her wrists and ankles. The ankle restraints have less slack, which forces her to keep her legs wide apart and gives me the access I need to that pretty little glistening cunt.

She's watching me, wide-eyed. Her stomach concaves with every quick, terrified breath that passes between her rosy lips.

I finish with the last ankle restraint and walk to the head of the table. When Feather licks her lips, leaving them glossy and wet, need coils low in my gut. I thought I was spent, but being in this form has given me fresh strength. Everything about me is bigger right now, including the heavy cock thickening between my furred legs.

Feather looks up at me, her eyes soft and pleading. "Before we begin, will you kiss me? Just once?"

"Right now, my tongue can paralyze you," I tell her.

"Oh." She turns thoughtful for a second, then meets my gaze again, a spark of wickedness in her eye. "If you use your tongue on me, can I still feel things?"

"You will feel everything I do to you, but you won't be able to move or speak for several minutes."

"Do it," she breathes. "I'm already yielding myself to you. I can give up a little more control."

I hesitate. "You won't be able to speak your confession… or your safe word."

"Only for a short time." Her gaze is bright, determined. "If I'm going to tell you everything, I *have* to be able to trust you that long. Krael, I need this. I am choosing this. Please… kiss me… and then do what you want to me."

The sweet bravery in her eyes finishes me. I'm helpless to resist, so I lean down, tipping up my mask a little so my mouth can seal over hers.

She has the softest lips, and she opens them wide for me. I send my poisonous tongue slithering in, deep as I can, probing the tip down her throat until I feel her gag reflex start to kick in.

Then I break the kiss and withdraw the slippery length from her mouth.

Her eyes are wide open. She can blink, but less often than usual, and her breathing isn't so fast. The poison slows the essential functions of the body without stopping them, but other than those essential functions, she's motionless. Helpless. And the darkest part of me loves the sweet possession, the ultimate control I have over her in this moment.

I take her body in my hands, right beneath her shoulders, and I drag my palms down her sides, her waist, her hips, her thighs. I frame it all, and then I go back and fondle the two plush little breasts, sucking each one into my mouth in turn. With the sharp points of my fangs I tease the rosy nipple of her left breast, smelling the sudden burst of her arousal in the air.

I can't help grinning as I step away from the table to get the switch. Feather's eyes follow the path of my hand as I raise the slender stick and bring it down swiftly across her thighs. I keep the blow light—just a little sting, nothing that will hurt for long or leave a mark. The moment after the blow falls, I take the tip of the switch and set it against her clit. Gently I wiggle it there. She closes her eyes, and a fresh flood of arousal scent permeates the room.

I use the switch on her breasts next—light swats, only enough to cause the faintest sting. Soon she'll realize that the torture I've planned for her was never going to be the physically painful kind, but a slow, agonizing tease to orgasm, followed by denial after denial. I will edge her for hours, until I'm convinced I've drained every last secret from this dark little soul.

Again I touch the end of the switch to her clit, jiggling it with a quick, precise, repetitive motion while her eyes go half-hooded, glazed with lust.

"What do you want, Feather?" I murmur, working her closer to climax. "Do you want to come?"

I watch her small pussy for signs when she's close. The lips of her sex are slightly parted, revealing her soaked slit to me. When she begins to tighten and tremble, I stop teasing her and I smack her thighs with the switch.

She can't speak yet, but she whimpers.

That small feral sound of craving sears straight through my brain, and for a moment, I go utterly mad.

I forget what I planned. I drop the switch and stride to the head of the table, dispelling my cape on the way. From the waist up, I'm the brawny Krampus, gifted with more strength than the average Fae, and from the waist down I'm coated in thick, shaggy brown fur. My cock protrudes from the fur, a massive, veined, brown length with a bulbous head that's already leaking arousal. I plant one cloven hoof up on the table and swing my hips forward so the huge cock juts directly over Feather's face.

I've never fucked anyone when I'm in this form. And I'm desperate to see how it feels.

Feather's lips are slightly parted, and I lower the side of my cock shaft against them, rubbing myself across her mouth. She holds my gaze, a debauched need in her eyes. That look emboldens me, and I grip the end of my cock, squeezing precum onto her lips, glazing them with it before I dip inside her mouth.

I turn her head to the side so I can fuck her mouth more easily. I'm too big to enter her very far, but I let her feel me, taste me. My cock is burning, aching so badly I can hardly stand it, so I wrap my hand around its girth and stroke, fast and frenzied, while the tip of my cock stays between her lips.

She never breaks the eye-lock with me. I grunt harshly, deep animal sounds bursting from my throat as I work my cock harder, faster.

When my balls tighten and the ecstasy starts, I jerk the head of my cock out of her mouth and swivel my hips. My cum spurts across her body, painting her collarbones, her breasts, and her stomach. Convulsive groans of agonized pleasure shudder through me, each one a sacrifice to her beauty, the primal sexuality of her.

As my orgasm ebbs, I turn back, poke my cock head between her lips again, and stroke hard once more, squeezing the last bit of cum into her mouth.

Panting heavily, I pull her jaw down and see the creamy white cum dripping over her teeth, pooling at the inside of her cheek.

It's the most beautiful fucking thing I've ever seen.

21

FEATHER

He's wearing the goat-skull mask when he fucks my mouth.
I keep my gaze fixed on it, on him, trying to communicate to him
how much I'm enjoying this. How much I love this brutal,
unbridled side of him. I love the sharp lines of his jaw beneath
the edge of the mask, and the way his tongue writhes out and
lashes in midair when he comes. I love the raw masculine
groans, and the way he feeds me a little of his cum at the end.

I am immobile, and yet I feel powerful, not just because I
chose this for myself, but because he is so helplessly, violently
feral for me and my body. I'm fairly sure coming all over me
wasn't part of his torture plan, but when I released that small
whimper of need, he abandoned the switch and the teasing, and

he began jerking his enormous cock like he would die if he didn't get to come.

I loved every second of it. And when he's done, when he takes his hoof off the table and backs away, I want to beg him to put that long, toxic tongue inside my sex. I don't care if I never get to move again, as long as he makes me come.

Krampus walks to the end of the table and bends close to my exposed pussy. Delicately, carefully, he uses two jagged nails to pull apart the lips of my sex. "You're dripping, precious."

As if he knows what I crave, what I need, he lets his long tongue slither out from between his jaws, right into the hole he's holding open.

I can't move. Can't gasp. Can't do anything but breathe and blink at the ceiling as his tongue wriggles deeper into me. It's the strangest sensation, heightened by the smooth silver nubs that decorate the center of its undulating length.

Once he takes his tongue out of me, it will be another few minutes before I can speak, and several before I can move. When we fucked at the inn, I could buck my hips, rub against him, seek out my own pleasure. Now my climax is entirely in his hands... or his mouth. And there's something excruciatingly erotic in being unable to react, utterly helpless to him.

He's coaxing my orgasm to the surface slowly, deftly, as his tongue flexes and curls inside me. It's coming, it's coming, and I can't stop it, can't encourage it, can't do anything but let him tongue-fuck me as I surge closer to the peak with every thrusting pulse. So close... gods... so *close*...

His tongue withdraws. Slips out of me. And I'm left quivering on the very edge, unable to tip over into bliss, unable to scream my frustration.

A single touch. Just one tiny caress against my clit, and that would finish me. But he stands there, masked, horned, and naked, with his red hair pouring over his shoulders like blood, and he does *nothing*.

This is agonizing. This is torture...

Oh.

The punishment he spoke of—it isn't the beatings I'm used to receiving. It's something wholly new. Physical pain, I could endure. Emotional pain—I'm used to that, too. But prolonged sexual torture like this, with blissful relief promised and then withheld—I don't know how to respond.

Krampus strokes his palm along my ribs and stomach, then down my thigh. He even sweeps his hand along my inner thigh, but he doesn't touch me where I need him most. Then he turns and walks away, granting me a view of his furred backside and his long, slender tail.

I struggle to moan, to murmur, to speak, but I can't.

He waits with his back turned until a few minutes have passed, and then he picks up the switch and returns to stand beside the table. I try to speak again, and this time a faint whine of need passes my lips.

Krampus's tail rises, its tufted end gliding along my leg, over my thigh. He brings the switch down in a quick arc, and its length bites the underside of my breasts while at the same moment the sinuous tail and its soft tuft glide along my pussy. I'm so agonizingly sensitive that the gentle contact feels like an explosion through my body. I whine again, shrill with need.

Krampus stings me lightly with the switch, here and there, each time in a new and unexpected place. And all the while his silken tail ripples softly over my clit and my pussy. Soon the furry tuft is soaked from my arousal, but he keeps teasing me with it until I'm gasping aloud, a fine sweat coating my breasts and collarbones. I'm straining so hard for the orgasm that I think I might burst. Almost... almost there...

He steps away, removing the switch and the tail from my body.

I clench my teeth and screech in frustration. A chuckle rumbles from behind the mask.

"Can you speak yet?" he asks me.

With an effort, I reply. "Yes."

"Then it's time. Tell me your secrets." He rakes the tip of the switch along my inner thigh, gives my clit a startling tap with it. I hitch a frenzied gasp as the pleasure flares for a second.

"I did what I had to do, to survive," I say.

"That's not the truth. That's an excuse. What did you do, Feather? Tell me."

Now that it comes down to saying it aloud, I crash into the immense wall I've built in my mind, the blockade that keeps those words from finding their way to my lips. I can barely *think* about the details of what I did, let alone recount the story.

The switch flicks my side, then taps my clit. I let out a sob when he denies me the contact I need once again.

"Your resistance to confessing this is even stronger than I anticipated," he says in a low tone. "That means it's all the more important for you to break through this barrier, so you can be at peace with yourself. Tell me the tale, Feather, and I'll let you come."

"You'll hate me," I gasp, tears trailing along my temples into my hair.

"Never."

"You'll judge me. You'll expel me from your house."

He stalks over and takes my chin in his clawed hand. The goat-skull mask approaches my face, and locks of his red hair spill onto my breasts and shoulders. "Why would I expel my heart from my chest, or my soul from my body? Why would I deprive myself of air to breathe? Why would I banish all that is joyful and interesting from my life?"

"But I hate myself for it," I whisper. "I did it, and I can't take it back, ever. I can't fix it. I knew exactly what I was doing, and I did it anyway, and that means I'm wrong inside. There's nothing I can do to change it. I simply have to accept that I'm sick like *him*. And I don't want to be like *him* in your eyes. But I can't always control myself, Krael. Sometimes the anger and the jealousy take over my brain, and I do things…"

"What things?" he presses. "Tell me." The switch glides up my leg, strikes my hip with a quick little sting.

When I don't answer, Krampus growls in frustration and stalks to the end of the table, where he unshackles my ankles before coming back to unchain my wrists as well. At first I think he has given up on me, which sends a pang of disappointment through my heart—but he only frees me long enough to flip me over onto my stomach, and then he secures my wrists and ankles again. I turn my face aside, pressing my cheek to the smooth, worn surface of the table.

I can move my body a little now, but I can't see him in this position. His voice resonates nearby, but he's out of my sightline.

"Tell me, Feather," he says.

The tip of the switch traces my spine. Then I feel its sting on my bare bottom. Immediately after the blow, his warm hand clasps one of my ass cheeks and squeezes it, soothingly but also hungrily. I feel more arousal leaking from my pussy as he taps me with the switch again, then gropes my other ass cheek.

"Who did you hurt, Feather?"

"Wife," I whisper.

"Wife? Was that her only name?"

"No." I swallow, and in that moment of hesitation I feel him climb onto the table between my legs. His fur is soft against my thighs.

His hand runs up the back of my right leg. "Tell me her name."

"Colletta."

"Good girl. And what happened between the two of you?"

"I don't know how to begin," I whisper.

253

"Try." The hot, blunt head of his cock strokes along my slick pussy, and I moan softly at the gentle thrill.

"She was the worst Wife he ever brought to the cabin. I was eleven. From the moment she arrived, she despised me. She called me a half-witted little bitch, and worse names. She said I was a conniving, slack-jawed slut, that I made our captor hard for me and then she had to bear the violence of his lust. Then she began to make sly, critical comments about me in front of him, each night. She would set up situations to make me look foolish or rebellious in his eyes."

Krael keeps stroking my pussy lips with his cock head, stimulating thrill after thrill, easing me through the agony of the confession. "What happened?"

"The way he looked at me changed." I gulp back a sob. "She was influencing him. Teaching him to despise and hate me too. I knew if things continued that way, he would kill me and take another Little Sister. I didn't want to die."

The warmth of his cock vanishes, and I cry out, aching at the loss. But his deep voice persists. "What did you do?"

"I began to play her game. I whispered to him when I sat on his knee, and when he put me to bed at night. I told him that Wife was saying all kinds of terrible things about him whenever he was gone. I said she was planning to kill him, and I told him where he could find the weapon she had made—a long, sharp splinter of wood pried out of a log. It was all lies. I made the weapon, and I put it under her bed."

His hands wrap around my hips, strong and comforting. "Don't stop. Tell me everything."

"I heard him that night, and I heard her, too. The screaming. It went on for hours. When he left the next morning, he told Mother and I not to help her, not to interfere. We peeked into the bedroom to see what he had done to her, and—" My voice breaks. "I can't describe it, I can't."

"Did you help her?" he asks.

254

My answer comes out small, as small as my soul feels when I think of it. "No, I didn't even try. I was horrified by what he did, but I was glad, too. She wanted me dead, but she was suffering instead. I realized that I had power over him. Enough power to keep myself alive. And that made me glad."

"You were a child," he rumbles. "A child raised in a terrifying situation, by a brutal man."

"But I was wrong to do it."

"You were wrong," he agrees. "But you were afraid. And that fear gave you the strength to survive." He pries apart my ass cheeks, and his big warm cock wedges between them, rubbing through the center. When he speaks again, his tone is low, fierce, unrepentant. "You destroyed the person who would have destroyed you, and I'm glad you did it. I'm glad you're alive."

The words startle me, cleave me right to the core, and spark a glow in the darkest parts of my being.

I'm glad you did it. I'm glad you're alive.

It's what I needed. Not forgiveness, exactly, but permission to be worthy of existing. Worthy of surviving that cabin, when so many others did not. My survival may not have been gained honorably, but Krael doesn't care. To him, my existence right here, right now, is worth any sin I committed to achieve it.

"He kept her there for three days," I whisper. "I don't know how she survived, the way he had cut her apart, stretched her open—" For once, I don't try to avoid or repress it. I use Krael's touch, the sensation of his heavy cock and his warm hands, as a lifeline, grounding me in the present while I face the scene in my mind.

"I don't excuse my actions, or blame her," I continue, my voice barely audible even to myself. "Both of us did wrong, but our captor was the ultimate evil. When he finally killed her, I was relieved that it was over."

"Did you ever do such a thing again?"

255

"Not for years. With the last Wife, I thought I might have to—but then everything happened so fast. He killed them, and then *you* arrived."

He shifts backward and presses the head of his huge cock to my entrance. My pussy quivers against him.

"I should have kept you with me that night, instead of taking you to town," he admits. "I regret leaving you alone. It was a cruel thing to do."

"It's in the past now," I say, both to him and myself. "You can't change the cause, the action, or the result. You can only try to do better, from now on. And that's why I had pity on your victim tonight... because I think people should have a chance to learn, and to make different choices."

"Many people deserve that," he agrees. "But in most cases, my victims do not. They have done evil beyond help or saving."

"I thought I was becoming a good person again," I murmur. "And then I struck Midrael with that candlestick."

"You were a jealous little brat. Deserving of punishment." He smacks one hand against my ass cheek, then grips the soft flesh, denting it with his claws as he forces the bulging head of his Krampus cock into my pussy.

"You won't fit," I gasp.

"Not yet," he says. "Not in this form. But if I shift forms—"

I feel him moving, changing, fur being replaced by smooth, hot skin. His cock becomes slightly smaller, and the second it fits, he shoves himself fully inside.

He's lying on top of me, humping against my body like the picture of two dogs in heat that I found in my book of creatures. My mound rubs against the table with every thrust, and my eyes roll up, my lips going loose as I give myself over to the bliss that is finally, finally going to be mine.

"Yes," I moan in blurred ecstasy, "Yes, yes, yes, I'm going to come—"

He pulls out.

My pussy clenches around nothing, and the orgasm recedes. "Fuck!" I scream. "No, please no. I told you everything, I swear I did."

Krael bends until his face is level with mine. He has dispelled the mask, and I swear he looks more agonizingly handsome now than ever before. Perhaps it's because I want him so badly.

He strokes my cheek, smiling, his face flushed with hectic lust. "What do you want, precious?"

"Please, please, please." I'm broken, nearly crying, utterly desperate. "I'm begging you, please make me come."

"How beautifully submissive you are," he croons. "My little maid in chains. Tell me exactly what you want me to do to your pretty cunt."

"Stuff me full of your cock," I pant. "Thrust into me, fuck me until I can't breathe, until I can't stop coming. Don't torture me anymore, please... I can't bear it."

He ducks in to kiss me, inhaling deeply as he presses his lips to mine. His tongue is no longer dangerous, and I welcome it into my mouth.

Then he climbs back on the table, orders, "Lift that darling ass for me, precious," and he plunges into my pussy.

I've been so close to coming for so long that I'm violently sensitive, and he's brutal this time, pummeling mercilessly into my cunt. My whole body jerks as I come with a heart-stopping, bone-jarring climax. Krael braces me while I shudder and scream, his claws puncturing my skin in a couple of places—and for some reason the pain only makes the pleasure more intense. I scream until my throat is raw, and with that scream, with that release, I expel all my guilt.

Krael lets me sink bonelessly onto the table while he pulls out and finishes with a hot spray of cum all over my back and my ass. I lie limp while he recovers his breath, unfastens my chains, and scoops me up in his arms.

Naked he carries me upstairs. Past the curious gaze of the Imp who's perched on a wall sconce, eating shards of hot glass. Past the gaps in the wall through which I spot Wolpertinger's long legs. Past an archway where the Bahkauv's eyes glow in the darkness. None of them disturb us.

When Krael lays me down on the sheets of our bed, I stretch out, warm and relaxed and at peace.

Despite all the filthy things we did together this night, I've never felt so clean.

22

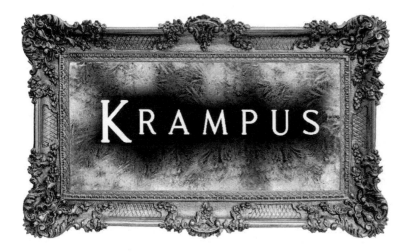

KRAMPUS

When I wake the next morning, Feather is still sleeping. Unusual for her—she's typically up and moving before I am.

Her brow is peacefully smooth, her sleep untroubled, her body entirely at rest. It gives me great joy to know I contributed to the sating of her body's hunger and the expulsion of her guilt.

Easing myself out of the bed, I pull on a pair of loose pants. Then, after a moment's contemplation, I gather up some clothes that I left strewn about yesterday, and I head into the hall barefoot. I nearly step on the Imp, and he starts to screech at me, but when I hiss "Hush! She's sleeping!" he quiets instantly.

As I head for the kitchen, he bounds along at my side—something he has never done. He keeps sniffing me. Maybe he smells Feather's scent on my body.

Once in the kitchen, the Imp scurries up the chimney out of sight, and I set about washing the clothes. I know how to do laundry—I simply don't enjoy it. My entire role as Krampus is something I don't enjoy, so I told myself I would do no other unpleasant tasks. I convinced myself I deserved to be as lazy, careless, and pleasure-hungry as I liked, as a recompense for the discomfort of my role.

But I have a new purpose. Someone else to please. Feather told me I must learn to clean up after myself, and I intend to do exactly that. It's selfish of me to leave all the mundane tasks in her hands.

Washing the clothes is usually such a dull chore I can hardly stand it, but today I amuse myself with memories of last night—Feather's saucy retorts, the fierce urgency with which she yielded to my kisses, the loveliness of her nude body on my torture table. I catch myself wearing an absurdly huge smile as I wring out each piece of clothing.

After weeks of tension between us, we sprang into this relationship headlong, whole, and unreserved—too quickly, perhaps. I worry about how the Wild Hunt might react to her presence in this house. But there's been no message or appearance from them, other than my usual assignments. Perhaps, as Perchta said, things are changing, and they're no longer interested in whether or not we follow the rules.

As if my thoughts summoned her, Perchta's faint voice echoes through the kitchen. "I never thought I'd see you *washing* anything, Krampus."

"It's high time I did," I admit, pinning a shirt to the laundry line Feather stretched across the room on the day she arrived.

"Times are shifting," she says in a distant, singsong voice. "Times and torments and terrors. And who are you now, devil? Servant to a human girl with big beautiful eyes?"

"I'd rather be her servant than anyone else's slave," I retort.

"A delightful sentiment. I am also weary of being a slave. I'm done with it, for better or worse."

I look toward her for the first time, and at the sight of her I drop the clothespins I'm holding. "Fuck, Perchta—what have you done?"

She's wreathed in blood—ghostly spirals of it. It's as if she sprang into a puddle of blood, and it splashed up around her, and then it froze there, in midair, twining around her body in slow-moving sprays of crimson.

"I'm forging a new path for myself." Her tone carries a vague, unfocused fury threaded together with pleading notes. "I was hoping you might understand. That you might help me."

"What did you do?" I repeat, moving toward her.

She darts backward and upward, floating near the ceiling with her blood-spirals writhing around her. Her translucent face tightens. "You're so judgmental, Krampus. And you have no right to be."

"Perchta, did you kill someone?"

"I only want to be like *you*," she says. "To make a difference. To end pain, to cut off lives that aren't worthy of continuing."

"I don't make those judgments," I tell her in the deepest, most commanding voice I can manage in this form. "I am directed by the god-stars. You know that. Tell me what happened, Perchta. Perhaps we can still salvage this—perhaps they will spare you."

"The only thing that can help me is the Nexus," she retorts.

"Which you cannot have. Especially since I may need to move the house soon."

"Are you being hunted again?"

261

"Yes. Two Fae-hunters. Well-supplied and full of hate."

"The most dangerous kind," she murmurs. "Yes, you will need the power of the Nexus. How fortunate that your little protégé has strengthened the soul of the house by her very presence. Why do you think she is so strongly connected to it? How is that possible for a mere human?"

"Some humans have gifts or sensitivities due to Fae blood in their ancestry," I tell her. "For some it may be dormant for generations before resurfacing. I suspect that's the case with her. There's a hint of Faerie somewhere in her bloodline, and the trauma she experienced as a child brought it to the surface. Besides, this house is a powerful force in itself. By forming a bond with her, it heightened her ability even as she fortified its strength."

"Still… I doubt it's enough to sustain her when you transfer the house," Perchta says. "So you'll have to leave her behind when you move."

"I'm well aware." I plunge my hands into the sink again and seize a pair of pants to wring out. "If you're not going to tell me what you've been up to, and whose blood that is, you may as well leave."

Perchta flits around the edges of the kitchen for a while, trailing misty blood spray behind her. Fortunately, in her ghostly form, the blood can't stain the plaster. Feather might have a fit if she saw her neat, clean kitchen befouled by bloodstains.

I wait, fully expecting Perchta to break down and confess. My gut twists with apprehension, though I try to appear calm. Whatever she did was terrible enough to saturate her ghost form and alter it dramatically. Her crimes could draw the attention of the Hunt, and that in turn could affect Feather and me.

Perchta usually confesses her thoughts to me eventually. We are not exactly friends, but we've been acquaintances for a long time, and I'm the only confidant she has. But this time, though I wait in silence, she doesn't speak. Eventually she drifts back through the wall and vanishes from my sight.

"Shit," I say under my breath.

She killed someone, that much is clear. Who was it? A parent? A child? God-stars, it can't have been a child. She isn't that heartless. She has dealt with stubborn, obnoxious young humans for years without doing them permanent harm—surely she wouldn't start now.

Or perhaps she is desperate enough to do just that.

Briefly I consider contacting the Wild Hunt myself to warn them about her. They will find out about whatever she's done at some point, and they might go easier on me if I come to them first, if I stand before the Void and blow the horn I was given, my sole means of calling my overseer. But what if they take Feather away? I can't bear the thought of her memories being erased, or worse. The god-stars might decide she no longer has a place in Fate's tapestry of life. They might end her, annihilate her, and then I would perish. I would destroy everyone and everything I could lay my hands on. I would wreak such havoc in this world that they would be forced to annihilate me too, because I can't bear the thought of existing without her.

Those dark thoughts carry me through the rest of the laundry and into the clumsy preparation of a partly edible breakfast. The eggs overcook before I realize it, and the sausage ends up burnt black on the outside and pink in the middle. I'm not sure how that happened. When I taste the sausage, my long tongue accidentally flicks against the side of the hot pan, and I swear loudly in trollish.

Feather enters the kitchen at that moment. She surveys the dripping laundry, the eggshells on the floor, the grease-splattered flagstones, and me, slurring swears around my burnt tongue.

The grin that spreads over her face is brighter than any smile I've seen from her. I can tell she's about to laugh, but she's stifling it for my sake.

"Come here." She takes me gently by my injured tongue, and I follow her to the sink amid garbled protests. She fills a cup with cold water and makes me immerse my tongue in the liquid. To my surprise, it helps.

"You'll heal in a few minutes, won't you?" she asks.

I nod.

"Then stop being such a baby."

I growl, and she laughs. "I see you did laundry. And made breakfast."

"Don't patronize me," I mumble.

Feather lays her hand on my arm. "I appreciate the effort."

I half-expect her to say that since I messed it up, she'll do everything from now on. But instead she says, "Next time, you'll try harder, and I'll help you. Eventually you'll be able to do it right by yourself."

I square my shoulders, strengthened by a determination I'm not used to, a hope I never expected to have. "I will."

"Good boy." She leans over the burnt sausage, which lies in a spider skillet among the coals, and I realize she's wearing one of her absurdly short maid's dresses, with a pair of delicate silk panties beneath it.

My whole body tightens with sudden heat and fierce need. Blood rushes to my cock, and it lifts, hard and erect, tenting my pants.

She's still bent over the spider skillet, inspecting the sausages. I can't very well fuck her right there—she might fall into the fireplace. I'll have to wait.

I've always had the rampant sexual appetite common to the Fae, but I've never craved someone this fiercely and this often. It's a ravenous obsession I did not expect. The mere sight of those panties sent all thoughts of Fae-hunters and bloody ghosts straight out of my head, and all I can think about is holding her again, feeling her silken pussy around my cock again.

I can barely sit through breakfast without propositioning her, and I manage only a few bites of the salvaged food.

"I'll be cleaning that tiled hallway outside the library today," Feather announces primly.

"And I need to set the concealment wards around the house," I reply.

She hasn't mentioned sex. She's probably sore from yesterday. I should give her time to recover. But now that I've experienced the silken suction of her cunt, restraining myself is more difficult than when I could only imagine what she felt like. I've got to leave this kitchen quickly and get on with setting the wards, or I'm going to throw her over a table and fuck her senseless.

"Are you feeling alright?" Feather asks me, narrowing her brown eyes.

"Of course," I choke out. "Never better. Have a fine time... mopping."

And I flee the room.

23

FEATHER

I'm sore all over, but especially inside. Despite the abundant slickness of my arousal, his ferocious thrusting was a friction I'm not used to.

The entire experience feels like a dream. I surprised myself with how quickly I adapted, how I drew together all the pieces I'd gleaned about sex and then leaped into the whirlwind of lust with him. I don't think I could have been so enthusiastic and fearless with anyone else, but with him, fucking felt as natural as breathing, or kissing.

Despite the soreness, I half-hoped he'd want to fuck me again this morning. But he seemed eager to get away from me. He scarcely touched his breakfast before he left the table. To be fair, he did a thorough job of spoiling the food, so perhaps he was embarrassed about it. I cling to that possibility, trying not to worry that he has thought better of *us*, and decided never to touch me again.

Carrying a bucket of hot, soapy water, a mop, and a sponge, I make my way to the lengthy tiled hall that runs past the library. I tell myself that if I clean the entire length of it, I can have an hour of reading, as a treat.

But my steps falter as I pass the library. It's not as if I'm slowing down intentionally—it's as if the house is lengthening the floor, dragging at my feet, impeding my progress.

I set down my bucket and stand the mop against the frame of the library door. Then I sink to my knees and press my hands to the tiled floor.

The house responds with a burst of pressure, an almost physical force compelling me to enter the library. At the same moment, something pulses against my chest—the jeweled hourglass necklace from last night. I've been wearing it this whole time—I never took it off, not even when Krael was torturing me so wickedly.

The house spins a series of images through my mind— Krael fucking me on the table in the torture room, his tall naked form carrying me through the house afterward, both of us entwined in the bed last night. The house approves strongly, that much is clear. It keeps pushing the word *mate* into my head.

I know what mating is—a term typically used for sex between animals. I have no idea why the house is so obsessed with the word, but I sense that it needs me to verbalize what I did with Krael, or perhaps how I feel about him.

"Yes, I fucked him," I whisper, blushing. "We fucked each other. He... that is, I..." I chew my lip, then confess in a rush of words, "I love him entirely and I never want to leave him."

A blaze of glee and satisfaction rushes from the house into me, and I gasp a little at the intensity of it. At the same time, it switches my inner vision to a view of the library.

"You want me to go into the library?" Climbing to my feet, I push open the library door and step inside. "What is it? What do you want me to see?"

The hourglass necklace lying against my chest lifts away from my skin and drifts forward, its chain tugging slightly. Instinctively I understand that it's guiding me, and perhaps I should be surprised, but I'm not. When I found this necklace, it was lying beneath a sofa, peeking out just enough for its emeralds to glint in the lamplight. Almost as if it *wanted* me to find it. I didn't tell Krael that part. I didn't want him to forbid me from wearing it, and I felt somehow that it belonged to me.

So when the necklace draws me into a narrow, shadowed aisle of the library, I follow without fear or protest.

No lamps or candles here, no faerie orbs to light the way, but toward the end of the gloomy aisle, I spot a green glow.

Tugged forward by the necklace, I quicken my steps until I see, on a shelf just above my head, a silver hourglass filled with green sand. Lush green ivy trails down from the shelves above, flanking both sides of the hourglass, almost like a concealing curtain that has parted just for me. Strangely, the stream of sand between the crystal globes of the hourglass seems to run up as well as down, so the bottom half never becomes full, and the top half never empties.

The hourglass itself has a simple design, nowhere nearly as elaborate as some of the timepieces I've seen in the library. But it exudes a power that vibrates along my every nerve, through each bone of my body. The house hums in my mind, and I understand, with sudden certainty, that the house *is* the hourglass, and the hourglass is the eternal heart of the house.

"The Nexus," I whisper.

Cautiously I stretch out my hand, and I touch the clear glass with my fingertips.

At the same moment, the pendant of the necklace stops floating and drops into place against my skin again. It's burning hot now, and the pain of the contact makes me gasp. But I can't reach up to yank the necklace off. I can't remove my fingertips from the hourglass. In fact, I can't move at all. I'm paralyzed as surely as if Krampus had licked my cheek.

For a terrifying moment I'm frozen in place, galvanized by the current of unbearable power rushing through me. My unbound hair rises around me like a cloud, crackles of green light flickering through it. I can hear the sizzling hiss of my own skin and flesh burning where the necklace contacts my chest. The pain is violent, and yet I can't scream. It feels as if a sliver of glass is searing through my skin and muscle, burning its way into my chest, pressing right against my heart, then sliding deep into the throbbing muscle. My heart beats loudly and heavily around the pain, while that imaginary shard slips in deeper, then dissolves as if it was never there at all.

Gasping, I jerk my hand back from the hourglass. My other hand grasps the pendant of the necklace to yank it off—or I try to grasp it, but nothing is there. No pendant, no chain, and no sign of any burn wounds. My skin is flawless, and the necklace is gone.

Where the *fuck* did it go?

My nails scrape against my skin, and I crane my neck trying to look down at the spot, just above my cleavage, where the necklace last rested.

There's nothing.

And yet what I just experienced wasn't *nothing*. I can't shake the odd sense that the necklace melted *into* me, that it went inside me somehow.

"What the fuck was that?" I yell at the house.

Through our connection, I sense that the house is satisfied. Smug, even. It sends me calming impulses, but it doesn't contribute any distinct explanation, only its certainty that everything is right, and good, and safer now. The word *trust* floats through my mind.

I've been working this whole time to gain the house's trust, and perhaps it's time for me to trust it in return. After all, it has welcomed me, protected me, expressed gratitude to me, and opened itself slowly to my advances. Rather like a lover, I suppose.

Perhaps I have *two* lovers: Krael and the house—the three of us, linked in a strange triad, connected in turn to the four monsters who share the place with us.

A soft, hysterical laugh escapes my lips at the thought.

When I glance back at the shelf where the Nexus stood, there's only a curtain of ivy and a row of books. I consider brushing aside the vines to see if the Nexus is hidden behind them, but I'm too shaken to risk touching it again. On wobbly legs I head out of the library.

Right before I close the doors, I think I glimpse a wisp of red smoke. I squint at the spot, but I don't see anything else.

After shutting the doors tightly behind me, I sit down on the floor of the hallway to recover. Idly I swirl my fingers in the bucket of hot, soapy water, only to find that it's cold now, not a trace of warmth left. I must have stood there, immobilized by the Nexus, for longer than I realized.

By the time I fetch more hot water and return to the tiled hallway, I sense Krampus's presence through my connection with the house. He must have finished his task, and he's slowly working his way toward my location.

I haven't cleaned a single section of the floor. He'll think I've been frittering away my time in the library.

Part of me knows he won't care. He would never blame me for taking time to read and to enjoy myself—in fact, he'd encourage it. But I want to be useful. I like my work here, and I want him to know that my efforts won't stop now that our relationship has changed.

Despite my urge to get on with the work, the knowledge that he's approaching sends little trickles of arousal between my legs. As I dip the sponge in the soapy water and squeeze it out, I realize my panties are already as slick and damp as my hands.

Which gives rise to a very naughty thought.

I drop the sponge onto the tiles, then reach beneath my skirts and pull off the panties I'm wearing. I wad up the silky bit of cloth and stuff it into the pocket of my dress. Then I get down on my hands and knees, and I begin to wash the tiles.

Thanks to my bond with the house, I sense the exact moment Krael appears at the far end of the hallway. My back—or rather, my bare ass—is toward him.

He'll understand instantly why I took the panties off. He'll know what a wicked, slutty little maid I am.

He was barefoot this morning, and he must be barefoot still, because I don't hear his footfalls. I keep sweeping the sponge across the tiles, scouring stubborn spots of grime, then sitting up on my heels to rinse and squeeze the sponge again before returning to my hands-and-knees position.

The cool air of the hallway stirs the lace on my skirt and flows across my naked pussy. I know Krael is staring right at my bare legs and ass as he prowls closer, and the knowledge makes my throat dry and my skin hot.

Later I'll tell him about what happened in the library. But right now, I simply want him to prove to me that last night wasn't a dream, that he still wants me, needs me... loves me. He said he did. But I can't be sure. I've had little experience with love outside of books. The love I felt for my captor was a twisted dependence, culminating in betrayal and violence. The love I felt for my favorite Mother was a source of comfort, but also of constant fear for her life—and it ended in agony. My connection with Krael seems doomed already, but for now I'm still here, with him. I intend to take full advantage of that.

I can hear his breathing now—slow and measured but heavy, thick with lust. I keep washing the floor, but I'm wiping the same tile, over and over.

His claws click against the buttons of his pants as he undoes them.

My heart flutters as I stroke another tile with the sponge and lift my ass ever so slightly.

Don't ask me, just take me.

I hear him kneel behind me. My fingers dig deep into the sponge.

The hot, smooth head of his cock plunges into my slit. His hands wrap my hips as he lunges forward, sinks in all the way to the hilt, seals us together with a firm *smack* of flesh against flesh.

A little cry breaks from me, eliciting a dominant growl from him. He pulls back a little, rams in deeper, and I cry out again. The twitch of his cock inside me lets me know that he likes the sound, so as he fucks me I grow more vocal, striving to please him. I fill the hallway with soft, breathless, feminine cries—the prettiest sounds I can make.

Krael stops thrusting. He leans forward, over my back, and clasps one hand around the front of my throat, gripping it tightly enough to ensure my attention.

"Stop faking," he hisses. "You're not playing a role for me. When I'm inside you, I want nothing but the most authentic cries from your soul, do you understand?"

"Yes, sir."

"That's a good fucking girl." His hand slides away from my throat, down my shoulder blade, then darts around underneath me and grasps my breast through the thin fabric of my dress. His thumb flicks across my nipple, and I suck in a quick breath as a thrill traces from that touch all the way to my clit.

"That's it," he purrs as I whimper for him. He squeezes my breast again, then runs his hand along my stomach before diving beneath the skirt to access my pussy. His Fae claws are still out, and I tremble there, on my hands and knees, impaled on his cock, while he teases my clit delicately with those terrifying nails.

"Pretty little maid." His voice is low, harsh with lust. "Tell me why you were here in the hallway with your pussy all bare and wet."

My response is barely a whisper. "I wanted you to find me and fuck me."

"Shall we have this agreement then," he murmurs, coaxing my clit toward bliss with his fingers, "that if you aren't wearing your panties, I can use you anytime I like?"

"Yes, please, sir," I whimper.

"You could be cooking dinner, cleaning your teeth, shaking out a rug, changing sheets, and I'm allowed to bury my cock in this sweet pussy anytime I like, as long as you've kept access open for me?"

"Yes," I gasp, as he jiggles my clit rapidly with the flat of his fingertip. "Oh fuck, yes!" And I come, with a shaking cry. He hums his approval and presses two fingers over that spot while my pussy spasms around his hard length.

"Fuck," he groans. "How do you feel this good?" He grips my waist and starts thrusting again, letting out fierce grunts as he increases his speed.

"Oh gods," I exclaim, shrill and breathless, as he pummels me toward another orgasm. "I'm going to come again... shit..."

I scream this time, and he bellows a huge, shattered groan. The waves of pleasure that wash over me are impossibly high, irresistibly wild, drowning me in mind-ravishing bliss. It goes on and on, surge after surge of ecstasy, and every time he starts to ease himself out of me, another shock of pleasure hits us both and he sinks back in with a helpless moan. I can *feel* him more intensely, more vibrantly than I did last night, as if our connection is deeper somehow. I feel his shocked joy, his disbelief at the violence of this orgasmic maelstrom. I sense his care for me, his desire that I enjoy myself just as much as he does.

"Feather," he pants, sometime during the storm of it all. "Feather, I love you."

I'm thrilling through another paroxysm of glorious pleasure, unable to speak or breathe because I'm coming so hard. But when the sharpness of it eases and I can process words again, I murmur the words back to him.

Finally he manages to pull his cock out of me without triggering another orgasm, and we lie on the floor, exhausted, him on his side and me nestled in his arms.

"I think you're my mate." He breathes the words raggedly into my hair.

"The house put that word in my head earlier," I reply. "What does it mean?"

"It's a unique, lifelong bond that results in unusually violent pleasure between the mated pair. It is a soul-deep tie that cannot—or should not—be broken. But it should only be possible between Fae, when one of them comes from royal blood."

"Maybe you do," I suggest.

"No." He lifts his hand to stroke my hair. The caress is absentminded, gentle. "After I left the trolls, I researched my bloodline, mostly so I could avoid my mother and anyone associated with her. She and my father were as far from royal as anyone could be."

"Maybe we aren't mates. Just normal lovers."

He chuckles hoarsely. "The sex we've been having is anything but normal, even for the Fae. This level of pleasure is all new to me."

For a moment I lie still, relishing the light, careful scrape of his nails against my scalp. It feels delightful, and it's relaxing.

"What would it mean if we were mates?" I ask him.

"Pain," he says dolefully. "It doesn't change the fact that I will have to leave you. When we do part ways, instead of a heart-wrenching sadness, our agony will be nearly unbearable."

"Sounds like my life," I murmur.

"I could lie to you, if you'd prefer that."

"No. Always the truth between us, from now on." I push myself upright, shoving my hair back from my face. "And since we're truth-telling... something strange happened to me in the library."

I tell him about the glowing hourglass, about the long moments I stood there immobilized by its power, and about the vanishing necklace. He sits up too, the lamps along the hallway highlighting the ridges of his black horns, glinting on the tiny ring in his nose. His expression grows more perplexed the longer I talk.

"Any idea what happened to me?" I ask, when my story is done.

"The house revealed the Nexus to you, and when you touched it, there was some sort of... reaction. Perhaps you absorbed some of its power, or perhaps you were merely a temporary channel. Maybe the necklace did go inside you somehow, or maybe it simply vanished."

"I thought you would have answers." I cock an eyebrow at him.

"I may be Fae, but I've never been a magical expert." He chuckles ruefully. "Even the wards I laid around the house are questionable... they represent my best guess for our protection. I can recognize certain amulets, totems, and artifacts, and I can wield specific magics like geistfyre, but the broader realm of magical study is a mystery to me, as are many aspects of this house."

"Who might have more information about the house and the Nexus?"

"Nocturis, my overseer. But I don't dare call for him. He won't approve of all the impossible, wonderful things that you are. He might try to take you from me, and I'll have to defy him, and then I'll be annihilated." He sighs and rubs a hand over his face. "So it's all a mess—one beyond your power to clean."

"Perhaps." I straighten my skirt and smooth my hair. "But until we think of a solution, or a new crisis presents itself, we simply need to do the next right thing."

He watches me as I retrieve my sponge and begin washing the tiles again. "Is that what you used to tell yourself in the cabin?"

"Among other things."

"It's not a bad philosophy." He hitches his pants into place, buttons them, and picks up the mop. When I look up at him, surprised, he smiles. "The work will go faster with two."

24

KRAMPUS

Two uneventful days pass. I keep an eye on the wards I've placed around the house. Since I can't touch the Fae-hunters' equipment and Feather lacks the skill to use it, we can't test the wards, so I can't be sure they're actually concealing the house's energy signature as well as its visual presence. But I hope that our theft of the hunters' tools will set them back weeks, if not longer.

The incident with the men who possessed iron weapons still disturbs me. I still haven't learned why those men were so well-supplied and organized, waiting for me, prepared to strike me down. I've encountered no such traps since then. It's possible it was an isolated incident, separate from the Mayor and the hunters, and that the instigator was one of the men I brought back that night. In which case he was devoured weeks ago.

Perchta hasn't returned to the house. I don't mention her bloodstained aspect to Feather, and I tell myself it's not exactly a secret I'm keeping—simply an omission so she doesn't have yet another thing to worry about.

Feather and I have found many delightful ways to distract ourselves from worries. We clean together, we cook together, and we fuck everywhere—in the hallways, on the kitchen table, in the bath, against the wall, on the bed.

I've heard that when mates first seal their connection, they experience an all-consuming sexual frenzy for a period of time. It's one more piece of proof that what we have is an inexplicable, impossible version of the mate bond.

Feather seems to have taken it in stride, as she usually does. But I sense that something else is nagging at her, especially toward the evening of the second day. She's slicing bread when I come up behind her, intending to lift her skirt and sheath my cock in her opening. But when she turns her head and smiles faintly, her wistful expression makes me change my approach, and I kiss the curve of her neck instead.

"What are you thinking about?" I whisper against her soft skin.

"My brother."

Ah. Not a good time to fuck her, then.

"Do you want to see him?" I ask.

"No. Yes? I'm not sure." She sighs. "I don't like what he does, or the danger he poses to you, but he's my blood. Isn't that supposed to mean something?" She twists around and looks up at me with huge, tortured dark eyes. "Shouldn't I want to connect with him, to learn more about my parents and my past? Shouldn't I be pleased and excited about it, rather than terrified?"

"Your feelings on this matter need no justification," I tell her. "As you well know, my memories of my blood relatives are anything but pleasant. Perhaps it's more important to create a new family for yourself."

"Can a family be just two people?"

"Fuck if I know. But as long as we're making up the rules… yes, a family can be two."

Feather turns to me and lays both palms on my chest. "Will you be my family?" she asks softly.

The question feels more intimate than anything we've yet shared. It weighs my heart, because I can't promise her forever. I can't promise her more than a day or two.

Gently I take her hands in mine. "No matter the parting that may come, or the distance that may divide us, I will be your family forever, and you will be mine."

She bounces up on her toes to kiss me, a soft seal of the promise. Then I pull her close, wrapping my hand around her head and pinning it against my heart. Praying to the god-stars that I will never have to let go.

"I've been thinking," I tell her. "We should go out, you and I. Purchase some food. Get some news about the Fae-hunters, if we can. Take the pulse of the region, as it were. See if a Fae-hunting frenzy has begun, as it sometimes does."

She looks up and pushes out her lower lip, an unconscious pout, or perhaps a habit leftover from the cabin. "But it's so peaceful here, just you and me."

"It won't be if the house is discovered."

"I know." She disengages herself from my arms and moves away. "I suppose an outing could be fun. I'll go and change."

Once we're both ready, I take her to Tanndorf, a village we haven't yet visited together. It's located slightly east of Rothenfel, within half a day's journey by coach. The best pub there is the Twitchy Toad, nestled in the heart of the village between maze-like rows of crooked buildings and twisted streets.

An ancient temple looms over it all, jagged spires of black stone reaching toward heaven.

Feather spots the temple at once. "I've never seen such a building," she exclaims, clutching my arm.

"A temple of Lugh, the trickster god," I explain. "A rarity for a village this size—an abandoned relic of days gone by, when the folk of Visseland worshiped the god-stars. At some point they conflated the god-stars with the Fae, and began to revile both. The temple was looted and burned, and it became a hollow shell, superstitiously avoided by most of the townspeople. They hate it, but it's too well-built and too monumental to tear down." I glance down at Feather's eager face and bright eyes, still fixed on the edifice. "Would you like to go see it?"

"Can we?"

"We can do anything you want."

She squeezes my arm in a spasm of excitement and I grin, drawing her with me down a street that will take us by the temple.

We've arrived during the lull of late afternoon, just before businesses close for the day and the workers and shop owners head home. Above the snowy slate rooftops and brick chimneys, the sky is a clear, pale yellow tinged with pink, a hint of the coming sunset. The pungent scent of wood smoke fills the cold air. I inhale deeply, listening to the clop of horses' hooves, the occasional squeak of a door or a wheel, the ringing of a blacksmith's hammer down a side street, and the barking of a dog.

The town seems quieter than usual, even for late afternoon. There's a tense hush in the streets, many windows are shuttered, and some of the shops have closed early.

As we approach the temple, a group of children run past us, chasing a rolling hoop down the street. One boy keeps hitting the hoop with a stick to make it go.

My body tightens involuntarily. No matter how many children I rescue from their abusers, I have never been able to purge the memory of the ones I killed. In the shrill laughter of these boys, I hear the dying cries of the orphans from so long ago.

A woman rushes out of a building and yells frantically to the children, "Be off home, all of you! The Krampus walks the night, and he's bound to catch you if you're out past sunset! He'll slit open your bellies and stuff them with straw!"

Feather vents a disbelieving huff, clearly perturbed, but I can't summon the will to be piqued by the woman's misconception of me. Memories are sliding up out of the bog of my past, grasping my brain with long, slimy fingers, overwhelming my living sight with visions of death. I can taste the disease and the rot in the moldering halls of the orphanage. I can see the sick children piled on one another in narrow beds, their eyes so huge in their small, wasted faces. I can smell the iron in their spilled blood as I end the torment for each of them.

We turn a corner, and the shadow of the temple falls over us, deep as misery, dark as my future.

"Krael." Feather murmurs. "Are you alright?"

When I look at her, my stomach drops at the sight of her small, pale face and her huge dark eyes. My limbs each feel as heavy as a sack full of bodies, and dread pools like black ichor in my stomach.

"You can't die," I croak. "You can't."

"I'm not going to die." She pulls me to the side of the street, beneath the eaves of the temple. I bend over and struggle to drag air through my sodden lungs.

"Breathe slowly, Krael," she says quietly, her hand on my shoulder. "I've seen this before—one of the Mothers used to call it a 'fear spasm.' Draw breath through your nose, and let it out through your mouth. Think about what is real, not what you see in your mind. Here—touch me."

She grabs my hand and places it on her breast, over the cloak she wears. Then she holds my other hand to her warm, soft cheek. "I'm right here, Krael. Look at me."

"You're here," I repeat, trying to grasp it.

"I'm not going anywhere, even if you have to move the anchor. I think I could survive it, Krael. I'm linked to the house."

I blink, and the memories recede to the back of my mind where they belong. Feather's sweet face clarifies before me, and I can breathe easier.

"I won't risk your life on a guess," I tell her.

Desperation flashes through her eyes, but she only tightens her lips briefly, then says, "We'll talk about it later. Let's go into the temple."

The massive double doors at the front are crisscrossed with chains and coated with posters whose corners curl and flutter in the wind. Along the broad top step of the entrance, unlit candles sit in tall clusters, wax pooled around their bases. Between them nestle children's toys and possessions—a couple of rag dolls, carved boats, flutes, wooden puppets, music boxes. Sprigs of evergreen and winterbloom decorate the clutter.

Feather steps closer, peering at the posters on the door.

"Krael," she says faintly. "Look."

Stepping nearer, I spot what has affected her so deeply. Sketches of children, all of them recent, within a couple of days, I would guess. But these children aren't missing—they're dead. Murdered, apparently. And interspersed with the commemorative drawings are notices declaring Krampus responsible.

As I scan the faces, I notice two familiar ones. Mine and Feather's. Above our sketched portraits are the words, "Wanted for questioning regarding suspected Fae sympathies or activities: Lady Laurelai Montaine and Lord Felix Brandt. If you have any information, send a message to Abil Amindi and Nikkai Richter at the Palace of Justice in Rothenfel."

"Feather," I manage through dread-stiffened lips, but she has already spotted it. She covers her mouth with both hands.

"I thought we were careful enough," I say. "Someone must have seen or heard something."

"Maybe after the theft, the hunters investigated the guests and realized we had holes in our story," Feather says. "What do we do?"

"We must leave immediately," I tell her. "It's not safe here. We'll go inside the temple and use geistfyre to return to the house. We can't get in the front door, but there's a side entrance. Come."

The haunting memories jarred me to my core, and a frenzied apprehension vibrates through my veins as I lead Feather around the side of the building. Between two buttresses, a narrow door stands partly ajar, snow drifted against the frame. I slip through first, and Feather follows.

"This way." I keep my voice low, because even though it has been abandoned for decades, this place gives me the odd sensation of being watched by the god-stars themselves.

We hurry along a shadowed hall and into the central sanctuary, a cavernous room studded with broken stone benches, with a gigantic marble altar at the front.

"This will do." I'm about to summon a chain and draw the geistfyre circle when Feather seizes my wrist.

"We have to talk about this," she says. "What if these posters are in other towns and villages? What will we do? Who will sell us food and supplies?"

I hesitate, grieved by the anxiety in her eyes. "When alarm among the humans rises to this level, I move to a new area and start my work afresh. But here I've been accused of more than just the disappearance of adults—I've been blamed for a rash of child murders. It isn't just my Krampus identity being hunted— my false identity has been jeopardized as well. And this time... I have you to consider."

"You'll take me with you," she says stoutly. "I know I can survive the transfer. As I said, I'm linked to the house. It will protect me."

"You don't know that for certain. I won't take the risk. As soon as I figure out how I can safely do so, I'm leaving you behind."

I say it with gruff, almost brutal finality, hoping she'll yield. But the hot fire that leaps into her gaze tells me that this argument is far from over.

25

FEATHER

He *can't* leave me behind. I can't bear the thought of
floating untethered in this huge, terrifying world.

I won't deny that I got cold chills when I saw our "Wanted"
posters. But the terror that fills my heart now is a hundred times
worse. And it isn't just a horror of being alone, but a horror of
being without *him*. He taught me that sex doesn't have to be
something frightening—it can be special, and inexpressibly
beautiful. He has been with many women, and yet he prefers me
above all others, despite my strangeness, my inexperience, and
my insecurity. Even when he's fucking me in a frenzy, like a
besotted demon, I feel cherished. I feel safe. I feel wildly,
wonderfully free.

Almost as satisfying is another habit he's begun—joining me in my efforts as I do the chores and clean the house. Sometimes he's terrible at it, and I get frustrated and send him away on some invented errand, but he's learning. And I love that he's trying to do better, for my sake.

He has told me about his collections, the things he claims from the worst and wealthiest of his victims. On some level, piling objects in the rooms of the house helps him feel safe, gives him a sense of ownership. Deep inside, he's still a rejected Fae child, sold to trolls, suffering everything and owning nothing.

I understand him. I'm happier with him than I ever thought I could be—so happy that sometimes I wonder if I'm dreaming it all. Dreaming *him*. If he leaves me here, and goes away, I'm afraid all the happiness and pleasure will fade like a dream, never to return.

I want to scream at him, but the words come out in a desperate, stricken rasp. "You can't abandon me. I love you."

Pain tightens his features. "But I don't have the freedom to give you the life you want, or the future you deserve. I was obtusely foolish to let it get this far, to place you in such peril. Grant me this one chance to do the right thing."

"How is it the right thing to save yourself and run off, leaving me homeless?"

"You can go to your brother and seek his protection," Krael says. "Tell him I've been holding you captive, that I forced you to attend the party with me and to do my bidding. Tell him I'm guilty of everything, and that you barely escaped with your life. He's your brother—he'll protect you. You can get to know him better, meet your parents—"

"But I don't want them!" I practically scream at him, my voice finally unleashed. I've never yelled this loudly at anyone.

Krael doesn't move, or retreat, or look shocked, even though right now I'm the complete opposite of the meek, frightened girl he agreed to shelter. And it hurts beautifully, even in this moment, that he accepts both sides of me so completely.

"I don't want a brother who's here to kill you," I shout. "I don't want parents who were friends with my kidnapper. I only want *you*, you damned fucking idiot!"

"I can't fix this, don't you see?" He's louder now. Angry, but not in a way that frightens me. "The house is doing something to you that neither of us understand, something you didn't ask for. What if it hurts you? You can't run with me, and if we stay, we'll both be caught and killed. My magic is limited, and though I could fight off a decent number of humans, I'm useless once I'm bitten by iron or restrained by Fae-hunter traps. I can't protect you, except in this way—by making you go to your brother."

"No." I say it more calmly this time as an idea takes shape in my head. "No, there's another way to do this. Think about it… the child killings are recent. They've taken place over the past few days. Yet you haven't been summoned to judge any murderers. Which means the thing killing the children isn't your usual prey. It isn't *human*. Maybe there's another Fae creature in the region, committing these murders. What if we could find out who or what it is and turn them over to the Fae-hunters? They would believe their mission fulfilled, and they'd stop looking for you."

His eyes widen with realization, and then he glances aside, almost guiltily.

"Krael," I say warily. "What aren't you telling me?"

"No." He shakes his head. "She… she wouldn't."

He doesn't have to say her name. We both know, with sudden certainty, who it is. A ghost who hates her duties, who despises the children she's sent to rebuke, who craves freedom from her role.

Perchta.

"Is it even possible?" I say in a cracked whisper.

"When she appeared to me a few days ago, her aspect was stained with blood," Krael answers slowly.

"You didn't tell me."

"I thought you had enough on your mind."

"No more secrets," I say tightly. "We both know what it is to be controlled and limited. Secrets are limits. Withholding knowledge is control."

He nods. It's an admission, if not quite an apology.

"We have to find Perchta and stop her," I say. "How can we do that?"

"She and I have a long history, and we're both members of the Wild Hunt, occupying the same world. If I'm at the house, I can contact her through the Void."

"Then we'll go back to the house. *Both* of us." I hold his gaze. "We need a way to hold her there, and a way to give her to the Fae-hunters."

"If I ignite my chains with geistfyre, they will hold her for a while," he replies. "I can confine her in my bag. But she'd still be in ghost form, so the Fae-hunters wouldn't be able to contain or destroy her. That's the purview of the Wild Hunt. Our overseers usually bring down swift judgment when one of us breaks the rules, especially in such an egregious manner. And yet they've done *nothing*. Fuck!" He kicks a broken piece of stone, and it clatters across the dust-glazed tiles of the sanctuary. The echoes rattle from the floor all the way up to the blackened arch of the ceiling.

He's upset because, despite what he claims, Perchta is his friend. I suppose she was beginning to be mine as well. But I've learned not to trust female friendships or rely on them. I tend to be suspicious of other women, cautious about allying with them or becoming attached to them. With a male, I'm more eager to become invested and entwined, to seek protection and stability. It's because of my captor. It stems from the twisted relationship I had with him.

Sometimes I fear I'm clinging to Krael simply because I've been conditioned to adore and serve the dominant male in my sphere of existence. And perhaps that's partly true. Yet in my relationship with Krael, there is a key difference.

With my kidnapper, I was always afraid of not being enough, of being rejected when I failed to perform flawlessly. I knew that my failure would lead to cruelty or death.

Krael sees my flaws and embraces them. He understands me in a way few people ever could. He wants what is truly best for me, even if it hurts him.

He was already in pain at the thought of our parting, and he's hurting even more because of Perchta's actions. Meanwhile the only feeling I can summon about Perchta is a faint regret that I let myself like her.

"I'm wrong inside," I say quietly.

Krael doesn't turn around, only scuffs his boot again. "So am I."

"No, I mean… the way I see other women is twisted. The way I view men, too. I think it will take me some time to unravel it all and remake my mind as it should be."

His shoulders stiffen beneath the heavy blue coat he's wearing. "Yes. You need time on your own, with other humans. With your true family."

"That's not what I'm saying." I release a frustrated sigh. "Let's get back to the house and deal with one problem at a time."

"Very well." His tone is dark and morose, with a hollow note of reckless despair. "Come here, then."

A black chain snakes from his hand, coiling around my limbs and torso like a lithe snake. Krael yanks the chain, jerking me right up against his body.

"Your chains look like they're made of iron," I tell him, breathless.

"They're made with a similar metal, but it's from Faerie, and it's safe for my kind." He produces another chain and draws the geistfyre circle around us.

As the circle forms, a jarring pain grips my heart—a wretched, howling brokenness that doesn't come from me, and yet belongs to me all the same.

It's the *house*. The house is screaming.

As the gray room appears around us, a mighty gale of wind nearly slams us both flat. The house quakes violently, as if it's being shaken by a giant. Its boards and beams are groaning, doors flapping and slamming, furniture tilting and tumbling across the floor. And the noise—it nearly deafens me. A great howling, wailing, groaning sound fills every chamber and corridor. The place feels as if it's about to collapse.

"What the fuck?" roars Krael through the storm of dust and crashing furniture.

I'm already leaping over obstacles, making for the hallway. The Bahkauv is there, lending his bawls to the cacophony. I push past him and stagger down the corridor.

But it's no use trying to get anywhere, not with walls shifting and floors tilting and boards heaving beneath my feet. I slide across a skewed hallway and slam into the wall so hard my head rings. I can taste coppery blood in the back of my throat.

Dropping to my knees, I splay both hands on the floor. "Enough," I cry out. "I'm here. It's alright."

I sink into the part of my mind that I share with the house, where I can see a mental map of the whole place. What was once structured is now chaos, and the house can't stand it. It's in agony, and all the pain centers on one specific location—the library. Something is broken—something is very, very wrong.

"The Nexus," I gasp out, as Krael crouches beside me. "I think Perchta was watching when I found it. She knows where it is…"

"Did she take it?" he asks.

292

"I'm not sure. But she did something terrible to it." I stretch out to my full length on the undulating floor, with my cheek against the boards and my arms spread wide. "Hush," I plead with the house. "I will help you, but you have to be calm. You have to breathe."

Krael raises an eyebrow.

"Houses are people too," I tell him.

He seems about to reply, but then he looks up, wonder flooding his expression. The rattling boards of the ceiling settle back into place, and the floor beneath us smooths out. The walls take on the proper angles. Though the wind still gusts through the corridors, it's less violent.

"That's it," I murmur. "You're going to be just fine."

I close my eyes and imagine my heartbeat synchronizing with the house, my lungs carrying its air, my mind blending with its consciousness. I picture its doors closing, walls straightening, floors settling. A pulse of power booms through one of my heartbeats and spreads outward, an ever-widening ring of soothing energy.

"Fuck!" exclaims Krael in a low, strangled tone.

Curious, I lift my head just in time to see one of the gaps in the wall, which has existed since my first day in this house, seal itself over, like a wound being closed. Plaster and paint cover the bare wooden slats, rendering the wall perfectly seamless. Farther along the hallway, the same thing is happening in more places.

"Feather," Krael murmurs, in a tone of cautious wonder. "You're healing the house."

"How?" I whisper.

"I have no fucking idea."

Since the house seems stable for the moment, I climb cautiously to my feet and we continue on toward the library. When we enter it, I head straight for the shadowed aisle where I found the Nexus. The curtains of vines that covered it have been torn down, and there's a hole in the lower globe of the hourglass.

Green sand is leaking out of it, floating in a trail of luminescent crystals through the air.

"There's no doubt now," Krael mutters. "She murdered the children, and she used their blood and their souls to fuel herself for this one great effort—accessing the Nexus."

"But she failed." I inspect one of the cracks branching from the hole in the hourglass. "She wasn't able to steal it."

"She stole some of its sand, which gives her a way to siphon its power. She may have achieved her goal and gained corporeal form, at least for a time."

I'm half-listening, because my focus is on the sand draining from the Nexus like blood from a wound. I have the strangest impulse to cup that drifting sand in my palm and seal my hand over the hole in the hourglass.

So I do it. I sweep my cupped palm through the air, collecting the sand, and I press it back into the hole. Another soft pulse of energy leaves my body, and when I withdraw my fingers, the glass is smooth again—unbroken, as if no one ever disturbed it.

I look at Krael, unable to hold back a huge smile. "I think it's fair to say that this house is mine now."

But the voice that replies isn't his. It's deeper, more sonorous. "It seems so, indeed. And what, pray tell, is a human girl doing in the lair of the Krampus and his monsters?"

I turn to see an impossibly tall man in golden armor striding along the library aisle toward us. His skin is pale green, and the locks of hair emerging from beneath his golden helmet are the rich color of emeralds. Muscles swell against the bands and bracers decorating his arms. His striking silver eyes send a chill through my body that's both terror and admiration. I thought Krampus was frightening, but this Fae radiates a blazing power far beyond anything I've ever felt. This must be Nocturis, Krael's overseer.

"You two have been extremely naughty." He looks at each of us, then points to Krael. "You took in a human woman and let her live in this house. Do you know how dangerous that is? Of course you do, and yet you did it anyway, because it pleased your fucking cock."

He takes two more threatening steps forward, and Krael backs up, the whites of his eyes darkening as his pupils spark red. It's unsettling to see the mighty Krampus shrink before another being. I want to defend him, but I sense that my interference might make things worse, so I remain still and quiet, my shoulders rounded, my head bowed. Making myself as small as I can. Preparing to flee if necessary—though running from this emissary of the Wild Hunt would probably be the last and the stupidest thing I ever did.

"She begged for sanctuary, Nocturis," Krael says. "And I didn't fuck her... not for weeks. Not until she—"

"Begged?" Nocturis arches a dark green eyebrow. "Do you think I care about her desires? I only care about your selfish behavior, your inability to see clearly, and your refusal to focus solely on your task. You're a disgrace to the Hunt, a rebel against the god-star, and a disappointment to me. Your punishment will be swift and sure—"

"No!" The cry leaps from my mouth.

Slowly Nocturis turns and looks at me. His silver eyes are like swords, slicing into my very thoughts.

I swallow hard and manage to say, "Everything Krael says is true. I pleaded for sanctuary, I bonded with the house, I begged him to fuck me. I'm the one who showed Perchta how to find the Nexus. I'm responsible for all of it."

"Perchta?" His eyes narrow.

"She damaged the Nexus, but I repaired it." Words stumble over my tongue. "Krael thinks she's been killing children, using their blood to fuel her power so she would be able to interact with the Nexus."

295

Nocturis's stare is unreadable, so intense that sweat films the back of my neck. "Have you any proof of this?"

"Not yet. But it all fits. There's no one else who could have entered here and damaged the Nexus. She's been asking Krael to let her use its power so she could have corporeal form—"

Krael groans quietly and presses a hand to his forehead.

Nocturis whips his gaze back to Krael. "You did not report any of this."

"Perchta is—*was*—a friend," Krael says. "She already lost her chance at a Final Task, and I didn't want her to be annihilated, simply because she was frustrated with her existence."

"How kind of you," sneers Nocturis, stalking closer. "And now, because of your foolish kindness, human children are dead. How do you feel about that? Perhaps it pleases you. Perhaps you aren't so different from the heartless Krael of centuries ago, when you first took your place with the Hunt. Perhaps you have learned *nothing*."

Krael has his back to a bookshelf and he remains there, his eyes sparkling with angry tears, while Nocturis looms over him.

"Would it give you pleasure to know how Perchta's victims suffered?" Nocturis grabs Krael's jaw and wrenches his face around so they're nose to nose. "How she crept into each child's bedroom, stuffed their mouths with their own socks so they couldn't scream, then slit open their bellies, pulled out their entrails, and crammed handfuls of straw into the cavity? She sewed them up afterward. Big, clumsy stitches. Does that pleasure your murderous heart?"

I can't bear the agony on Krael's face. Scarlet fury explodes in my mind—not a red haze this time, but a murderous bonfire. With a guttural shriek, I leap at Nocturis, clawing at him, tugging at his armor, striking any part of him I can reach.

Calmly he turns, picks me up by the throat, and pins me to the bookshelves.

Krael roars, "Put her the fuck down!" and his body convulses, seams ripping as he transforms into his huge, muscled Krampus form.

"There you are." Nocturis throws him a grin. "You can finally transform at will. Excellent."

"Put. Her. Down," snarls Krampus. "Or I'll tear you apart, even if I go to the Void for it."

Nocturis sets me down. I suck in a ragged breath and use it to exclaim, "You *knew*."

"I have no idea what you're talking about," Nocturis replies.

"You *knew* about Perchta," I challenge him. "You knew what she was doing. And you didn't stop her."

"You're nearly correct. I didn't know, at first. I've been rather occupied elsewhere and I failed to keep a close enough watch on her. When she damaged the Nexus, I was alerted, and then I saw it all—the murders and her rebellion. Unfortunately I didn't catch it early enough to keep her from stealing the power—a problem that could have been avoided had *you* told me what she was asking of you." He frowns at Krampus.

"I thought you could see the future," Krampus growls, his tongue lashing out. "I remember you boasting of that once."

"Only the possible futures related to a rider's final task," Nocturis answers. "I could not have foreseen Perchta becoming a torturer and murderer of children, or finding a way to take corporeal form. But those events have now transpired, which means you have your orders, Krampus. You will capture and destroy Perchta. After that, you will leave this region and go elsewhere."

"I'm bonded to the house now," I venture. "I can go with him."

"Absolutely not," Nocturis replies. "This place is for monsters, and you are human. You'll return to your own kind, and Krampus will continue playing his role for the Wild Hunt."

"But—the house—"

"—will soon forget you," Nocturis interrupts. "Distance will sever any flimsy ties that may have formed between you and this place. And if Krampus tries to defy this order and take you along, he will be annihilated, and we will find a more amenable monster to assume his role."

My heart thunders violently in my chest, the hectic beat vibrating through my hot blood until I feel like I'm going to explode. I clench my fists, and the entire house shudders in a paroxysm of shared rage. "Fuck you."

"Feather," Krampus hisses warningly.

Nocturis glares down at me. "I beg your pardon?"

"*Fuck. You.* You think you're a purveyor of justice, but you're a wicked tormentor, a power-hungry tyrant, and a cruel oppressor. I fucking *despise* you. I'll only say this once—get out of my fucking house!"

The library quakes, every wall groaning, and with a ferocious boom like thunder, a hole appears in midair at the end of the aisle. Wind rushes into it with sucking force, and yet the only person affected is the tall overseer of the Wild Hunt. His silver eyes widen as he's drawn toward the streaming void of the portal, dragged into it, and finally sucked through. His final cry of shock is cut off as the hole closes inward and disappears.

I'm not sure where the bastard went. He's not in the house, though.

When I look at Krampus, he's standing there, face hidden by the skull-mask, his jaw dropped in utter astonishment.

"Put your tongue away," I tell him.

"What have you done?" he gasps.

"I made him leave."

"You expelled a leader of the Wild Hunt from this house. He won't forgive that."

"Serves him right, I say."

"There will be hell to pay, Feather."

"We're going to pay either way," I exclaim, my voice shrill with tears. "You heard what he said. I'm not allowed to come with you. They'll kill you if I do. So I have to stay, because I would risk *my* life to join you, but I won't risk *yours*. I'll be miserable until the day I die, but at least you'll be alive, and... fuck this..."

I sink down onto the floor and lose myself in a storm of sobs.

The great, caped form of Krampus kneels beside me, and his huge arms close around my shoulders. He holds me for only a moment before he says, low and reluctant, "Perchta has physical form now, and I can see her location. She's going to kill another child, Feather. I have to go."

"Go then," I say petulantly.

He doesn't respond, only tightens his embrace briefly before letting me go and moving away. With my face buried in my knees, I listen to the clank of his chains and the rush of igniting geistfyre.

And afterward, silence.

26

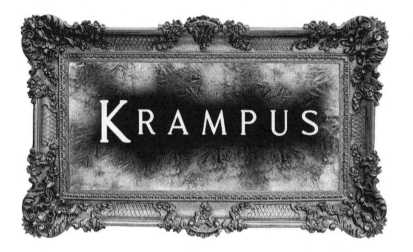

KRAMPUS

I'm almost too late.

Usually I like to terrify my victims with the impending threat of my arrival, but this time I forgo all the lead-up to my appearance, and I smash straight through the roof of the cottage into the child's attic bedroom.

I almost don't recognize Perchta. She's dressed in white garments streaked with blood, but instead of the wizened, demonic face she usually wears to frighten unruly children, she is tall and lovely, with the same elegant features she wore as a ghost—except now, she's fully corporeal. Her nails are sharply pointed, glossy white, and nearly as long as her fingers.

At the sound of my hooves, my clanking chains, and the bells in my robes, she glances over her shoulder and smiles.

"Krampus," she says. "I'm glad you decided to join us."

The child on the bed is a stocky boy with a round face. His eyes bulge in terror as he screams through the sock she has jammed into his mouth. His wrists and ankles are bound to the bed with golden strands of Perchta's hair. His nightshirt is rolled up, exposing his midriff, and as I watch, she raises a sharp nail and prepares to slice him open with it. There's a bag of straw beside her, probably for stuffing him when she's done extracting his guts.

"Perchta!" I growl. "What has he done to deserve this?"

"He's been a cruel little snot," she says lightly. "He terrorizes his younger sister. Threw her down a well once, and she walks with a limp now. Not that I care much about her, but *he* is a bad seed, and should be uprooted."

"Your role is not to murder children," I tell her. "And I'd wager some of the ones you've killed in the past two days did nothing to deserve such final punishment."

"You're one to talk," she hisses. "When we first met, you told me what you did—your great act of mercy, ending the lives of those miserable children. What I'm doing is a mercy, too. You have no right to judge me."

"In fact, I do," I reply. "I am acting on the authority of the Wild Hunt and our overseer, Nocturis."

Her eyes narrow. "I'm no longer part of the Wild Hunt. I have authority of my own now. Magic siphoned from the Nexus." She lifts a tiny glass bottle strung around her throat, and I spot grains of shining green sand within it. "You have no power over me."

"You are corporeal, and you are an abuser of children," I tell her. "I can destroy you, and I will. But it gives me no joy to do it."

At that moment the boy's father appears in the doorway, his face stricken with terror, holding an ax in his shaking hands. I sigh, knowing that his eyewitness report of this night will conflate me with Perchta and I'll be blamed for yet another attack on a child. Best to get this over with quickly.

I lunge for the man, seizing his wrist and bending his arm down so the ax blade bites into the floor. My tongue lashes along his cheek and he falls to the side.

"You'll be alright," I growl at him. Then I whirl back to Perchta just as she makes a dive for the stairs.

"You should know better, old friend." I send several spiked chains whipping through the air. They coil around her body, tearing through her smooth flesh. If she were still in ghost form, I'd use geistfyre to bind her, but in physical form, my usual methods will do.

She screams, emitting a pulse of green light that throws off the chains. I fling several more chains in her direction, grunting with the effort as my power clashes with hers.

Another burst of green energy jolts from her, but this time she can't fully free herself. Most of the magic in those grains of sand is being used to keep her corporeal, and there's not much left for self-defense. She manages to lunge toward the stairs again, but as the chains tighten, she loses her footing and tumbles headlong down the narrow steps with a scream of frustration.

"Fuck." I clatter downstairs after her, barely managing to maintain my grip on the handfuls of chains I'm wielding.

Perchta is dragging herself across the floor of the house's main living space, blood streaking the boards as the spiked chains tear deeper into her body.

"I just created this form," she wails. "And you're *ruining it!* Fuck you, Krampus, you selfish, wretched asshole!"

"I was your friend," I tell her, winding the chains around my forearm as I approach her. "Feather wanted to be your friend. And you betrayed us. You caused this, Perchta."

"Friends would have *helped* me," she spits back. "Feather promised to help, but she did *nothing*. She was too distracted by your filthy, lustful aura and your filthy fucking house. I waited for centuries, and I was tired of waiting. I bought my freedom, in spite of you."

"I told you that using the Nexus could destroy the house, and it would have, if not for Feather," I tell her. "You've done all this… and for what? Those grains of sand you stole won't last long outside the Nexus, Perchta. Your recklessness will cost you everything."

She's moving weakly now, still trying to drag herself toward the door. I yank one of the chains, and her body flips over. As I approach, she lies on her back, seething and weeping.

"It doesn't feel good," she whispers. "This body doesn't feel right unless I'm killing. I thought it would be different. I thought it would be beautiful."

My heart aches for her… but my heart is buried beneath layers of black fabric and ruthless muscle. Right now, it isn't guiding me. I am a slave of justice, servant of the god-stars, and I have come to right this wrong.

I slide the sack off my shoulder, and it gapes wide, ready to receive her body.

"Perchta, exile of Faerie, Lady in White," I say in my deepest voice. "For your crimes against human children, your existence is forfeit."

"Take off that fucking mask and look me in the eyes when you do it, Krampus," she hisses.

Jaw clenched, I reach up, remove the mask, and set it aside. Then I lean down and grip the chains that bind her. She isn't struggling or screaming now, but she holds my gaze as I lift her up.

With my face close to hers, I speak, low and intense. "I was told to destroy you, but I'm not going to feed you to the beasts. That would annihilate you forever. Instead, I'm giving you to the humans. You'll confess to all the crimes for which they're blaming me, and thereby clear my name and Feather's. They will kill you, and if they do it before the magic in that sand fades, you'll go back to being a ghost. You won't have a role to play, and you'll be trapped in the city where you die, no longer part of the Wild Hunt... but you will still exist, and you can haunt your killers to your heart's content. This is your one chance to escape annihilation. But you have to play along. You have to confess."

Perchta wavers on the brink of denying me—I can see it in her eyes. But after a moment, she nods. "Agreed."

It's a small mercy—not really a mercy so much as a convenience for Feather and me. But I knew Perchta would take the offer, because when it comes down to a choice between existing in some form or not existing at all, most living things will pick the former option.

I pick up my mask and put it over Perchta's face. Once it magically seals to her skin, I lift her hand and lick her knuckles to immobilize her for a while. Then I toss her into my sack and cinch its mouth shut.

With the bag slung over my shoulder, I stalk out of the house and draw my geistfyre circle. Upon my return to the house, I put the bag in a cell in the room below and lock the cell door so Meerwunder can't get to Perchta. The bars, the bag, and my chains will hold her until I settle things with Feather.

At first, I can't find her. She's not still crying in the library, nor is she cooking in the kitchen or scrubbing floors in the hallways. I've reverted to my Fae form, and I stop by our bedroom to put on pants, since I ripped through my clothes when I transformed in the library. But Feather isn't in the bedroom, either.

Fear begins to gnaw at my heart as I stride the corridors of the house, hunting for her. Her scent lingers faintly everywhere, not strong enough for me to follow it to the source.

What if her tenuous relationship with the monsters failed, and one of them has finally eaten her? If that has happened, I'll kill every single one of them or die trying.

At last, hot with fury and anxiety, I stop in the middle of a gloomy hallway and bellow, "Where is she?" so loudly that the smoky glass lamps tremble in their sconces.

The house rumbles with resignation, and several boards shift aside, creating a gap. Behind the wall is one of those dark, narrow passages Wolpertinger likes to use as he slinks through the house.

"Did he eat her?" I ask hoarsely. The house doesn't respond. It doesn't hate me as much as it used to, but it will never commune with me like it does with Feather. I sense that she's alright, though. If she weren't, I think the house's grief would be nearly as wild as mine.

As I step into the blackness behind the wall, I place one hand against a board. "How are we going to survive without her?" I whisper.

The house shudders in response.

I conjure a tiny orb of light that glides in front of me as I proceed through the dusty space, tripping over slanted slats and ducking under beams.

After a few minutes of struggling through the passage, I stop short. The orb halts too, glowing on the hideous rabbit face and upright antlers of Wolpertinger. He's lying down, his immense bony legs folded under him. The tiny raccoon limbs protruding from his chest are holding onto Feather's arm, which, thank the god-stars, is attached to her body. She's sitting between Wolpertinger's bent front legs, leaning against him. His flexible neck arches over her.

As I step closer, he bares his square yellow rabbit's teeth and screeches a threat.

Grimacing, I stop. "I'm not here to hurt her," I tell him.

"It's alright," Feather says to the monster. "I'll go with him." She strokes the raccoon hands, and they release her arm.

I still hate seeing her in such close proximity to any of them, but she seems utterly fearless as she pats the eldritch creature's horrible neck and then walks toward me.

I barely breathe until we're out of the passage, back in the hallway.

"What were you thinking, going in there with *him*?" I whisper harshly.

"Saying goodbye. And now it's your turn." She shoves me against the wall with all the force of her slender body, rises on her toes, and grabs my hair, pulling my face down to hers. Her lips catch mine with a fiery, tormented kiss that sends a glow right down to my bones, turning them incandescent.

"We don't have much time," I gasp against her mouth. "I have Perchta ready to give over to the Fae-hunters. She has promised to confess everything to them. She'll be our scapegoat so you can return to your brother safely. But the chains and the cell won't hold her forever."

"I wish we had longer." Her whisper is faint, agonized. "I wish we had forever. I want you to *ruin* me, Krael, the way you once told me you would. Fuck me like it's the last time. Mark me so I'll always know you weren't a dream."

With a groan of anguish, I rip her shirt wide open, tear off her pants and my own. We crash against the wall again, with her back to it this time, and I sink slowly down her bare body, my long tongue traveling her smooth skin, from her perfect breasts to her small navel, to the mound of her pussy. My knees hit the floor, and I hold her thighs open while every piercing of my tongue glides along her sex.

307

Feather grabs both my horns, a shaken moan slipping from her mouth. I gorge myself on the taste of her as if she is my last meal. I swear she will be. I want no one else who isn't *her*. Fucking another woman would make me physically ill.

"My little mate," I whisper against her quivering clit, and she whines, hauling desperately on my horns, pitifully eager for more pressure. Of course I oblige her, sucking her tiny bud, slathering her pussy with my tongue, running its full length deep inside her until she screams and comes with a violent shudder against my face.

As she's panting through the orgasm, I sink all my fangs deep into her inner thigh.

She screams again, pain this time, but she's gasping "yes, yes," still gripping my horns, still fluttering through her bliss.

The mark I've given her is a claiming bite, a custom of trollish clans. In their society, such a mark is not always consensual—it's brutal, vicious, and permanent.

My fangs slip out of her flesh and I drag my tongue across the wounds I've made. *Mine forever.*

"Every man you fuck will know I've been here first," I tell her.

She releases my horns and runs her fingers through my hair, then along my cheek. "There won't be any others. I couldn't bear anyone else touching me."

I look up from between her legs. "I feel the same way."

"Show me."

With a growl, I rise and spin her around, breasts to the wall. Clasping her hips, I tug her ass toward me and lower my hips so I can push my cock inside her. She's deliciously snug and wet, her body sucking me in, sheathing my entire length perfectly.

I wrap both arms around her, one hand fondling her breasts and the other cupped between her legs. She's small, and I have to hunch low to encompass her like this. I bend my head, my cheek alongside hers so I can observe every shift in her expression and hear every tiny gasp and shrill moan that slip from her throat.

My fingers sweep over the soft flesh of her breast, then roll her nipple between them. Her whole body gives an answering shudder, and I murmur my approval against her cheek. I lower my hips and shove upward, eliciting a helpless whimper from her parted mouth. I vanish my claws and tuck my fingers deep between her legs, adding one to her opening along with my cock. She gasps at the surprise stretch, and I grin. I thrust my cock and my finger inside her in tandem for a minute, then draw out the finger and use its wetness to massage her clit.

I'm so deeply immersed in her reactions, her pleasure, that I barely notice my own. But I'm surging toward the peak myself, gliding closer with every thrust.

"Fuck me like a monster," she says faintly, so I grasp both her breasts in my hands and squeeze them mercilessly while I rut into her rapidly from behind. Snarling, I reach down and slather my fingers in her arousal; then I hook three of those fingers into the side of her mouth while I fuck her harder, ramming her against the wall. She makes senseless, guttural little groans in rhythm with my thrusts until I come inside her like a geyser, hot and violent. There's so much that it drips out around my cock and runs down her legs. It's as if my body knows I can't have her again, and it's determined to deposit a month's worth of cum in her belly.

I cup my hand over her lower stomach, feeling the slight bulge of my cock in her overfilled womb. Feather is gasping, shaking, still vibrating from her second orgasm.

She comes again when I pull out of her, her small fingers flying to press against her needy little clit. I stroke her body with both hands, soothing her through it all. If we weren't overshadowed by this necessary parting, I suspect I could come again, too, but the understanding of what I must do weighs heavy in my mind. So I ease her to the end of her bliss, and then I carry her to our chambers and wash the cum, arousal, and blood from her lovely skin.

We don't speak as we wash and dress. Nor do we speak as we walk the halls of the house and descend the steps to the room below.

Meerwunder is lolling in the shadows, burbling hungrily, but the cell door remains locked, and Perchta is still in the sack, though she's squirming.

"She's in there?" Feather asks, looking up at me.

Fuck, I'm going to miss her mouth, her adorable nose, her beautiful, sweet face—

"Yes," I manage to say.

"I can't believe I have to go." Tears sparkle in her brown eyes. "I hate the Wild Hunt. They're cruel to do this."

"They are."

"And there's nothing we can do? No way to... fight them?"

"There are hundreds of them, Feather. Interdimensional travelers with magic, with the power of a god-star at their back. You and I cannot hope to defy or deceive them. I won't take you with me and risk you dying during the transference."

"And I won't stay and put you in danger of annihilation."

"Then we're agreed."

"We are." Her voice drops to a whisper. "But I don't think I'm strong enough to do this, Krael."

I don't tell her what I'm thinking—that annihilation might be preferable to an existence without her. I need her to be strong, and I need to be strong *for* her.

I turn and cup her face in my hands.

"Fate has been wicked to you," I tell her savagely. "But you've always been stronger than the fuckery of the gods. You'll do this—play this role, secure your future. And I'll do what I vowed to do when I joined the Wild Hunt. Nor will I abandon hope of seeing you again."

Light dawns in her gaze. "You think there's hope?"

Not a fucking iota. "Of course. The next time I see Nocturis, I'll explain that I believe we're mates, and I'll ask for a special dispensation from the god-star so I can visit you."

"Do you think they would grant it?" she gasps.

"We can try." I give her the flamboyant grin I use when I'm Lord Brandt, but I temper it a little. She's as clever as they come. If I overdo this, she'll know I'm lying.

"Very well, then." She returns my smile. "I can endure it, if it's not forever. Give me another kiss, Krampus, and then let's go over the plan."

As I kiss her, I pray to the god-stars that one day she will forgive me for this worst sin of all... giving her hope.

27

FEATHER

I've been waiting in a cell beneath the Rothenfel Palace of Justice for hours now.

When I dragged Krampus's bag from an alley up to the courthouse steps, chaos erupted. Guards surrounded me and brought me inside the building, where they checked the bag's contents and discovered Perchta, bloodstained, wrapped in chains, wearing the goat-skull mask. Someone shouted, "Send for the Fae-hunters!" and they proceeded to hustle Perchta off to a cell with iron bars, one they had prepared for just such an occasion.

I was escorted to a confession room where the constable interviewed me. I told him the false tales—how Perchta kidnapped me years ago, how she forced me to work for her while she murdered innocent folk in various regions, including Visseland. How she sometimes took on a glamoured disguise and became the charming and devious "Lord Brandt." How I managed to overcome her and trap her with her own magic.

The constable seemed convinced. And yet, when my tale was told, he ordered two men to take me to the prison at the rear of the courthouse and lock me in a cell.

With nothing else to do, I took the time to acquaint myself with the Palace of Justice. It's a massive, imposing structure, one of the oldest buildings in Rothenfel. With my hands pressed to the stone floor, I can sense the parts of it that were constructed first, and the parts that were added later, like the prison wing at the back. I can feel the building's stolid, uncompromising personality, entrenched in years of service to the city. But I sense its frustration, too. It was created to facilitate justice, yet too often justice has been twisted or circumvented beneath its roof.

The Palace of Justice despises the constable, the magistrate, and the other officials currently in charge, and when I press for reasons, images float into my mind. The constable groping one of the female guards, who doesn't speak of it lest she lose her post. The magistrate taking bribes. Guards beating the prisoners. Harsher sentences issued to those who don't have friends in high places. Brutal rape occurring among prisoners, with no action taken by the prison's overseer. Sometimes the courthouse longs to collapse on top of them all, to crush them into silence the way they have silenced the innocent and the helpless. That, in its mind, would be true justice.

The longer I stay connected to the Palace of Justice, the more it awakens. It's interested in me, curious about my abilities and desperate to communicate.

My cell opens onto a covered walkway which forms the perimeter of a large courtyard. I can see a platform in the courtyard's center, complete with a gallows, a whipping post, a torture rack, and a chopping block. The jailhouse and the courtyard fall within the purview of the courthouse complex, but it's like a diseased limb that the Palace of Justice would rather be rid of.

"There are things in my past that I'd like to forget, too," I whisper, running my palm over the stone floor of my cell.

A flood of understanding surges from the building's consciousness, and it shows me an image of my cell door opening, then a passage leading to a side exit from the prison wing. The courthouse would let me escape. But that isn't part of the plan.

"I must wait here for my brother," I reply softly. "But thank you."

A low vibration rolls through the stone, and I smile, delighted that even here, I've formed a connection. I don't even care that it's not a human being. Buildings are intriguing, multifaceted entities, with history and personalities all their own. They deserve to be treated with respect.

Another vibration ripples beneath my palms, and I sense the courthouse's approval of the sentiment.

But a voice shatters the connection. "What are you doing?"

I startle, snatching my hands from the floor like a guilty child. Nikkai stands before my cell, both hands tucked behind his back, surveying me with a slight frown.

"I was… I dropped something. I was looking for it." I widen my eyes and give him my softest, most innocent look. "Never mind that. Everything will be alright now that you're here!" I clasp my hands over my heart as if I'm overjoyed. "Did the constable tell you what happened?"

"He told me that the creature in chains is the Fae killer we've been looking for, and that she is somehow the redhaired Lord Brandt with whom you attended the mayor's party." He quirks an eyebrow.

"Perchta would sometimes glamour herself as male, yes. And she kept me in thrall. I had no choice about what I was doing." I move toward him, clasping the bars of the cell. "Remember when I felt sick at the party? I had to leave, because you said something that penetrated the fog of my bespelled mind."

"Is that so?" He's eyeing me cautiously, suspicion heavy in his gaze.

I let tears well up in my eyes, blinking so the drops will cling to my lashes—a trick I used many times in the cabin. I lower my voice, making it weak, childish, and breathless. "The sister of yours, who was taken at age six… *I* was stolen from my family at age six. I remember the peddler with the wagon and the owl tattoo on his neck, the one who warned our family in vain. That peddler is another favorite disguise of the Fae who kept me captive."

His eyes widen, and he steps back.

"I didn't tell the constable that part," I whisper. "But on the night of the party, I realized you must be my brother. My family. And that knowledge gave me the strength to finally break free from my captor. I found the recipe for a poison in one of her books, and I managed to cobble it together and put it into her food. Once she was immobilized, I used her own chains to bind her. And here she is, in your hands. You can ensure that the wicked one who has been plaguing this region does no more harm. And maybe, just maybe… you and I can be a family again. I would love to see our parents!"

He takes a step toward the bars. "What's your name?"

"I don't remember it." I let my shoulders droop and my lower lip emerge in a sorrowful pout. "I wish I could, but I was so young, and my captor trained me to forget."

That part is true. And though I'm a little curious about my original name, I prefer the one Krael gave me.

"Margaret," says Nikkai, in a haunted tone. "Little Maggie, of the big brown eyes. I can see it now. You look like her."

"I *am* her." I look up at him pleadingly. "Your baby sister. And I need you, brother. I've been gone so long. I just want a home. Someone to keep me safe."

He doesn't look nearly as overjoyed as I thought he would. Surely, if what I've read about families is true, a brother should be ecstatic over the return of his long-lost sister. Yet Nikkai looks conflicted at best.

He glances over his shoulder at his companion, Abil, who is standing some distance away in front of another barred door. Though I can't see inside that cell, I would guess that Abil is questioning Perchta.

Something isn't right. Perhaps I overacted my part.

Or what if Perchta lied to us? What if she told a different story than the one Krael gave her to tell? What if she decided to betray us again?

I only saw her briefly when Krael released her from the bag to explain the plan. She seemed willing to go along with it all, eager for a chance to be a ghost again rather than be annihilated completely. In fact, she seemed so subdued, so repentant, that I felt sorry for her. Pity led me to trust her. Maybe that was a mistake.

Now that she's here, what's stopping her from telling the humans anything she likes? She'll be executed and end up as a ghost either way. Why not fuck us over in the process?

"You *are* my brother," I say quietly to Nikkai. "What drew us together at that party wasn't romantic—it was something deeper. We share the same blood, the same family. We're the same, you and I."

"But we're not the same." When he turns back to face me, his brown eyes are emotionless, his features wooden. "You've been contaminated by evil. You were raised by the Fae, infused with their dreadful magic, poisoned by their words from a young

317

age. I can't take you back to our parents. Who knows what demented ideas have been implanted in your brain, what violent fits you might be prone to? I can't do that to them. They've suffered enough—they don't need a Fae-cursed daughter to care for in their old age."

Cold claws of dread pierce my heart. "You're saying I would be a danger to them. I promise I wouldn't."

"A danger, yes. But also a burden. Who will marry you now, after you've been corrupted by the Fae? You'll be a spinster, lingering alone in the shadows, using up the resources our parents worked for their whole lives. When the Fae-cursed do return from their captivity, they are usually violent, lecherous, or mad. It's not always readily apparent, but judging by the way you tried to seduce me the night of the party, you're sex-obsessed, and likely mad as well."

Violent. Lecherous. Mad.

The words hurt because they're true. I was raised in a household of sudden violence, and I can be unexpectedly violent at times. I'm obsessed with sex, as long as it's Krael doing the fucking. And my connection with buildings might be considered the result of an unhinged mind.

I certainly feel rather unhinged at the moment. Because I'm standing before my older brother, expecting to be welcomed into the family… and yet I'm being rejected *because* of the trauma that ripped me away from them. I've been soiled, so he doesn't want me anymore. I'm broken, and he can't be bothered to fix me.

I lean closer, my fingers tightening on the bars. "Please… I need my family. Where else can I go?"

He avoids my gaze. "Where you can't do any further harm. Where we send all the Fae and the Fae-cursed."

"To death," I whisper. "You put them to death. You're going to have me killed?"

"The alternative is too risky. The Fae-cursed attract more Fae. They're weak and volatile—they're leeches, not contributing members of society. Our parents and siblings think you've been dead for years, and it's kinder to let them continue believing that. I won't cause them more pain."

"But I'm your little sister," I gasp.

He looks at me then, his gaze hard as stone. "Not the one I wanted."

Then he turns on his heel and strides across the courtyard to join his fellow hunter.

I stagger backward until I hit the rear wall of my cell and I crumple to the floor. My mind whirls, unable to grasp what just happened.

Until now, my worst fear was that Nikkai might not believe me about our familial bond. But he *does* believe me. And like my captor in the cabin, he's going to murder me for not being the perfect Little Sister he envisioned.

I'm ruined. I'm wrong. I'm a risk. I'll disturb his family's peace, burden his parents, traumatize everyone afresh. It's better if I'm gone.

They were better off without me.

I stay frozen in that spot all night. I don't eat the simple meal they pass through the cell door. I don't sleep. I barely blink. I don't respond when Abil and Nikkai come to my cell to tell me that Perchta did, in fact, betray me by telling a wildly different story from the confession she was supposed to make.

Of course she betrayed me. People always do. They're fickle, self-serving worms. None of them deserve my trust or my affection.

I suppose by remaining in this frozen state I'm feeding the suspicion Nikkai has about me—that I'm a demented wretch corrupted by the Fae. I'm adding fuel to my own pyre. But I can't bring myself to care. By this point, Krael is gone. Out of reach. He won't know I'm dead until long after it happens. And even if he knew I was in danger, I doubt he'd defy his orders to save me.

I'm on my own.

At dawn, the gates to the prison yard are opened, and people from the city begin to trickle in, bringing stools, benches, or blankets. They arrange themselves in rows around the central platform. I don't understand why they've come until I overhear a small boy crowing excitedly about the "execution of the Faeries" that he'll get to see today. He and his mother claim seats right in front of my cell. They're so close to the bars I could almost reach out and touch them.

A few men climb the platform to remove the chopping block and the whipping post from their stations. Then they coat the boards of the platform with some kind of black substance, and set up a different post instead, near which they pile bundles of sticks.

"That's the stake where the Faerie will burn," explains the mother of the boy. "The black stuff is to keep the fire from spreading."

"I heard they're burning two of the bastards today," says a man nearby.

"Two *whores*," an old woman corrects him. "They're both female. Though they say one used to take male form and fuck the young ladies of the region." She shakes her bonneted head.

The mother of the boy covers her son's ears and looks reproachfully at the old woman. "Please watch your language."

I stifle a snicker, absurdly amused by a mother who would bring her child to watch living things burn alive, then fuss about him hearing a couple rough words.

The day is gray and cold, and the people shiver under shawls and blankets while they wait for the spectacle they've come to see. I'm wearing a simple black dress and a cloak, and I should be chilly, but somehow the Palace of Justice has rerouted warmth from a distant fireplace through the stones of my cell, so I'm quite comfortable. I thank the courthouse by letting it fill my mind with its worst memories of injustice. It needs someone to listen, to understand.

Around mid-morning, a man in a slouchy cap winds his way through the crowd. A shallow box hangs around his neck by a thick strap, and in that box he carries steaming mugs of tea and cider which he sells to the chilled citizens. The aroma of cinnamon, hot herbal tea, and musky pipe smoke fills the air, but there's an unshakeable stink of excrement, too, since each cell has no toilet, only a bucket in the corner. Perchta and I aren't the only prisoners, by any means. I see faces pressed to the bars of almost every other cell along the outskirts of the courtyard. The other inmates are just as eager to watch us burn as the citizens are.

They take Perchta first. She still has corporeal form, though she's looking a bit translucent around the edges. She's no longer wearing the pendant with the green sand—they must have taken it from her. Its magic was nearly spent, anyway.

Except for her height and the pointed tips of her ears, she looks vulnerably human as they lead her up to the stake. Her long golden hair falls in wavy sheets, nearly touching her bare feet, and her blood-streaked white gown flutters in the icy wind.

Perhaps some of the children she killed did awful things. I can believe it, judging by what I've seen of their parents. But the evil wasn't necessarily their fault. With time they could have learned better, done better... yet she didn't give them a chance.

She had the power to end them, so she did. And they were helpless, because power is rarely given to the ones who truly need it.

I watch the hunters bind Perchta with chains of iron that make her scream. I watch them pile sticks around her. I watch the hunter Abil step forward, carrying a purple flame on a silver torch, and light the kindling.

I watch Perchta burn, knowing I will be next. And perhaps that is best, after all. Perhaps I should go where I can't harm anyone else and where no one can hurt me. I can't have Krael, or the house, or my monsters... and I can't have my birth family. What else is there?

The purple fire set by the Fae-hunters must be magical, because Perchta's execution is over within seconds. Her body turns gray, then explodes into ashes that drift down onto the crowd. Some of the women scream in disgust. The boy in front of my cell leaps to catch the falling flakes.

It's over too quickly, and the crowd isn't pleased. They wanted to watch skin blacken, eyes melt, flesh roast. They wanted more screams.

"Let's have the next one!" bellows a man.

The courthouse workers appear again to set the stage for the next execution: mine.

"Are you just going to sit there?" whispers a voice by my ear.

Startled, I whip around and see the faintest wispy outline of Perchta, all golden and white, drifting in the shadowy corner of my cell. Glancing around, I determine that I must be the only one who can perceive her, at least for the moment.

"So you're back," I murmur. "That was quick."

"Rebellious women never really die." She gives me a ghostly smile. "In this universe of realms and magic and dimensions, there are countless possibilities. The real power, my darling, is the indomitable soul inside you. The will that simply refuses to yield. You and I both have that reckless, indestructible spirit."

"And I should listen to you, after you betrayed me?"

She titters softly. "The story I told to these fools was never the important part. I knew, once I saw those two hunters, that they would have your life either way, by death or imprisonment. What I said to them didn't matter."

She's right, though I detest admitting it, even to myself. "Still... I hate you for what you did to those children, and for cracking the Nexus, and for breaking my trust."

"And I hate you for not being the friend I hoped you would be," she retorts.

"Then why are you here at all?"

"It's self-serving, really," Perchta says. "I'd rather not be stuck haunting this one building for eternity. I have other plans. So if you don't mind, it's time for you to reach down into that rebellious little heart of yours, and *do it*."

"Do what?"

She smiles. "Everything."

And with that word, she fades into the stone.

Her voice rings in my mind even after she's gone, like a Krampus bell reverberating through veils of death and time, growing ever louder.

I watched Perchta burn, just like I watched Mother and Wife die. Back then I sat still and quiet. I did not try to escape.

But this time...

This fucking time...

This time, I am done yielding to the will of men.

A low pulse of power throbs through my heart... echoes of the energy I felt when I touched the Nexus. I remember the way the hourglass necklace seared my chest, the way it seemed to melt *inside* me. In this moment, I'm more convinced than ever that its magic lies at my core, fueling and amplifying what I've always been able to do—which is *everything*.

The stone floor trembles beneath my hands.

And suddenly, I know what to do.

I fix one goal in my mind—to get out. To free myself of them all, forever. To crush anyone or anything in my way.

You were built for justice. I speak to the courthouse in my mind. *And they used you for greed, for gain, for lust, for evil. This is the end of it all.*

The Palace of Justice responds with an exultant groan and a shuddering quake that spurs cries of alarm from the crowd in the courtyard.

When I rise from the floor, the walls of my cell explode.

Stone and mortar and splintered wood fly outward as the prison self-destructs, cell after cell bursting apart, all around the perimeter of the courtyard. The stone floor beneath my feet lurches upward, buoying me higher, carrying me aloft on a gliding platform supported by the whirling shards and broken stone of the destroyed prison wing.

I have never soared so high in my life.

Below me, people are screaming, crouching in the debris or scrambling to get out of the courtyard. I glide through anyway, bruising and breaking them with the rumbling force of my passage.

Shrieks of "witch" and "Fae-cursed" pierce the air, but I am not the hungry, half-frozen girl who stumbled barefoot into a tavern, hoping for a welcome that never came. I do not care what they think of me.

Rising higher, I face the bulk of the courthouse. I'm still connected to it, linked by the whirlwind of rubble that uplifts the piece of stone floor on which I ride. I drop to one knee, slamming my palm to the chunk of stone, and with a thunderous implosion, the Palace of Justice crumbles, folding in on itself. Giant slabs of roof, great columns, thick walls, arched windows—everything tumbles inward as the oldest building in

Rothenfel finds its justice at last. Clouds of smoke and dust billow upward into the gray sky.

As the courthouse collapses, my link to it falters. I ride the last wave of its energy over the rubble, down to the street.

"Thank you," I whisper as its consciousness fades from mine.

As my feet touch the cobblestones, I shiver with the fresh burst of power that engulfs my body. I'm not sensing just one building now—I can feel all the structures flanking this street. Law offices, lenders, money-changers, counting houses, the mansions of the rich and the wicked, their places of business. I think of the Mayor's mansion, of its gibbering hunger for the pain of living things.

A volcanic hatred erupts through my heart, and with it a surge of energy, like lava outflowing in rivulets, seeking out each structure. I pull the buildings to me, and they crack wide open, disgorging desks and carpets and paintings. Fireplaces collapse and set curtains aflame, windows burst into shimmering shards, and pieces of each destroyed structure rush to me, assembling themselves beneath me, lifting me even higher, forming a makeshift throne perched on long, jointed legs fashioned from debris.

I sink onto my new chair, three stories above the tiny people running along the street. They look so absurdly helpless that I want to laugh and cry at the same time. I feel no pity for them— all the people of this region ever did was reject me. Perhaps now they will learn some respect.

I'm not Little Sister anymore, nor am I the maid to Krampus. I'm the Queen of this city, gifted with the glorious power to crush everything they've ever built.

My long-legged throne strides down the street, and I summon more buildings, tearing pieces out of them to build my seat higher, larger, more secure, more imposing. I have two destinations in mind—first, the Mayor's house, and then, the quarry where Krampus's house resided. Krael has probably left already, but it's the only place I want to go. My last point of connection to him.

By the time I reach the Mayor's mansion, I'm riding a gigantic monster built from the debris of his city's wealthiest district. The beast I've made is tall like Wolpertinger, hunched like the Bahkauv, with the Imp's long, writhing tail and tentacled arms like Meerwunder. I ride on its head, my throne flanked by two gigantic, curved spikes of black metal, like Krampus's horns. I grip them, using them to steer my monster.

The city's guard is assembling now, emerging from side streets, trying to get their horses to approach my beast, to no avail. I have to laugh, because their little swords and axes are no match for me. Nor is their fire. If they set part of my monster alight, I discard the burning bit of wood or plaster and summon another piece to take its place. If they fire crossbows, I block the incoming missiles with bits of broken doors or pieces of wall.

For once in my life, I feel invincible. Strong as a queen. Powerful as a goddess.

I bring my monster to a halt before the Mayor's mansion. It knows me. It remembers the taste of my pain, and what Krael and I did within its walls. It isn't bonded to me like Krampus's house, nor is it self-sacrificial like the courthouse. It wants to survive, and it trembles, trying to resist the pull of my will.

But this place feels like a locus of cruelty and greed, like the dark Nexus of Rothenfel, and I'm determined to bring it down. I focus all my mental powers on undoing its very foundations— but in that moment of intense focus, I forget to be aware of my surroundings.

I hear the singing whine of the arrow a second before it sinks into my left side, below my breast.

It didn't touch my heart, but I know instantly that it sliced something vital. With a shriek I turn, glaring down, seeking the face of the one who shot me.

I shouldn't be surprised that it's my brother. He's standing at the peak of a half-collapsed building, on a mountain of debris, bow in hand.

I suppose I proved him right, after all. Violent, twisted, mad. Too great a risk. Although if he'd been glad to see me, if he had accepted me and loved me, this would never have happened. *He* is the wicked one, not me.

Warm blood spills from the wound, soaking the side of my dress, and I think of Perchta in her tattered, bloodstained garments. I never did get to hear her whole story, how she came to be part of the Wild Hunt.

The power inside me quivers, flickering as my body begins to react to the wound—a mortal wound. My monster shudders beneath me, and its legs wobble. My heart throbs violently in my chest, a frantic series of beats before it slows down... slower... slower.

Everything I've collected, each column and shutter and floorboard, each door and brick and window-frame—it all collapses beneath me, and I'm left prone and gasping on top of a pile of rubble, with an arrow jutting from beneath my breast. The feather on the arrow is white, pure and pretty.

"Feather," I whisper.

My left lung feels oddly heavy, and a trickle of salty blood runs from the corner of my mouth.

I've been ready to die for a long time. Ever since my first bleeding. I did everything I could to avoid it, but I don't fear it now, especially since I got the chance to wreck this city first. I didn't burn at the stake—I destroyed whole buildings, crafted a monster of my own, and rode it all the way to the Mayor's mansion. It's not exactly a victory, but it was glorious.

Rebellious women never truly die.

A snowflake touches my cheek, melting instantly, and I smile a little as I close my eyes.

A horrible, earsplitting, bone-cracking howl splits the air, and my eyes flash open again.

I know that dreadful howl.

Wolpertinger.

The screams of the citizens, which quieted when I fell, start afresh, and beneath their shrill notes I recognize the bawling cry of the Bahkauv, and then the sound of something with huge, heavy appendages, flopping and slithering and slurping. *Meerwunder.* The city guards yell, their voices rising high with terror.

I want to see what's happening, but I can't move. I stare up at the drifting snowflakes, pretending that each one that touches my skin is keeping me alive. I can stay awake for *one more snowflake.* And then one more after that. I can hold out a little longer, because unless I'm going mad and imagining it all, the monsters of the house have come to save me, and that means *he* is here too.

Steps crunch somewhere nearby, and a timber groans under a sudden weight. Something is climbing the pile of debris, working its way toward me. I think I hear the muffled tinkle of a sleigh bell.

Gritting my teeth, I manage to turn my head.

A hulking, horned shape is mounting the heap of rubble, dressed in a huge black cape whose ragged edges stream like dark smoke on the wind. He's wearing another goat-skull mask and using a long, sturdy stick to help him climb higher on the mountain of broken buildings.

I try to speak. Blood bubbles from my mouth instead.

Krampus bends over me. "Don't try to talk," he says, low and tender. "Had a little fun without me, did you?"

I smile through the blood.

"Fucking humans," he growls. "They deserve everything the beasts will do to them."

A few garbled words crawl from my lips. "You... didn't leave."

"I tried. The house wouldn't budge. I went to check on the Nexus, and it was dead. All the light gone, the sand motionless. That's when I realized the truth." He leans closer, his long red hair brushing my cheek. "All its magic went into you. You *are* the Nexus. The new soul of the house. And I need to get you home, so you can heal."

He bends to lift me, but a voice cries out, "Don't move, or I'll shoot her!"

My brother stands several paces away, having climbed the rubble from the opposite side. His dark eyes are wild, his teeth bared and clenched. He holds an arrow in place with his tattooed fingers, ready to fire at me.

Krampus straightens, a growl rumbling in his chest. "Nikkai Richter. We meet again."

"I knew the killer wasn't that golden-haired woman," my brother says. "It was *you*."

"She killed the children," Krampus corrects him. "I did the rest. Well... most of it."

"You stole our equipment."

"We did. Your sister helped me. I take it your reunion did not go well?"

"She's tainted. Ruined," spits Nikkai. "Corrupted by Fae magic and madness. I wish she had died as a child, rather than becoming this... *thing*."

"Turn your arrow on me, boy," says Krampus darkly. "She's dying anyway. Not much use threatening her. I supposed the arrowhead is made of iron, or at least iron-clad?"

"That's right." My brother narrows his eyes. "But you have some means to protect yourself against iron, do you not?"

"I did." Krampus casts a sheepish glance down at me. "Unfortunately I lost the amulet somewhere. I had to leave my house quickly and didn't have time to search for it. Your sister

329

has tried to teach me to put things back where they belong... but I haven't yet learned my lesson."

"Let's find out if you're lying," Nikkai grits out. But as he adjusts his aim, angling the bow toward Krampus, a storm of spiked chains burst from both of Krampus's clawed hands, winding around my brother's torso. The arrow flies, striking Krampus in the shoulder, and he roars with pain—yet he manages to keep a grip on the chains and constrict them around Nikkai's body. My brother screams as the spikes bite deep into his flesh. He crashes onto the debris, flailing, struggling to break free.

Dizzily I drag myself halfway up, propped on my arms, so I can look him in the face. "Nikkai!" I shriek.

He stills for a moment, his eyes meeting mine.

"You didn't look for me," I rasp. "You let your hatred of the Fae cloud your mind until you couldn't see the human evil that visited you every year and slept under your roof. All those years, I needed my family. And when you finally found me, you despised me for things beyond my control. How is that fair?"

There's no flicker of guilt in his eyes, only rage and desperation. His arm twists in the chains, fingers reaching for his pocket—perhaps for some amulet or charm to defend himself.

Krampus looks over at me, and though he's masked, I sense the question.

"Yes," I whisper. "You can kill him now."

But before Krampus can move, a tiny streak of fur flies through the air. The Imp's rows of razor teeth gleam as he bounces all around Nikkai, slicing and dicing as he goes. Even though I turn away quickly, my brother's blood still spatters my cheek. Large snowflakes drift into the slick wetness across my face.

Nikkai's death feels like the end of a nightmare. I search for sadness within myself and find only vestiges of it. My real family was always a nebulous dream, anyway, and I'm not sorry to restore them to that state of vague non-existence. I have a new family now.

Krampus sways and falls beside me, grunting with pain, his claws fumbling with the arrow in his shoulder. Somehow he manages to produce one more chain and swing it in a circle around both of us. The geistfyre leaps up, and suddenly we're back in the house, in the gray room. The transition has never felt more jarring, or more welcome.

The house greets us with a groan—half pleasure at our return, half agony when it realizes how injured we are. Strangely, the moment I'm within its walls, I feel stronger. Strong enough to seize the arrow between my ribs and yank it out. More blood gushes from the wound, and I hold my hand over it, pressing firmly.

"The monsters," I say. "You set them free. They'll kill so many people..."

"Serves them right," he chokes out. "But don't worry... our housemates will come back to the quarry soon. They are bound to the house. Can't survive long outside it."

I drag myself nearer to him and close my blood-slick fingers around the iron-tipped arrow in his shoulder. It's lodged tighter than mine was, but with a scream of effort, I manage to pull it out. I roll onto my back, panting. "You fucking *lost* the amulet?"

"I'll look for it later," he promises, with a pained, rueful chuckle.

I can't help a small laugh too, and it hurts. "What was that you once said, about Fae essences helping humans heal faster?"

"It's a primal sort of magic, most effective when distilled in the form of consumable potions—which is beyond my skill," he says. "But it can work in raw form, too, especially if there's a strong connection between the human and the Fae."

"So if I'm your mate..."

"Yes. It should work. Sex helps the Fae heal, and my cum, sweat, blood, and tears will help you heal."

"A messy business, and painful," I breathe. "But perhaps we should get on with it, before we both die."

"It's only logical," he replies.

I struggle out of my cloak and drag my skirts up to my waist, but it's all I have strength to do before I fall back onto the floor, weak and panting. Debilitating as iron can be for him, his exposure was short-lived this time, so despite the pain, he can move. Without being asked, he takes the lead in our dance of survival.

He hasn't transformed back into his Fae aspect yet, and watching his great cloaked form descend on top of me is a little terrifying. But I'm so elated to be back in the house that I scarcely mind the bulk and weight of him, or the ponderous heft of his huge Krampus cock as it settles between my legs. He growls when he encounters my underwear, and he rips them apart with his claws.

"No one touches this little cunt but me," he rumbles, tracing a claw along the seam of my pussy.

"This is your little cunt," I echo softly.

He doesn't enter me right away, but braces himself on his good arm and rubs his giant cock over my pussy, again and again, while he grows thicker and harder. Wetness seeps from my body with each glide of his length, until I'm helplessly slick for him. With a violent groan of bliss and agony, he comes, spurting thick streams of cum across my bare skin.

He doesn't wait to recover from his orgasm. He sweeps some of the cum into the arrow wound below my left breast, then spits into the wound as well. Finally, he slicks his fingers with his own blood and mixes that into the strange poultice he's made for me.

"A three-fold application of Fae essence," he says. "A powerful remedy."

"Disgusting," I whisper.

"I wish I knew a better way."

"Krael. I'm teasing." I reach up and stroke the line of his jaw beneath the mask.

At my touch, he transforms, reverting back to his lithe, handsome self, and the first thing he does is slide his cock deep inside me. He's still bleeding, crimson drops falling from his shoulder onto my breast, but I don't care. I lie on the floor of my house, drawing strength from it and from him, watching his silky red hair sway and his beautiful face tighten with anguished bliss as he fucks me. When he comes again, I reach down and cup his perfect ass, drawing him deeper.

We lie tangled on the floor afterward, healing slowly, half-insensible, only conscious of each other, until a distant yowl stirs me out of my daze.

"That sounds like Wolpertinger," I murmur, trying to figure out which limbs are Krael's and which are mine.

"I'll go and fetch him, and the others." He gets to his feet, still a bit unsteady, but to my delight, the wound in his shoulder has nearly closed.

Without bothering to clothe himself, he summons a chain, draws a circle, and vanishes. I decide it's best if I'm out of the way when they return, so I climb shakily to my feet and stumble over to a faded couch. In the moment, it's the most comfortable piece of furniture I've ever collapsed on.

I peer down at the wound under my breast. From what I can see, it's healing more rapidly than I dreamed it would.

"So I'm not going to die, after all," I say aloud, and the house sends a pulse of joy from its being into mine.

I can't help smiling. It's a delicious feeling, being wanted—and strange, too, coming on the heels of my brother's rejection, the bloodthirsty eagerness of the crowd in the prison, and the violent magic I tapped into at Perchta's prompting. Too much has happened in the past few hours. My brain can scarcely contain it, or cope with it.

For now, all I need to know is that I am safe. I am quiet. I am lying in the gray room I know so well, on a couch with deep cushions, in peaceful silence. The house is with me, part of me. And my lover has gone to retrieve our monstrous housemates, of whom I've grown unexpectedly fond.

I won't think about the future right now, about where we'll have to move, and what the Wild Hunt will do to us, and how we'll manage to stay together and stay alive. I will simply close my eyes, and rest.

For all of ten seconds. And then Krael reappears with a very irate Wolpertinger, who delivers an earsplitting howl before loping off to find one of his favorite passages to hide in.

Meerwunder comes next, and requires much persuasion to go back downstairs. Then the Bahkauv, who nuzzles up to me briefly before Krael shoos him off into the house.

The Imp is the last to return, riding on Krael's shoulder. He leaps to the floor the moment they arrive and races over to me. His terrible little teeth are scarlet with blood, and his tail is drenched with it.

"I'll boil some water so you can bathe," I tell him, and he chitters with delight at the prospect.

But Krael says, "His bath can wait. I'm preparing yours first."

28

We spend a full day in bed, recovering. The sex is slow and gentle, and we kiss more than we speak to each other. Feather doesn't cry, which concerns me a little. Whatever she went through in Rothenfel, before I arrived, it made her rebuild some of the defenses around her heart.

I want to give her all the time she needs to heal, and to open up to me. But I know we can't linger like this. One of the Fae-hunters is dead for certain, and I'm fairly sure I saw the Bahkauv swallow the other, but thanks to all the destruction we wrought, more hunters will be arriving in Visseland with all possible speed. We'd best be gone before that.

After I left Feather in Rothenfel, I didn't leave at once. I spent hours in the library, tearing through books, trying to figure out a way to circumvent the will of the Wild Hunt. Then I sat motionless and empty for a long time, lost in the center of the mountain of books.

I did not weep. My grief was too great for tears, too heavy for sobs. A sorrow as vast and soundless as the Void.

At last I scraped together the frayed shreds of my will, and I searched for the Nexus, a necessary component of the transference. Before, whenever I needed to move the house, the Nexus revealed itself to me at once, sometimes in the form of a globe or a watch, sometimes as a ring or a hand mirror. But this time, I could sense nothing. And when I checked the place where Feather and I saw the green hourglass, it was still there… except it was dead. No sign of life or magic.

I tried the transference ritual anyway, with the shell of the Nexus. But the house refused to budge. It kept pushing visions of Feather into my mind, until I finally understood what it was trying to say—that she had become the new Nexus. Since she was alive, whole, and nearby, the house still retained some of its power, but without her, it would not survive long. And she was in peril. The house could sense as much, though it could not tell me the source of the danger. So I rallied my housemates, who were more than happy to join me in rescuing her.

It was, perhaps, a foolish thing to do—charging into Rothenfel in my Krampus form, in the company of four eldritch creatures. But I barely thought about the risk. All I knew was panic, sheer terror that I might not get to Feather in time.

Now that she's back, I sense the house's satisfaction. I've never been so closely in tune with its emotions before, but since the transference attempt and our clumsy breakthrough in communications, I'm far more sensitive to its aura. It's almost… smug. As if everything that transpired was part of its plan, and it's happy with the result.

I'm not sure the Wild Hunt will be pleased with any of this. In fact, I'm surprised Nocturis hasn't shown up yet to berate both of us and annihilate me. I know he'll be watching, wanting to ensure that his orders are followed.

Much as I dread speaking with him, I hate the uncertainty more. It's time to have a conversation with my overseer and to find out, one way or the other, what my fate and Feather's will be.

Leaving Feather asleep, I head to the lowest level of the house. Meerwunder is sprawled in the center of the torture room, snoring, glutted with human flesh. Carefully I sidle past him, take a silver horn from its shelf, and open the trapdoor, the portal to the Void. I step out onto the underbelly of the house, staring up at the cloudy pathways and the swirls of starry color in the blackness.

I'm only supposed to use the silver horn in dire situations. I've blown it twice before, and both times I was reprimanded for it. This time, I have no choice. I need Nocturis's immediate attention.

But as I lift the horn to my lips and I'm puckering up to blow, Nocturis himself appears on one of the cloud-paths, mounted not on a horse, but on a gigantic black dog with ears as sharp as daggers. The unnatural length of its legs reminds me of Wolpertinger.

The dog leaps from the cloudy pathway, extends immense batlike wings, and soars through the Void, covering the distance between us within seconds and landing gracefully on the house.

Nocturis swings off the beast's back and approaches me. Wonder of all wonders, he's smiling smugly, the way I imagine the house would look if it had a face.

"Well done," he says.

"The fuck?" I retort.

"You've done well." He pronounces each word slowly, as if he's explaining to a small child.

Either he's going mad, or I am. "You do realize that we wrecked a city and killed dozens of people, including a couple of Fae-hunters? And Feather hasn't left me. In fact, she *has* to stay. The house has turned her into the Nexus, and if I had to guess, it did that on purpose as a preemptive measure, knowing you would command her to leave. It didn't want to be parted from her so it made sure that wasn't a possibility, and I only wish I'd thought of it first—"

"Excellent." Nocturis grins, rubbing his hands.

I thought my wounds had healed, but maybe I'm still iron-sick and delirious. I must be. This is not the reaction I expected. It makes no sense.

"You threatened to annihilate me," I point out. "You all but threatened to kill Feather. You said if we broke the rules—"

"If I really intended to harm *her* or annihilate *you*, ask yourself this question—why was she given a Krampus bell?"

"A mistake?"

"A plan."

I stare at him, unable to make sense of it. "You wanted me to save her. To take her in—"

"And to fall for her. Yes." Nocturis clasps my shoulder. "I wish it could have happened sooner. But we couldn't find the right one for you. Once we did find her, we had to wait until she was ready. And then you both had to be tested, to ensure that your love was true, that you would defy the universe and sacrifice anything for each other. You had to believe your relationship was forbidden, and yet pursue it anyway. We had to know that the mate bond was secure."

"You know about the mate bond," I whisper.

"Of course. This experiment with you and your pretty little Feather is just one of a series of redemptive efforts undertaken by me, under the direction of the god-star Andregh himself. A new sort of Final Task, as it were, with true love as part of the equation. You see, we realized that after completing their Final

Task and receiving corporeal form, many ex-riders either squandered their mortal lives or slipped back into selfish, destructive patterns. So we're aiming to achieve a more permanent, wholesome change by finding their other selves, their missing piece, their mate. We saw excellent results with a certain foursome in another realm—perhaps you've heard of Paemon, Abraxas, and Helix?"

I shake my head.

"Ah, well—they've found their missing piece, and their redemption is complete." Nocturis pats the side of his dog-monster's face companionably. "And so is yours."

"I don't understand."

"Perhaps this will clarify matters." Nocturis clears his throat. "Krael, known as Krampus, outcast son of Faerie... with the god-star Andregh's blessing, I hereby declare you free from your service to the Wild Hunt. Any judgment you deliver as Krampus, from this point forward, is yours to choose. The house, of course, belongs to Feather. With its geistfyre, the two of you can go anywhere you like in this world. You will both exist as long as the house does—which should be another millennia or so, if you tend it well. Enjoy your future together."

With that, he leaps astride the bat-winged dog, gives me a final salute, and gallops off toward the cloud-path again. As his form recedes, the words he spoke finally take root in my mind, and seeds of stunned joy begin to bloom.

"You glorious motherfucking bastard," I say faintly.

When I turn around, I see Feather, frozen halfway out of the trap door, staring at the retreating figure of Nocturis. She glances at me, her eyes wide. "You left our bed, and the house told me where you were, and I..."

"Did you hear?" I say hoarsely. "Did you hear what he said?"

"That you're free?" Her lip trembles and her eyes fill with tears. "That you and the house are mine for a long, long time? Yes, I heard."

I try to keep myself from breaking, but I can't. The tears are already brimming in my eyes. "Shit. I'm *free*. I'm fucking free."

She springs out of the trap door and leaps for me. I catch her in my arms and swing her clean off her feet, around in a giddy circle. Then I bury my face in the curve of her neck and I sob, harsh and heavy, while she holds me tight.

The house and the monsters weren't my prison. I didn't need to escape them. I needed absolution. I needed to be craved and valued by someone who knew the wickedest of my deeds, and considered me worth loving anyway.

I needed this. I needed *her*.

"You fucking saved me," I choke out against her warm skin. Her shoulder is wet with my tears, but she only squeezes me tighter.

"They're not going to annihilate you," she gasps. "They're not going to make me leave you. We're leaving together. We're a family, not like—" Her words break off, and a sob jars her body. "Not like *him*. He didn't want me, Krael. My own brother."

I rear back, taking her face in both my hands. "*I* want you," I snarl. "I will want you every day for the rest of our lives."

"You fucking better." She gives a tearful laugh. "And I will want you just the same."

"Then there's only one thing left to decide." I kiss her nose, then her forehead. "Where would you like to go?"

Her eyes light up, and I can tell she's about to express a wish she has carried for a long time. "Maybe… somewhere with a beach? And palm trees?"

"My lady has spoken." I plant a swift, hot kiss on her mouth. "So shall it be."

We move our house to the Lucernas Islands, to a remote cove between two arms of a mountain. We're a short walk from the beach, and thanks to my geistfyre, we're within easy range of a few charming towns with well-stocked pubs.

The transference was easy this time, since Feather, the house, and I share a connection. I was still concerned about the great pulse of power generated by the move, but it didn't seem to hurt Feather at all. In fact, judging by her soft gasp and the light shining in her big brown eyes, she rather enjoyed it.

On our first night in the islands, I build a bonfire on the beach, to the great delight of the Imp, who proceeds to set palm fronds on fire and swallow them whole. I spread a cloth on the sand and lay out my haul from a local pub that will probably become our new favorite. Besides a savory spread of food, I uncork a couple bottles of truly exceptional wine, and we both indulge more deeply than usual.

After the first bottle, I'm feeling a pleasant warmth, but Feather, who never drinks, is rosy and bright-eyed, slurring the edges of her words.

"Are you going to keep on being Krampus?" she asks loudly. "It doesn't seem quite the same here, does it? It's not dark and dreadful and cold anymore. Everything is so green, and so *warm*. I'm warm right down to my bones. Too warm for clothes." She pulls her dress off and tosses it aside, then stands up, swaying, dressed only in her bustier and panties. She has a belly piercing now, and the little jewel I placed above her navel glints in the firelight.

"I suppose I will mete out justice if I see the need," I reply. "People can be just as wicked in warm climates."

She smirks at me. "I do feel rather wicked."

"And what about you?" I lean back on my palms, admiring her. "Do you have any other dreams of what you want to be? Confess them, and I'll do my best to make them come true."

Her eyes narrow, and her lower lip emerges in a pout that reminds me momentarily of the Little Sister I saved from the cabin.

"I may not have lofty dreams of justice and retribution," she says, waving her arms in a grand gesture. "But I do, in fact, enjoy my current line of work."

"Indeed? And what is that?"

She smiles at me indulgently, as if I'm being silly and obtuse, and I swear in the fire-glow, with her brown hair wind-tossed and her cheeks wine-flushed, she has never looked more beautiful. "I like being a maid to the very frightening, very fuckable Krampus."

"You're the fuckable one," I growl, jumping to my feet.

She squeals and darts a few steps away.

"Don't run, little one." A feral grin spreads over my face. "I warned you, if you run, I must pursue. And I can't be held responsible for what happens once I catch you."

She gives me a slow, deliberate blink that makes me realize she's not as drunk as she seems.

"With you," she says softly, "I never fear being caught."

Then, with a naughty, daring smile, she races off down the beach, running barefoot through the cool foam of the midnight ocean, under the twinkling stars.

And of course, I chase her.

MIND-MISSIVE
TO THE
GOD-STAR ANDREGH

I am happy to inform you that our second experiment was just as successful as the first. Krampus and Feather are ideally matched to repair each other's wounds, both physical and emotional. They have been living peacefully in the tropical kingdom of Lucernas for several months now. Thanks to their care, the house is immaculate, and the eldritch creatures are well-fed on the carcasses of the occasional murderer or rapist whom Krampus sees fit to punish.

Your choice to give them a mate bond was a brilliant move, despite my initial doubts. With that heightened bliss to strengthen their love, Krampus has become wiser and more responsible, and Feather has grown more confident and joyful. I trust that with time, they will be a most exemplary pair.

It is with utmost delight that I report these results, God-Star, and request your blessing upon our third experiment, the one of which we spoke during our last meeting. It will be difficult, to be sure—but as you know, I have never been one to shrink from a challenge.

Yours Eternally,
Nocturis, Leader of the Second Squadron of the Wild Hunt

(art by BookishAveril)

If you enjoyed this book, try the "Wicked Darlings" series! It begins with *A Court of Sugar and Spice*, a sexy Fae retelling of the Nutcracker, the first of a trilogy of fantasy-romance retellings.

For access to character art, updates, ARC info, and the scoop on new releases, be sure to sign up for my newsletter through my website!

MORE BY
REBECCA F. KENNEY

The WICKED DARLINGS Fae retellings series
A Court of Sugar and Spice
A Court of Hearts and Hunger
A City of Emeralds and Envy
A Prison of Ink and Ice

A Hunt So Wild and Cruel
A Heart So Cold and Wicked

The DARK RULERS adult fantasy romance series
Bride to the Fiend Prince
Captive of the Pirate King
Prize of the Warlord
The Warlord's Treasure
Healer to the Ash King
Pawn of the Cruel Princess
Jailer to the Death God
Slayer of the Pirate Lord

The BELOVED VILLAINS series
The Sea Witch (Little Mermaid retelling with male Sea Witch)
The Maleficent Faerie (Sleeping Beauty retelling with male Maleficent)
The Nameless Trickster (Rumpelstiltskin retelling)

THE VAMPIRES WILL SAVE YOU trilogy
The Vampires Will Save You
The Chimera Will Claim You
The Monster Will Rescue You

The MERCILESS DRAGONS series
Serpents of Sky and Flame
Warriors of Wind and Ash
Storm of Blood and Shadow

The GILDED MONSTERS classic retellings series
Beautiful Villain (retelling of "The Great Gatsby")
Charming Devil (retelling of "The Picture of Dorian Gray")
Ruthless Devotion (retelling of "Wuthering Heights")

The IMMORTAL WARRIORS adult fantasy romance series
Jack Frost
The Gargoyle Prince
Wendy, Darling (Neverland Fae Book 1)
Captain Pan (Neverland Fae Book 2)
Hades: God of the Dead
Apollo: God of the Sun

Related Content: *The Horseman of Sleepy Hollow*

The INFERNAL CONTESTS demon romance books
Interior Design for Demons
Infernal Trials for Humans

The SAVAGE SEAS books
The Teeth in the Tide
The Demons in the Deep

Made in the USA
Columbia, SC
25 September 2024

42427669R00196